The Invisible Exchange

Also by Brian Woolland

http://www.brianwoolland.co.uk

The
Invisible
Exchange

Brian Woolland

Matador
Unit E2 Airfield Business Park,
Harrison Road, Market Harborough,
Leicestershire. LE16 7UL
Tel: 0116 2792299
Email: books@troubador.co.uk
Web: www.troubador.co.uk/matador
Twitter: @matadorbooks

ISBN 978 1803132 105

British Library Cataloguing in Publication Data.
A catalogue record for this book is available from the British Library.

Printed and bound in Great Britain by 4edge Limited
Typeset in 11pt Minion Pro by Troubador Publishing Ltd, Leicester, UK

Matador is an imprint of Troubador Publishing Ltd

Dedicated to the memory of my beloved son, Tom

Praise for
The Invisible Exchange

Matthew is a great character. He has a distinctive voice, he's engaging and fascinating... He's playing power games all over the place... His point of view is intriguing ... *The Invisible Exchange* is a real page-turner.

Lesley McDowell, author of
Unfashioned Creatures

Brian Woolland has produced a superb plot, a complex and entertaining protagonist, all set against an impeccably researched backdrop where Jacobean England comes vividly to life.

Michael O'Byrne, author of
The Crime Writers Guide to Police Practice and Procedure

The Invisible Exchange is an immersive journey through the halls, hidden pathways and corridors of power in Jacobean London. Brian Woolland paints with equal verve the London underworld and the grand houses of the aristocracy. Vivid tableaux for engaging characters and an engrossing plot. A distinctive, gripping historical thriller.

Stevie Simkin author of,
What Makes The Monkey Dance

A gripping journey through the murky underbelly of Jacobean London, guided by a cunning rogue who finds himself entangled in a deadly web of power politics and Court intrigue. Vivid, suspenseful, compelling!

Tim Grana

CONTENTS

Cast of Characters

In order of appearance:

Matthew Edgworth

Viscount Rochester (formerly Robert Carr), favourite of King James and Gentleman of the Royal Bedchamber

Alice, found at the House of the Vixen

Bradshaw, Rochester's coachman

Katherine Garnam (Kate), Frances's personal maid

Frances Howard, Countess of Essex

Alexander Colquhoun, Rochester's steward

Amos Appleby, cook at Sherborne Castle

Doctor Simon Forman, physician, astrologer and sorcerer

Anne Forman, married to Simon Forman

Jacob, Matthew's half-brother

Master Bailey, steward at Audley End

Master Shackles, Matthew's nickname for the master of The Bridewell

Pieter Vancy, Alice's older brother

Frans, Alice's younger brother

Richard Weston, servant to Anne Turner

Anne Turner, close friend of Frances Howard

Mary Woods, who claims to be an astrologer

Doctor Savory, who claims to be a physician and astrologer

James Franklin, apothecary

Hannah, wise woman

Christopher Mountjoy, French tire-maker, who has a workshop that also makes theatrical props

The Earl of Essex (Robert Devereux), married to Frances

The Master at Bedlam hospital

Bill Carter, carter whose yard is in Southwark

Sir Thomas Overbury, close friend and adviser to Rochester

Henry Howard, Earl of Northampton, great uncle to Frances Howard

Jack, kitchen boy working in the household of Sir Thomas Overbury

Lawrence Davies, servant of Sir Thomas Overbury

Matthew's London

MOOR

TYBURN

COPE CASTLE
&
OXFORD

ALDGATE

WHITE HART INN

DRURY LANE

WESTMINSTER

TO WHITEHALL
PALACE

3

4

5

6

7

8

9

10

River

LAMBETH PALACE

PARIS
GARDENS

BEAR PIT

BANK SIDE

THE GLOBE

SPITAL FIELDS

OLD PRIORY

FIELDS

BEDLAM

MOORGATE

N WALLS

TO EPPING FOREST & ESSEX

13

TOWER OF LONDON

Thames

LONDON

TO THE PALACE OF GREENWICH

BILL CARTER'S YARD

SOUTHWARK

KEY

1   Doctor Forman's House

2   Lambeth Palace

3   Salisbury House

4   Essex House

5   The Bridewell

6   Fleet Bridge

7   Matthew's Lodgings

8   Newgate Jail

9   The Mermaid

10   Anne Turner's House

11   St. Olave's Church

12   Mountjoy's House and Shop

13   The House of The Vixen

I

The Sign of the Vixen

If you're going to beat a man, no half measures. That was their mistake. They broke my left hand. As if that alone would crush my sinister, ill-omened nature. But they didn't kill me. And they didn't cut out my tongue – nor my balls come to that, though I can but dream of the time when I might have use for them again. And if a man with cracked ribs and crushed hand can be said to have his health, I have that too. Maybe even some of my wits, for I managed to make my escape from London and I'm writing this in what seems, at least for now, a place of sanctuary. Matthew Edgworth, who no longer has the use of his left hand, writing with his right. And right has never come easy.

Same with beatings, same with lies. The halfway house on any journey's the place most fraught with danger. Half-truths, half-lies – they're the ones that ambush you. So this is a whole truth. The truth that's missing from the chronicles of these dark times.

Why do people never stumble on the name of Matthew Edgworth when they read the pamphlets about Frances Howard, Robert Carr, the Earl of Essex, Thomas Overbury and King James? The answer's simple. I don't exist. I never did. If that's a pretty riddle, think on this. To be truly useful to nobility, you have to be trusted with secrets. But a servant with a store of secrets is a threat. So now I'm dead – so they suppose. But they should beware, for I'm no ghost who's writing this, and I have grievances to settle.

When I first started working for him, Robert Carr had the appearance of an innocent, fair-haired boy, and the beauty of both sexes – fragile and delicate, soft-skinned and beardless. Not to my taste, but I could see why the King might want such a body in his bed. I've never had Carr's looks but I'm no fuckwit. If a smockfaced page could rise to favour, I too could make my way in the world, even if my scarred face will never decorate the pillows of the powerful.

When Robert Carr wasn't attending to his duties as Gentleman of the King's Bedchamber, he was pursuing Frances Howard, the renowned beauty and daughter of Thomas Howard, the Earl of Suffolk, the wealthiest man in all England. But Lady Frances was already married to another Robert – Devereux, the Earl of Essex. Her father had arranged the marriage some seven years before, when Frances was just fourteen. Thus it was, Essex had a wife, but my master had an appetite. And in me he had a servant who was far more artful than himself. I took letters between them. I'd seen the lady herself, but never spoken to her. My contact was with the maid, Katherine Garnam. Cut from the same cloth as the mistress. If I could woo Kate and gain her trust, I'd have a spy in the lady's household. Sweetening profit with pleasure. Kate spurned me at first, but all things change. You see what's possible. You make it so.

The liaisons between my master and Lady Frances worked well enough until the husband grew suspicious and had her removed from London to Chartley Manor, his rotting pile in Staffordshire, where she was removed from the gaze of her admirers at the court and delivered from temptation.

The King, meanwhile, had ennobled his beloved Robert Carr. Dear sweet Robbie became the Honourable Viscount Rochester and grew a fashionable beard in the Spanish style. Such a delightful, witty young man whilst with the King. Foul-tempered, petulant and mean when prevented from seeing Lady Frances. And he blamed whoever was nearest when thwarted. I don't take kindly to a tongue-lashing, whoever's dealing it out, and often had to restrain myself from giving him cause for his misery. But I had good reason for staying in my master's employ. So, when he ordered me to arrange for the lady to be smuggled out of Chartley, I agreed to make plans. Somebody had to, for he had none of his own.

But in truth, I was at a loss. I could get her out of Chartley. And I could get her back to London. Then what? Lord Essex would know she was missing. Only a matter of time before her escape was common knowledge. The world might mock Essex for such a public cuckolding, but the scandal would ruin the lady, and even Rochester could see that wouldn't further his cause.

A week passed. And then a fortnight. Rochester was growing impatient, and I could quickly fall from favour. Were it not for a happy accident, I'd have lost all.

I was visiting the House at the Sign of the Vixen in Petticoat Lane. I'd come to see Diego, the broker for the house. He owed me favours. He was sitting at a table in what passed for a kitchen. Diego's long, black curls framed his dark scowling face, contrasting with the golden tresses of the tall, slender young whore who stood facing him with her back to me.

'You get the portion that I say you get,' he shouted, banging the table with his fist.

'Diego,' I called out.

He was about to rage at the intruder who dared interrupt him, when he recognised me.

'Who's the girl?' I asked.

'A common strumpet. New to the game. Thinks what the vaulter pays is hers.'

I shook my head in disbelief that anyone could be so raw.

'Her name?'

'We call her Alice.'

I took a closer look. She was uncommonly tall for a woman, her turquoise eyes were sparkling jewels in that dingy kitchen, and she held herself upright with a self-assurance I'd rarely seen in any woman outside of the nobility.

'New to the game, you said?' Me to Diego.

'Been here a week.'

'Clean?'

'Course she's clean.'

'One hour with her.'

'Ten shillings,' he said. 'An angel for an angel.' But despite his slithering, dirty little laugh, he was worried. He knew I could have called in what he owed me and saved myself ten

4

shillings. I chose to pay and leave his account open. Debts, like revenge, are often best kept in storage.

Alice led me upstairs. Once in the room, I led her across to the window to look at her in the light. It was only then that I really saw it. I could charm my way through Whitehall, pick the most intricate of locks, cut throats for my master if necessary and on occasions play the courtier, given time enough to paint my face and dress in doublet and hose. But nothing had prepared me for Alice. The likeness to Lady Frances was uncanny. The beginnings of a plan began to hatch.

I paid Diego another angel, hired a coach, and instructed the coachman to take us out of London, past Whitechapel out into the country, where the roads were even more rutted than those inside London's walls. While the carriage rumbled and groaned, she sat facing me, smiling softly. I could have taken her to a hostelry instead of driving out east, but the stench of the Whitechapel tanneries is guaranteed to dull a man's yearning for the pleasures of the flesh. And I didn't want to be distracted by Alice's obvious charms.

'What is it you want, sir? Shall I play your fine lady?' She wouldn't have sounded out of place in my master's withdrawing room. 'Talk rough and dirty? Or be your little girl?'

She has all the voices, I thought. Good enough to appear in a playhouse, if women could have joined the players – although she did want for a little practice, for there was still a hint in all of them that she'd not been born in England.

'Alice your real name?'

'It's what they call me, sir. I can sing or be silent or whatever you will. What would you call me, sir?' She put her hands to her mouth, playing the innocent.

'Keep things simple. I'll call you Alice. I'm here on behalf of my master. A wealthy man. Powerful. One of the noblest in the land. He's charged me to bring you into his household.'

I thought the news would please her. But she scowled. 'I didn't come to London to become a whore.'

'Then what is it you think you are?'

'What I am and what I do are not the same.'

'What you do, sweet Alice, *is* what you are.'

'I shall not do it for long. Do you think I want to be treated as a nag with a broken leg at the first sign of wrinkles on my skin?' The precisely chosen words of someone fluent in English, but who'd learnt it as her second tongue.

'I'm offering to buy you out of that.'

'I will be no Dutch Courtesan to your ... great lord.'

'You Dutch then?'

She didn't answer. Her eyes glinted with the ferocity of a she-wolf.

'You'll be very well paid.'

'I will never see it. The bawd and the broker at The Vixen take all but a tiny portion.'

'You misunderstand me, Alice. I've money enough to buy you out.'

'The bawd will never agree.'

'Mistress Fox will do as I say. And Diego knows better than to start a fight he cannot win.' That gave her pause. I waited a while before adding, 'Whatever you and I agree between us will be yours to keep.'

'How much?'

'Twenty-five pounds.'

She tried to show no feeling. But her eyes widened. Those beautiful eyes.

'Five pounds now. Twenty when your employment ends.'

That pricked her interest. Twenty-five pounds. More than she'd earn in a year at The Vixen. The coach lurched on as Alice withdrew into the soft mists of her thoughts. Better she change her own mind than me try to persuade her. A mile or more must have passed before impatience got the better of me. 'Listen, Alice. It's simpler than you think. We go back to the Vixen. I reach an agreement with Diego and Mistress Fox. I come back tomorrow. I pay them off, you come with me. I give you five pounds. I take you to my master.'

'You ask me to sell myself to a man I have never met. Your 'great lord' will throw me off as soon as he tires of me. Better to be a whore in the stews than a rich man's discarded plaything. I have chosen to survive by doing this until I can live without recourse to sin.'

'A whore living without sin!' I laughed.

She snarled and looked away.

'I leave the offer with you. Think on it.'

'Leave it as long as you want. I shall be steadfast.'

'Most would sooner work in a palace than a common house.'

'I shall not be long at The Vixen.'

'So be it then. Dig your own way out of the pit you've dug for yourself. Stay there, filthy common strumpet that you are.' I couldn't help myself. I raised my arm in frustration.

'Your lord sent you to the market,' she said, victorious in my flash of anger. 'Will it please him if you return with bruised

7

fruit? Go on. Strike and walk away. You will never find another such as me.'

And she was right, damn her. So I didn't strike.

'Think on it,' I said. 'You'll soon see the benefits.'

Had I shown too much interest? Was she playing a game to get the offer raised? Or did Alice have a secret she was holding back?

I took her back to the House of the Vixen, then found the Boy of the House. I paid the young fellow to spy on her for me. He'd never before had a whole sixpence of his own.

While the Boy was playing spider and I was waiting for a tug on his web, I sought an audience with my master. When Rochester deigned to meet me in person it was usually in the stable block of Cope Castle, a grand house near the manor of Kensington owned by one of his cronies.

'A double?' He turned on me, as if I'd spat on his shoe. 'You dare to suggest you can find a woman to match Frances Howard! You think a common strumpet could take her place? You think our love so cheap?'

'Forgive me, sir. I didn't mean to offend. The double takes Lady Frances's place in Chartley so the lady can take her place with you.'

'Even Essex is not so witless as to be fooled by that.'

'You told me he has no interest in his wife's happiness.'

'None whatsoever.'

'Suppose the woman feigns melancholy and retires to her bed, refusing to speak to anyone except her maid. Would Essex not leave her alone? May I be so bold, my Lord, as to ask whether it's still possible to get letters to Lady Frances?'

'Houses have servants, Edgworth. Servants can be bought.'

'Then perhaps, my Lord, you might write to Lady Frances.'

I gave him time to considered this before adding, 'There is but one problem, my Lord.'

He looked crestfallen. 'You have yet to find a woman who bears a resemblance?'

'No, my Lord. I have the woman. But I cannot think how to get the double to Chartley and bring Lady Frances to you.'

He thought about this for a while, and then told me how it could be done.

'Oh, excellent,' I said. 'Most excellent.'

With Rochester, the trick of it was to plant the seed, give it time to grow, then be astonished at his razor wit as the seed sprouted and the plan became his own.

2

A calling in of debts

My little spy had excelled himself, though it took a while to tease it out from the tangle of his nerves.

'When she leaves The Vixen, sir,' he squeaked. 'When she leaves Petticoat Lane, sir, when – '

'Slow down.'

'She goes to Paul's, sir. Down Petticoat Lane and then Cheapside.'

'I know the way to Paul's, boy. Just tell me why she goes there.'

'Buys food on her way, sir. From the market. Apples. Bread. Cheese. Takes food to a fellow in Paul's.'

'And who is this fellow.'

'Gives 'im money.'

'Who?'

'Alice. The one they calls Alice. What you give me the shilling to keep an eye on.'

I'd have cuffed him if I'd thought it would speed the telling, but we got there in the end. The man she visited was tall and strong, but half his face was stained purple, 'Like someone's smeared port wine and treacle all over it.'

'Easy to recognise then?'

"Cept it wasn't treacle, sir, 'cos I got right close when he's asleep. It's 'is skin. 'Orrible. Honest, sir I – '

'I believe you, boy.'

'Giant of a man he is. And when she's talking to 'im, they don't speak English. Every day he looks at the notices by the *Si Quis* door. Every day, sir. Looks at the door, then off 'e goes. Always comes back, so what I reckon is 'e en't getting no work.'

'Maybe they don't like his face.'

The boy thought that funny. 'Or maybe it's 'cos he's Dutch, sir. That's what the other beggars told me. One day I follows the Alice woman to Paul's. Master Stainface en't there, so she heads out through Bishopsgate to Spital Fields. And all the time I'm follerin', though she don't know it. An' when she gets to Spital Fields she goes into a little wooden shack just past the old ruins. I hides round the back. Chillun in there by the sound of it, but I can't make no sense of it. Reckon them's all Dutch too.'

So … Alice had come to London from Holland. And this purple-faced giant and her family – if that's who it was shacked up in Spital Fields – needed her money as much as she needed mine. Maybe she told them she'd found honest employment in some wealthy household? No concern of mine. What mattered was that she wanted to support them, though she'd struggle to do that by doing turns at The Vixen. The longer she was there, the less the bawd would pay her. My taking her for Rochester would be a blessed act of kindness.

I gave the boy a penny.

'Show you the place at Spital Fields, shall I?'

'No.'

'Won't take long. Few hundred yards past Bishopsgate and Bedlam.'

'I said no. Begone before I cuff you.'

The mention of Spital Fields had set me on edge.

Diego was sat in the kitchen. I could barely see him for smoke.

'I need to see your Alice.'

'Take your turn, Matthew Edgworth. She's working.'

It took some bargaining and a few well-chosen threats – reputations in the stews are hard won and easily lost. Word of the pox or the plague can get a House closed sooner than any magistrate can do it. But I'm a fair man and I offered a fair price.

Alice's client was kicked out, and the gallant hoping to be next in line was turned away. She was brought down to the kitchen, where a sticky, sickly fug hung in the air from Diego's tobacco pipe.

She knew, even before I told her. 'I told you before. I will not do it.'

'I offered a price, Alice. And Mistress Fox has agreed to sell. You work a trugging house like this, you become another's chattels.'

'I will not do it.'

'So how will you find the money to support your motley crew in Spital Fields? Your man in Paul's can't provide for himself, never mind the children.'

The colour drained from her cheeks. 'I will find another place to work.' She was trying to sound calm, but was shocked that I knew.

12

'And where do you imagine you'll find this work? There's more honour than you might think amongst the London bawds. They may not have a Guild with livery, but those who run the better houses all know each other. And good Mistress Fox would be most unhappy if a girl she'd sold in good faith ended up working for a neighbour. Or would you join the Winchester Geese in Southwark? Once a girl starts working there, she never sees the light of day again.'

She clenched her fists and scowled, as if it was me ran the Bankside stews.

'Come with me, Alice. I give you the five pounds now. You choose what you do with it. Keep it for yourself, or we can take it to your fellow in Paul's.'

'Twenty-five pounds you said.'

'Five now. Twenty when you leave.'

'I cannot abandon them.'

'Five now. Five when you leave. And five at the end of every month between now and then. I deal plainly with you, Alice. I take five pounds to your man in Paul's on the last day of every month until my master no longer has need of your services.'

'How do I know you speak truth?'

'Because I give you my word.'

She shook her head in disbelief.

'You may think me a rogue, but when I say I'm going to do something, be certain that I will. Why else do you think that when I call in debts they're paid so very quickly?'

'Swear it.'

I swore. And that was that. The deal was done.

From there we went to Paul's, where she doled out a little of her new-found wealth to the stained-face Dutchman.

13

'Who is he to you, Alice?'

'Who is who?'

'Master Plumface?'

'His name is Pieter Vancy. He is my brother. And now I have to go to Spital Fields.'

'I'm not going to Spital Fields.'

'I do not ask you to. I go alone. It is not far. Through Bishopsgate and – '

'I know where the Spital Fields are.'

She took hold of my hands and looked me in the eye. She could cheat a man with charming as well as any of her trade. 'Matthew,' she spoke softly. The first time she'd spoken my name. 'I wish to say goodbye to my family. I wish to give them money to live on while I'm away.'

'Tell me where they are, and I'll take the money to them.'

'If I don't see them, they will look for me. They will ask where I've gone.'

'We haven't time. Your brother can tell them you're safe.'

'If I cannot see them, I will not do it.'

I came so close to cutting her... Who was she to set the terms? But she was steadfast. So I agreed – but with conditions. 'When we're there you speak English. No Dutch. I stay with you all the time. You tell them you've found work as a maid with a family who'll be spending the summer in Kent.'

'Why Kent?'

'Because that's where the better class of people go in summer, when London stinks even worse than it does now.'

She reluctantly agreed. But I insisted we'd go out of the city through Aldgate to Whitechapel and up Brick Lane.

'You said to make haste. That is much longer.'

'Alice. This is the way we're going.'

'What is it so troubles you about Bishopsgate?'

'If you want to see your family, we'll talk no more about it.'

And we didn't – talk about it. But she was right about going through Aldgate. It did take longer. The stench from the leather tanneries and brick kilns was foul. And Brick Lane was clogged with overladen carts coming down from the kilns and the claypits. Our destination? A squalid little wooden shack on the edge of the Spital Fields themselves, where the miserable little band had a roof over their heads. Alice knocked the door. It opened. A rat scurried out. A woman appeared. She smiled when she saw Alice. Then she caught sight of me. Two small girls and a boy followed her out. The girls were maybe five and six years old, the boy a little older. All had runny noses and rheumy eyes. So this was Alice's raggedy Low Country, Arselander family. Alice did as I'd instructed. The woman was close to tears at the news that Alice would be in Kent for the summer. Alice knelt, took the girls in her arms. The boy looked on. When she embraced him, he froze at first. Then wept. I tapped Alice on the shoulder. Too many tears. We had to leave.

'You need to prepare yourself for your new life, Alice,' I said as we walked back.

'You'll bruise my arm if you hold so tight. Would your great lord want that? You say you are a man of your word. And I am a woman of mine. We have an agreement. I will not flee. I promise you.'

'Doll Common, a woman of her word!'

'I am no Doll. And if I were common you would never have hired me for your master.'

I smothered the provocation with a gracious smile, and led her through a maze of alleys to the back gates of a house in Warwick Lane. Another debt called in.

'I was expecting a grand house in The Strand.'

'You expected wrong. Call this the tiring house, where you prepare yourself. The mistress of this place is a widow. She prefers her cousin's house in Tunbridge to London in the summer months. She's taken the household with her. My brother lent me the keys.'

'Your brother?'

'My brother Jacob. He's the gentleman usher here.'

She harrumphed in disbelief.

'Do as I ask, Alice, and you'll meet your employer tomorrow.' I led her across the courtyard to the stable block. 'But tonight you stay here.' I opened the door to the coachman's bedchamber. I'd laid out the clothes she was to wear: bodice, petticoat, red velvet gown and, on the bolster, a wig of hair, dark as a raven's breast.

'You would have me play a lady, and yet these are my lodgings! Do I not deserve better than a chamber furnished with a louse-ridden pallet bed and stinking pisspot?' She gave me a look. She knew, damn her. She knew full well how much I wanted her for myself. Any man would have.

But I resisted temptation. I bowed and took my leave. 'Sleep well Alice. I'll see you on the morrow.'

Her top lip twitched in a sour-faced sulk.

I shut the door and turned the key.

3
Spanish miracles

I returned to Warwick Lane early the next morning, dressed in honest plain livery – borrowed from the tiring house at Blackfriars Playhouse. So many tales to tell, but that one's for another time. The door to the room in the stable block was swinging open.

'Alice?'

Nothing. No Alice. Nor even the clothes I'd left for her. Nothing except the raven wig neatly arranged on the bolster.

She was sitting at the kitchen table, dressed in all her finery.

'You took your time. And I was hungry.' Treating me as if I were her manservant. Knowing I couldn't strike her.

'How did you get in here?'

'Did you think you are the only pick-lock in London?'

'My master awaits.'

'I'm ready.'

'Not yet you're not. You have to colour up your face and put on your wig before we go. Anybody looking at you sees a Spanish lady. I have to hire a coach. Be ready when I get back.'

What greeted me on my return was little short of a miracle. I was astounded at the elegance of her deportment, at the effortlessness with which she'd assumed her disguise. She stood before me, maybe half a head taller than me – and I'm no short-arse – almost as tall as Frances herself. A sight to behold. We journeyed out of London in style, the Infanta della Vixen and her manservant, Don Matteo, heading west down The Strand.

'Who is this brother of yours who loaned you his keys?' she said.

'He's gentleman usher to Lady Tellebouche of New Place, Warwick Lane.'

'And you, Master Edgworth, are not so good a liar as you think.'

'It's as good as you'll get this morning.'

She wafted her fan in haughty contempt, then looked at me in brazen defiance before turning away to admire Charing Cross and the entrance to the Royal Mews. The coach clattered on its way. We sat in knotted silence until we reached Cope Castle near Kensington. The coachman took us up the drive to the great front doors of the house. The usher greeted us, led us straightway into a grand entrance hall. From there he took us through to a large withdrawing room, where he asked us to wait. Alice feigned the haughty indifference of one born to wealth, but I could see she was astonished by the size of the room, the quantity of paintings, the thickness of the carpets and the sheer size of the Chinese vases standing either side of the fireplace. She took my arm and eased herself down onto the couch, while I stood beside her in attendance. Her self-possession set me on edge – which amused her.

'Remove the wig now,' I said. 'The raven-haired Spanish lady was for the journey. She is not required here.'

'To be dressed in the Spanish style and show my own fair hair. Would that not –'

'Do it, Alice. Do it now before I rip it from you.'

Too late. The door opened. The Vice Count stood there in all his court finery. He glided into the room, a slow dance on velvet shoes. His legs were silk-stockinged, and he wore a starched ruff in matching cream, set against a black velvet cape, with wine red lining.

Most women would have looked look away out of deference. Alice met his gaze. Playing her part to perfection, she hardly moved from where she sat, except to tilt her head slightly to one side and extend her hand to Rochester, who seemed at first to enjoy the game. He bowed and kissed her outstretched hand. I retreated to the wall and watched the scene play out. Rochester's lips were full, his cheeks rosy pink, his skin unblemished. Were it not for the slender goatee beard and moustache, his face could have been that of a girl. Although Alice did not for a moment lose her composure and dignity, I sensed that she was more unsettled by his epicene appearance than by the conspicuous display of vast wealth.

He stood back and gestured for her to rise. I stepped forward, assuming he was about to bid me unlace her, put the goods on display. But it seemed the game was over.

'Most amusing, Master Edgworth. But hardly the perfect match you promised. She is tall, I grant you that.' He paused, assessing the quality of what was on offer. 'And the turquoise eyes. I like the eyes.' He looked at her closely. 'But she will not pass.' Then he turned his attentions to me. 'I am an impatient man, Edgworth. I warned you not to disappoint.'

'One minute, sir, I beg you.'

'No more tricks and false promises. I'm done with her. And with you.'

'What you see before you was the cheat, my lord. Give us one minute and you will see the truth.'

Alice knew what was required. She had already looked away. When she turned back, she'd removed the dark wig, combed her fingers through her own golden hair, and wiped one cheek clean of the dark-skinned Spanish lady to show her own fair complexion.

Rochester's eyes widened. He took a step back, then glided slowly around, appraising a fine work of art.

'Miracle of miracles.'

'May I speak, sir?' said Alice, her voice as soft as velvet. I dreaded what she might say. Her voice and her manners were impressive, but she could ruin everything in seconds, and there was nothing I could do to stop her talking.

He nodded approval.

'Am I to live here, my Lord?'

This amused him. 'The same height as Lady Frances. The same eyes. The same hair. And now her spirit too. I will speak with you anon, mistress.' Then he called for his steward, Colquhoun, and had him escort me from the room whilst he gave Alice her instructions. It was, after all, his plan.

Colquhoun ushered me through passages at the rear of the house and up a narrow back stair to a small room on the first floor, saying nothing until he'd closed the door behind us. He stared at me. Cold blue eyes in his Scottish granite face. 'A word o' warning for ye, Edgworth. Don't think my master's soft because he's fey.'

'I think nothing of the kind. I think he means what he says. I think he's used to getting what he wants. And he employs me to make sure of that.'

'Aye. But ye're nae the only one to work for him, though ye'll nae meet any others. He'll pay ye well, until you cross him.'

'Why would I cross him?'

'London is a dangerous place, Edgworth. You'd nae be the first of his fixers and spies to drown in the Thames.'

That came as no surprise. But I thanked him for his advice. Rochester hadn't yet asked me to spy on the spies. But I knew I'd been watched.

I could see a time when Colquhoun could become a valuable ally, but cultivating such a sour-faced Scot would take a deal of wit.

He grunted, which I took to be his leave-taking.

When, eventually, Rochester appeared, he allowed himself a smile. 'This Alice of yours is everything you claimed,' he said. 'You shall be well rewarded.' He handed me a small leather purse, heavy with coins. I thanked him.

'She is valuable. But she does not exist. I trust you understand me, Edgworth.'

4

Charity to the poor

'Where are you taking me?'

'I'm escorting a lady to Chartley Manor in Staffordshire.'

I'd fondly imagined we might pull down the blinds of the coach, shut out the dreary wastelands that stretch out interminably between English towns, and find some amusement in each other's company. But all Alice wanted was to talk about how I came to be working for Rochester and why I'd been so reluctant to go through Bishopsgate.

'I'll not speak of it. And nor will you.'

'Are you in debt to a gatekeeper?'

'I owe no-one, Alice. Debts are what's owed to me.' It was the old priory that troubled me – not Bishopsgate. It's not something I talk about. She retreated into stubborn silence. You might wonder why I didn't force myself on her. A little jiggy business could have been most entertaining. But perhaps, with Bradshaw within earshot, abstinence was wise. Rochester saw Alice as his property now. If word reached him that I'd had her for myself, my own bollocks would be fed me on a plate.

I banged on the roof for Bradshaw to stop. I climbed up to sit with him, leaving Alice to her sullen distemper. He knuckled the reins, and we were on our way again. But Bradshaw's conversation was as lumpen as his heavy, lumbering gait. The roads became ever more rutted, the journey passed ever more slowly. What could I do except make plans for pleasures in store? Delivering Alice to Chartley would at least give me the chance to charm Lady Frances's maid.

We arrived in Oxford in the early evening. The city teemed with flocks of scholars, chattersome as crows. We drove between college buildings, golden stone glowing in early evening light, until we arrived at The Star in Cornmarket Street.

We had no difficulty getting rooms. The landlord saw a lady and her manservant. A maid took supper to Alice while I ventured out to find some gaming. I could have filled my purse with coins that night – what a blessing to work a place where your face isn't known – but I was cautious and made do with what I could take in five rounds of Primero. For the first three I was a little drunk and reckless. By the fourth I came into surprisingly good fortune. Then Prudence whispered in my ear, and in the next round I lost a little of what I'd just taken. Prudence was right, bless her. I could foresee a time when Oxford would offer rich pickings. And besides, I wanted to get back to The Star to make sure that Alice was comfortable. The damned hussy had bolted the door.

'Where is the coach?' said Alice, indignant, the following morning.

'I sent Bradshaw back to London. From here we travel on horseback. You'll be smuggled into Chartley Manor as a serving maid. There you change places with a true lady.'

'I am no serving maid.'

'And you're no lady either. But we still have to get the maid to Chartley. Out of your finery, mistress.'

'We travel to Chartley on horseback?'

'Would you rather walk?'

'One horse?! You expect me to ride behind you? Are you mad?'

'I expect you to wrap your arms around my waist and hold tight.'

'I'm perfectly capable of riding – '

'Rochester gave me a purse to cover costs. That doesn't include the hire of two horses.'

She argued and she sulked. She threatened to walk back to London. But once mounted on the horse, she did hold tight. She could hardly do else. We rode through Woodstock, and on, stopping for rest and food and drink at an inn close by Banbury Cross, though Cock Horse missed out on his ride that fine summer's day. Alice's spirit was far from broken, but she wanted to get the journey done. We'd seen too many haystacks and hedgerows, pigs and ponies, sheep and shit. Little wonder that so many country folk are thronging into London!

And beggars. So many beggars. Sometimes alone, sometimes in pairs. They looked at us and reached up imploringly. And cursed us when they thought we were out of hearing.

'Why do you spurn them?' asked Alice.

'You think we should take pity on every lame sow?'

'I think they are people, not pigs.'

'They should be soundly whipped, then set to work.'

'We don't have to treat them worse than beasts.'

'We stop for one, and a dozen will appear and take us for every last penny we have. Would you have them sit and yap like household spaniels while we feed them titbits?'

'We should treat them as we'd want them to treat us if we fell on hard times.'

'They don't fall on hard times, Alice. They're too idle to work. Nothing noble about beggary.'

'Do you know nothing of compassion?'

'I've known poverty. And I know where I'm going. But I'll not get there by giving dole to beggars.'

'You're a mean man, Matthew Edgworth.'

'I'm a loyal servant. My master charged me with getting you to Chartley. Not to dawdle and gossip.'

But the warmth of a body like Alice clinging to your waist has its effect on a man. We were five miles out of Warwick when I caught sight of two beggar women trudging towards us.

'Look you, Alice,' I said. 'Mistress Fewclothes and Lady Bonnyrags. Will you throw them scraps, or shall I?'

'If you mock poverty, Matthew, then Heaven make you poor.'

'Not mockery, Alice. I say what I see.' I pulled up the horse and held it on a tight rein.

'Good your worships,' called the younger of the two. 'May goodness soften your hearts to the poor.'

She gaped up at us, while the elder, who must have suffered the punishments for begging, stared at the ground.

Alice's grip tightened on my waist. I could tell she feared a trick. I reached into my purse – bulging from the winnings that Dame Fortune had thrown in my direction in Oxford. I dropped a couple of coins.

'Charity to the poor. Oh, thank you sir,' said the elder. 'Charity to the poor! We will duly and truly pray for you.'

'Feed yourself up,' I said to the young one. 'Get some flesh on your bones, and you'll be a good catch for someone.'

'Duly and truly we pray for you.' Now I could see it. Mother and daughter.

'Half-crowns!' said mother, in disbelief.

'Charity to the poor,' I said. 'Spend it well. Good day to you both. I trust that will be enough to get you food and drink and shelter.'

'Duly and truly we pray for you,' they chorused as we rode off.

By the time we reached Lichfield, Alice had grown easier with me. We dined together in the King's Head that night. She was in good humour. Dropping the two half-crowns seemed money well spent.

'You should do it more often,' she said. 'It becomes you well. Robbing from the sons of moneyed men in Oxford and doling out their wealth to poor deserving women. Duly and truly, I think all of my sex might pray for you!'

'We will regret it tomorrow.'

'I think not,' said Alice.

'Do you suppose that Lady Bonnyrags and her daughter will keep their good fortune to themselves? Drop money for beggars and you're ripe for the picking. My guess is we'll be safe until we're about three miles out of Lichfield. Then the highwaymen will swoop.'

'So why give them money?'

'For you, sweet Alice. So you'd know that beneath my roguish manners I am truly the most kind-hearted of men. Now let's be done with games and get us to bed.'

'By all means to bed. I am weary and saddle sore. But I will not lie with you tonight, Matthew.'

'I found you in a whore house, Alice. I can pay – out of my own purse, not my master's.' I'd hoped it wouldn't come to that. But what's the point of money if you have no use for it?

'I told you before. No matter where you found me, I'm no whore. And I cannot be bought.'

'You have been bought, damn you.'

'But not by you, Matthew Edgworth.'

Has any virgin ever been as tight with her favours? Perhaps she was distracted by what lay ahead, for she knew as well as I did that if Essex discovered his melancholic wife was an impostor, he'd despatch Alice with no more conscience than a cook disposing of rats. So maybe it was for the best to sleep alone that night, for we'd need to be up early, and there were other matters to attend to. I stayed up long after Alice had gone to bed, and fell to drinking with the rustics. In my cups, I let slip that my companion and I were on our way to Derby – travelling East from Lichfield.

The art of playing drunk is greatly underestimated. For who doesn't believe the confessions of a man whose tongue is looser than cockerels at daybreak?

When I could barely stand – or so they thought – I took my leave and stumbled off, as if to bed. Alice was dressed and ready. We'd already discussed the plan. We tippy toed down the back stairs and out to the stables. I tied sacks around the horse's hooves, and we made our escape before sunrise.

It wasn't until we were well out of Lichfield – heading West towards Stafford and Chartley – that Alice broke the silence. 'Is this how you expect Lady Frances to ride with you? Clinging to you like a child to its mother?'

'Quicker than me walking alongside while she rides. But if that's what she wants, then so be it. Unlike you, Alice, I know my place. Lady Frances is high born. She has choice in these matters.'

'Not much of a choice from what I can see. Not much of a choice if she was married off to the Earl of Essex at the age of fifteen.'

'You weren't born for this world, Alice.'

The sky was lightening as I tethered the horse in a copse near what Essex fancifully called his manor house. Rochester had briefed me well and sent word in advance to the real Lady Frances. Chartley Manor might pretend to be grand, but it was a timber-framed house, not a castle under siege. At the back of the house, a narrow bridge spanned the moat. The lady's maid was waiting by a door into the kitchens. The rest of the household hadn't yet risen. She let us in. But I barely had the time to greet her before she whisked Alice away, up back stairs to the lady's chambers.

She said she'd return shortly with Lady Frances.

I waited.

The place reeked of its master – cold, musty and foul smelling.

I waited some more.

5

Changing places

The kitchens of grand houses are usually most welcoming. They smell of wood smoke, fresh bread, roast meats and herbs. The kitchens at Chartley Manor were cold, dank and sour. The fire had been allowed to go out overnight. The servants cared no more for the place than they did for their master.

At last, the maid returned.

'You must leave now. Before the kitchen boys and scullery maids come down.'

'My instructions are to leave when the lady is ready to travel. Not before.'

'And my mistress's instructions are that you leave now, Master Edgworth.' A brave spirit! She knew my name, too. Her wide eyes and flushed pock-free cheeks betrayed the spark of interest she was trying so hard to conceal. 'My mistress says the woman you brought with you is not yet ready to take her place.'

'Bring her back down here. I'll remind her what's required.'

'You misunderstand. Your woman knows what's required, but – '

'Her name's Alice.'

'She has to learn how to become Lady Frances. That will take more than a simple change of clothes. My lady said two days. In two days, Master Edgworth – '

'You may call me Matthew.'

'In two days, Master Edgworth, they will both be ready to play their new parts.'

'Call me by my name and tell me yours, and then we can discuss the matter.'

'There is nothing to discuss. I will meet you outside the kitchen door at sunrise two days from now. Wait on the moat bridge. As you did today. Now you must leave.'

'First, tell me your name.'

'My name is Katherine. Now leave.'

'Ah. Kate. Such a beautiful name.'

'Katherine, not Kate.'

'The sweetest of Kates.'

'I care not for Kate.'

'But I would,' I said. 'I would dearly love to care for Kate.'

'Begone. If you are found in the kitchens you will ruin all.'

'First, let me hear you say my name.'

'Edgworth.'

'Matthew.'

'Matthew. There. I have said it. Now leave.'

'I shall indeed – if you'd you be so good as to take me to my chambers, and show me the bed where I can lay my head and rest?'

'Stafford's an hour's ride from here. You'll find coaching inns there.'

'So much easier to stay here. Tell me, good Kate. Do the servants at Chartley talk to you? Alice and I stayed briefly in Lichfield, and I confess I found the accent hard to understand.'

'You'll find a bed in Stafford.'

'You could find a bed for me here. Then you and I could get to know each other better. I warrant you have your own tales to tell. A woman as spirited and witty as yourself. Are there are no empty bedrooms in the house? Or should I sleep in the stables? A better man than me was born in one of those.'

She scowled.

'And you will not inform on me because if they arrest a trespasser in the stables, he couldn't escort your mistress from this place.'

She glared at me. Eye to eye. Unflinching. In return, I smiled. Her cheeks were colouring. She was angry, but she'd not forget me.

'Come with me,' she said.

She led me out of the kitchens and over the moat bridge, shutting the door behind us.

'You cannot stay in the stables. If you are discovered –'

'I shall not be discovered. Invisibility is … how shall I call it? … a skill of my trade.'

'The valley road below leads straight to Stafford.'

I could have pressed my case. Instead, I lifted my arms in surrender. 'Just say goodbye to Matthew, and I'll be on my way.'

'Goodbye Matthew.'

31

'Goodbye, sweet Kate.' I kissed her on the cheek. She stiffened but didn't turn away. 'Two days,' I said. 'Just before sunrise. I'll be waiting for you by the moat bridge.'

Finally, a smile. And she still had all her teeth.

I turned on my heels and set off for Stafford.

I took a room at The White Hart, where Colquhoun had arranged for two post horses to be prepared for the next stage of our journey. He'd been diligent in making the arrangements. Colquhoun might be a miserable fellow, but Rochester had good reasons for bringing him South from Edinburgh. He managed his master's affairs with great skill and little fuss, so there were some things he and I had in common.

I explained to the innkeeper about the change of plan and asked him to be sure the horses would be ready when we needed them. I was tempted to seek out games of cards or dice, or stealthily make my way back to Chartley and try again with Katherine. But the risks of being discovered were indeed too great.

Two days later, I returned as arranged. Kate was as good as her word. She'd been watching from an upstairs window. She opened the door before I could knock.

'Is she ready?' I whispered.

'Sit you down. I'll be back soon.' She disappeared up the back stairs.

I hate waiting. Leave butter out and it turns rancid. Leave wine and it turns to vinegar. Same with thoughts. Give them time and they too turn sour. Another man might have said his prayers, but on the rare occasion I do get an answer it's never what I want to hear.

Finally, the stair door opened. Kate came back into the room, followed by a heavy, buxom woman, her hair concealed beneath a dowdy blue bonnet. Were they still not ready? Was I now to entertain this Staffordshire sow?

'Matthew Edgworth?' She spoke without so much as a glance in my direction. 'I believe you are here to escort me from this place.' Her voice as pure as crystal. I gaped in amazement. Was this Lady Frances herself, transformed from renowned court beauty to a corpulent drab? Given Alice's miraculous transfiguration from Smock Alley doxy to raven-haired Spanish lady, I shouldn't have been so startled, but to dress lamb as mutton – that was somehow more surprising. The transformation was perfect – except that she'd need to keep that face concealed and stay silent. Her skin had been made to look ruddy and her cheeks were puffed out, but no paint could conceal the beauty of her eyes. It was the first time I'd seen her close to. Later, as we journeyed together, often not speaking for miles on end, I mused about Frances and Alice – not merely the uncanny likeness in appearance of each to the other, but their manners, their wit, and even the circumstances of our first meetings in dark, cheerless kitchens.

'From this place, Master Edgworth. Without further delay, and I thank you.'

The exchange was complete. And no-one had seen it, except for Alice, Kate and Matthew Edgworth. I led the way across the moat, down the hill and into the wood on the other side of the valley. On seeing the horse, she looked dismayed.

'Did Lord Rochester not send a coach?'

'He feared it might have been noticed, my lady.' In truth, Rochester didn't have the wit to think such a thing. It was

Colquhoun and I who planned the journeys, Colquhoun and I who made the arrangements.

'We need to get clear of Chartley before sunrise. The coachman will meet us later. Shall I walk beside you, my lady?'

'Do you take me for the simple-minded nursemaid that appears before you? The journey would take a week. The horse is surely strong enough to bear us both. I am thankful it's not a mule. Just get me away from this god-forsaken place.'

We didn't speak again until we reached Stafford, where the two post horses had been saddled and were waiting for us in the yard at The White Hart. From Stafford we rode to Worcester, from Worcester to Stroud, and from Stroud to Wells. We broke our journey and took simple food in those coaching inns where we changed horses. Night was falling when we arrived at The Crown Inn at Wells. We'd been riding most of the day and had barely spoken in all that time. I know when conversation isn't welcome.

She was an excellent horsewoman, but anyone would have been exhausted after a ride such as that, especially when her disguise demanded so much padding beneath those drabbest of clothes.

The ostler dealt with the horses. A maid showed us to our simple bedchambers. Had this common nursemaid and her companion paid for anything better we might have been suspected of being thieves on the run from our master. Lady Frances made no complaint. It impressed me that she didn't think herself above spending the night in such a place.

My room overlooked the yard. Hers was on the opposite side of a dark narrow landing.

I ate downstairs. A couple of dozen men were drinking in the hall, which was quieter than any London tavern. I chose to sit alone on a rough bench at the end of a long table. I wasn't seeking profit from the evening. I needed food, then sleep. Nobody came to bother me – until I became aware of a large, dull brown presence standing close by. I looked up. Frances, the nursemaid. I resisted the urge to scramble to my feet and indicated she should sit on the bench opposite me.

She leant across the table and whispered, 'Tell me, Master Edgworth, what is the custom in a place such as this? The etiquette? Do men and women eat together?'

'Servants do,' I said. 'I thought you'd want to eat in your own chamber.'

'I have spent too long in forced confinement these past two months. For weeks I have been forced to endure the tedium of Chartley.'

I called the serving maid over, who duly brought mutton pie and ale for us both. Frances ate everything before her, as if it were appetite and not rags and pillows which had endowed her with such ample hips and belly.

She did her best to be cheerful. But memories of Chartley weighed heavy upon her, and soon seeped into her talk. 'Scottish Queen Mary spent her last year in that damned house,' she said. 'Now I know for certain it was Chartley that finally broke her spirit. The place would surely have broken me if I'd had to stay a day longer. And I fear it will yet break my beloved Katherine. She is almost a sister to me.'

I murmured my commiserations, and hoped my face didn't betray my thoughts. Kate, the maid, was almost a sister! A sister who was surely entrusted with the most delicate of confidences. All the more reason to pursue my seduction.

'But now I have my liberty, Matthew Edgworth.' She looked me in the eye. 'And I intend to live my life.' I could see why every red-blooded man in court was so taken by her. I had the wit to know she was playing me. And the fire in my blood to enjoy it.

But there was more. I escorted her to her room, and was about to bid her goodnight, when she asked, 'Are you left-handed?'

'I confess it. Yes.' Did she imagine my left-handedness was a curse on the venture?

'Most men open doors with their right hand. You use your left. Do you think I don't notice such things? If I have ever met a left-handed man before now, he has concealed it very well. You make no attempt to do so. That intrigues me.' Then she wished me goodnight.

I was woken by a gentle knocking on my door. 'Woken' is an exaggeration, for I sleep like a dog. Eyes shut, but one ear always half-cocked. I have no intention of waking to find my throat slit and my life blood draining away. So even when I share my bed, I sleep with a dagger close to hand. Live your life the way I've lived mine and you'll know better than ever to relax. I opened the door with my right hand – my left held a dagger behind my back.

Frances standing in the doorway. She'd removed the padding and let her hair fall loose. The nursemaid's clothes hung loose about her.

'I cannot sleep.'

36

I intrigued her, and she couldn't sleep! If this were my invention, I might tell you that we sat together on the pallet bed and kissed, that she implored me to pleasure her as no man had ever done before. The truth is stranger than that. She wanted to talk.

'I have never felt so tired, but I cannot sleep.'

And I am rarely so tongue-tied.

She looked at me. 'I know who you are, Master Edgworth.' If she were not so highborn, I might have thought she was flirting with me. 'You are a rogue. I know that very well. A rogue and a villain. But you are also most resourceful.'

She spoke quietly, almost under her breath, then smiled again. And in that soft, almost shadowless light of a waxing gibbous moon – for I had not closed the shutters, wanting first light to wake me in the morning – she looked more beautiful than ever. I had never before been so awed by the presence of a woman. She wore no perfume – she had been travelling as the plainest of nursemaids – but the sweet smell of her breath in that chill midnight air left me weak.

'The names of the places we have ridden through mean little to me. But I have heard of Wells. I know it has a fine cathedral church. And I know it is not on the way from Stafford to London. Where are we going?'

'Sherborne Lodge. Lord Rochester's instructions.'

'He has often spoke of it.'

'In Dorsetshire, my lady. Bradshaw, my lord's coachman, will meet us by the church tomorrow morning. That will be more comfortable than riding.'

'I don't recall complaining about discomfort.'

Frances sitting on a plain wooden stool in the plainest of

rooms. A few rushes on the floor and plain whitewashed walls. Nothing but a simple pallet bed and a joint stool for furniture. And me. And Lady Frances.

I'm not used to silence. London is never silent. I could hear my own breathing.

'Lord Rochester will be there,' I said. 'At Sherborne Lodge.'

Despite her apparent calm, she was angry that we weren't going to London. I was uneasy. I know where I am with the likes of Rochester. But I'd never been alone with a Countess.

She walked over to open the small glass window. A draft of cool night air lifted her hair. 'I can breathe' she said. 'After the privations of Chartley I can at last breathe freely. Do you know how welcome that is?'

I said I could imagine it. That seemed to satisfy her. But I could smell something other than fresh air coming in from outside. The faintest hint of tobacco smoke. I'd kept a watchful eye throughout our journey and was certain we hadn't been followed. But then, from the yard below, came the sound of a horse stamping its hooves.

'They do that in their sleep,' I said. 'Stamp their hooves.'

'Maybe they too have dreams.'

I wondered whether it had been spooked by someone skulking in the yard. 'Perhaps best we do not leave the window open in case we're overheard.' I ventured. 'Gossip travels faster than the fleetest of thoroughbreds.'

She turned and looked at me, tilting her head to one side as if wondering whether she should take advice from this upstart rogue. Then she took a deep breath before shutting the window and returning to sit on the stool.

'I would fain talk to you, Matthew Edgworth.' She was whispering. Matthew it was now.

She turned and looked at me directly. 'When it comes to matters of the heart, Cupid's arrows sometimes land in the most unexpected places.' She let that lie a while before adding. 'I would never have imagined I could fall in love with a Scotsman.' She laughed quietly at the thought. 'And who would have thought that Katherine should be so taken with you.'

She wanted to inflame me, using Katherine as kindling. I may well have blushed.

'Tell me, Matthew Edgworth, you speak well for a rogue. Did you go to school?'

'For long enough to learn to read and write. My father was a lawyer at the Inns of Court. He died. My brothers and sisters too. And my mother.'

'How distressing.'

'No time to grieve, my lady. I had to make my own way in the world. A scrawny little orphan who can read and write is a valuable commodity for a certain kind of folk.'

She clasped her hands together and looked down, as if seeking forgiveness for what she was about to say. 'Have you ever broken into a house?'

'I confess it. Yes. But I'm no common thief, my lady. I do what I have to for my master.' She looked quizzical. 'When he needs me to seek intelligence for him.'

'You act as his spy?'

'Sometimes.'

'Did he ever send you to Doctor Forman's house?'

'Doctor Forman? The Cunning Man of Lambeth? Yes.'

She didn't ask why Rochester sent me. Perhaps she already knew. 'When you return to London, pay another call on Doctor Forman. He has something of mine. He cast my nativity for me. I paid him well for his time, and for the horoscope he promised to cast for me. He wrote to me at Chartley saying he'd completed it. But he trusts no-one as a courier. Can I trust you, Matthew Edgworth, to collect it on my behalf?'

'What if he refuses to give it to me?'

'I've no doubt you have powers of persuasion.'

I thanked her for the compliment.

'Will you do it for me?' We both knew what she was asking.

'Whatever you ask of me, my lady.'

'You will be well rewarded.'

Then she got to her feet and walked to the door. She was about to open it when she turned back.

'Will you make me a promise, Matthew Edgworth?'

'Willingly.'

'If ever my husband forces me back to Chartley, follow me. Break into the house. Do it at night. Let no-one know you are even in Staffordshire. Find me. And take me and Katherine from that dread place to a port where we can take ship for Virginia. If I cannot live as I choose in this country, we will make a new life for ourselves in the new world.'

Soon after dawn, the nursemaid and I walked a hundred yards or so from The Crown to the cathedral church – which is more than a match for Paul's in London. Its towers are taller, its stone is cleaner, its sculpture finer, its windows brighter. As grand a building as any I've seen in England. But the world comes to Paul's, and the world goes about its business beneath its roof.

It sleeps, it trades, it hornifies and cuckolds. It whispers and it shouts. Oh yes, it preaches too, though most who visit Paul's aren't there for the sermonising. There was none of that in Wells – except the preaching. The place was full of clergy and choir. What purpose all that magnificence and sanctity when me and a buxom nursemaid were the only ones present who'd sinned enough to make us worth the saving?

But we weren't there to be saved. We merely did as others did. When we emerged from that cavernous hall of devotion, Bradshaw was there, as arranged. He ushered the nursemaid into the coach and me up to his bench to sit beside him. We travelled about five miles south before he stopped to allow Frances to change into the clothes he'd brought for her. She pulled down the blinds and, hidden from view, she discarded her disguise and took on new clothes and a new name. Thus, she became the fragrant, slender Lady Isobel, Viscount Rochester's English cousin.

For the past day and a half I'd been the nursemaid's travelling companion. Now I was the lady's manservant. When we arrived at the gatehouse at Sherborne Lodge I jumped down, unfolded the steps and held the door open, bowing as she descended.

'Lady Isobel,' I said, extending my arm to steady her.

'I thank you Master Edgworth. It has been a long journey. You have been a good travelling companion.'

Few words, I grant you. But it assured me I'd not dreamt her midnight visit to my room at The Crown.

Rochester appeared in the main doorway. He walked slowly forward and bowed. 'Welcome to Sherborne Lodge, Cousin Isobel.'

I was the only servant close enough to notice that Lady Isobel removed her glove before offering her hand to Lord Rochester, and that the lady's breath came a little quicker as his lips touched her skin.

Colquhoun led me off to the kitchens. After what had passed between myself and Frances, I could tolerate banishment to the kitchens. And, besides, the company of cooks and maids offers its own pleasures.

6

Intelligence in
the guise of drudgery

Why do so many women bestow their tenderest affections on undeserving, tedious men? I could see why Rochester was obsessed by Frances, but I could never fathom what she saw in him. She was as wasted on him as she was on Essex. She was shrewder and more quick-witted than either of them. I guessed it wasn't Rochester she wanted, but the ear of the King.

Sharing King James's bed had swollen Rochester's pride and made him complacent. He, of all men, should have known that kings have Divine Right to be fickle. Rochester's enemies were already queuing up to strike as soon as James grew bored, biding their time like vipers, venom sacs filling through the chill of winter.

My fortunes were still tied to Rochester's, and he paid well for my services. But I was already thinking about a time when I might have to break my ties and raise myself up in different ways. Where better place to start than Sherborne? When men long to know their fate, some ask an astrologer for a reading of their stars, some study *chiromanty*. In times past, they examined the entrails of a goat. A messy business! It was the rise and fall of my master's fortune that interested me. No better way of gleaning that than spending time in his kitchens.

Walls may have ears – but it's servants who talk. I let them all think that it was Bessie who'd caught my eye. Bessie, a rosy-cheeked kitchen maid with fine figure, full lips, a quick tongue and a laugh that gave her away. But I had other interests in that kitchen than who might share my bed that night.

No-one had a bad word to say against Rochester – not with anyone else in earshot. So I showed willing, offering my services and doing whatever was asked of me. This is called intelligence in the guise of drudgery. And, sure enough, when nobody was around to eavesdrop, out slipped the grievances. But you have to be cunning if you want more than day-to-day whinging. I asked about Bessie. So what the kitchen staff remember is Edgworth, the lecherous Londoner, not some foxy intelligencer.

'How long's young Bessie worked in the Lodge?'

'Why you asking?'

'As if you don't know. Go on. How long's she been here?'

'Year or so. Her mother and father used to work here. Both got sick. Good Sir Walter would have kept them on.'

Good Sir Walter. Mark that. Ralegh still remembered fondly some eight years since he was last seen at The Lodge. From one and then another, the yarns of the story came together.

'Good master was Sir Walter.'

'Kind man.'

'Wise man.'

'Terrible thing, man like Sir Walter imprisoned in The Tower.'

The unspoken, badly kept secret in that kitchen was that every one of them who'd known Ralegh despised their new master. Given the history of Sherborne Lodge, that wasn't surprising. Fearing Ralegh's popularity, King James had him imprisoned in The Tower on charges of treason, and his lands taken into Crown ownership. Then James leased Sherborne Lodge for a pittance to his favourite, Robert Carr – now Viscount Rochester. Such generosity.

Not one word spoken directly against the new master. But the damning stories kept tumbling out. I wanted more.

Amos Appleby, the cook, had been drinking, as cooks do. And when cooks drink, they often grow garrulous. I guessed he'd been at Sherborne for most of his working life. The kitchen maids and scullions kept well clear when he shouted and cursed. His face glowed red and his great belly quivered as he roared and he raged. But his hot temper was my opportunity. I accompanied him to the kitchen garden to help gather fruit and vegetables. 'Dinner tonight. For himself and the fancy cousin.'

Did he expect me to speak up for Rochester? He was, after all, my master. Thankfully, he didn't give me the chance.

'Miserable bloody Scot, our new master,' he continued. 'Nothing ever good enough. The Lodge not big enough. The lake not deep enough. My fish not salty enough. Venison not hung long enough. And he hates my quince pies. Hates any pastry. Shouldn't be saying this to you, should I.'

'What you tell me, stays with me,' I said.

'Go tell the Scottish shit-licker for all I care. He daren't dismiss me. He'll never find another cook – not in these parts. Needs a good cook, don't he, if he's gonna impress the jumped-up strumpet what he calls his cousin. See her, did you?'

'Fine looking woman,' I ventured.

'Wasted on himself.'

We saw eye to eye on that, but I didn't comment. My job to gather peas and beans, carrots and parsnips. He pointed to them. I picked them.

'I've filled two trugs,' I said.

He grunted. But his eyes were closed. He was sitting on a stone bench, slumped against the wall.

'Can I trust you, Master Appleby?' I asked – not that I cared one jot for his trust. But if he thought I was revealing secrets, I might get some in return.

The prospect of gossip roused him from the edge of slumber. He chuckled and took a swig of brandywine from a flask concealed beneath his apron. I began cautiously, as if worried I might be overheard. My prologue, if you like. I started with talk about the court in Whitehall, the painted ladies and their trains of suitors, the fanciful fops with hats like shuttlecocks, and heels so high they could hardly balance.

There is nothing quite so certain to arouse righteous rage amongst the rustics as ranting about the manners of the court. I had my audience's attention. It was time to begin the play. It opened with a series of petty little grievances. How Rochester was the meanest master, how he never thanked me for covering his mistakes, how he gathered about him a parade of flattering, talentless sycophants, Nathaniel Smoothfleece,

Crispin Wellbourne, Sir Wellbred Golding. I was enjoying myself, although I hoped I hadn't overreached myself when I started moaning about Nick Stuff, the master's personal clerk. Appleby's raucous laughter, and his offer to share his brandywine suggested otherwise.

'You might, laugh, Master Appleby. But his enemies are gathering like wolves by night.'

'Why d'you stick with him then?' he grumbled.

'Would that I could leave. But I daren't. Not yet.'

'Not yet?'

'Forgive me,' I said. 'I've drunk too much. And said too much. I shouldn't burden you with my troubles. I brought them on myself.'

He eased himself back, lifted his bum off the bench and let rip a fart so noxious that it surely killed all garden pests within twenty yards. One way of keeping caterpillars off the cabbages.

'Better,' he said. 'That eased a burden.' And his belly rippled with laughter.

Needing fresh air in my lungs, I got to my feet and turned away, as if deliberating on whether to take him further into my confidence. When I turned back, I lowered my voice.

'He will be brought down soon enough. The fall will be heard a hundred miles away. I don't want to be taken down with him, but that's not what troubles me. I can look after myself. My great worry is...' I paused. A short interlude before the next act.

'What? worries you?'

I took a long slow breath. 'Ralegh's fate.' His eyes widened. 'Rochester and his toadies are conspiring against him. They never miss an opportunity for defamation. I have heard...'

and then I took a pause – you see how many lessons I've taken from the players. 'I have heard it said that good King James had been planning to pardon Sir Walter. And he would have done so, … I shouldn't be telling you this. Forgive me.' I dropped my voice to a whisper for the epilogue. 'The thing is this, Appleby, our master fears Sir Walter. Even in The Tower. You see, Ralegh has befriended good Prince Henry – which means Sir Walter's regaining influence.'

'That's good.'

'It should be. But my fear…' I paused again. 'My fear is that Viscount Rochester will persuade the King to have Ralegh executed before Prince Henry comes of age.'

Appleby groaned in rage, a bear who's seen the dogs, and cannot wait to be unleashed into the pit. And then, in a low rumble, out came what I'd been hoping for, '*The School of Night* will see to the Vice Cunt. Them'll destroy him.'

'I thought *The School of Night* passed away with Doctor Dee and Kit Marlowe.'

Appleby got to his feet and stumbled forward before turning round to look me in the eye. His breath reeked and he couldn't walk straight, but he somehow focused his bloodshot eyes on mine.

'There are some… Some men,' he began, but then his thoughts slipped out of reach.

'Some men?' I prompted.

'Men who won't… Men who won't rest until… Viscount … Rochester stripped of title. And plain Robert bloody Carr takes Sir Walter's place in The Tower.'

Two turtle doves were perched cooing on the high wall opposite. The lavender bed was alive with bees. But no other sound broke his silence. An age seemed to pass. I wondered if Appleby had fallen into the arms of brandywine and I'd lost him for the afternoon. Then, without opening his eyes and barely moving his lips, he mumbled something that sounded like 'Gervase Chapman. Chapman the man to talk…' His head slumped. His mouth fell open.

'Gervase Chapman?' I said. 'Is that right?'

He grunted. And dribbled onto his belly.

'Where? Master Appleby? If I'm to speak to this Gervase Chapman, where will I find him?'

'London.'

'Where in London?' He was slipping away again. I shook him by the shoulder.

'Phoenix.'

'The Phoenix tavern? Which? There are several.'

'Bowden landlord.' He lurched. Opened his eyes wide. 'Phoenix in Something Street.'

There's a great many Something Streets in London, but by then the brandywine had taken him for its own, and there was nothing more I could get from him.

7

The egg and the mirror

Rochester sent word through Colquhoun for me to meet him in a room above the stables at Cope Castle which the grooms and the stable boys never used. It was where we usually met. I arrived in good time. The room was bare except for a joint stool and a stack of firewood in a corner. A raw wind was blowing from the north. I lit a fire in the hearth. I always carry a tinderbox, and there was no shortage of straw. I liked to make him feel welcome. The fire drew well, very little smoke blew back into the room. Even the stable block chimneys were well built at Cope Castle.

My thoughts drifted to Appleby in the walled garden at Sherborne. He'd been so drunk he'd probably not remember his indiscretions, but I had them firmly rooted in my memory. Gervase Chapman, *The School of Night*, The Phoenix tavern. The first thing I'd done on getting back to London was to find out which Phoenix. There was a Phoenix in Drury Lane, but the landlord there was a John Goodstock. The Phoenix out in

Whitechapel wasn't it either. Richard Bowden ran the Phoenix in Lombard Street. I drank and ate there one night but decided not to seek Gervase Chapman just yet. It could work against me to show myself too soon. To strike a good deal, you must be clear about what you want, precise in what you offer in return, and get the timing right.

For the moment I could get more from working for Rochester.

I was kneeling in front of the fire, warming my hands, when I heard boots on the stairs. By the time the door flew open I was standing.

'Good day, my Lord.' I bowed. But not too low. I'd hate him to think I was mocking.

He grunted a response, slammed the door behind him and strode over to the fire. He removed his sealskin gloves and stood before the fire.

'When did you last see Doctor Forman?'

'A fortnight ago. The day before I set out with the whore for Chartley.'

'What did he say?'

'That he would do everything he could to ensure that Lord Essex would never consummate his marriage. But he refused to supply poisons.'

He gestured for me to bring him the stool. He sat down, holding his palms to the fire.

'You don't accept refusals, Edgworth. That's why I employ you. Go back to him.'

'Doctor Forman is not like other men.'

'Does he frighten you?'

'Not in the least, my Lord. But he pretends to be a Godly man, and threats don't work with him.'

Rochester stood up, knocking the joint stool over as he did. It clattered to the side of the room. He turned on me.

'Are you deaf? Do you not hear what I'm saying? Or are you fucking witless? I employ you to do what I ask. Don't tell me what doesn't work.'

'You're right, my lord. Everyone can be persuaded. With some people, it takes minutes. With Forman, it may take longer.'

'I don't like that word 'longer'. Soon, Edgworth. Soon. Every minute that man Essex lives is an offence against nature.'

'I will speak to Forman again. But best not push him too hard. The last thing we want is for him to leave London.'

He glared at me.

'But if he does, my Lord, I track him down. I bring him back. He will agree to what you ask, I promise you.'

He turned away, took hold of a stick, and angrily poked at the fire.

'I will go to him tomorrow, my Lord.'

'Days, not weeks,' he said. Then he stomped from the room, as if petulance would speed my negotiations with the doctor.

I took a wherry across the Thames to Stangate Stairs, the landing stage close by Lambeth Palace. Forman's stone-built house stood on its own about a quarter of a mile up the track to Camberwell.

The wooden door creaked as I entered the flint-walled garden. It was a hot September day, and the air inside was heavy with the scents of herbs, roses and gillyflowers. But the sweet perfumes and rich colours of Forman's garden aroused misgivings. If the devil had all the best tunes, it seemed he also had the best physic gardens. His wife opened the door to my knocking.

'The answer is no, Master Edgworth. I have told you before, you are not welcome in this house.'

'My brother Jacob is sick,' I said. Something of an understatement given how long he'd been in his coffin.

'The last time you were here you tried to intimidate my husband. I do not wish to see you in this house again.'

'Hear me out, Mistress Forman. That is not why I'm here today. My brother has a fever. And I fear for his life. I've come to seek your husband's advice.'

'I doubt you even have a brother.'

'Dear Jacob is abed at New Place, a house in Warwick Lane, and is much too sick to walk. I don't ask you to like me or my master, but my brother is as honest a man as any in London.' If dead men tell no lies, that was indeed a kind of truth.

'An honest man in London!'

'There are times when I despair of our dear Jacob's honesty! He's not like me at all!'

Mistress Forman scowled, as if that would drive me away. What I saw was a fine-looking woman, some thirty years younger than her husband. Tall, but slight of frame. Strong features to her face, and piercing eyes of deepest green.

'Will you at least ask the good doctor if he'll see me? I can pay very well.'

'I will take you to him. But I will stay while you speak with him. Follow me.'

As shrewd as she was shrewish.

I followed her through the dark passages that led to the doctor's room at the back of the house. She knocked on his door. We waited awhile. The door opened. Susan, the maid, scurried past with her head turned away, not saying a word.

'Susan has been helping me with the ledgers.' The doctor was seated behind his table. Curtains had been pulled across the window, and lanterns had been lit despite the time of day. Mistress Forman ushered me in and shut the door behind us. I'd been to the room before, and had seen the shelves of books, the gleaming instruments, the multi-coloured bottles and jars of powders and pastes. But that sweet scent of lavender oil – so unexpected the first time I'd visited – was tainted with the reek of exertions with the maid.

'Master Edgworth's brother has a fever,' said Mistress Forman. 'He needs your advice.' Her feigned composure barely concealing a furious heart.

'He is near death,' I said. 'If it was me was sick, good doctor, I wouldn't expect you to attend to me. But our Jacob is a good man.'

'I cannot heal someone I've never met.'

'I'm here to ask advice. I'll pay well for it.'

I produced a purse and emptied the contents into my palm.

'Do I have to remind you, Simon,' said the wife, 'That you have it in your power to do some good in this world?'

'I have no need for you to remind me of anything. I did not ask for your interruption.'

'Save your indignation,' said Mistress Forman. 'I am sure it will keep. This man's brother is dying.'

They were well practiced in the art of quarrelling. Not my place to intervene. Her anger soon grew so intemperate that she turned on her heels and left me and the doctor to our dealings.

'If anyone can help my beloved Jacob, it's you, good Doctor.'

He looked up and sighed, his high forehead creased with deep furrows. The intensity of his gaze made me uneasy. 'If your ailing brother is another of your crude devices to gain access to my presence, there is nothing you can say or do will make me change my mind.'

'I am not here today for my master. If there's a more honest man in London than my brother –'

'But you are not honest, Matthew Edgworth. And your master is a scheming catamite.'

I raised my hands in submission. How could I disagree?

He shut the ledger he claimed to have been working on and took out a leather-bound casebook from a drawer beneath the table. He asked for a detailed account of my brother's fever, how long he'd been suffering, whether he had any swellings or rashes. Where he lived and worked, where he slept in the house, when and where he fell ill. I was wary of Forman, but he was no charlatan, whatever others might say. And I was interested in how he worked.

He rested his elbows on the table, folded his hands together as in prayer, then leant forward resting his chin on his hands. I would have shut my eyes if that could have prevented him from reading my thoughts.

'You want to leave my house with something for your brother?' Was that a statement or a question? 'An ointment, a poultice, or powders? An elixir of life, perhaps? Or a salve for your own conscience?'

'Not me. My brother's health.'

55

'Your beloved brother's health.' Then he leant back in his chair. 'You want to take him something to show your concern. I can give you advice. But this most honest brother of yours deserves better than that. I have a duty to make something for him. So… we must go to my workshop. Take off your boots. We walk on stockinged feet. We make no noise, we carry no lights. My wife would smell the candle smoke. Stay close.'

I suspected a trick. But I had my wiles too. And the further away we were from the interference of Mistress Forman, the more likely I was to get what I wanted. Or so I thought.

He led me down a long dark corridor at the back of the house. I was wary, silently counting every step, committing to memory every door and unlit wall-lantern. He opened a door, steered me through, shut and locked it behind us, then led me down a narrow stone stairway, into the darkness beneath the house. A few yards along another passageway. He stopped, unlocked a door and ushered me in.

Even before he'd lit two wall lanterns and a candle, I knew from the pungent combination of smells that this must be the place where he made his potions and poisons, syrups and salves. I could smell some of the same herbal essences that were present in his study – aromatic and musky – but beneath that, and catching in the throat, the whiff of sulphur and coal smoke and something metallic and acrid, as when a kitchen pot boils dry.

He sat behind a table, making notes and diagrams in the casebook he'd brought with him. In the far corner of the room was his furnace with a large copper alembic hanging over it, and all manner of apparatus I'd never seen before. On one of the shelves, in the opposite corner, stood a large bell jar, containing the embalmed bleached corpse of a small animal. The horn of a unicorn hung over his table, suspended on a golden braid.

It was Forman's silence that most unsettled me. As he scratched away, scribbling in his casebook, I felt his power growing, mine draining away.

'I have cast your brother's nativity from what you have told me,' he said, without so much as a glance in my direction. 'It is never wholly accurate without the subject present, but taken with your account of his symptoms, I can prepare a poultice. Sit down. Do not disturb me while I work.'

I did as he said. This business of my brother's sickness had started to trouble me. Did Forman know about Jacob and the darkness surrounding his death? I should never have invoked his memory. But if I paid him well for the poultice, I might yet persuade him to let me take away Lady Frances's horoscope, for I had not forgotten the promise I'd made at The Crown in Wells. First Jacob's poultice, then the horoscope, and finally the poison.

He got up from his chair, collected some vials and wooden boxes, measured various powders into the pans of the scales. He poured the concoction into a mortar, added a little oil then ground all to a paste, which he smeared onto a bandage. He went about his business as a cook might prepare a dinner, confident, unhurried, unconcerned by my presence.

'There,' he said, laying the poultice on the table.

'How much do I owe you, doctor?'

'Your brother is an honest man. None more honest in all of London. Isn't that what you said? How could I ask payment for speeding such a man's recovery?'

'I thank you, doctor.'

'Don't leave. Not yet. I have something to show you. Something that I'm sure you'll find of interest.'

He took me by the arm and led me over to the bell jar in the corner, which I'd thought contained the preserved corpse of an animal. I felt a sudden surge of turn-sickness – not so much at the hideously swollen head with giant bulbous eyes, but at the perfection of the tiny human hands.

'Do you know what it is?'

'You don't frighten me, Doctor. I've seen much worse.'

'Why would I want to frighten you?' His voice was quiet. Barely louder than a whisper. 'A woman lost her life giving birth to this. It didn't long survive her. What is frightening, Matthew Edgworth, is how little we understand. What terrible thing caused it to grow like that? All is not perfect in this world, as you very well know. But it is you who trades in fear, Edgworth. My life's work is to seek to understand a little better, not to frighten people. If we are to understand, we have to speak truth. You are easier to read than a sign outside a tavern. You and I both know your brother died many years ago.'

That chilled me. I tried to make light of it: 'How foolish then, to make a poultice for a man who doesn't exist.'

He gave a sly little laugh and walked back to his table.

'Don't take me for a fool. The poultice is for you. Not your imagined brother.'

'A bandage for my redemption? To transform me into a God-fearing churchgoer? If I'd told your wife the truth, she'd never have let me in. But now we are here. You and me. So let us waste no more time.'

'You are here for your master. He wants me to make a poison that will kill Lord Essex. And if I don't do as you say you will force me to your will.'

'My master awaits your decision.'

'He knows my decision. I said no before. I say it again now. I will never make a poison to kill an innocent man. Frances Howard married a man she despises. That is a misfortune shared by many women, not justification for taking a life.'

'You could make a poison that would make it seem his heart had given out.'

'There are many things I *can* do. But what you and your master seem not to understand is that I will never be bought.'

I stood up. Reached beneath my doublet and withdrew my dagger. He didn't flinch.

'I am not going to kill you. You're no use to me dead. But I have skills, too, doctor. I can cut flesh in ways that'll leave a man in pain for the rest of his days.'

He shuffled back, lifted his hands in the air and gulped as tried to swallow.

'Then you and I ...' he paused, took a breath, and started again. 'Then you and I must reach an understanding.' He laid the poultice on the table.

'Very good, I said. 'That's all I ask for. A little understanding.'

He held a finger up to bid me wait. Then opened a drawer in the table and took something out, which he concealed in his hand. He walked over to my side of the table, then opened his hand to reveal what I thought was a quail's egg. Flattening his palm, he held it up to show me.

'I can make you a poison. See this little egg. I suck it clean. Then I fill it with powders and seal them inside.' He picked up the egg and held it up for me to look at. 'Then I shake the egg.' Slowly, gently, back and forth. 'If there were powders inside, they would mix, creating vapours. Vapours so powerful that if the egg were then to break, and the poisons inside were released, you and I would each suffer convulsions and a seizure of the heart. What do you know about snake's eggs?'

How could I know about snake's eggs? I'm a Londoner.

'The shell is soft and pliable. Not brittle like a hen's egg. Watch.' And he gently squeezed the little egg. It didn't crack. 'But in time it weakens. A baby chick has a beak to peck its way out. Baby snakes must wait for the shell to decompose. Which it surely will. Take care what you ask for, Matthew Edgworth.'

He removed a small black velvet cushion from the drawer and placed the pure white snake's egg on it.

'Take it. Put it in your purse. Or a pocket. But never forget what it is you're carrying, and how fragile it is.' He knew I'd not touch it. He opened the daybook which lay on the table. 'You know what this is? Look. What do you see?'

'Numbers. Symbols. Lines on a page. Writing.'

'What you see is the nativity I cast for Frances, Countess of Essex.'

'Her horoscope?' He nodded. How could he have known I wanted that?

He lit an incense burner with a taper. The room quickly filled with sweet-smelling smoke.

'No man can foretell the future, however learnèd and wise he might be. The Countess has the same free will God gave us all.' His voice becoming distant. 'A nativity is but a map of possibilities.'

'Let me take it for her.'

'My casebooks are precious. They never leave here.'

'Then copy it. I'll pay you well. I promised Lady Frances I would collect it.'

'That was a foolish promise. She must be present when I read it to her. But you may look at it. You can assure her that you've seen it.'

'It's written in a language I've never seen before.'

'A man can look. You have a memory.'

There was an object lying on the table beside the casebook. I hadn't noticed it before. The light was low, the room had filled with herbal smoke. Sweet, but not so sweet as incense, more like woodland after rain.

Forman lowered his voice. 'Do you see?'

'The mirror?'

'An obsidian mirror. An object of unimaginable power. The great John Dee's legacy to me. Gaze into it, Matthew Edgworth. That too gives a glimpse of possibilities.'

I reached to pick it up. He took hold of my wrist.

'Put it back on the table. Look at it there.'

A black glass framed in finely wrought silver. Black glass lying flat. Myself leaning over. I saw the outline of my face. Highly polished black glass, but nothing more than a mirror. I had an urge to laugh.

'Stare into it.'

'And see what?'

'Breathe slow and be patient, Matthew Edgworth. The scrying mirror will answer your question.'

I was minded to pick up the damned mirror and beat him with it. But I did as he bad me. I looked. Time itself seemed to shiver. My own face dissolved.

I caught sight of something… deeper than darkness. A bottomless void that snuffed out all sound and light, a void that swelled, and grew, expanding in the deeps beneath the mirror. Darker than a raven's wing. Darker than coal. Darker than the abyss. I knew it straightway for what it was. The same darkness I'd glimpsed once before. In the priory near Spital Fields.

It chilled me in a way that visions of demons with horns and cloven feet could never do. And yet I couldn't look away.

Have you ever woken alone in the darkest hours of a moonless night, alone yet knowing there's a presence in the bedchamber with you? Tried to dismiss it as the lingering taste of fear spilling over from a nightmare? Got out of your bed and willed yourself awake, but still unable to banish it?

Whatever I saw in that obsidian mirror was more powerful, more real than any ghost.

'Did you see it?' came Forman's voice. He was staring at me. 'A forewarning. Take heed, Matthew Edgworth. You are ruthless and ambitious. You despise your master, yet you will do whatever he asks in the interests of your own advancement. Never again ask me to make poisons – whether for your own use or your master's. I will not do it – for we can never know what tides of darkness our actions might unleash.'

I left the Forman house trying to convince myself that the snake's egg and the scrying mirror had been nothing more than the kind of tricks so often turned by mountebanks and magicians who lighten the pockets of gulls at fairs. I cursed myself for allowing him his moment of triumph.

As weeks and months passed, however, I came to realise

that I had indeed witnessed true dread in that obsidian mirror. And that still haunts me, even now.

I duly delivered my message to the Vice Count: 'Doctor Forman has agreed to continue to work his magic to prevent Essex from consummating his marriage.'

'Did he agree to provide poison?'

'He did, my Lord. But it might take him several weeks to find all the ingredients.'

'Several weeks! Which could mean several months. What fucking use to me is that?'

He was a child who refused to be gainsaid. He would have what he wanted, no matter what the cost. His shouts and curses were ridiculous, but I wasn't the only rogue in his secret employ, and he wouldn't hesitate to have me cut down and disposed of when he no longer had need of me. So I listened meekly to his rantings.

'Do you not remember why I hired you? Dragged you out from your wretched life with the flesh-brokers, whores and rats in the stinking Southwark stews?'

'How could I forget, sir? I am forever indebted to you.'

'Rid me of Essex. Or I will rid the world of you.'

'Allow me, sir, I beg you.'

'Allow you what, you insolent scoundrel? Now is not the time to be begging favours.'

'I've been thinking about what you once told me about old Walter Ralegh,' I said.

'I've said many things about Ralegh.'

'Did you not once tell me that it was you who dissuaded our good King James from having him … contract a disease that might prove fatal?'

'Ralegh is harmless in The Tower,' he said. 'In death he would be mourned and celebrated.' Parroting what I had said to him a few months before.

'Very wise,' I said.

'But bloody Essex is not imprisoned in the Bloody Tower. And he is far from harmless.'

'But if Essex were to die a young death, Lady Frances would be forced to play the grieving widow. She could not be seen with you for many months. Might it not be better to see Essex dishonoured than mourned?'

His puckering lips twitched into the semblance of a smile.

'And how do you propose we bring disgrace to Lord Essex?'

8

What you learn in theatres

Lady Frances wondered how I learnt to read and write. My days in school were only half a truth. The other half is this – I learnt as much from theatres as from books. The actors and their playwrights taught me more than they could ever know. Indeed, I owe my life to one of their murderous tricks, as you'll hear tell in due course.

I first went to a playhouse to cut purses with Jacob, the boy they called my half-brother. A bully and my tormentor, but a well-practiced foist. My job to make a nuisance of myself. Distract the chosen victim while Jacob took his purse. For every ten shillings he took, he gave me a penny. I was too frightened of Jacob to complain, so I stuck with him and learnt the trade. Cutpurses usually work in pairs. But long before Jacob died, I could see that a skilled cutpurse could work alone in public theatres like The Swan or The Globe. The jostle and roar of the crowd makes it possible to work alone. I'd see the same play twice, get to know when the crowd was silent, when they got excited, and when they wouldn't notice a young lad squeezing by. Do nothing first time – except watch, listen and learn. Cut purses the second. A good cutpurse has an eagle's eye, a lion's heart, and a lady's hand. The eye to spy the soft victim, the heart to be fearless and the hand to slip lightly in and nimbly out.

Comedies are best for cutting purses – there's hubbub at a comedy. But there's much to be learnt from them all. If a boy can play a queen, a rogue can play an angel, and an innocent the devil, what was to stop me from playing the courtier? I'd need the clothes of course – and where better to look than The Blackfriars tiring house, where The King's Men kept their costumes and their face paints. I made it my business to learn how a king can be cut down in battle, how an actor can be hanged from the gallows the same time each afternoon, how a man can be stabbed and bleed to death and live to play it all again the next day. And many other tricks besides.

I also like the words they speak, the tales they tell.

9

Traps and curses

As I stepped from the wherry at Stangate Stairs I caught sight of Doctor Forman standing by a mooring on the south bank, a hundred yards or so downstream. There were several rowboats tied up, and he was talking to a boatman. When the fellow went off to tidy his oars, or whatever it is boatmen do in their sheds, I walked over. Forman had his back to me.

'Good day to you, Doctor.'

He turned round, startled, staring wide-eyed, as if I were an apparition he'd conjured from Hell.

'Going far?' I said.

'I have business to attend to, and it's none of yours. You're not welcome here, Edgworth. None of you are welcome here.'

'None of us? I'm alone, my friend.'

'I will have nothing to do with your master's depravity.'

'I'm not here for my master. I have business for myself, in Lambeth Palace. I saw you here. It seemed courteous to walk over and wish you good day.'

'If you think you can force me to your master's will with hidden threats,' he whispered, 'Think again.'

'What threats? I'm grateful to you. You've been most kind to me.'

'You're scum. All of you. Everything you say is a lie or a threat.'

'Why ever would I threaten you, Doctor?'

He glared, as if that alone could lay a curse upon me. And then, slow and soft: 'You reap what you sow, Matthew Edgworth.'

'Then I shall sow goodwill! Take your time and travel well.'

'What do you mean by that?' he snapped.

'Travel safely. God be with you, Doctor.' I turned away and walked along the bank towards Lambeth Palace a hundred yards or so. I looked back. Forman was already in his boat. I stood watching for a while as the boatman handed him the oars, undid the mooring rope and pushed the boat off. It looked like Forman was rowing over to Whitehall Stairs. He caught sight of me. I waved. He scowled and pulled harder on the oars.

I was troubled by that 'none of you are welcome here.' Had Rochester sent another of his men before me?

I had no more business in Lambeth Palace than I did in the King's bedchamber. It was Forman's house I was heading for. I'd not planned on the good doctor's absence, but it would make things easier. His wife was visible at an upstairs window, watching the river intently. She seemed not to notice me, and it seemed best not to disturb her or the maid by knocking the door. On a previous visit I'd found a side door giving entry to a small room filled with wooden shelves and used for drying herbs. It was unlocked. Clearly, Forman didn't expect to be away for long.

I make it my business to get to know the intricacies of every house I visit. It's in my nature to be curious. Doesn't the Good Book tell us to make the most of our talents? Forman's was a warren of dark-panelled passages and unexpected stairs. From the drying room, an interior door opened onto a narrow passage. His workshop was in a cellar, but I needed to find his ground floor study to orientate myself. I removed my boots and shuffled silently on stockinged feet with only touch and memory for guidance, stopping every few yards to listen for movement in the house. Silence. Was Mistress Forman still upstairs? Was he visiting a lover in Westminster? Was that why she was watching him so intently? Or did she have a lover of her own?

I found an unlit lantern hanging from a wall bracket beside a heavy wooden door. I recognised the triangular pattern of iron studs of his study door. I'd memorised the route through passageways and down stairs from his study to his workshop. One day, I'll write about the under-rated craft of picklockery. In the meantime, suffice it to say that the lock to the door which led down stone stairs to Forman's workshop yielded quickly to my tender tickling.

No natural light down there. But I always carry a tinderbox and small candle. I shut the door behind me, then lit the candle. I locked the door behind me, then eased a small, tapered dowel into the keyhole. If anyone came to the door while I was inside, they'd see no flickerings of light, nor be able to insert a key.

Forman's workshop. Where he wrote up his casebooks, made up ointments, mixed poisons and worked the dark arts.

Everything was as it had been when I was last there. The shelves with yards of books, the glass jars and flasks, the bottles and boxes. The furnace, the alembic and gleaming instruments, the balancing scales. The unicorn horn hanging over the table. I tried to avoid looking at that vile deformed foetus in the bell jar in the corner, but I couldn't shut out its ghastly presence. The only thing different was the smell. The acrid, cloying smell of overheated metal and sulphuric fumes was stronger, and not masked by the scent of lavender, sage and marjoram which had so surprised me on my earlier visit.

A folio book lay open on the table. An inkwell and goose quill beside it – as if Forman had just left the room to visit the privy. After pausing to take stock and reassure myself I'd seen him setting out across the river only minutes before, I sat on the chair where he made his notes. I placed my candle on the table. The flame was steady, but the light seemed somehow contained. From where I sat, I couldn't see the walls, as if I had wandered into some vast cavern on the edges of Hell itself. I have never been frightened of the dark. I'm wary of people who hide in dark corners, but darkness itself holds no terrors for me. But this… This was different. The very light from my candle made the darkness blacker, more profound. And the air itself was heavy, burdened with the weight of that darkness. I slowed my breathing, calmed myself. I had plenty of time. Forman could be away for hours.

I leafed through pages of charts, diagrams, exotic occult symbols, most of it in a language and characters I didn't recognise. Lists, tables, inventories, and what I presumed were ingredients for recipes with quantities attached to names. The word *belladonna* caught my eye. I knew that for a poison. My fingers were sweaty, although the air in the room was cold as midwinter midnight. The book might be useful if I were ever to meet Gervase Chapman and make an alliance with Ralegh's *School of Night*. What better way to introduce myself? I could come back for it – and more. If I could break in once, I could do it again. But it was the casebook containing Frances's horoscope I was looking for. And the belladonna book wasn't it.

I pulled gently on the drawer beneath, slid my hand inside. It was lined with velvet – soft, inviting to the touch. But I knew Forman to be a cunning man in every sense. Move too quick and my fingers could have been crushed in a sprung trap. Or worse. The snake's egg full of poisonous vapours could be lying in the dark, waiting for an intruder to break it open. My hand sliding slowly, silently, half an inch at a time. Fingertips touching sheets of parchment. A spare quill. A metal bowl. Small candles. A tinderbox. I took them out, laid them on the table. Then slowly eased my hand in again. At the back of the drawer … cold leather. Another casebook? I grasped it with fingertips and was slowly removing it when my hand brushed against something that felt like sharpened teeth. Instinct made me snatch my hand back. And in that moment of weakness, I betrayed myself. My sudden movement jarred the table, knocking the candle over, extinguishing its flame. I heard it fall from the table and roll across the floor.

The air grew heavier around me. Instinctively, I shut my eyes – to protect myself from Forman's darkness. On hands and knees, I crawled until I found the candle.

Footsteps on a wooden floor above. Hurried woman's footsteps. A door slamming shut.

My heart beating fast. I stopped where I was, clasping the unlit candle. Breathe slow, breathe deep. A door shutting heavily. More footsteps. Anne Forman clomping through the house in fury.

Think simple, think straight. Light the candle from the tinderbox.

Sparks in the darkness. No flame in the tinder.

Patience, Matthew.

More sparks. No fire.

Seven, maybe eight attempts. At last, a timid flame.

Holding the candle before me with one hand, shielding my eyes from the light with the other, I remove the casebook from the drawer. Figures, diagrams, writing in strange characters. I turn more pages. These are the names I'm looking for – Frances Howard, Robert Devereux, Anne Turner. Others too, all connected with Lady Frances. I shut the book. A good day's work. I should pocket the book and leave. But reading the word *belladonna* has planted its own seed. On a shelf near the door is a wooden box with a dozen empty glass vials, each with cork stoppers. I take a couple, wrap them in my kerchief and pocket them.

Then back to the table. Everything taken out has to go back in the drawer. Forman mustn't know there's been an intruder. That's when it catches my eye. There, on a corner of the desk, a black pool of darkness. The scrying mirror. So that was the trap that Forman had left. His damned mirror. I look away. I'd not allow a child's night fright to startle me a second time. All I have to do is return everything to the drawer. Never mind the jaws of whatever it might be. A cat? A snake? A succubus? No matter. Teeth or no teeth, a skull is but a skull. No more frightening than the *memento mori* in every household.

I take a casebook from the shelves to put in place of the book with Frances's nativity. The books on the shelf are tightly packed, so I jiggle them around a bit until the gap's not noticeable. I slide the casebook from the shelf to the back of the drawer. Then replace the quill, the sheets of parchment, the little metal bowl, the candles…

But as I'm doing this, the scrying mirror's luring my gaze like a flash of sun on distant glass. I shut my eyes. But still I'm dazzled by a tiny pulsing zigzag circle. I turn away. Wherever I look – eyes shut or open – the pattern's growing ever brighter, and gradually expanding. Time seems to falter, to hold me in its grip.

Then my throat cramps tight. I can't swallow. An expanding ball of thorns inside my gullet. Behind my right eye a growing pain, something trying to burst out from inside my head.

The room shifting beneath me. I'm losing balance. Can hardly see. I sit down in Forman's chair. But that, too, is moving.

Forman's surely placed a curse on the mirror. I have to escape. But my fingertips are tingling. Then throbbing. As if I've grasped a bouquet of nettles armed with vipers' stings.

I've no idea how I unlocked the door, for I struggled to grasp my picklock wires, and could barely see my own hands before my face. I must have stumbled up the stairs, along the corridors and out through the drying room. By then the zigzag lights had gone, but the light outside was so bright I could barely open my eyes.

I remember glimpsing a small gathering at the water's edge where Forman kept his rowboat. I remember paying the wherryman an extra threepence to get me back across the river because he thought me blind drunk. I remember falling as I stepped onto his boat because by then the turn-sickness was such that I could hardly stand. And I remember realising that I'd left the casebook with Frances's nativity on the table. All I had for my pains were a couple of empty glass vials.

I don't know how I got back to my Broad Lane lodgings. Nothing I could do to stop the pain. An iron band around my head growing ever tighter. I was desperate for the sanctuary of sleep. Those hours were the closest I have ever come to willing my own death. But that would have offered no release. I was certain that Forman's curse and that appalling, blinding headache would accompany me forever in my own perpetual night.

10

School and university

There is truth in the story I told Frances. My father had indeed been a lawyer at the Inns of Court. There was always writing in our house on Gray's Inn Road: legal documents in Latin which I didn't understand, pamphlets he picked up from the churchyard at Paul's, and books. He loved books, and I loved the leather, the paper, the words. The rustle of secrets, the smell of mysteries. Even before they sent me to school I wanted to learn to read and write, though I never got as far as Latin and Greek.

My sister, Beth, died first. Seven years old when she was taken by scarlet fever. Six weeks later my brother, Sam, lost to smallpox. Then father fell sick and couldn't work. It was all mother could do to care for the babes. She took me to Aunt Grace, who lived near Christ Church, just inside the city walls. She was already a widow with no babes in the house. Just one son still lived – Jacob. And now me. Aunt Grace said Jacob should look after me. 'You must treat our Matthew like he's your own younger brother.' Jacob thought that funny.

No books in that house. No more chalk and slates for Matthew.

Soon after moving in with Aunt Grace and Jacob, I heard the plague had come to Gray's Inn Road. I disobeyed my aunt and went back. The house was boarded up. All dead.

Jacob thought it useful I could read and write, but he still mocked me for my book learning. But Jacob was a teacher, in his own way. Picking locks and cutting purses. And many other things besides. Until he died – in that accident near the Spital Fields.

After that I had to work the theatres on my own.

Not just books and plays I learnt to read. So many bawdy houses are close by the theatres. Their business is the same. Little wonder we have so many names for our whores: Guinea-bird, Moll, Punk, Doxy, Wagtail, Doll Tearsheet. All finely tuned performers. I got myself work at the Cardinal's Hat, one of the best houses in Southwark. I was barely thirteen, but fleet of foot, skilled with my hands and quick in my wits – a good combination, highly prized by the bawd. She soon made me Boy of the House. I kept a watchful eye and a twisted smile, always reporting what I saw. The Hat taught me much. The bawd and her dolls and their broker: all in their way fine teachers.

I was a quick learner. Easy to spot those who feigned wealth with borrowed clothes but could ill afford the pleasures on offer. Why waste time on them? It was the moneyed men feigning poverty who interested me. How can any man aspire to rise in this world if he cannot recognise at one swift glance the gullers and the gulled? Jacob had been my cruel tutor. Theatre was my grammar school, the Cardinal's Hat my university. I learnt who to fleece and who to charm. Amongst the latter was a gallant, whose name I've long since forgot, who gave me employment as a messenger. My reputation spread. I was reliable and discreet. Errands led to commendation, led to employment with the king's own favourite, Robert Carr.

II

Letters and dolls

I was lying abed, my head still raging with pain. Made worse if I opened my eyes. I wanted to close the shutters but when I moved, I threw up. Forman's curse was worse than the most vicious of hangovers. And I've known a few of those. I don't often drink much these days – in my trade you need your wits about you – but there was a time I played the drunken rakehell as often as any roaring boy.

I remember little of those hours, except that they stretched out longer than a lifetime. I drifted in and out of sleep, but there was no avoiding the curse. My dreams were filled with head-crushing tortures. My head inside Forman's bell-jar, his dark eyes staring at me through the glass.

Then there was Colquhoun. Washing my face with a flannel. I opened my eyes. What I saw was not my room. At that time, my lodgings were above The Painted Tavern on Broad Lane, not far from Three Cranes Wharf. The place stank of stale beer and rotting fish, but the landlord asked no questions, and very little rent.

But I was lying on a bed of straw and the place smelt of fresh hay.

'Where…?'

'The stable block at Cope Castle. Lord Rochester gave instructions.'

I was surely still dreaming.

'I brought ye here. Ye missed your meeting.'

'I had a fever.'

He shrugged. Colquhoun seldom had much to say for himself except when in his cups. And I was in no state to ask how he'd brought me from Broad Lane to Kensington. But even in my battered state, I had the wit to realise that if he could track me down so easily, I needed new lodgings.

'Ye'll be staying here tonight,' said Colquhoun. 'Himself will see ye i' the morning.'

He brought me bread and cheese, small beer to wash it down, and a chamber pot.

'You think of everything, Colquhoun.'

'A word o' warning, Edgworth. He's nae happy wi ye.'

'Have you ever seen him happy?'

'Don't mock. Not me. Nor him. I've nae idea what he wants from ye. But believe me, the moment you're nae longer o' use ta him, ye may as well be deed. Loyalty's that fine thing he demands from others. He'd think nothing o' having his closest friend killed if he ever felt betrayed.'

I thanked him for his advice.

He locked the door behind him as he left. I could have found my way out easily enough, but I didn't have the energy, and soon slipped back to sleep. I was woken by cock crow the next day. The headache was gone, but I still felt turn-sick when

I got to my feet, and barely had the strength to make a fire.

The sound of Rochester's foul temper stomping up the wooden stairs preceded him. The door flew open.

'What in Hell's name did you do?'

'I had a fever. I am deeply sorry, my Lord. I must have slept a whole day and a night. Please forgive me.'

'A fever?! Is that why you killed him?'

'Killed who, my Lord?'

He glared, his lip twitching beneath that manicured moustache.

'Forgive me, my Lord. I don't understand.'

'No concern of mine how you go about your business. But why? Why in Hell's name would you be so reckless?'

'Who is it you think I've killed?'

'You know damn well. Forman, you half-wit.'

'Doctor Forman?'

'Who else?'

'Forman is dead? I didn't know that, my Lord. I had no part in his death.' I was shocked to hear it. That gave him pause. I waited while he took stock.

'Doctor Forman had a seizure of the heart while rowing across the Thames. I assumed that was your doing.'

'Most certainly not, my Lord. I would never have done such a thing without your instruction.'

He must have died soon after pushing off from the mooring near Stangate Stairs. I was confounded by his death.

'I never liked the man,' said Rochester. 'I like him even less now he's dead. His legacy's a buried powder keg, threatening to destroy everything we have.'

'I agree, my Lord.'

'I instructed you to collect Lady Frances's horoscope from Doctor Forman.'

'He showed it to me, but refused to let me take it. He said he was the only one could interpret it for Lady Frances.'

He sighed.

'But he did supply the poison, my Lord. In case you do have use for it.' I reached inside the pocket of my doublet and pulled out one of the small glass vials I'd taken from Forman's workshop. The liquid inside was dark yellow.

'It's warm,' he said, wary.

'It was warm when he gave it to me,' I said, as if that explained anything. 'It will be safe so long as it remains tightly stoppered. He said not to sniff nor breathe in the vapours, for they alone can kill.'

'How should it be administered?'

'A couple of drops on food or in drink will be enough. There will be no effect for several days. Then the victim will lose all appetite and slowly sicken. And die within six weeks.' Tell him what he wanted to hear. That was always the trick of it.

'Very good,' he said. 'The cruellest of poisons. And undetectable.'

'Exactly. But once the potion's been unstoppered it must be used straightway.'

'I am not yet ready to make use of it.' He handed it back to me, unable to hide his nervousness. 'When the time comes, you will administer it. You understand the business.'

'Forman told me it must be kept in a cool, dark place,' I said. 'So long as it's kept sealed it will remain effective for up to two years. I believe there's an ice-house here at Cope Castle. If you lend me a key, my Lord, I will secrete it in there.'

He thought this a good idea. 'Was the doctor in good health when last you saw him?'

'He was his usual self, my Lord. A curmudgeon, and a pinchpenny. But, as far as I could tell, in excellent health.' I made no mention of stealing into the doctor's workshop. Better that he thought Forman and I reached a deal before he died. If he found out I'd been prey to the doctor's curse, he'd be as wary of me as I was of the scrying mirror.

'You have done well, Master Edgworth. But know this: you are not my only source of intelligence.' He let the threat of that hang in the air. 'The Privy Council will be sending men to scour the Forman House for evidence of corruption and wrongdoing. Lady Frances wrote letters to Forman while she was in Chartley. They must never fall into the hands of those who could use them to sow mischief. Conceal the poison, then go back to Forman's house. Bring me those letters and the casebook with Lady Frances's nativity, and any letters which mention me, Lady Frances or the Earl of Essex. No delays, no excuses. Get there before the Privy Council's officers do.'

He gave me the key to the ice-house and a purse containing five sovereigns. Whoever could have imagined my piss worth more than its weight in gold?

I've taken on men twice my size in knife fights, faced down half a dozen roaring boys all armed with pistols, floored a Thames wherryman who tried to short-change me. But I was filled with dread at the prospect of returning to the Forman house. But if a tiny vial he thought was filled with poison was worth five sovereigns, what would he give for letters and casebooks that could destroy him and his mistress if they fell into the hands of their enemies?

When first I saw the scrying mirror, I lost all sense of time. The second time it nearly killed me. This time I prepared with great care. Along with my daggers, picklock's tackle, tinderbox and candles, I carried a blindfold.

I'd watched Mistress Forman and the maid leave not long before, but even so, the house was unexpectedly silent. I entered through the herbal drying room and made my way through the labyrinth of passages to Forman's study. The door wasn't locked.

Could Forman's heart seizure have been another of his tricks? What if he'd faked his own death on the river? I knocked quietly. Loud enough to be heard by someone in the room. Not by anyone in the kitchens.

Nothing. No sound. Silence growing deeper than death itself.

I put on the blindfold and let myself in.

I felt my way across to the table. No instruments, no books. No quill nor inkwell. I edged around the walls. Found the shelves. Not one book on any of them. I felt every inch of the floor. Nothing in the room except the table with a chair on each side, bare shelves, and a day bed. No books, no letters, no small objects. Nothing that could have been weighted with a curse. But no treasures for me to take away.

Only when I was outside again in the corridor did I remove the blindfold and look back into the room. The shutters had been opened. The room was bare. Officers of the Privy Council had got there before me.

There was still Forman's workshop. The door to that was locked. A good omen. I picked the lock, then waited, steeling myself for whatever might greet me. I blindfolded myself again, felt my way inside and shut the door behind me. As my hand alighted on a shelf, I knocked a jar to the floor. It smashed. I froze. My heart thumping, as if a pistol had been fired in the room.

I stepped forward slowly and slid my hand along the edge of a shelf, filled with the paraphernalia of sorcery. Small skulls, measuring scales, mortar and pestle, glass jars and boxes.

Another step forward. Boots crunching on broken glass. I found a leather pouch and then a root. Was that a mandrake? Parchments scrolled and sealed. More jars and boxes. A metal sphere, cold and harsh, its polished surface studded with rivets. An hourglass. And then, just before I reached the far wall, I found it. Circular. Polished. With embossed metal handle. Heavy for its size. The scrying mirror. I clenched my eyes tight shut behind the blindfold, though I could have sworn I saw a flickering of light around my fingertips as I wrapped it in the leather I'd brought for the purpose. I removed it from the room, leaving it on the floor in the passageway outside.

Back in Forman's workshop, I removed the blindfold and lit a candle. On the shelf to my right were a collection of small figurines, some made of clay, some of metal, all bare-arse naked with all their parts. A little clay doll about six inches high with long black hair, moustache and goatee beard was surely an effigy of Essex. It had a pin stuck through its bollocks. Painful! Next was a little sculpture made of black lead, a man and a woman naked, belly to bum in bestial fashion. With the scrying mirror safe in the passage outside, I could afford a wry smile. I slipped the figures into my shoulder bag.

The casebook was there on the table where I'd abandoned it before. I flicked through the pages. In amongst the charts and diagrams, the lists in Greek and Hebrew, surrounded by a buzzing cloud of arcane symbols, I found those three names that gave the book its value – Robert Devereux, Frances Howard, Robert Carr. Birth names. The casting of nativities.

I still needed the letters. A small, black, polished wooden casket sat on one of the shelves. The lock was small and fiddly. Slowly. Gently. And then the faintest whisper of a click. Open. Inside, a dozen or so letters had been bundled together, tied with red velvet ribbon. I looked at a couple. Frances's signature. I slipped them into my bag. And laid one of the figurines in the casket in their place. Let the men from the Privy Council make what they could of that. I locked the casket, extinguished the lantern and returned everything in the workshop to its rightful place. The difference between a journeyman picklock and a true craftsman.

The air in the passageway was still and cold. Silence filled the house like mist rising from the river on a chill autumn morning.

I had the letters and the casebook, a couple of figurines and dolls. But the scrying mirror, wrapped in leather, was still lying in the passageway. It had made my heart pound just to hold it, even though it was wrapped in leather. Forman had thought it would kill me. But I'd survived, and was stronger and wiser for it. I went back for it.

Once Dee's, then Forman's. Now mine. I was not such a fool as to imagine I could ever learn its secrets. But better to take a thing of such power than leave it for some other who could use it against me.

12

Sir Haughty and the Ladies Frances

'I have what you asked for, my Lord. Doctor Forman's casebook.'

He flicked through a few pages.

'Does it have the horoscope?'

'It's the book Forman showed me last time I saw him.'

'And the letters?'

I handed him the bundle tied in red ribbon. He walked over to the window to read what he could by the fading light. He sighed in relief. If he'd known I was keeping a couple for myself, he might not have been so pleased.

'You have done well, Edgworth. I have another task for you.' He lowered his voice. 'The whore you escorted to Chartley.'

'Alice?'

'You will collect her from Audley End. Lord Essex is at his house in The Strand for the duration of the Parliamentary session.

Lady Frances wrote to him, asking him to send a coach to take her to her family at Audley End. He believes the letter came from Chartley and has agreed to her demands.'

'Is Alice already at Audley End?'

He sighed, as if he'd been talking to a fool.

'At Audley End they change places. That is where you collect the whore. And then dispose of her.'

I'd been expecting that. 'Yes, my Lord.'

'No matter to me how you do it. No-one must know that a double for Lady Frances ever existed.'

'I understand, my Lord.'

'Bring me proof when it's done.'

'Proof?'

'Proof that she...' He stopped himself. Was he so squeamish?

'Proof that she cannot tell tales?' I offered.

'Exactly. Bradshaw will take Lady Frances to Saffron Walden. You meet them at The Eight Bells, a coaching inn. Then you smuggle her into Audley End. You get the whore out of the house and away. Bring me proof that you've dealt with her and you'll be well rewarded.'

His upper lip was twitching and his hand was trembling. Whether with elation at commanding the murder or relief, I couldn't tell.

'You are cunning. And ruthless. That's why I employ you.'

'Thank you, my Lord.' I bowed my head. Such compliments. 'You can rely on me, I assure you.'

'Tomorrow morning. Take one of my horses. I will speak with the groom.'

That was a surprise. He treasured his horses. I nodded agreement.

He walked over to the window, looked down into the yard before turning back. 'This matters to me. You do know that?' Was that a threat or a confession? I took it as both.

'I am careful who I choose as friends.' He spoke softly. 'The English court is full of flatterers and sycophants. I know you for what you are, Matthew Edgworth. But there are few amongst the English nobility as capable as you.' Nothing surprising in his words, but there was something close to affection in his tone and the way he looked me in the eye. I saw a sad and lonely man in that moment, a man with few friends, a man who understood how fragile his position really was.

I often wondered what Frances ever saw in him. He was powerful and wealthy, he had the ear of the King, he was unmarried, he could be charming and generous to his friends – all of which made him attractive to the Ladies in court. He was most surely the one they'd want to catch. But Frances was different. None of that would be enough for her. But in that glimpse of Rochester's weakness, I saw an unexpected capacity for gentleness; a gentleness that was so different from the brutishness of Essex and the swaggering bombast of her father. Perhaps that was what intrigued her.

'When I make a promise, I always deliver,' I said.

He gave me a smile that was unusually generous, and then, as if embarrassed, quickly added, 'You must be gone before sunrise tomorrow.'

'I will need a purse in advance, my Lord. The horse will need fodder and stabling in Saffron Walden. And there will be bribes to pay.'

'How much?'

We agreed a figure. 'And I will need a letter of introduction if I'm to get access to Audley End.'

'From me? To whom?'

'You misunderstand me, my Lord. I'll need a letter sent from Lord Essex to Lady Frances. Any letter. No matter what he writes. I need a sample of his handwriting and his seal.'

I set out from Cope Castle before dawn, arriving at The Eight Bells soon after midday. Rochester's coach was already in the yard, with Bradshaw in attendance. Frances had already taken a room at the inn. I waited out of sight while he informed her that I'd arrived. Bradshaw came back out accompanied by a tall woman dressed in widow's weeds, a dark veil covering her face. Lady Isobel Monson, I presumed. Formerly a long-lost cousin, now a mourning widow. Not so colourful as the roles she played in court masques, but most convincing.

Bradshaw helped her climb up into the coach.

'You're to join her in the coach,' he grumbled. Bradshaw knew his place, and resented me not knowing mine.

Frances bid me join her inside. Bradshaw walked away.

She spoke quietly in sombre tones befitting a widow's grieving state: 'You have ridden from Cope Castle this morning. You must be hungry. Do you need to eat?'

'I thank you, my lady. I can wait.'

'Then we must talk about how to proceed. You have a plan?'

'I thought we could do the same we did at Chartley. We go in through the kitchens. I get word to your maid. She takes us to the room where Alice is hiding.'

'Until the exchange is effected,' she said, 'Alice *is* Frances. Remember that. So she is in Frances's room. *My* room. Refusing contact with anyone – even mother and father. That is not 'hiding', as you call it. She is following instructions.' A reprimand. Mild, but firm. I had never seen her so close in daylight. The woman I escorted from Chartley to Sherborne, who came to my room in The Crown at Wells, had her face painted a glowing rustic red, a couple of teeth blackened, and cheeks puffed out. The woman who sat in Rochester's coach was even more beautiful than her reputation. I was struck by the contrast between her fragrance and the musty well-worn leather of the coach.

She unrolled a piece of parchment. 'Audley End is not Chartley Manor. Let me show you. This is a sketch I made from memory. But it should suffice. I grew up at Audley, but there are rooms in the house which even I have never seen, corridors I've never walked. You will lose your way if you venture in alone.'

I nodded – doing my best to appear wise. But I was scarcely able to believe the situation. Her hand brushed mine as she used her sketch to point out the formal entrances and those for servants, the terraces, the walkways, the bowling green, the kitchens.

'Could you arrive as Lady Isobel?' I suggested. 'Then seek an audience with your mother, and discreetly announce yourself to her?'

'No-one must know about the substitution. Not even my parents. I need my father's sympathy and support. Your scheme must remain forever a close secret.'

My scheme! She knew, even though Rochester had claimed it as his own. How much sharper-witted she was than the men who fawned on her! And I could see why they did. She was playing me, reprimanding while keeping me in her thrall.

I suggested disguising her as a serving maid. She'd go to her room, Alice would leave as the maid.

'Audley End is not Chartley. My father has a household staff of more than two hundred men and women, each with their allotted task. The only maids allowed on that floor of that wing are personal maids. Frances always has hers with her. An unfamiliar face would stand out. Servants do not skulk about the house with their faces veiled.'

We sat in silence. From the stables of the inn came the sound of horses whinnying.

'Damn him,' she whispered under her breath. 'Damn him to Hell.' Her husband, I assumed. 'Damn him that we have to scheme and plot to break into my own house.'

'What if Alice comes to us?'

A look of irritation crossed her face.

'How in Heaven's name do you propose luring her out alone?'

At first, she didn't like the plan, perhaps because she had to remain at The Eight Bells while I arranged for Alice's departure. But she agreed to it. And I took that as a compliment.

I'd ridden with saddlebags, and carried a change of clothes and face paint – taken from Blackfriars Playhouse tiring house several months before. A man never knows when he might need to be a courtier. I had the horse for it – one of Rochester's fine black geldings – and I had a letter purporting to come from the Earl of Essex secured with his very own seal. It took two hours to prepare my appearance, just minutes to ride to Audley End.

It was late afternoon when I presented myself at the gatehouse, dressed in a cape, black leather gauntlets and riding boots, a costume I'd once seen a nobleman wear in *A Wintry Tale* or some such trifle. With my face painted and powdered sickly white, and no trace of my scar, I sat on horseback, waiting for the gatekeeper to come to me. I announced in the voice of Sir Haughty Disdaine that I carried with me a letter for delivery in person to Lady Frances. He beckoned me through.

And there before me lay the Audley End estate. Frances's sketch of the house should have prepared me, but I was still taken aback. Some half a mile away, at the end of a long, gently curving drive, stood a vast palace, not a house. Compared to this, Cope Castle was a poor man's cottage, Whitehall Palace a sprawling shambles. I rode to the principal entrance and announced myself as a representative of the Earl of Essex. The steward was called. He looked furious that anyone should arrive at this door without prior invitation.

'I am here to deliver a private letter to the Countess of Essex.'

'Lady Frances is not well. Give it to me. I will ensure delivery.'

'The Earl insisted that I deliver it in person.'

'The lady is receiving no visitors.'

'The letter contains something that will please her. Her husband has an offer to make.'

'You do not wear Essex's livery.'

'I am not Essex's man,' I said as I dismounted from my horse. The steward didn't like my perfume – but then nor did I – and so he kept himself at some distance. Eventually, he agreed that I could take the letter to Lady Frances, provided he accompany me. He called for a servant to have the horse stabled, then escorted me through the house. Neither of us attempted conversation – which gave me an opportunity to study the place. We crossed the first courtyard. Up semi-circular steps, across a paved terrace, and into the great hall of the main house. Frances's map had showed large double doors to the left leading from the hall to the kitchens. The steward took me through a much smaller door in the far right hand corner, into a picture gallery which gave onto a staircase. These stairs led to a wide corridor with doors to the right and windows to the left, overlooking an inner courtyard. Even these corridors were light and airy. No need for candles or lantern light. Frances was right. This wasn't a place where an intruder could prowl unnoticed.

The steward stopped. 'Tell me your name,' he said.

'Sir Martin Farnworth,' I said.

He harrumphed his derision – more for the King than for me. It was well known that James tossed out knighthoods with the same abandon that Queen Elizabeth doled out groats on Maundy Thursday.

The steward knocked on the door of Frances's apartments. The maid half-opened it. Katherine.

'My mistress is still plagued with the most melancholic humour,' she said. A quick glance in my direction was enough to convince her that the visitor was the kind of parasitic fop she so disliked. 'She will see no-one, Master Bailey.'

The steward turned to me and scowled. *There. Did I not tell you so?*

'This is for the Countess of Essex.' I held up the letter to show Lord Essex's seal. 'I am charged to give this to her, and not to leave until she has it in her hand.'

'She will not read it. You master imprisoned her in Chartley. It broke her heart. And she is still sunk low in deep despair.'

That's good, I thought. Alice and Katherine playing their parts to perfection.

'If she chooses not to read it, so be it,' I said, keeping the plum firmly in my mouth. 'But I must see it in her hand.'

'She will see no-one.'

'Then tell her this. The Earl of Essex is willing to make her an offer that will be to her great benefit. The details are within.'

'She will not –'

'And tell her this also. These words. These precise words. Tell her that her husband wants her to know that he *Duly and truly prays for her.* Those words. Tell her.'

She hesitated before opening the door, letting us through into a small ante-chamber. The steward came in with me. We sat down on two of four upholstered chairs, each decorated in fine needlework, and arranged in a line to face a tapestry hanging on the opposite wall – a biblical scene, one that Frances's father perhaps hoped visitors might find edifying.

Katherine returned. 'She will receive you.'

Master Bailey looked astonished. He tailed me into Frances's room. Alice stood silhouetted in the long south-facing window, which overlooked a garden. She jolted as she heard our footsteps, but didn't turn round.

'I thank you my lady,' I said. 'I thank you for your *Charity to the poor...* poor messenger.'

I wondered whether she was so deep in her part that she hadn't heard my words. Then she stretched out an arm behind her. I gave the letter to Katherine, who placed the letter in her hand.

If the steward hadn't been watching, I'd have stolen a kiss from Katherine. But I was the very model of courtly decorum.

'*I will duly and truly pray* for your return to good health,' I said.

Alice gave a slow nod in reply.

The steward accompanied me to the stables. He asked if I could find my way out of the estate on my own. I thanked him and assured him I could. But the sun was setting, and in dark and unfamiliar surroundings I strayed from the drive that led to the main gates. In such a vast estate it was all too easy to get lost. Although the perimeter wall was several miles in length, it led back to the main gates. I bid the gatekeeper a good night as I left Audley End.

'Suppose Alice doesn't read the letter?'

'She will. I promise you, my lady.'

'What if the groom cannot be persuaded to give them horses for an early morning ride. You have another scheme if this one fails?'

'I do, my lady.' I was glad she didn't ask me what it was.

She did, however, ask about Alice. 'Where will you take her?'

'To her family. Near the Spital Fields.'

'I do not want her harmed. She must never tell her story, but she is not to be harmed.' I'd thought that she and Rochester would have agreed Alice's fate between them. She offered no solution to the riddle of how I was to silence her whilst ensuring she came to no harm.

Early in the morning, just before sunrise, I accompanied Frances on foot to a small door in the estate wall that I'd unbolted on my wanderings the previous night. With the sky lightening, we walked to a wooded area that Frances had marked on her map as *The Wilderness*. No brambles. No fallen boughs. No wild beasts. Just trees and grass with a path winding through, wide enough for two to walk side by side. As wild as Queen Anne's poodles! We followed this path til we reached a clearing. Frances sat down on a bench, carved from stone with the seat supported by two rampant stone lions. I stood nearby.

And there we waited.

13

A kind man in the mist

Low-lying mist lay soft on the ground, chilling the air and dulling the sound of the horses. Katherine was riding side saddle on a dark bay mare, holding herself as proud as a lady. Alice, her mock mistress, followed some ten yards behind. Her horse seemed infected with its rider's lethargy.

Katherine jumped down, overjoyed to see the true Lady Frances. They greeted each other with a warm embrace. My job to deal with Alice. She seemed barely conscious of her surroundings. I helped her dismount, tied her horse to a tree. She didn't speak.

I was about to take my leave and escort Alice to the Eight Bells where Bradshaw was waiting for us, when Frances called out that she wanted to talk to Alice.

I led her over.

'Katherine, you may talk with Master Edgworth.' It was an instruction, not permission.

We walked to the other side of the clearing, but she kept a watchful eye on Frances. The sky was lightening, the sun just visible over low distant hills, a faint white disc behind gauze grey cloud.

'Do you fear for your mistress's safety?'

'Not now. Not hers. Not now she's home.'

Audley End gardeners had raked the first fallen leaves of autumn into a bonfire close by where we were standing. The fire had burnt out overnight. A layer of ash surrounded by a ring of half burnt leaves was all that remained, but the air still smelt of smoke. A puff of wind. Leaves shivered. A few more fell.

'More work for the gardeners. Everything in its place at Audley End. The master of the house wants leaves on the trees or not at all.'

'It's Alice I fear for,' said Kate, ignoring my attempt to amuse. 'She and I have grown fond of each other.'

'Just as well. The two of you cooped up together at Chartley.'

'Don't mock.'

'I'm not mocking. I merely say what I think. It would have been Hell on earth if you'd had a falling out.'

'Alice is a brave woman. And very quick-witted. She saved me from Essex when we were at Chartley.'

'Tell me more.'

'Another time.'

'And when will that be?'

'Who knows?' she said with the faintest of smiles, teasing and taunting, every bit as self-willed as her mistress.

Alice and Frances were sitting together on the bench. Alice, stiff and uneasy, but they were talking.

'Alice likes you, Matthew Edgworth.'

'I didn't see much sign of it in the time I spent with her.'

'Where will you take her?'

'Rochester's coach is in Saffron Walden to take us back to London.'

'And when you reach London?' She lowered her voice. 'What then?'

'Her family live in a hovel near Spital Fields.'

'You've not answered my question. What happens to Alice?'

My instinct was to lie – to tell her that Alice would be reunited with her family. But I could see that she knew. She and Alice must have talked about it.

'I have my instructions, Kate.'

'From Viscount Rochester?'

'That's who I work for.' This wasn't the conversation I'd hoped to be having.

'Will you do it yourself? Or hire another to do it for you?'

'I never talk about such things.'

'Which means it will be you. How will you do it?'

Frances's horse whinnied. I glanced across. Frances and Alice were still rapt in conversation. I'd not seen them together before. They could have been twins. Kate was waiting for my answer. I took her hand in mine. She didn't resist. Her skin was soft and warm. A lady's hand, not a maid's.

She gave me a look I couldn't read.

'I like you, Kate.' I spoke as softly as I could. 'When you and your mistress are returned to London, will you meet with me?'

I thought I detected her eyes widen and the promise of a smile. In that soft shadowless light, standing there on the edge of that manicured wilderness, Kate was almost as beautiful as her true mistress. Her skin was ruddier than Frances's, and she was not so tall. But she'd have stood out in any other female company. She might not be nobility, but she'd grown up with Frances. Neither high-born nor a commoner. Somewhere in between. We were well matched, for that's me too. Forever lodging in half-way houses.

'Alice told me about your journey,' said Kate. 'From Oxford to Chartley.'

'And what did she tell? That Matthew Edgworth was not to be trusted? That he took money at cards from Oxford scholars?'

'She told me about your encounter with the beggar women.'

'Ah. Charity to the poor. Mistress Bonnyrags.'

'You are the strangest of men, Matthew Edgworth.'

'What did Alice tell you?'

'That you're not what you seem. Every man I've ever met pretends at first to be kind and considerate, but they think only of themselves. And what they hide is the bullyboy and the lecher who lurks behind the easy charm. Most men are as boorish and as selfish Lord Essex. They'll stop at nothing to get what they want.'

'Every man you've ever met?'

'What you choose to hide, Matthew Edgworth, is different. You want people to believe you're an unscrupulous, mean-minded scoundrel. But...' she hesitated.

'But what?'

'You give money to beggars, then you hide your good nature by pretending to mock them.'

'Is that what Alice told you?'

'Beneath your show of villainy lies a kind heart.'

'You sound like my mother!'

'I sound like Katherine Garnam, who says what she thinks.'

'Shall I confess all my sins? Is that your game?'

'You are not so heartless as you pretend.'

'Who am I to argue with that?'

She smiled. 'I have something to ask of you Matthew Edgworth.' So that was it – flatter, then beg the favour. 'Alice can read and write. So cutting out her tongue wouldn't be enough to ensure her silence. Which means your instructions must be to kill her?'

'My instructions are between me and Viscount Rochester. And I am sworn to secrecy.'

'You're not a man who does as he's told. You are your own man, Matthew Edgworth. You are not so easily bought.'

'Depends how I'm being paid!'

She edged closer, her eyes now just inches from mine. Something stirred in my britches.

She whispered, 'Keep Alice safe, and I will meet you when my mistress and I return to London. She had to playact the melancholic at Chartley for so long that she may have been infected by it.'

'What will you have me do?'

'Take care of her, Matthew. Take her to a place of safety.'

On the other side of the clearing, Alice got to her feet and curtseyed. Frances called for Katherine.

'Agreed,' I said, squeezing her hand. 'I give you my word. The word of a kind man.'

Except that Alice knew very well there was nothing kind-hearted in my charity to the beggars. I smiled wryly to myself as Katherine helped Frances onto her horse, then mounted her own, following her mistress a few yards behind. Who was playing who?

14

A place of safety

Kate turned back as she and Frances rode out of the clearing. She looked directly at me and waved. The warmth of her smile could have lifted the mist. I was amazed that a woman could have such an effect on me. I still intended using her as a spy in Lady Frances's household. And if that meant taking her to bed, so be it. I could warm to the task.

I walked Alice out of the estate through that same small door in the wall I'd unbolted the previous day. From there to The Eight Bells. Bradshaw drove us back to London, with Rochester's black gelding trotting behind the coach on a leash. Alice was still dressed in Frances's finery, but there was little else noble about her. She'd lost much weight at Chartley. Her cheeks had hollowed, her skin looked sallow.

I asked what she and Frances had been talking about.

'I've been playing Frances these past months. She wanted to thank me. She wanted to know what happened at Chartley. She wanted to know whether Frances surrendered her virginity.'

'Did she?'

'Not at Chartley. No. But if Katherine hadn't stopped me, I might have killed Lord Essex.'

'You have it in you to kill a man?'

She stared at me. An unfathomable look, as fixed as a mask.

'Could you? Could you do that, Alice?'

'Where are you taking me?'

'Spital Fields.' The lie was in her interest. The journey back to London would be easier if she travelled in hope.

She didn't respond.

I was surprised by Frances's insistence that Alice wasn't to be harmed. It seemed to imply that Frances kept secrets from Rochester. A spy in her household would be more than useful, so I would do as Kate asked and find a place of safety for Alice, though I hadn't yet worked out where that might be.

Twice we stopped at coaching inns to break the journey. Alice wasn't hungry, and she spoke very little. Her silence gave me time to unravel the knot at the heart of the bargain I'd struck with Kate. I'd need proof for her that Alice was alive, proof for Rochester that she was dead. And that set me thinking. Who else knew about the exchange, besides Frances and Rochester? Colquhoun, Bradshaw, myself, and Kate. Were any of us any safer than Alice?

Not long after passing through Ilford, Bradshaw pulled the coach to a halt. We'd reached a dilapidated old stone bridge over the river Roding, the trackway barely wide enough for the coach. We waited while a drover herded cattle across the bridge. Bradshaw climbed down to inspect the bridge and be sure it would take the weight of the coach.

'Course it'll take the bloody coach,' I said. 'There's carts and wagons crossing all the time.'

He pointed out a gap in the parapet, where a stone had fallen into the river below. I have never known a man slower about his business or more averse to taking risks, although the curses of carters queuing behind us didn't seem to bother him. Alice and I crossed the bridge on foot. Bradshaw followed. Slowly, slowly, ever so slowly.

'How much further?'

'Nine, ten miles,' I said. 'Maybe less, maybe more.'

'Depending on where you're taking me.'

'You know where I'm taking you.'

'I know what you told me.'

She gazed out of the window as the coach trundled on, occasionally jolting and lurching from side to side. The featureless flatlands and marshes of Essex seemed to energise her. She persisted with her damned questioning.

I drew my dagger.

'Ahh, there's the truth. You plan to slit my throat.'

'If I wanted to kill you, Alice, I'd have done it hours ago. The truth is Rochester has no more use for you. It's dangerous to be discarded by a man of power.'

'Is that where you're taking me? For him to see me die?'

'You think Rochester has the stomach to witness a killing? Of course he wants you dead. That's why I'm taking you to a place of safety.'

'Why in God's name should I believe you?'

'No matter to me what you believe. But if you try to escape, I will cut you, Alice. I'll not kill you. But if needs be,

I will cut you. And you should know by now I don't make idle threats.'

I waited for another mile or two before breaking in on her grim-faced silence: 'Is it true you told Kate you thought me kind?'

Nothing.

'Very well, since you ask. We're going first to Blackwall docks.'

'I want to see my brother before you slit my throat and dump my body in the Thames.'

'I've told you. I am not going to kill you.'

'Those were your instructions, were they not?'

'I interpret instructions as I see fit. No more chatter. Do exactly as I tell you, and I swear you'll be safe. And your brother too.'

She glared at me. The look of a falcon when its hood's been removed. Fierce. Cold. When it can see at last what's been shielded from its gaze. Still on its leash, but all too ready to take your eye out.

'Do as I say, and your family will get the money I promised.'

'How can I trust anything you say?'

'Kate trusts me.'

'More fool her.'

'Enough. Don't try me, Alice.'

We were assailed by the smells of London long before we heard the screeching of gulls mobbing the docks. The acrid stench of tanneries and brickworks, the slops and dung heaps, the butchers' waste, the rotting fish. All those things that make London what it is.

We passed through the dock gates, and the erratic lurching

of the coach became a thumping and squeaking as the wheels rattled over cobbles. I'd instructed Bradshaw to take us to The Anchor and Hope, a low tavern where I'd had dealings before. He drew up in the yard. I helped Alice down, and sent Bradshaw on his way.

'I have business to attend to. Get word to our master that that you left me here with the whore. Tell him I'll report to him at Cope Castle at midday tomorrow.' I lowered my voice. 'With the proof he requires.'

I hired a room in the tavern, where I had Alice switch clothes with one of the house drabs, who could hardly believe her good fortune.

'What now?' said Alice.

'Scruff down. Dirty your face. And make haste. We need out of this place before the drab starts swanking about in her new found finery.'

Blackwall boasts the busiest docks in all of London. Carriages are as easy to hire as wherries across the Thames at Paris Gardens. I opened the door for Alice, whispering our destination to the coachman before joining her inside.

We headed north, then west, entering the city through Aldgate, rattling down Cheapside, through Ludgate and across Fleet Bridge. It wasn't until we drew to a halt, and the coachman rapped on the door that Alice spoke again.

'The Bridewell? You bring me to a House of Correction and call it a place of safety!'

'You'll be here no more than a matter of days, and I'll pay the warden well to ensure you're protected.'

'My brother will hear about this. And he will hunt you down, Matthew Edgworth.'

'Your brother will hear about it because I'll be the one to tell him when I give him the money I promised.'

'You take me for a fool? You think I don't know about The Bridewell? Women and beggars rounded up off the streets. Torments and beatings. It will make Chartley seem a haven.'

'Which is why Rochester's men will never think to look for you here. If he thinks for one moment that you're alive, he'll have us both hunted down and killed. But they will never look here. Just days. That's all. While I find a safe place for you and your family.'

'Where?'

'Away from London. Somewhere you will all be welcomed.'

The coachman was getting impatient. I grasped Alice's arm. She trudged beside me, in through the wooden gate that had once been a side entrance to the royal palace that the last King Henry built for his Spanish Queen Catherine. Distant memories. And certainly not mine. The place had been a workhouse for longer than my quarter century on this blighted earth, the most dismal House of Correction.

I'd had business there before. The gatekeeper looked at Alice with a knowing smirk and called a guard, who cuffed her hands and escorted us to the warden's room. Muffled, tormented cries echoed through the wide, unlit passageways – wolves howling on distant hills.

The warden was sitting behind a large desk in a dark little room, making entries in a ledger by the light of a smoky, spluttering lantern.

'What you got for us this time?'

'She needs a place of safety,' I said.

He was short and fleshful, with overflowing chins and sunken eyes. His skin was pale and oily. Laughing left him wheezing.

'A place of safety!' he coughed out, struggling for breath.

'She is not to be hired out and not to be harmed,' I said, placing a gold sovereign on the ledger. 'Item in. One woman, who shall be nameless, accepted without further question. Not one finger on her. Not yours. Not your guards'. And she is not to be seen by any of those painted courtiers wanting to sample your wares and plunder your brood for a cheap half hour of rough pleasure. I'll return in two weeks. If she's untouched I'll buy her back for three pounds. With the sovereign you've just had, that's two pounds for each week she's here.'

'I don't run a pawn shop.' His idea of a jest.

Alice started to scream. The guard slapped a hand over her mouth.

I leaned forward, rested both hands on the ledger. I spoke slowly and quietly. 'If she is harmed or abused in any way it's you who'll pay. You understand?'

He nodded. His several chins wobbled. It seemed we were agreed.

The guard led Alice away, her screeching echoing through dark corridors long after she was out of sight.

'Now. Master Shackles –'

'My name's not Shackles.'

'If that's what I call you, that's what it is. I need to speak with you alone.'

'We are alone.'

I shut the door. 'We are now. You know me for a man of my word?'

He nodded again. Not a pleasant sight.

'I will return for her,' I said.

'Two weeks?' he said.

'Probably more like three months. I want her to think two weeks. At the end of three months, if she comes to no harm, you get twenty pounds.'

He was wide-eyed. 'She will not be touched. I swear it.'

'Good. Then keep what I'm about to tell you a very close secret. Swear that too.'

'I swear.'

'I've been charged to dispose of her. I need proof. Of her death.'

He looked confused. 'You said to keep her –'

'In a place of safety. Precisely. A great man has had knowledge of her. And the poor punk has knowledge of him. You know what they say? *Great men do great good.* He will not have people talk of him otherwise. Which is why he wants rid of her. But I don't want her dead. I want her safe. And alive. And healthy. And nobody lays a finger on her. Understand?'

'You want proof you can take to him.' His voice as much a-quiver as his jowls. 'Proof of her death while she stays safe?'

'That, Master Shackles, is exactly what I want.'

He struggled out of his chair. 'Come with me,' he said. He ushered me from the room and led me out of the building into a great inner courtyard, maybe forty yards long by thirty yards wide, surrounded by The Bridewell's high walls on every side.

I guessed this had once been an interior garden – not unlike the Principal Court at Audley End. Now a muddy, bare-earth yard with a large wooden platform about five feet high and twenty feet square erected in the centre. Two pillories and a whipping post stood on the platform. The wooden boards dented by stones, stained with fruit and blood. We crossed the courtyard, into another passageway. I noted every turn, counted all the doors and every pace. By my reckoning we were close to the River Thames. The warden stopped for a moment, out of breath from all this exercise.

'Will a finger do yer?' he said.

'An eye and a finger. And her head of hair. Her own hair. You shave your fallen women, do you not? I'll wait while it's done.'

He unlocked and opened a door. I gagged at the stench of decomposing flesh.

'The recent dead,' he said, without expression. 'Not diseased, mind. No plague or pox in here. What colour eye we looking for?'

Alice's hair was duly delivered with a red silk ribbon tied around it. The other tokens of proof came wrapped in waxed paper.

For once Rochester was in the room above the stables before me. He had his two favourite hounds with him, who greeted me with furious barking.

'Lady Frances awaits you at Audley End, my Lord. She's recovering from her melancholia.'

He smiled. 'Bradshaw tells me that you brought the whore back and took her to Blackwall.'

'To a tavern,' I said. 'I wanted some pleasure from her before despatching her on her final journey.' He found this amusing. 'But she'll trouble you no more, my Lord. Her corpse is in a sack in the Thames, keeping company with fish and eels.'

I took the waxed paper from an inside pocket in my doublet, placed it on the table and unfolded it, revealing the finger and the eye. He recoiled slightly before moving the lantern closer.

'She was dead when I took them from her,' I said.

I saved the hair til last.

'Sell that to a wigmaker,' he said. 'They pay well for quality, so I hear. You've done well. It's why I employ you.'

He gave me a purse with another five sovereigns. I thanked him for his generosity.

Then he took a kerchief from his sleeve. Wrapping it around his hand like a glove, he picked up the eye and the finger and tossed them to his hounds. The bitch caught the eye and swallowed it as you might an oyster. They snarled and fought over the finger.

'Will they never learn to share?' he said. He expected me to laugh, so I did.

15

Paul's

Throughout the time that Alice was at Chartley I called in once a week at Paul's to give dole to Alice's brother for him and the family. I thought sixpence a week exceeding generous. Alice would never have known if I'd abandoned them. But despite what she might think, I am indeed a man of my word.

I continued with these visits even while she was in The Bridewell – until one cold morning a few days after Christmas. Every puddle frozen, every muddy rut in all the lanes turned to rock. More beggars in Paul's than seagulls at Billingsgate. The fellow not there. I called back later that same day. Still no sign of him.

A sour-faced deacon was studying the notices on the *Si Quis* door. He tore down half a dozen, grumbling loudly about blasphemy. I suspect those that offended were not those touting the wares of nearby vaulting houses, but those posted without the bribe he thought his due. Beggars and clergy, doctors and lawyers, they all have an eye for easy money. I'd seen Master

Deacon before. He'd never seen me. I'd been quick as an eel slipping in and out of Paul's.

He was dressed in what might have once been white vestments with a purple stole, now faded to a shabby grey slashed with blue. 'God be with you, sir,' I said.

He muttered something about his work being a thankless task. And there was me thinking a man of God would be totting up the rewards he'd get in Heaven. I tutted and shook my head in sympathy.

I described Alice's brother, asked if he knew him. 'Giant of a man. So tall he has to duck his head to pass through doorways. Left side of his face stained purple, like port wine on a white sheet.'

'The mark of Cain,' said the deacon.

'You've seen him?'

'What do you want with him?'

'Not me. My cousin, John Butcher of Cheapside. Needs a good strong man to work for him.'

'Then John Butcher, should put up a notice.' And pay the bribe, I thought.

'His name's Pieter Vancy,' I said. 'He did a good day's work for Cousin John last summer. Says Vancy's the man he wants to hire. But I'd value your opinion, sir, before I go chasing after him.'

I guessed nobody ever talked to Master Deacon, except to hurl curses at him. A little respect from John Butcher's well-mannered cousin must have come as a pleasant surprise. Deacon's face grew slightly less sour.

'Keeps himself to himself. Most people who take shelter in here huddle together for warmth. Floor's cold. But your fellow Vancy sleeps alone, even in winter, wrapped in a blanket. Keeps his own company. Never bothers no-one. No-one bothers him. He's strong alright. Looks after himself. But that doesn't usually stop the rakehells and beggars come crowding in here. Blood spilt here most nights. But what can I do? I'm a man of God, not the sword. But that one, they never go near him. Curse like that mark of Cain keeps even thieves away. You sure your cousin wants to employ him?' He looked suspicious, as if I might be a spy from the Bishop of London come to check on how he was attending to his duties.

'Certainly,' I said.

'Vancy's Dutch,' he said. 'Knows that, does he?' He tore down another notice.

'My cousin wants him to carry meat. Not write verses.'

'Not what I meant,' said the deacon.

'My cousin knows he's Dutch. Says it's worth the risk for a strong, hard worker. And between you and me, you can pay them less.'

'Rather him than me.'

'You know where I might I find him?'

He looked at me, saying nothing, his head turning slightly to one side. I knew the expression. I took out my purse.

'I'd like to donate alms. If I give to you, will you see that my humble offering is used for the benefit of the poor?'

He smiled and nodded. 'Your fellow sometimes goes to Spitalfields. That's where he went the day before yesterday. Not seen him since.'

I gave him a farthing. 'Every little counts,' I said.

He didn't seem to think so. He scowled and stomped off in a dudgeon.

Nothing for it but to walk to Spital Fields.

16

Darkness at the Spital Fields

When I took Alice to say her goodbyes, we'd walked past the stinking Whitechapel tanneries and up Brick Lane. She thought going the long way round was a strategy to tame her. But it had nothing to do with Alice. There's a weakness in me that I can write about now, because it's so far away. But I didn't want Alice to see it.

Rumour has it, there were vast burial grounds at Spital Fields long before The Tower was built, long before the Priory Hospital gave the place its name. Maybe the Priory was built to sanctify the place. But the Priory's long since fallen to ruin. And that tells you more than any churchman would ever admit. It's what lies beneath the ground, what lurks within the very stones themselves that chills me deep. Whatever it was I saw in Forman's scrying mirror was a darkness more powerful than any ghost. There are places where that same darkness seeps through. Spital Fields is one of them.

I felt pleased with myself for the deception of Alice's mock death. Maybe that's what gave me the confidence to confront this other darkness. If I could master that, then maybe I could turn my attentions to the scrying mirror – still carefully sealed in leather. I walked through Bishopsgate, past the wailing walls of Bedlam. Spital Priory ruins loomed.

I never admitted to Jacob how frightened I was of the place. Twelve years old, and he already had his own crew. I was the one they dared to do things. Me that climbed over the walls of Finsbury Court to scrump for apples and pears. Me the first to slide on the Thames when it froze. Me the stall to Jacob's foist when we cut purses in the playhouses, me who had to be the decoy while they thieved from the Cheapside costermongers. Me who burglarised the grand houses, while Jacob stood guard.

First time in Spital Fields, Jacob told me we'd be digging for treasure. Just him and me. We found a few old coins. But nothing you could use to buy things. I found two skulls. Jacob stuck one on a pole to stake out our ground. Took the other back to show the crew. Jacob said he'd dug it up. 'Make a good football.' First kick, it shattered into fragments.

I'd never have gone inside the ruins on my own. But Jacob was a brutal persuader. First time, he's more nervous than me, though he'd never admit it. We go round the back and creep in through a doorway with no door. Neither of us speaking. Walls blackened with age and mould, roofs long since collapsed. We climb over rotting beams which have lain where they'd fallen for longer than I've been on this earth. Twigs piled up in corners, dropped from the nests of rooks and ravens. Jacob looking at me, his face a mixture of terror and can't-stop-now. Neither of us speaking.

An explosion from the Artillery Yard nearby. And another. Half a dozen. Silence. Then a dozen more. Thuds shaking the very ground below as cannon balls hammer into a great earth mound piled up against one of the thick stone walls of what had once been the Priory Hospital.

Second time in the ruins, we find a spiral staircase, and climb to a narrow walkway along a wall. Roof's long since collapsed so it's open to the sky. Jacob says I have to walk it. Then a magpie flies off screeching from the tower behind us and he changes his mind. I have to climb up and look for jewellery in its nest. Half a dozen eggs. Nothing shiny.

Third time we go to the ruins, Jacob's in a dangerous mood. He cackles with high-pitched laughter as we pass the wails of Bedlam. His eyes are wide. He's jittery. Nobody must see us. Soon as we're inside, he whispers, 'Say the Lord's prayer backwards.'

How can he think of calling up the devil when the place is already so full of darkness?

'Go on,' he says, a thin little grin twisting his mouth.

'You do it,' I say. And he does. Slowly. Stumbling over words. But he does it. And I have a horrible feeling he's done it before. I'm shivering with fear. What if the devil comes for both of us?

'Can't let that hang in the air,' he says. 'Got to burn the place now. Clean it with fire. Get all the wood you can.'

How can we burn it? Nothing to burn. It's stone. But I never argue with Jacob. And he's already crouched in a corner where twigs have fallen from a crow's nest above.

'Not enough,' he says. 'Look. Up there.' He's pointing to a large nest in what had once been a fireplace on the second floor. 'Best kindling, is that.' Up the spiral staircase I go again. At the top I look down. He's on his knees. Tinderbox out. Sparks in the gloom. Hints of smoke. That nest is at the other end of the wall. But it's thirty feet away, and I'm forty feet up.

'Get it, Matthew,' he shouts. Then he's back to blowing on tinder.

I hate him for that. Always making me do the things he's too frightened to do himself. *Damn you, Jacob. I hate you, hate you, damn you.* I could gob on him and pretend it was birdshit, if only I dared.

So now I'm on hands and knees. Inching forward. The Artillery Yard has fallen silent. The only sound is Jacob cracking flint against steel. Cursing that the tinder won't take.

A raven lands on the wall just six feet in front of me. It folds its wings. Stares at me, looks at Jacob, who's still clacking and cursing. I don't move. The bird's beak is black. Its eyes are black. A bird-shaped window into the darkest of nights. A bird-shaped glimpse of that darker world beyond.

It stares. Fixes me with its gaze. Loose mortar dust trickling from a joint by the stone where it landed.

It opens its beak wide, and squawks. The sound unlike anything I've ever heard before. Closer to a startled dog bark than a bird call. I swear it cries out, 'Jay Cob', before opening its wings and taking flight. Flying towards me, talons outstretched. I wrap my arms round my head. Feel the air from its wings. Then it's gone. I drop my arms. Open my eyes. There's a great stone falling from the wall.

Jacob doesn't hear it fall. Doesn't look up. Doesn't see it.

By the time I get down, his fire's well alight

'It wasn't me,' I say. 'It was you, Jacob. You forced me up onto the walls. You said the Lord's Prayer backwards. It was you brought in on yourself.'

But he doesn't hear me. Doesn't feel the heat of the flames. Doesn't smell his own burning flesh. Jacob's head is smashed. Splinters of bone, blood and pulp.

And every time I think about the scrying mirror, I see the blackness of the raven, feel the dark breath of its wing beats.

The place was cursed long before the priory was built. You can never cheat a curse.

That's what I'd seen in Forman's scrying mirror. A window onto that same raven-black darkness.

I walked on towards the hovel in search of Vancy. The first time I'd been that way in more than ten years. The Spital Priory ruins were still slowly rotting, the curse still lingering in the walls. I walked past without stopping, without turning back, my head filled with thoughts I didn't want to think, pictures I didn't want to see.

The sky was clear that day, but the wind was blowing from the north, so cold it pained to breathe. I walked as quickly as I could, trying to think of Kate and pleasures in store, past wooden skeletons of buildings rising out of frozen mud. Too cold even for bricklayers to infill the frames that day. I'd thought it would be easy to find the place where Alice's family were shacked up. But twice I walked past it. In the six months since last I was there a dozen new houses had appeared. And their little hovel stood in the shadows next a roped-off area in the shape of a house-to-be. A miracle it hadn't been knocked down.

I understand why penniless beggars seek out shelter wherever they can find a roof, but did rich merchants really imagine that people would someday choose to live on that cursed land?

No lock on the shack door. Only a flimsy latch to hold it shut. There were still four of them – which was another kind of miracle because they all looked thin and sickly: the woman I presumed to be Alice's mother, the two girls and the boy. But no Pieter Vancy. The females looked frightened. The boy did his best to stand tall and look brave.

'What you want?' said the boy. His Dutch accent stronger than was good for him. He wouldn't last long when the building work started in earnest on the roped-off patch. I said I wanted to talk to Alice's mother.

'She speak not the English.'

'She'll understand my English,' I said.

'I say the words,' said the boy.

'No, you don't. I say the words. And I say them outside.' I gestured for her to come outside with me.

'I come met her,' said the boy. Brave little fellow! Foolish. But brave. It must have been Kate's talk of Matthew Kindheart that persuaded me to let him help with translation. But there wasn't much to be said. Every week Pieter Vancy had taken them the money I'd given him. But they hadn't seen him for more than a fortnight. He'd gone to Canterbury.

'Pieter the Pilgrim?'

They didn't understand the jest. Vancy had heard that families they knew who were fleeing the killings and the midnight house fires in their part of Holland had sought refuge in Canterbury and Faversham, where they were establishing themselves as weavers.

I gave the woman the rest of Alice's money, and took my leave. She thanked me in her own tongue. The boy chirruped a translation that that didn't sound much different. I bid them goodbye, then the mother said, '*Waar is Aeltje?*'

'Alice? She's safe. You'll see her again soon enough.'

'*Waar is ze?*'

But I was already on my way. The boy came running after, shouting 'Where is *Aeltje?*'

'I've told you, somewhere safe.'

He tugged at my doublet. 'Where?'

I turned and crouched down. I spoke loud and slow. 'Listen to me. I have never hurt a child. But I've killed more men than I care to remember. So do as I say. You understand?'

He swallowed. His colour had drained. But he didn't flinch.

'Say you understand.'

'I understand.'

'Good. I like you, young lad. Tell me your name.'

'Frans,' he squeaked.

'Frans. I like your name too. You're a brave boy.' His mouth twitched in a nervous grin. 'Now listen. I swear to you that Alice is safe, and I will make sure she comes to no harm. But now you must swear to me you will take care of your mother. And the little ones. Keep them safe. You understand that?'

'Yes, sir. I swear it.'

We shook hands on that, and I went on my way.

I did indeed like the boy. He had the same spirit about him as Alice. Like brother, like sister. But I lied to him. I remember very well who I've killed because I never do it lightly.

17

Chapel

The streets were full of winter, the skies were thick with it. Two days of snow. Then slush and mud. Then rain. Then freezing fog. And then more snow. But all was not bleak. Katherine had moved back to London with Lady Frances. I'd heard they were living at Essex House on the Strand.

After Colquhoun found me at the Painted Tavern and took me unconscious to Cope Castle, I sought new lodgings. I took rooms on the top floor of a house in an alley just off Water Lane in Blackfriars. I paid my rent in advance. It was quiet. I told nobody where I was living. It had its own staircase. And the arrangement I struck with the landlord was that no servants would ever come in. There are benefits to renting a room at an inn – not least that there are always fires burning in the colder months – but I was pleased with my new lodgings. What I'd lose in winter warmth I'd gain in privacy. First thing I did after moving in was pay for the finest new lock that money could buy.

I made an arrangement with Colquhoun. When Rochester needed to contact me, Colquhoun would leave a coded letter for me at The White Hart in Drury Lane, which was outside the walls and the jurisdiction of the City. The tapster and the landlord knew me for an honest man. I never took whores there, and never played cards or dice.

About a week after my excursion to Spital Fields, there was a letter for me at The White Hart. I deciphered Colquhoun's instructions, and got to the room above Cope Castle stables as arranged. I lit the fire – which Rochester expected of me – and was warming myself when the door opened and an elderly man entered.

'Good day to you, sir,' he said, giving a slight nod of his head. He shut the door behind him, then removed his hat. A little cautious deference never goes amiss. He had a small white beard and greying hair, but plenty of it. He was a wiry looking fellow with sunken cheeks and yellowing eyes. My immediate thought was that he worked for Walter Cope, but he was too well dressed for stables work and I'd never seen him about the place. He extended his arm. We shook hands. Right hands. But I was watching his left. He seemed an unlikely killer, but he wouldn't have been the first to set a man at ease before pulling a knife.

'My name is Richard Weston. I work for Mistress Turner, who is a close friend of Lady Frances, the Countess of Essex.'

Rochester and Frances had both spoken of him, the man who'd carried letters to and from Chartley. I'd imagined him to be younger.

'Then you won't object to being searched.'

He put both hands on his head. 'I have a dagger in a scabbard at my hip,' he said.

I removed it, threw it to the far side of the room.

'Sit on the floor. Back against the wall. Remove your boots.'

He did so without complaining. No weapon.

'Now stand up, hands flat against the wall. Keep them there until I say. Why did the Turner woman send you?'

'Mistress Turner recommended me to Lady Frances. I bring a message for Matthew Edgworth.'

I looked at him.

'Lady Frances said she'd make the arrangements through Rochester's steward. She wishes to talk with you.'

'Does she indeed?'

'She says it's urgent.'

'And that's your message, old man? Lady Frances wants to talk to Matthew Edgworth?'

'In the Chapel Royal at Whitehall Palace. Tomorrow at noon. After mattins and before evensong.' He described in detail the pew where I should wait for Frances. 'She said the place would be quiet at that time.'

I put my dagger to his throat.

'And what makes you so sure I'm Matthew Edgworth?'

He was breathing fast. His reply came fitfully. 'Lady Frances told me you'd be here. She gave me a description.'

I held him there awhile. There was moisture on his forehead. Little beads of sweat like early morning dew.

'Just suppose, Master Weston…. Just suppose you delivered your message to the wrong man? You want me to trust a man who's so reckless? Do you know how sharp this is?'

I ran my dagger slowly across his beard. His eyes now wide with terror.

'Pick them up,' I said.

'Pick what up?'

'The hairs I just cut from your beard. Only the sweetest, sharpest blade will cut so cleanly with so little effort.'

I took a step back to give him space. He hesitated as if uncertain whether I meant it. Then he bent down, picked them up and held them out to me, as if offering titbits to a slavering dog.

'Not for me. For you, Weston. Keep them safe. A reminder to be more careful in future.'

He swallowed.

'Now, take a message back. Tell her I'll be there. Tomorrow at noon.'

I picked up his dagger. Mine in my left hand, his in my right. 'And think on this, Richard Weston. I know you could be leading me into a trap. But if you are, I'll be well prepared. And it'll be you who wakes one night for just long enough to feel your life blood draining away.'

I put on the same wig of long black hair I'd used at Audley End, and dressed in the same linen shirt, doublet, black cape and boots.

The Chapel Royal at Whitehall stands between the Great Hall and the Thames. Small compared with Paul's or Christ Church, but grander than either of them. But it's a chapel, not a church, so there's no nave where common folk can come and stand or kneel in prayer. I arrived well ahead of the agreed time. The place was empty. Two doors – one at the front, the other to the side of the altar. Picklock wires can be used to jam a lock as well as open it. I didn't want anyone creeping in from the vestry. It would never do to be murdered in a

House of God. The box pews were all arranged down the sides and facing inwards, as the choir stalls are at Paul's. But I hid behind a pillar at the back and waited close to the place we were supposed to meet, watching to see who came in.

I heard the front door creak open and bang shut. Someone who looked like Frances came in alone. She walked slowly, bowed to the altar, then sat down in the pew where Weston had said she would. I walked over and sat behind her. She heard me, but didn't look round.

'Do you know the cathedral at Wells?' she said quietly.

'It is beautiful' I said. 'I attended a service after staying at The Crown.'

'And where else have you been that might be of interest to a traveller?'

'The Eight Bells in Saffron Walden. Not far from – '

'Enough.' It seemed I'd passed her simple test, although she hadn't so much as glanced at me.

'You made me a promise, Master Edgworth.' She was whispering, but her tone was sharp as a blade.

'I did indeed, my lady. And I – '

'You assured me you would bring me the casebook where Doctor Forman wrote my horoscope. That was five months ago.'

'I have retrieved it, my lady.'

'Then why do I not have it? Why did you say nothing when we were at Saffron Walden?'

'I delivered the casebook to Lord Rochester.'

'That was not what I asked, and not what you promised.'

'It was my misunderstanding.' I'd assumed that Rochester would give the casebook to her, and I said as much – without directly maligning my dear master.

She was silent for a while.

'I apologise for not bringing it to you, my lady.'

She bowed her head, clasped her hands a few inches in front of her lips. 'Come, sit beside me and join me in prayer,' she whispered. 'There is something I need to ask of you.'

'Please you, my lady, ask.' What manners hath the fellow!

'Did you know that Doctor Forman has passed away?'

'I had heard that.'

'You swear that Lord Rochester has the casebook?'

'I delivered it to him myself. He said he would look after it for you.'

'I will ask him for it. But that still leaves me in need of someone to interpret it. Everyone forever talks of what's *not* possible. Forman's horoscope will tell me what *is* possible. That is I want to know.'

My task – to seek out that someone to interpret Forman's writings – no matter whether that person was man or woman, necromancer, sorcerer, witch or cunning woman.

'Hear this, Edgworth. I will not be cheated.'

'I understand, my lady.'

'Can you do it?'

'Most certainly.'

'I now live at Essex House on The Strand. Use Richard Weston as your messenger to contact me. I will do the same.'

She gave the slightest nod of her head, suggesting that our conversation was over. I said a quiet 'Amen' and sat upright in the pew.

'Wait here until you hear the outside door bang shut. My maid and I will leave first.'

She got to her feet and seemed about to walk off when she

said, 'My maid, Katherine, tells me that she would like to meet with you in private.'

If the place hadn't been so dark, she'd have seen my cheeks colouring.

'Find someone to take Forman's place, and I'll reward you with a good purse. And I will allow you a meeting with Katherine. But I warn you, Edgworth, if you try to pass off some street corner conjuror as a true divine, I will see you dismissed from Lord Rochester's employ, and you will never again see Katherine.'

18

The apothecary, the cunning woman and the tailor

I find someone to interpret Forman's horoscope, I get paid for my pains in time with Katherine. Frances the bawd!

I thought of disguising myself and renting a darkened room. Go back to the Forman house and furnish myself with the astrolabe, a few pelican jars, some glass vials and half a dozen books of arcane wisdom. The tiring room at Blackfriars Playhouse surely has a costume for it. The thought amused – Matthew, the cunning man, speaking slowly in Forman's dark treacle tones, conjuring up a reading from his spidery squiggles, goading Lady Frances into revealing all her darkest secrets. And then slowly teasing it all out to tell her what she wanted to hear. But the risks were too great. Her warning about conjurors had been heartfelt. I suspected she'd already been cheated. And if I failed to convince, my chances with Katherine would be as naught.

So I set about finding a genuine sorcerer or cunning woman. I know better than most that London seethes with more quacksalvers and mountebanks than maggots in a dead dog. And in answer to my queries I heard all manner of mouldy tales. Witches whispering their charms in Edmonton – I wasn't going to walk three hours there and three hours back to meet with two old hags who could barely manage to curdle milk on a hot summer's day. A wise man in Deptford who had in his possession the philosopher's stone – if the man was so wise, why was he living in Deptford? I paid a visit on a Thomas Bretnor, a maker of almanacs and prognostications. He dismissed Forman as a dangerous quack. I knew for myself how dangerous Forman had been, but it was Bretnor who was the fake.

I saw a woman called Mary Woods, recently arrived in London from Norwich and claiming to be learnèd in astrology. She did her best to conceal her accent, but the traces of her Norfolk drawl were as hard to remove as slug trails in a kitchen pantry. The words she used reminded me of Forman, and at first I was taken in. Then I asked her to cast my nativity.

'A relative you have not seen many years will return.'

'A close relative?'

'A cousin.'

'I have no cousins.'

'A sister then? A long-lost brother?'

'Ah!'

'A brother. Yes.' She looked pleased with herself. But not for long. Her smile turned sour when I foretold her own bleak future if she wanted payment for her cheating.

I tried a Doctor Savory, who lived in a cottage in Hackney. With his long white hair and beard, he looked the very picture of a cunning man, immersed in arcane wisdom. But that's what raised my suspicions. Had I known then what I found out a few days later, I'd have given a good yank to that silver beard and put him to the test. He'd been an actor with the King's Men for longer than he'd been a doctor. I'm sure they'd have been delighted to have their false beard returned.

Of all the people I saw, the only one who showed any promise was a Doctor James Franklin. Remember that name. He was a crook-shouldered Yorkshireman with reddish beard and pock-marked face. When I entered his lodgings in Monkwell Street, near Cripplegate, such was the stench I could barely stop myself from retching. At first I thought a dog had died. But it was he who smelt so rank. He said it was because he was an apothecary and the smell of ingredients he worked with clung to the skin like wet shit to a sheep's arse. But I knew that smell for what it was. He had the pox. He was rotting from the inside out. In other ways he seemed honest. He told me plainly that he wouldn't know where to begin with horoscopes. But he did know about herbs and roots, powders and potions. I didn't like the smell of Doctor Franklin. But he was a man I could deal with. And when needs must, I hold my breath.

I thanked him for his honesty and asked him whether he could recommend anyone who could cast a nativity.

He'd heard rumours about a cunning woman named Hannah who lived in an abandoned charcoal burner's hovel in a wood beyond the heath at Hamsted. He'd heard she was a gifted healer and could read men's signs and stars. I thanked him and paid him for his advice.

And so it was, on a cold, dry night in mid-April, with a half-moon in a cloudless sky, I made the journey out of

London to find this cunning Hannah. I took Forman's scrying mirror with me – still carefully sealed in leather wrapping. But that hadn't stopped me wondering how I might use it. In my fancies I imagined it as a weapon. Oh yes, Matthew has his fancies! But a wiser Matthew knew he'd not be able to stop himself getting drawn into its darkness. Like the mewling infant left alone with a stiletto. Pudgy little hands near gleaming blades. It always ends in blood. I took the mirror with me that night thinking that this cunning woman could teach me how to master it. And if that weren't possible, I was certain there'd be many in London's dark underworld who'd pay dearly for such a thing. Perhaps even Gervase Chapman and *The School of Night*?

I'd never before seen a charcoal burner's hovel. It took a while to find it, but there was no mistaking it when I did. A small circular building in the middle of a clearing, its walls made of rough stone to a height of about three feet, and then long timber poles reaching up to a point and covered with turf sods creating a kind of shaggy, living thatch.

I looked round, then went back to sit on a low ridge overlooking the clearing. I waited and watched. Only one way in and out of the hovel – a low opening covered with a sheepskin. I didn't want to be caught inside if anyone else came visiting. But the only sounds were the hoots and keewicks of a pair of owls and the occasional rustling of mice and woodland animals.

I checked both my daggers before pulling the sheepskin aside. A woman was sitting on a joint stool in front of a fire burning low in the middle of the hut. Nobody with her. I ducked down and went inside. Despite the hole in what passed for a roof, the hovel was thick with wood smoke and a strange combination of smells. Two spluttering candles gave off the acrid, cloying stink you always get from mutton-tallow, but there was something else besides, something sweeter which I couldn't place.

Two cushions lay nearby, each covered in green damask, frayed at the seams. When new they might not have looked out of place in Frances's apartments at Audley End. A large black cat lay curled asleep on one. The cunning woman's bare feet rested on the other. Her clothes were rags, her long black hair was greasy and lank, her feet were muddy, but her face was startlingly fine in its features, and her skin, though smudged with soot, was pale and unblemished.

She looked not much older than Frances. I glimpsed a reminder of Alice as the Spanish lady. Franklin's talk of a 'cunning woman' had conjured a picture of an elderly crone. Hannah wasn't old. She was almost beautiful. There was a time I might have taken an interest.

There was a hole about the size of a large plate in the middle of the roof. The wooden poles on one side were about two feet higher than the other, to keep out the worst of any rain. No decorations and none of the paraphernalia Doctor Forman had in his workshop and study.

I stood there, just inside the hovel. She stared at me.

'I mean you no harm,' I said.

'I'm glad of that.' A long silence. And then: 'Your face is in the dark. If you mean me no harm, come close.' She moved her feet from the cushion. 'Sit if you wish.'

'I'll stand.'

'As you please,' she said. Well mannered, I thought. Well bred.

'Are you Hannah?'

'Do you bring food?'

I hadn't thought to bring food, so I took out my purse.

'Some people bring food. Some people bring clothes.' She spoke slowly. 'But coins, I have no need for coins. What use are coins?'

'I will bring you food. And clothes. If that's what you want.'

'When? When will you bring food?'

'Next time.'

'You will come again.' It sounded more a prediction than a question.

'Yes.'

'You want something from me.'

'They say you can cast a nativity.'

She stroked the cat, which purred and flicked its tail. She took a stick and poked the fire. Sparks flew up and out through the hole above.

'They say many things. Do they say I can cast a nativity?'

'That's what I was told.'

'They say I should be cast out to a place where madness can be cured. Did the moon make me mad?'

She gathered a handful of herbs and sprinkled them on the glowing embers. The smoke smelt sweet and musky.

'There is no light without darkness. The brightest lights cast darkest shadows.'

'What does that mean?'

She stared at me, her gaze unwavering.

'What does that mean?'

'I am who I am.'

'Are you Hannah? Is that who you are?'

'A nativity. You want me to cast a nativity.'

'I can pay you well.'

'I have no use for your money. What use is money?'

'I will pay with whatever you choose.'

She shut her eyes and seemed to drift away. I had to be certain she'd be willing to see Frances. But I suppressed my impatience while she floated in and out of her dreams. Time passed. She spoke again.

'Who are you wants to know if I can cast a nativity?'

I had thought to use a false name – perhaps Martin Farnworth again. He gets around does Martin. But she drew the truth out of me.

'Sit you down, Matthew Edgworth.'

She put wood on the fire, and then more herbs.

I was watching the cat grooming itself. My limbs relaxed. My breathing slowing. But why that mention of bright lights and darkness? Did she know about the scrying mirror? A knot was tightening in my stomach.

'Do I frighten you?'

I didn't answer.

'There is no hiding things if you want the truth of your nativity.'

The fire crackled. She was staring at me, looking into me.

'Not fear,' I said. 'Not frightened. Wary. I am always wary.'

One of the candles spluttered. The flame died. She spoke again, softly, gently. 'What is it you want?'

I told her about Forman and the nativity he'd cast for a noble woman, about the casebook and the horoscope it contained.

'You want me to interpret a horoscope that Simon Forman cast for this woman you care not to name.'

'She can tell you her name herself. When you meet her.'

She shut her eyes. She rocked slowly back and forwards – in time with her own breathing? Or to some distant music she alone could hear? And then quietly, without opening her eyes, 'The lady will need to come here herself. She must bring Forman's casebook. She must be truthful. No hiding of names. No dissembling.'

I walked from her hovel to the Cock and Hen in Highgate village. The tapster was locking up when I arrived. He wanted me to take a room. I said I had to continue with my journey, but needed to eat.

'We got no food left at this time o' night.'

I offered him a silver angel. He remembered they might have some food after all. That's what coins are for, Hannah, I thought to tell her when I returned.

He served up a tankard of ale and a large wooden trencher heaped with bread and cheese and apples. I drank the ale, put everything else in my bag and made my way out of the back door quietly.

Hannah was asleep when I returned. The cat had gone out mousing, or whatever familiars do when they're not being familiar. I laid the plate down and hoped Hannah would wake to find the food before the cat did.

It was long past curfew when I got back to Aldersgate. When the gatekeeper realised who was knocking, he slid back the bolts, opened the door within the gate, and allowed me through. It's as well I have as many friends in low places as patrons on high.

'Why you out so late? Out for sport? Or hunting witches?'

'Gaming,' I said. 'Where I'm not known. Money to be had in Highgate.'

He laughed and waved me on my way. But it gave me pause for thought. Hannah might be shielded from the wind and the rain in that smoky little hovel. But there was nothing to protect her from those who would sooner burn her alive than allow the presence of a witch in the woods.

She'd been cast out before. She told me so herself. I needed to get word to Frances and take her to Hannah before the hovel caught fire.

Contacting Frances meant seeking out Richard Weston. He was easy enough to find. He lived in the servants' quarters at Anne Turner's house in Paternoster Row. Unsurprisingly, he was a Mermaid man. The inn was less than thirty yards from her front door. He was sitting in a corner, drinking alone. I thought it wise to get to know him better. If he could carry messages between me and Lady Frances, he could take mine to Katherine. I guessed he could be useful in other ways too.

He recognised me and was in want of company. I bought him a jug of Canary sack – I told him it was my way of apologising for treating him so roughly a few days before. He was easily won over. We played a few games of dice, which he won. I took a little back at cards – but only enough to stay in pocket and stir his interest. And then we drank awhile. And we laughed. I asked him about Mistress Turner. We drank and laughed some more. He'd been employed by Doctor Turner – Anne's husband before he died – and had remained in Mistress Turner's service after her husband's death. And thereby hangs a tale, I thought.

He was neat and well-dressed, the very model of a gentleman of virtue. But by that stage in the evening, not quite so sober as his appearance. It was easy to lead him into indiscretions. He'd started life as a tailor.

'And is it true what they say about a tailor's prick, Master Needle?'

He laughed as if he'd never heard such a merry jest before. The Canary was flowing fast, and he was growing too relaxed for his own good. Unless he was playing me at my own game?

I tried him again. 'Such an honest man, Master Needle. I'm sure you never took advantage of the ladies.'

He grinned, and took another drink.

'Aha! I have it now. Is that why Mistress Turner employs you, Master Needle? To examine her seams and keep all in good repair.'

He laughed again, but somewhat ruefully. 'My tailoring days are long since gone. Mistress Turner has a lover a good deal younger than herself.'

'Oh, shame on her,' I said. 'So she employs you because you are steadfast and dependable. Yet you allow your reputation to be sullied by drinking with a rogue such as me!'

He seemed to take this as a challenge. And with a little gentle prodding and encouragement it soon slipped out. He'd once been charged with coining.

'Oh Richard Weston, you could have been hung for that. Master Weston, the well-hung tailor!'

'No witnesses came forward to testify against me,' he said. 'And when they asked me how I came by a pocketful of sixpences, I told them that a fishmonger down at Billingsgate passed them to me in change.'

'You expect me to believe that?'

'They did.'

He offered to buy another jug of sack. I said I'd had enough and needed to be up early the following morning, and it was time to take my leave. He was unsteady on his feet, so I walked him to the back door of Anne Turner's house, reminded him to take my message to Lady Frances, thanked him for his good company and bad him goodnight.

There was more to his story than he was telling, but I had enough to be getting on with. Weston was a man who had a history, and a man's history lays him open to persuasion.

19

The silence of the night

Weston took my message to her ladyship early in the morning. By noon he'd returned with a reply. Frances wanted to meet me that same evening in the private chapel in the large walled garden which backed onto the river at the rear of Essex House.

I walked down Milford Lane, found a small door in the garden wall and picked the lock. When I left my lodgings that morning the sky was blue, the air warm. By late afternoon, there had already been several showers. Any gardeners at work that day had taken shelter from the heavy rain. The door to the small porch at the front of the chapel was unlocked. It squealed as I opened it. The hinges would warn if anyone followed me. The chapel was small and plain, with a black flagstone floor, old grey glass in meagre windows, and little decoration of any kind – except for a tattered flag of the Earl's family coat of arms hanging limp from a pole by the altar. What might have once been white and red had faded to grey and shabby pink. The place was dark, musty, damp and cheerless. Rain was dripping into a pool of water close by the altar. Little danger of anyone coming here to seek comfort, but I was still wary. I searched the chapel, even lifting the cloth that covered the altar to see if anyone was hiding beneath, and making sure there was no other way in.

I positioned myself on the edge of a choir stall, where I could see anyone entering, and placed my dagger on the seat beside me. The thick stone walls blocked out the screeching of gulls and the shouts from the wharves and quays. The only sound was water dripping, regular as the ticking of a long case clock.

The porch door squealed open, then closed. A hooded figure walked in alone. I took firm hold of my dagger. Whoever it was stood still. I leant forward, bowed my head as if in earnest prayer.

Slow, deliberate steps on the flagstone floor, over to the stalls behind me.

I could hear her breathing.

'Good day to you,' she said. 'I am looking for the priest who presides over this chapel.'

'I am here to pray and give thanks,' I said. 'But I've not seen a priest.'

'Are we alone?'

'I came here alone.'

'My maid's keeping watch in the porch.' It was Frances. She moved forward to sit beside me and threw back the hood of her cape. 'Katherine has her instructions. If anyone comes, she will engage them loudly in conversation to warn us. I will stay here in silent prayer. You will hide yourself. Now, to the business.'

'I am sorry it's taken longer than I'd hoped, my lady. I've seen dozens claiming to be seers and sages. All of them of cheaters and frauds – until yesterday, when I met a cunning woman by the name of Hannah. And she, I believe, is a true divine. I made no mention of you by name, but she understands what's required. She says that if Forman cast the nativity, she can read the horoscope. She thought most highly of him, where others were jealous of his wisdom.'

'And I now have the casebook from Rochester. You say the cunning woman's name is Hannah?'

'Yes, my lady.'

'Bring her to Anne Turner's house in Paternoster Row.'

'She refused to come inside the walls of London.'

'I have waited months for this.'

'She will not be persuaded.'

Frances said nothing for a while. The water dripped on.

'You believe she can do it?'

'I'm convinced of it.'

'Then I must go to her. Tell me how to find her.'

'She is wary of strangers. Her hovel is well hidden in dense woods near Hamsted. Allow me to lead you to her. I can ensure your safety on the journeys there and back. And keep guard outside the hovel while you talk privately with Hannah.'

Silence except for the dripping water as she gave this some thought. 'Very well. But be warned, Matthew Edgworth, if this cunning woman is not what you say, you will regret it.'

'She will not disappoint.'

'Good. And who better to escort me than a man who knows the ways of scoundrels and highwaymen?' There was a wit about Frances that I admired, although I knew very well that her candour with me was no less of a performance than my own good manners.

'When will we go?'

'As soon as possible, my lady. I fear that Hannah will not be long in Hamsted.'

'Then we go tomorrow night.'

After we'd made arrangements for when and where to meet, I suggested I should leave the chapel first.

'So you can speak alone with Katherine! No, Edgworth. You stay here until you hear the door close. Then wait a good while after that. I made a promise that you may speak with Katherine. And I will keep it. But the cunning woman must first prove herself. When you and I are safely returned from Hamsted, then you may meet with Katherine.'

She stood up, bowed her head to the altar, then turned and walked out.

Frances was putting trust in me. But that made her vulnerable – which made the situation dangerous. Did I trust her in return? Only for so long as she needed my services. After that, I'd be chaff thrown to the wind. Frances was renowned for her charm and her beauty. I'd seen that even when she was disguised as that ruddy buxom nursemaid on our journey from Chartley to Wells. But I also knew she could be as ruthless as any of the men in her family, and far shrewder than her lover or her husband. I understood why she was so keen to hear Forman's horoscope, but there was surely another reason for offering Katherine as bait. As yet I had, no idea what she wanted from me, but I sensed that taking her to Hannah was to be a kind of test.

We'd arranged to meet in the yard of a merchant's house on the north side of The Strand, less than a hundred yards from Essex House. Being outside the city walls, The Strand's not subject to the curfew laws. It was a warm night for the time of year, and no hardship to wait in the yard.

Frances appeared when we'd agreed, accompanied by fair Kate. She was wearing man's clothing, as I'd suggested. It wasn't unusual for men to ride out to Highgate at night, but a woman would be noticed, even in the company of a man. I never asked how she obtained the clothes. Maybe her friend Anne Turner found them for her.

I'd hired two horses, both saddled for men. Kate looked disappointed. Did she expect a third horse? Had she imagined she'd be chaperone to her fair mistress?

'What shall I do, my lady?' said Kate.

'Go back to Essex House. Lock the doors to our chambers. When I return I'll give the knock we agreed.'

'Yes, my lady.'

Frances took hold of the reins. I cupped my hands for her to use as a mounting block. She mounted and adjusted the reins. Kate looked at me. Hard to read her expression by the light of a half moon. But there was a question in there somewhere. Was she asking about Alice's safety? How I'd gained the trust of her mistress? Or whether she and I might meet? I nodded yes to whatever.

Frances was clearly well-practiced at riding astride. I tightened her saddle straps and adjusted the stirrups. She called out to Kate. 'Go now, Katherine. Have no fear for my safety. I will be back before sunrise. Now go.'

I caught a glimpse of Kate's scowl before she turned and walked off.

Frances pulled the hood of her cloak forward to conceal her face and we set off, trotting slowly west along the Strand, taking the right fork at Charing Cross and up Saint Martin's Lane before leaving the road to use tracks and byways. The houses were fewer and smaller. About a hundred yards before the church of St Giles in the Fields, the track passed through a small copse. I held up my arm and reined the horse in. I turned round, drew close to Frances, leant forwards in the saddle.

'We're going to gallop through the copse,' I whispered. 'Stay close.'

I saw the flicker of a smile. Maybe she thought of this would be the kind of adventure she'd always been denied. It boded well that she felt safe in my company. I rode with her as far as the church, and then dismounted.

'Why have we stopped?'

'I chose this route to avoid highwaymen. But I thought I heard something in the copse.' My caution was genuine. It was a quiet byway, too narrow for a coach. 'Probably just a fox or dog. But I need to be sure we're not being followed. I prithee take both horses and wait for me. On the far side of that yew tree there's a horse shelter that can't be seen from the track. You'll be safe there.'

She led the horses through the churchyard. I walked back into the woods. I stood still, in the shadow of a large oak, holding my breath, listening intently.

A rustling not far away. Then a gasping cry. Had a traveller been snatched from the track in the minutes before we rode through? I listened intently. Someone was panting, gasping, short of breath. Finally, a series of wheezing moans. I followed the sounds. In the middle of a clearing, an old boy was lying on the moss, his britches cast aside, a young woman sitting astride, her skirts spread round, concealing the fellow's legs and chest, so all I could see of him was his head turned away and his arms stretched out.

The woman caught sight of me. A look of panic on her face. I put my finger to my lips. She took my meaning and leaned forward to cover the old fellow. I looked through the pockets in his britches for a purse. What I found was a small prayer book. Inside the front cover, the inscription:

This Book of Common Prayer belongs to the Parish of Saint Giles in the Fields. In the care of Roger Manwayring, Rector of the Parish.

Roger Manwayring. Remember that name, I thought. I borrowed his little prayer book as a kind of *memento mori*. Make the most of this life while you have it. A thousand gasping little deaths before we die. What the parson at St Giles got up to with his parishioners was no concern of mine, though if I ever needed sanctuary in his church, I had the prayer book with his name inside to remind him of what I'd seen that night.

'It was nothing,' I said to Frances. 'Foxes rutting. It's that time of year.'

20

Reading figures

From St Giles we used tracks and byways, until we reached the edge of Highgate. I knew the village by reputation for its numerous taverns and the pleasures of the flesh they offered, though I said nothing of that to Frances.

A nearby church clock struck eleven. I pulled my horse to the edge of the road and gestured to Frances to do the same. I turned and looked back, wanting to be sure we weren't being followed. Seeming to think I'd stopped for the view of London, Frances looked round and gazed back over the city.

'It is beautiful,' she said. 'I've never seen it like this.'

A half-moon picked out the Thames, a snake of gleaming silver winding through the landscape, splitting it in two. North of the river, the great bulk of The Tower and Paul's church loomed over the dark formless shadow that was London under curfew. Beautiful? Not to my mind.

Somewhere in that darkness, somewhere close to the river were my meagre lodgings. To the West, a myriad of lights were glowing even at this late hour. How many thousands of candles and lanterns still burning bright in Whitehall Palace and the great houses on The Strand? Frances seemed deep in thought. I wondered whether Katherine would still be fully dressed in Essex House, waiting all night to welcome Frances on her return.

To the east of Paul's on the far side of the river, more lights. 'Is that Greenwich Palace?' said Frances.

Was she thinking about her beloved Rochester with the King? Was she jealous? What would Rochester think if he ever found out that Frances had been to Highgate with the rogue Edgworth?

'I think it is Greenwich, my lady. But I've never been there myself.'

She looked at me and smiled. 'The quality of the night seems different here. The air so clean and fresh. When I came back from Audley End, it struck me how smelly the place is. Even Westminster and Whitehall. The smoke, the tanneries, the brickworks. I like it up here.'

She pointed out what she could see, as if that was why we'd ventured out. The noblewoman enjoying her great adventure.

I humoured her. But I sensed beneath the cheerful chatter she was nervous, the excitement of the journey giving way to apprehension. All the more reason to press on.

'We have to leave the roads and byways now, my lady.' I pointed out a pathway leading into the woods. 'Best stay close behind.'

The tangled undergrowth on either side of the path soon blocked out all sight of London, Westminster and Greenwich. The thick summer canopy screened out much of the moonlight. Spring hadn't yet turned to summer, but the path was already entangled with brambles. It was well she was wearing long boots and men's britches.

Neither of us spoke until we reached a mossy clearing, where I suggested we dismount and sit for a while on the bough of a great tree which must have fallen in last year's autumn storms.

'Are we near?'

'Not far now. We must take care in these woods.' I raised a finger to my lips. Something was moving not far away. I drew my dagger.

A badger waddled into the clearing, snouting for grubs. Scenting humans, the half-blind beast looked up, then scurried off into the undergrowth.

An owl hooted nearby.

'The sorcerer's bird,' she said. Her thoughts lay ahead, with the cunning woman of her imagination. I'd not described Hannah, and she hadn't asked.

We continued on our way, soon reaching the bank of a large pond, the half-moon reflected in its still, dark waters. The sky was clear, although from many miles away there came a booming roll of thunder.

The path grew narrower, barely wide enough for horses. We climbed a steep hill before reaching a low ridge. From there we looked down onto that strange circular building in the middle of a clearing. The hovel that had once been a charcoal burner's hut.

'Does she really live in that?' whispered Frances.

'For now she does.'

I tethered the horses to a low branch of an ancient yew tree.

'I'll go in first,' I said. 'Make sure she's alone.'

I walked down into the clearing, pushed aside the sheepskin hanging over the entrance, and crouched down to go inside. As before, the place was filled with smoke from the fire and tallow candles, and that unfamiliar other smell, sweetly aromatic, belying the grimness of the clay earth floor and bare turf walls.

'I have returned. My name's Matthew Edgworth. I came before.'

She was sitting cross-legged before the fire on one of those damask cushions, the cat curled up beside her. She didn't move, gazing ahead, as if entranced by the flames. She gave no indication that she'd heard me.

'I have brought the lady with me.'

Distant thunder rumbled. I tried again.

'The last time I came, we spoke about a noble lady.'

'You came before.' Her voice was barely audible.

'I came back with a plate of food later that night. You were asleep. I left it for you.'

'Your name is Matthew.' As if this were something she had just divined. 'Was that an act of kindness?'

'You wouldn't let me pay you in coins.'

'Are you kind?'

'You can trust me.'

'You don't answer my question. Are you kind?'

'Not for me to say.'

'Do you not like being kind?' She was still looking into the fire, not at me, and yet I felt that she was seeing deep inside me. With Forman I'd fought it. But Hannah's world was warm and comforting. I'd said I'd bring food the next time I came. I didn't have to go back with it that same night. So maybe it was indeed an act of kindness.

'Yes. There are times I am kind.' My mind was wondering. Time already slowing down and drifting. I knew Frances was waiting outside. I knew she was nervous. I knew she'd be impatient. But the way Hannah spoke…

'Sit down, Matthew.' Her words so soothing.

'I spoke to you before about a lady.'

'A lady who wants me to read the horoscope that Simon Forman made after casting her nativity. Sit down, Matthew.'

'She is waiting outside.'

'She will come in when she is ready.'

I allowed myself to be enchanted. Maybe I wanted to be. I sat down.

'You bring something with you, Matthew.'

Silence wafting gently through the room. Time slowing.

'You bring a heavy darkness. I do not mean your dagger. Nor whatever it is you're hiding. I mean the darkness within.'

Did she mean Jacob or the scrying mirror? I don't remember how much I told her, nor why it was easy to do so when it wasn't something I ever spoke about. But I do remember the cat jumping from the cushion to sit on her lap. And I do remember saying again that Frances was waiting outside.

Hannah looked up. Frances was standing in the doorway. 'It is raining.' She sounded almost apologetic.

I got to my feet and bowed, then moved away. Habits of deference die hard. But Frances hardly noticed me. She was looking at Hannah.

'Come closer.'

Frances took a step forward.

'Tell me your name.'

'You know why I'm here.'

'I do indeed. But I can do nothing for you until you tell me your name.'

'My name or my title?'

'The names you were given at birth. I have no interest in titles.'

'Frances Howard. I came for an interpretation of the nativity that Doctor Simon Forman cast for me. I have here the horoscope he cast for me. Master Edgworth told me you'd understand. He said you'd be able to interpret it.'

'That is why you came.'

'Yes, it is.'

'Come closer. Kneel. I need to see your face.'

Frances looked nervous, but did as Hannah asked, kneeling on the bare earth floor, as if awaiting benediction.

'Reading figures is private,' said Hannah. 'Matthew should leave.'

I didn't move. Whatever the spell that Hannah cast over me started to wane in its powers when I backed away. Rain drops spattering onto the fire. Thunder in the distance.

'He brought me here safely,' said Frances. 'I owe him thanks for that. Let him stay.'

'It is a private matter.'

'And it will stay private, said Frances. 'If I tell him not to listen, he will hear nothing. It is raining heavily outside. Stay by the doorway, Matthew.'

I was foolish and arrogant enough to feel flattered by her trust in me, and touched that she didn't want me getting soaked in the storm.

Hannah put kindling on the fire and sprinkled herbs into the flames. The hut filled with smoke again, the unfamiliar scent masking the acrid tallow candles. I made a show of moving off into the shadows.

'Do you know what your nativity contains?' asked Hannah, her voice so gentle it could have been a lullaby.

'I have only my hopes and my fears.'

'It is not prophecy.'

'Doctor Forman explained that.'

'Hopes and fears,' said Hannah. 'First tell your fears.'

'What I fear … is that there will be no escape. That I will spend my life in the prison of my husband's dreadful house. That I will suffer for the sins of others.'

Hannah waited. She must have known there was more.

'And poisons,' said Frances. 'I fear that Forman's book contains recipes for poisons, as well as the nativity that was cast for me.'

'Nothing in this world is wholly good or wholly bad. Hyssop heals cuts and bruises, gives relief from congestion of the chest. Belladonna lessens women's pain in childbirth or at her monthly bleedings. Poppy sap aids sleep. Too much and you never wake. All of these are poisons. Love can heal or mortally wound. It is the same with poisons.'

'I know that Forman could make poisons so powerful they'd make the plague seem like a summer sneeze,' said Frances. 'Poisons give power to those who understand their secrets. But I want no part in that.'

Hannah leant forward, threw another handful of herbs onto the fire. The hovel filled again with scented smoke.

'And now your hopes.'

'I tell you my hopes, then you tell me what I want to hear. I know your trickery.'

'I have no tricks. If you don't wish to speak aloud, then keep your thoughts silent. But think them clearly.' Her voice was gentle, soothing.

And Frances did speak aloud, although her words came soft and quiet. 'To be freed from my hateful marriage. To be free to marry a man I choose. Not be judged by mean-spirited men. Not to be constrained by the fears of others.'

'Wise hopes. Fair hopes,' said Hannah. 'Now, hold the candles for me while I look at Forman's charts.'

Frances took the candles. Hannah opened the book. She leafed slowly through.

'What do you see?'

'Hold the candles closer.' She leafed through the book. Forwards, then back to check on something. Forward and back. Until: 'There are five. Forman drew up five charts for you. Reading charts drawn up by someone else is never easy. Give me time.'

Frances was sitting cross-legged, gazing into the fire as Hannah studied the charts. From where I stood, I could just make out Frances's expression. She looked at peace with herself and the world. Strange days.

Time flowed.

Hannah spoke again. 'A mother can abandon her child, but she will never forget it. The same is true of knowledge. You may not like what I tell, but once heard it will never leave you. Are you sure you want to hear?'

'Tell me.' An edge of fear in her voice.

'A reading cannot be rushed.' From outside, the sound of

falling rain. Inside, the crackling of logs and the occasional hiss as raindrops fell onto the fire.

Then it began. 'It was the conjunction of your birth chart with the circumstances of your consultations which caused Doctor Forman such tribulation. You are a good woman, Frances Howard. But your fate has become entwined with dangerous men.'

'Have I come out here in the middle of the night, risked my life and my reputation for you to tell me what I already know?'

Untroubled by Frances's irritation, Hannah spoke slowly, choosing each word with great care. 'Five. Forman saw five. It is a sacred number. Again and again he saw this number in your horoscope.'

'What in heavens' name do you mean?'

'Five men. Five forces on your life. Five points of the star. Five senses. Five fingers. Five wounds of Christ. Within the pentacle lies a void, a dark abyss where fallen angels are fettered in perpetual pain.'

'Brave language, but leave off the decoration. Two men, not five. My life. I should know. Two men. One loves me. The other wants to hide me from the world, deny me everything that makes a woman whole.'

Hannah continued as if Frances hadn't spoken. 'The first – your own father. He wanted you to be the agent that would heal great rifts. The second – your husband, the man chosen by your father.'

'Lord Essex.'

'His birth name, not his title.'

'Robert Devereux.'

'Forman saw disharmony, disjunction, deceit in your husband and your father.'

'You tell me what I've known for years,' snapped Frances.

'To understand future possibilities, we have to know the present and the past. Father and husband, the first two men. Then a third, and soon a fourth. Each has great power. Each is dangerous.'

'All men of power are dangerous,' whispered Frances.

Hannah flicked between the charts.

'Forman was troubled by what he saw.'

'Don't protect me from the truth. I get my fill of flattery at court.'

'These next two men. The charts say you love them both. In different ways. Do you know who he meant?'

'I know one. Not two.'

'Give me his name. To interpret further, I must –'

'Breathe a word of this outside this hovel and your corpse will rot in Fleet Ditch.'

'Without a name, I cannot be sure –'

'Viscount Rochester.'

'Titles change at the whims of kings and queens.'

'Robert Carr. No. His Scottish name was Robert Kerr. He changed it when he came to London.'

'And the other? Who might that be?'

Frances shook her head.

'There are many kinds of love,' said Hannah.

'A different kind of love? My uncle then. He loves me the way my father should.'

'Your uncle?'

'My great uncle. His birth name. Henry Howard.'

'Two of these men ….' Hannah faltered. She was gazing into space as if waiting for a mist to clear. 'Two of these men …. The lines are broken in each of the charts…'

'Meaning they die? Is that what it says?'

'This is not prophecy.'

'Which men die?

'Forman's figures show lines growing tangled, then moving apart. '

'Two lines broken… One must be my dear Uncle Henry. He's in good health, but very old.'

Outside, the roaring of thunder. Rockfall in the heavens. A storm approaching. The hissing of raindrops on the fire more frequent. Hannah looking closely at one of the charts, tracing lines on it with a finger. Matthew silently watching, glad not to be out in the storm.

'Five men,' said Frances. 'You said there are five men. Tell me of the fifth.'

'There is love, but not for you. A friend who becomes an enemy, who stands for, then against.'

'A friend of mine? A friend of my husband? Or a friend of Robert Carr?'

'The interweavings become tightly plaited.'

'What does that mean?'

'I know not,' said Hannah.

'A friend of Robert Carr? Is that possible? Who stands for me then against me? I know the man. His name is Thomas Overbury. Is he the fifth man?'

'I only know the names that you tell me.'

'Say what you think. I've come to hear what Forman saw – not turn away from it. Is he the other man who dies?'

'One of these men dies in great pain. He suffers a long, drawn-out death.'

'The friend of Robert Carr who becomes an enemy dies in great pain?'

'Maybe him. Or maybe another. There are always several possibilities.'

Hot candlewax dripped onto Frances's wrist. She flinched. 'What else do you see?'

I saw Hannah show Frances one of the charts in Forman's book.

'I see your husband's line breaking from yours.'

'Essex. Robert Devereux?'

'Your line and his grow far apart.'

'What then? After my husband's line has broken from mine. What then?'

'Possibilities, not consequences.'

'Just tell me what's there.'

'It tangles again. Your line and this conjoin.'

'What does that mean?'

'Two lines joining together sometimes means a wedding.'

'And that line could be Robert Carr's?'

'It is possible.'

'Thank you,' said Frances, triumphant. 'The marriage I deserve.'

'And after the conjoining, a period of great happiness,' said Hannah.

'Thank you.'

'The charts never give certainties. There are no certainties.'

'Enough. No more.' Frances reached out for the book.

But Hannah held it tight. 'Forman also saw darkness,' said Hannah. An odd growling sound was coming from the cat. 'On all these charts, one of the five dies in great pain. Forman may have known which one, but I cannot read his cyphers. There is also darkness. Darkness and fog. An abyss of darkness.' I shivered at that mention of the abyss.

Outside, the storm was roaring.

Hannah had to raise her voice 'Forman saw beyond the second wedding.' A moment of silence, except for the dripping water and the hissing fire. 'He saw someone sucked into the void. Powerless to escape.'

Neither woman spoke until Frances whispered, 'Is that me? Does that mean me?'

'Too far into the future to see clearly. But someone is accused and vilified. Someone brought low after rising to great heights.'

'Five charts. Five different possibilities. That's what you said.'

Hannah was silent.

'What do *you* see?'

'I see a void. A dark abyss at the centre of the pentacle.'

'What does that mean? Me in that void? My world destroyed?'

The fire hissing. Raindrops falling through the hole in the roof.

'What does that mean? I command you. Tell me what you see.'

Hannah flicked the pages back to Forman's notes. 'There is always darkness after light,' she said in a low murmur. 'Night follows day follows night follows day.'

'Where? Where is light?'

'Two lines here I do not understand. There are obstacles. So many entanglements.'

'Whose lines? What obstacles? Who is entangled?'

Hannah shook her head. 'I think…' Her voice faded.

'You think what?'

'I think Forman did not complete his work. If he had lived, he would have wanted you to go back to him for another consultation.'

'I know that. He wanted me to go to him.'

'He would have wanted to cast a second nativity.'

'Is that possible?'

'He would have asked different questions.' And with that, Hannah closed the book.

'Is there nothing more?' said Frances.

'Nothing I can see.' Hannah shut her eyes and lowered her head. 'I am tired.'

'If I return, would you be able to cast a nativity for me yourself?'

'During the day. When there is light.'

'Would you be willing to do it?'

'Yes. I am willing.' She folded her arms around the casebook and held it to her breast.

Frances was trembling. 'I need to take the book with me.'

'It is too dangerous for you to take.'

'Give it to me,' snapped Frances. 'It will be safer with me than here with you.' The great turmoil within that she'd been keeping in check since leaving Essex House was coming to the boil.

'It is the book itself that's dangerous,' said Hannah.

'You think I want to make poisons? Is that it? How dare you! Give it to me,' she shouted. She grabbed for the book, dropping the candle onto the fire as she did so. The melting tallow spat and flared. The cat yowled, leapt from its cushion and ran out into the night. Hannah clung to the book.

Frances grabbed Hannah by the hair, twisting it round, pulling her down to the fire.

'Give me the casebook. Give it to me, or I will burn your face in your own damned fire.'

21

Glimpses of what might be

The Countess of Essex as vicious a fighter as any brawling whore in a low tavern rowdy. Hannah's hair would have been ablaze if it hadn't been raining. But the hovel offered scant protection from the storm, and rain had nearly extinguished the fire.

Both women struggling on the bare earth floor. Frances holding tight to Hannah's hair, trying to force down her into the embers of the fire. Hannah clutching Forman's casebook to her breast.

I stepped out of the shadows.

'Best leave now, my lady,' raising my voice to be heard.

They held still for a moment. Had they forgotten I was in the hovel with them? 'We should leave before the storm gets worse.'

'Get the casebook,' said Frances.

'It is best we leave, my lady.'

They held off for a moment. Then Frances let go and got to her feet, breathing heavily, red-faced from the struggle.

Hannah's arms were still wrapped tightly around the book. She rocked back and forth, staring at the hissing embers of the fire and whimpering.

I edged Frances away and whispered, 'Hannah is still of use to you. We mustn't turn her against us.'

'She cannot keep Forman's book.'

'Allow me to deal with it, my lady. The yew tree where we tethered the horses will give shelter. I'll get the book. I swear it.'

Gently, I led Frances to the doorway. I pulled back the sheepskin and she made a dash through the rain across the clearing.

I liked the way Hannah thought. Stay alert to possibilities. When Lady Luck smiles, be sure to smile back and accept what she's offering with good grace, for she'll turn on you and damn you quick as blink. You see a possibility. You make it happen. Or be forewarned and do your damnedest to prevent it.

With the fire almost out, the only source of light came from a candle spluttering on the bare earth floor. I offered to help rebuild the fire. Hannah looked at me, suspicious, still clutching the book as I added straw and kindling, then small pieces of wood. A few drops of rain were still getting through, but the worst of the storm seemed to have passed.

'I want advice, Goody Hannah.'

She said nothing.

I sat down. Hannah poked at the fire with a long stick. From the corner of my eye I saw the blanket hanging over the doorway move. A black shadow slipped through and padded over, walked round several times, then curled up by the fire and licked its paws.

'I have something in my possession that once belonged to Doctor Dee.'

'Something?'

'Doctor Dee bequeathed it to his pupil, Simon Forman.'

She stared at me, but I couldn't read her expression.

'You seek advice?'

'Forman warned me that even he had only ever glimpsed the true extent of its powers.'

'What advice do you seek?'

'His widow was fearful that men from the Privy Council would come to the house and search for anything that might incriminate her deceased husband. She asked me to look after this something that I have. She asked me to keep it safe. She feared she'd be accused if they found it.'

'You're lying.'

I shrugged. 'But I do have Forman's scrying mirror.'

'Then you're a thief. Doctor Forman's widow would never have given it to you.'

'I am many things, Goody Hannah. But I have the scrying mirror, and I can prevent it falling into the hands of men who would use it for evil.'

'You should never have it.'

'Should or shouldn't. No matter to me. What matters is I have it. But what am I to do with it? That's the advice I seek. I want someone who understands its powers to keep it safe.'

Almost imperceptibly, she started rocking gently back and forth again. Her gaze switching between me and the fire, me and the cat.

I unbuttoned my doublet, reached into the secret pocket and withdrew the leather-bound package. After all that talk of *the dark abyss* and *darkness after light,* I wanted rid of the wretched thing. Since walking past the ruins of the Spital Fields Priory I'd been minded to hurl it into the Thames and let the river mud swallow it. Now I saw a different possibility.

'I could give it to you, Goody Hannah. A token of thanks for your good work this night.'

'Frances tried to burn my face.'

'She's not used to people speaking truth to her. When she thinks back on what she heard this night she will be well pleased.'

'The charts are not truths. They offer glimpses of what might be.'

'So be it. You keep the scrying mirror for safekeeping. I look after the casebook.'

'Let me see it.'

And thus the deal was done. I let her unwrap it, shielding my eyes as she did so. When she was satisfied that it was what I claimed, she handed me the book.

'I will return with the lady. And we'll bring the casebook with us. Keep you well, Goody Hannah.'

She was already staring into the depths of the obsidian glass as I left the hovel. I was glad to be relieved of it. But it was a loan, not a gift. Hannah could look after it til I had use for it.

Frances was sheltering beneath the old yew tree. I showed her the book.

She smiled. 'So you are true to your word.'

'I only ever make promises that I know I can keep.'

'I shouldn't be surprised. But I am. Thank you.'

'And you surprise me too, my lady, if I may say so. Where did you learn to fight like that?' I'd seen a glimpse of another Frances in Hannah's hovel; a Frances who could fight with her hands and lose her temper was a Frances who might warm to teasing – at least out here, away from the stiff formality of nobility and the stuffed etiquette of their grand houses.

'Are you being insolent?' She was smiling as she said it.

'Far from it. I am full of admiration.'

'I fought with my brothers when I was a child in Audley End. That taught me never to give up. Will the cunning woman agree to see me again?'

'I am certain of it.' She seemed convinced by that, though I had my doubts.

The rain had stopped. The journey back was quick and without incident. The sky was lightening as we neared The Strand. Crowing cocks set the dogs off barking. Westminster and London were waking up. Frances turned to me and thanked me for 'A good night's work.'

We left the horses in the merchant's yard. Katherine had hidden Frances's own clothes in the chapel of Essex House. I led her down Milford Lane until we reached that door into the walled garden – the same way I'd found my own way to the chapel. She looked on in amusement as I picked the lock.

'You're a useful man to know Matthew.' Praise indeed, I thought, and addressed by my Christian name.

Some call me a patter merchant, but now that we were back in the world of grand houses and walled gardens I was tongue-tied as I wondered how I might ask about Kate in a way that didn't seem like calling in a debt. But it was Frances who asked me, 'Would you still like to meet with my maid?' I must have looked surprised, for she added, 'You see, I too keep my promises.'

22

Saint Olave's

I slept for much of the next morning, then woke to the strangest of sensations, for it was Kate who had woken me. She'd appeared in my dreams. I could still hear her voice and almost taste her sweet kisses. I knew what I wanted her for, and if I could take her to bed in the process, so be it. But appearing in my dreams – I hadn't planned for that.

Had the smoke in Cunning Hannah's hovel infected my mind? How else could I have allowed myself to become so obsessed? I was like a stripling boy who thought that playing the two backed beast was a game of piggy-back, as if the only paps I'd ever seen were my mother's.

Given the chance, I'd have happily bedded Alice, or little rosy-cheeked Bessie at Sherborne, or even Anne Forman, for behind her shrewishness the doctor's widow was a good-looking woman. I know about lust and how to slake it, but there was already something else with Kate. And whatever it was, I'd not felt it before.

I headed for The Mermaid that night, hoping that Richard Weston might have a message for me. Nothing from Lady Frances. But we played a few games of dice. We both won, we both lost. I didn't want him getting wary. And we drank a little – not too little, not too much. Without Weston knowing, I had already enlisted him into my own little band of intelligencers.

A couple of days later, he handed me a letter. 'From her ladyship,' he said. But it wasn't. It was from Kate. Frances had used her own seal and written my name in her hand on the envelope. But Kate had written instructions inside.

> **I go the tire-maker shopp of Cristofer Mountjoy for MY LADY on Tusday morning nex wek. His shopp on corner of Silver Strete and Muggle Street, close by city walls. Oppersit the churchyard of Saint Olave. Meet under the syn at noon.**

And there she was – a fine lady in flowing golden periwig – the sign of a tire maker, painted on a wooden board, swinging from a bracket above the door on Silver Street. But no Kate. The clock at Saint Olave's struck twelve. No Kate. Was her appointment with Mountjoy taking longer than expected?

I'd had dealings before with Mountjoy. He sold me the sleek, raven black wig that Alice wore when I delivered her to Rochester. And it was Mountjoy who bought the hank of Alice's hair which Rochester so generously gave me to sell.

Mountjoy had a reputation. Indeed, he had several. It was said he made the best tiaras and headgear in all London. It was also said he was mean and conniving. I once heard that Will Shakspere had lodgings in his house, though why anyone would want to lodge with Mountjoy was beyond me. Maybe Mountjoy's icy surliness acted as a shield, protecting Master Shakspere from actors who demanded he rewrite their parts.

I was hoping to find Kate in the shop. But there was only a long table with a dozen wig-stands on it. Twelve eyeless mannequin heads. As wooden and witless as blind justice. The last time I was here these wig-stands and mannequins had been laden with a glittering array of headbands and circlets, wigs and tiaras, the finest of them in the form of a little ship, with sails of pure silk and pearls for portholes, riding high on a sea of curled hair. No wares on display this time. Trade must have fallen off with so many wealthy folk leaving London for the summer months. Or had Mountjoy's reputation as a mean-minded killjoy finally caught up with him?

I rang the bell on the table. A prentice boy came through from the workshop.

'What do you lack, sir?'

What I lacked was Kate to warm my bed.

'I'd like to sample your wares, for my master can't decide whether to commission a periwig from here or from the tire-maker in The Strand. Is Master Mountjoy here today?'

'In the workshop, sir. He's busy.'

'Then I shall speak to him in the workshop.' I pushed the boy aside and walked through.

What a foul combination of smells – the acrid stench of a browny-green dye bubbling in a crucible, animal bones reducing for glue in a cauldron hanging over a smoky coal fire. Over in the far corner was Mountjoy, a tall man with gaunt face and thin wiry beard, talking earnestly to a woman who had her back to me.

A wig of sleek, golden hair crowned a wooden head on the workbench beside the prentice boy. It could have been fashioned from Alice's fine mane. A pair of false paps lay beside it. Much of Mountjoy's work came from the playhouse companies. I wondered what pretty boy player those paps were destined for, and who he'd be personating when he wore them. I ran my hands over the pale calfskin, cold against my curious fingertips yet perfect in shape and soft and yielding to the touch. I shuddered, stricken by the strangest foreboding that a woman's corpse would feel like this.

Mountjoy caught sight of me.

'No,' he shouted in his Frenchie accent. 'No touch that.'

The woman looked round. I smiled. It was Kate. She smiled back.

'Oh, Master Mountjoy,' I said. 'I see you're busy. How pleasing. I'd heard your trade was falling off. No matter. I shall wait outside. The sun is shining.'

Mountjoy looked suspicious. The Matthew he'd met before had never shown much patience. But the Matthew he'd met before hadn't come to his shop to find Kate. And this Matthew, who smiled sweetly and bade him a polite goodbye, didn't want him asking if I had any more hair to sell – not with Kate in earshot.

'Where shall we go, sweet Kate? Perhaps we might sample the sparrow grass at Paris Gardens? Or to The Globe? Better still, I hear Ben Jonson's *Alchemist* plays at The Blackfriars.' That would have suited very well because my lodgings off Water Lane are less than fifty yards from Blackfriars Playhouse.

'What I would like,' she said, 'Is for you and me to talk.'

'Then allow me to escort you to Hyde Park, where we can talk as we walk.'

'I'd like to sit here.'

So that's what we did. We found an old wooden bench in Saint Olave's churchyard. It was encrusted with birdshit, so I laid down my cape for Kate to sit on. She allowed me to hold her hand and kiss it. Such a well-mannered gallant wooing his fine lady!

'I like you, Matthew. What I said in the Audley End Wilderness was true. I do think you're a kind man.' Something ominous in that.

'Then kiss me Kate, for you've been forever in my thoughts since the happy moment we first met.' I'd have said the same words had I still been trying recruit my spy in Frances's household, but the words came in a nervous flutter, fledglings taking first flight.

'You and I first met in the kitchens at Chartley,' said Kate.

'I remember it well.'

'The day after you tried to bed Alice.'

'You talked to Alice?' My hopes were sinking.

'We shared an apartment for more than two months.'

'Was she good company?'

'Where is she?'

'I did as I promised. I escorted her to a place of safety.'

'Where is she, Matthew?'

'She is alive and she is safe.'

'I want to see her. I want to thank her for what she did in Chartley.'

'What was that?'

'I will tell you whatever you ask after I've spoken to her myself.'

'I visited her family. I've given them all the money I promised. Her mother, her sisters and her little brother. All well provided for.'

'Where is Alice?'

'And I gave money to her elder brother, Pieter Vancy, the giant with the stained face – until he took himself off to Canterbury to seek employment.'

'Answer me, Matthew. Where is Alice?'

I looked away. A blackbird with a worm in its mouth flew into its nest in the yew tree.

'Matthew.' She took hold of my hand. 'You made me a promise.'

I could so easily have lied, told her I'd taken Alice to Canterbury to join Pieter Vancy. She'd never have known different. A well-chosen lie is so much less painful than a tiresome truth. But I didn't lie. That squeeze of her hand kept me honest.

'I've kept my promise, Kate, though you may not like what I have to tell you. I had to tell Rochester that I'd had her drowned.'

'I know. Frances receives letters from Rochester most days. She told me that Alice drowned. And now you say she's safe. What really happened, Matthew?'

'Bradshaw, the coachman, left us at Blackwall docks.'

'Where is she?'

'I took her to The Bridewell. I paid the warden well to ensure no harm comes to her.'

Kate got to her feet and walked away. I thought I'd lost her. But she stopped about twenty feet away and stood with her back to me, staring out over the graveyard. Most of the headstones were covered in moss, many of them cracked, and all crammed together, tight as flints in church walls.

I gave her a little time, then walked quietly over and stood behind her. 'Alice is in The Bridewell,' I said, as gently as I could, 'Because that's the safest place for her.'

'One week in that place is enough to destroy a woman.'

'And one day out of it would have been enough for Rochester's men to track her down. If they found her, she and I would both have been food for fishes. She had to be in a place where no-one knew her. Where no-one would come looking for her. I paid the warden well to ensure she was well fed and not harmed or abused in any way.'

Kate stood where she was. Silent. Staring straight ahead.

I explained about needing to show Rochester proof that I'd disposed of Alice. Still, she wouldn't look at me. I couldn't tell whether she was furious or distraught. Probably both.

'Tell me, Kate, what would you have me do?'

She turned round, looked me straight in the eye. But didn't speak. Then she went back to sit on the bench. I followed her over. The church porch was covered with flowers. I picked one and gave it to her.

'It has no scent, I fear. But it is pretty.'

'It's honeysuckle, Matthew. They keep their scent for evening.'

'Then we must come back one day, as the sun is setting, and I'll pick a posy for you.'

'I'll agree to nothing until you get Alice out of The Bridewell.'

'And where in Heaven's name would you have me take her? Essex House? So you and Lady Frances can keep her like Lady Wellborn's tame spaniel?'

'Where are your lodgings, Matthew?'

I looked at her in disbelief. 'You're not suggesting I remove Alice from The Bridewell and take her to live with me?'

'Only until she's ready to travel out of London. And while she's there I will come to your lodgings and help nurse her back to health.'

'What makes you think she's sick?'

'How could she not be after six months in The Bridewell?'

'Do you know what you're asking?'

'I know exactly what I'm asking. And if you'll not lift her from The Bridewell, then I'll ask Lady Frances to help me do it.'

'That would be utter madness.'

'So you must do it, Matthew. And if you don't, I'll not speak to you again.'

A gust of wind. From atop the church steeple came a screeching as the weathercock turned on its rusty mast. The chill wind brought with it a whiff of the gluepot in Mountjoy's workshop. Saint Olave's was not the most romantic of places for a lover's tryst!

'You will come to my lodgings?'

'If Alice is there I will.'

'I will lift her from The Bridewell tomorrow.'

'Then tell me where to find your lodgings.'

23

That fine palace on the banks of the Fleet

'You got more wagtail for us, Edgworth?' The warden was sitting in the same dark little room, behind the same desk. He'd put on weight and his forehead gleamed with sweat, for the weather was much warmer than the last time I was here, but little else had changed.

'I've come to collect.'

His eyes opened wide. 'You said three months.'

'We made an agreement – I'd pay you well, and you'd see she was safe and in good health. I've come to collect. Have her brought here.'

'Three months is long past. Didn't think you was coming back.'

'You thought wrong. Have her brought here.'

He sniffed and got to his feet. He was shuffling over to the door to call a guard, when I caught hold of his arm.

'Where is she?' I had a terrible suspicion that he'd sold her on.

'This place is too big to keep track of all the commodities what we have in. She was well looked after for the three months you said. I swear it.'

'Swear as much as you fucking like. I'm here to collect. If she's not here, or not in good health, you'll suffer. Understand?' He swallowed. 'Where is she?'

'I … I'm. I'll go and find her.'

'You and me will go together.'

We climbed a wide stone staircase, pausing at the first-floor landing for him to regain his wheezing breath. He led the way down a long wide corridor, glancing back every few paces like a fearful dog. After thirty yards or so he pulled out his keys and unlocked a room. We were greeted by the wailing of infants. Perhaps in former times this had once been a great room of state with rich tapestries, oak panelled walls and Turkish carpets. Now the only lingering grandeur was the height of the windows – three in the far wall, all of them barred. The air in this fine palace on the banks of the Fleet might once have been fragrant with the perfumes of the Spanish Queen and her Ladies in Waiting. Now it stank of infant shit, mothers' milk and crumbling lime-wash plaster. The women, all heavily pregnant or nursing young babes, were confined to wooden-sided stalls littered with straw, shackled with iron collars and heavy chains.

'Why are we looking here? She wasn't pregnant when I brought her in.' At least I'd assumed she wasn't. Could she have been carrying the child that Frances didn't want, a child fathered by the Earl of Essex?

Shackles walked into the room and looked around, oblivious to the stench and the wailing of infants. I waited in the corridor until he came back, shaking his head. He slammed the door shut.

'Why look in there? Does she have a child?'

'Sometimes we puts a healthy one in to act as midwife. Those what come in here knows what's what. They help out, they get privileges.'

He led me on, deeper into the labyrinth, our progress accompanied by muffled cries of rage and distress, echoing down the long wide corridors.

He opened another door. 'Take a look in here.'

A keeper by the door with a whip. Shackles gestured for him to stand back while we looked for Alice. Thirty, maybe forty women, all sewing, spinning or weaving. The fetid air heavy with the smell of stale sweat. Most of the women had blistered fingers and blood on their smocks – some fresh, some dried. The looms, the wheels and the needles as unforgiving as the keepers.

Their heads all shaven bare, and all wearing shapeless, tawdry grey smocks and the same lifeless expression, as if that, too, were part of the uniform. Alice could have been working the spinning wheel in front of us, and I wouldn't have known it was her without a close inspection.

So this was what the City Fathers meant by cleaning the streets. I don't know quite why I was so shaken by what I saw. I've seen far greater suffering before and since. I don't know what happened in that room at The Bridewell, but I found myself choking back tears. Tears of rage, tears of frustration, tears of... what? I don't know. I've said it before: this is no place for half-truths. So I confess it now – I'd always known what went on in that dread place, that she'd become another commodity to be used and hired out when I didn't come back for her at the end of three months. Rochester might have forgotten about her, but so had I. I'd chosen to put her from my mind. So maybe my tears were for shame. Or maybe it was because I'd surely lose Kate if I couldn't rescue Alice.

'I don't think she's here,' I said.

'She's not dead,' said Shackles. 'We keeps a tally. If she wasn't in the nursery, she'll be here. The female factory we calls it.' He flapped his hand to indicate I should take a close look. 'But beware. The devil's in them.'

I walked into the room. I approached the woman closest to the door. She stank of incontinence, rank as a polecat's arse. Did the keepers not even allow them to piss? I looked up, hoping to breathe clean air. The ceiling was the kind of ornate plaster work I'd only ever seen before at Audley End. There, above my head was a Tudor Rose in white plaster and full-breasted Justice holding her scales – blind as ever to the cruelty beneath.

I walked on. Whenever I caught a woman's eye she looked away, flinching as if I were there to test their attention to their work.

I wanted to see the colour of their eyes. 'Look at me,' I said to one, shouting to be heard about the squeaking wheels, the clattering of shuttles and treadles. 'I mean you no harm.'

One of the keepers strode over. 'Do what the man says. Look at him if that's what he wants.' The woman got to her feet and lifted her smock.

'Not that. We're looking for Alice. You know her?'

She looked blank. The keeper cuffed her and walked away.

The warden waddled over. 'She's here somewhere. I know she's here.' He looked worried. He was right to be.

And then I saw her. In a dark corner away from the others, just as her brother Pieter Vancy used to be at Paul's. She was seated at a small table, sewing sleeves onto the body of a smock. Her cheeks were hollow, her skin was ashen, grey as her smock.

'Stand up. Look at him,' said the warden. Her eyes were vacant, no trace of thought nor feeling behind them. But she did have Alice's eyes. And she was tall.

'That's her.'

'I'll have a guard bring her down,' said the warden.

I did my best to look pleased that we'd found her. I didn't want him bringing in his deputy for the negotiations.

'I need to pay you, Master Shackles. Settle my debts. Pay you what's owed.'

He led the way back to his room. He sat back down behind his desk and opened a ledger. He wanted the full twenty pounds I'd offered in October.

'She's at death's door. If you call that safekeeping, I call this twenty pounds.' I counted out ten shillings and laid it on the table.

'You said three months. If you'd come for her in January, you'd have found her in good condition. You only had to send a message.'

'I'm sending it now.' I drew my stiletto.

'I have men waiting outside.'

'They're outside. We're in here. I'm not paying twenty pounds to take her out in that condition.'

'I can shout.'

'Don't. They won't be in time to save you.'

He blustered and gave way a little. But my heart wasn't in it, and my thoughts were elsewhere. I was keen to get Alice out of there, and back to my room, though I was dreading what Kate would say when she saw the state she was in. In the end we agreed on five pounds.

I put the Spanish Lady wig on Alice, the one that Mountjoy had made a year or so before.

'Where are you taking me?' she said. Her voice sounded pitifully weak and resigned to whatever fate awaited. Her spirit seemed finally broken.

'I'm taking you out of this place. I'm taking you to Katherine.' She didn't seem to recognise the name.

I waited until dark before leading her the few hundred yards from The Bridewell, over Fleet Bridge and down Water Lane to my lodgings, where Kate was waiting for us with food and ale. I knocked the door for Kate to let us in. She barely gave me a glance. Her attention was all on Alice, but I felt I was returning home. Kate had lit a fire and laid fresh rushes on the wooden floor. Instead of the smell of mould and damp which I'd grown used to, the room was fragrant with pomanders filled with lavender and rosewater.

She said nothing then about Alice's bald head and pinched features, although she couldn't disguise her dismay. She took Alice by the hand and led her through to the room at the back where I had my pallet bed. She offered food and drink, all the time talking quietly as a nursemaid with a favoured child. Alice was suspicious and hesitant, but after a while she ate a little.

'Lie down,' said Kate. 'Lie down and sleep. Matthew will not trouble you.'

Alice lay with her eyes open for what seemed an age. Kate sitting beside her on the only chair I have in the bedchamber, and me standing by the door, watching.

You might wonder that I'd given Kate the key to my lodgings. Maybe when it comes to matters of the heart we simply have to trust. Or maybe I was going mad, for I was certainly being driven by something other than reason. Lust is so much more straightforward.

I'd brought Kate there from St. Olave's – to show her where I lodged and how to get there without being seen. I'd hoped we might find out more about each other before I collected Alice, but Kate was as resolute as any puritan preacher: no kissing before the business between us was sealed with proof that Alice was safe. So I'd left her there to prepare the room, and in my madness, I trusted her. She swore she'd tell no-one where I lived. And I believed her. Greater love hath no man.

Kate held Alice's hand, gently reassuring her that she'd never have to go back to The Bridewell, nor Chartley Manor, nor the House of the Vixen. After Alice had finally fallen into sleep, Kate turned to me. 'You said she'd be safe. She is barely alive. You placed her in The Bridewell as punishment.' The words were fierce, her voice as quiet as if she were singing a lullaby.

'Punishment for what?'

'For being so strong-willed. For her strength. For selling herself to protect her family.'

'You really think that's why she did it?'

'I know that's why she did it.'

She laid Alice's hand gently down on the bed and gestured that we should go back into the other room. Kate shut the door on the bedchamber, but we still whispered. The window in that room didn't close properly. A gust of wind brought the stench of rotting fish up from the river. Kate grimaced, almost gagging. She'd brought pomanders for good reason.

'I chose my lodging for privacy, not comfort.'

'Alice isn't here for luxury. She will need to stay. She's too frail to travel. After the tortures of The Bridewell, she'll need peace. She must stay here until we can nurse her back to health.' I liked that 'we', although I knew as little about nursing as I did about mending stockings. I agreed to let Alice stay. And although Kate still refused to let me kiss her, she did soften. We talked for a while longer before checking on Alice. She was still asleep and breathing heavily. I closed the door.

'Did you and Alice talk much at Chartley?'

'Not at first. I took against her. I thought she was common. I thought she was insolent, haughty and sullen. But what I really couldn't abide was that she looked so like Frances. That above all – that she wasn't Frances. I didn't want her talking because her voice is different and might have raised suspicions. Frances gave us instructions that she was to continue to play the melancholic. Alice playing at being Frances feigning melancholy.

'I didn't like the arrangement. If Alice had been discovered, she'd have been hanged for personating nobility, and I'd have been thrown into the Bridewell for abetting the deceit. I missed Frances terribly, and I took it out on Alice.'

'But something changed? In the churchyard at Saint Olave's you said you wanted to thank her. To thank Alice.'

'You did her a terrible wrong to put her in The Bridewell. I know why you did it, Matthew. I understand your thinking. You thought it for the best. But it wasn't right to leave her for as long as you did.'

I don't take kindly to women who are scolds. With anyone other than Kate, I'd have thrown them both out. But with Kate it was different. I was different. Maybe I wanted to believe she'd glimpsed something in me that I'd not seen in myself.

'I know,' I said, quietly. 'It was wrong. Now I want to do right – by her and by you.' A younger Matthew would have mocked, marvelling that I'd have gone to such lengths to bed sweet Kate. 'You wanted to thank her?'

'She saved me from being raped by Essex.'

'*She* saved *you*?'

Outside, the shower of rain had turned to hail, scattershot driving against the window's thick glass.

'What happened? At Chartley. Between you and Alice and Lord Essex?'

'Why do you want to know?'

'Because I care about you.' Words I'd never spoken before. Not to a woman. Not to anyone. I thought she might scoff, but she smiled, and indicated I should sit beside her on the old chest where I kept clothes and secrets.

'Even before the exchange, Essex rarely visited us. When he did, he spent most of the time reminding Frances that she was his to do with as he chose. He took no interest in her as a woman. He's a blustering, drunken bully who wants an heir, not a lover. For him, a wife was but a means to an end. There was much gossip in the kitchens about whether he kept a catamite. The first time he came to visit, Frances told him she was bleeding heavily and suffering cramps from her monthly courses. He cannot abide the thought of women's blood. A few weeks later, he crawled into her bed. He was so drunk he was incapable.'

'Frances told you that?'

'Frances tells me everything. After the letter from Rochester advising her to feign melancholia, she told Essex that she'd suffer from it since childhood. The doctors at Audley End warned it would prevent her from conceiving a male child. I don't know if there's any truth in that, but Essex seemed to believe her. He left us alone for a while. But with Alice there in place of Frances I dreaded him coming back and forcing himself on her.'

She got up and went to look into the bedchamber again. Alice was still asleep and snoring quietly. It must have been months since she last slept uninterrupted.

Kate came back to sit beside me. Alice sleeping in my bed. Katherine sitting on the locked chest where I keep clothes from the Blackfriars tiring house and other tools of my trade. And there was this strange new Matthew listening attentively with Kate just inches away, talking soft as silk, and he'd not so much as brushed her cheek.

'About a fortnight after the exchange, we heard Essex's footsteps on the wooden stairs. Slow and steady. Not the usual clomping. He knocked gently. We'd been dreading the day he came to us sober. Without drink in him he might even be man enough to follow through on his intentions. Before I let him in, Alice went to her bed, I closed the shutters and blew out the candles, so the bedchamber was as dark as he believed my mistress's mood to be. I unlocked the door and welcomed him.

Instead of his usual roaring he was polite and ominously quiet. He asked to see Frances, I said her condition had worsened. He soon abandoned his show of restraint. "I am her husband, damn it," he roared, and pushed me so hard that I fell to the floor. He threw open the door to Frances's bedchamber. Alice lay there, arms wrapped around herself as if it were midwinter. I tried to plead with him. He ignored me and raged, insisting she answer him. Alice appeared not to see nor hear him. He screamed at her. Still, she didn't speak. "Speak to me, you sullen bitch. Damn you, damn you, damn you." He slapped her, the woman he thought was Frances. I was praying he'd stop there, and that Alice wouldn't respond in kind. But she gave a stifled cry, and her head rolled to one side like a broken doll. The performance was perfect.

'He seemed suddenly shamed by what he'd done. He caught a breath, then dropped to his knees and took her hand. Still Alice made no sound. I begged him to leave. The sound of my voice seemed to shock him, as if he'd forgotten I was there. He turned. A look of panic. A bullyboy caught tormenting his sister. He scrambled to his feet, grabbed me by the arm. Dragged me from Frances's room into my own bedchamber, threw me onto the bed, his breath as foul as a rotting carcase. He was snarling like a rabid dog, saliva dripping from his mouth, one hand pawing at my breasts, the other tugging at my skirts.'

'Oh Kate. If I'd been there – '

'It wasn't lust. It was rage and spite. Raping me was to humiliate the woman he thought was Frances. He didn't see Alice come into the room. I did. I saw her pick up his dagger which had dropped on the floor. There was a moment when

I wanted her to kill him, but that would have been the end of all of us. I shouted, "No" to Alice. That seemed to excite him, as if my 'No' was the confirmation he needed of his manliness. But it was enough to make Alice hold off, thank the Lord. She grabbed his hair from behind, pulled his head back and held the blade to his throat.

'He squealed. And still Alice didn't speak. Not one word. Essex's pig-stuck panic turned to whimpering as he struggled to catch his breath. "I think she means for you to leave, my Lord," I said.

'He pulled up his britches and left without looking at either of us After he'd gone, I realised I had a long splinter deep in my hand from when he'd thrown me to the floor. In the weeks Alice had been at Chartley I'd not had one kind word for her. Despite that, she bathed the wound and removed the splinter. We were both so frightened that neither of us said much that evening. The next morning, we began to talk. That's when she told me where you found her.'

'The House of The Vixen?'

'And the terrible misfortunes that brought her and her family so low. Maybe she'll tell you herself if she ever learns to trust you. What she told me was in strict confidence.'

She got up and went back in to Alice, who was whimpering in her sleep. Kate stroked her head. Slowly, Alice calmed. A nearby church struck four. Kate got to her feet and tippy-toed away. 'I have to go, Matthew. Lady Frances will be expecting me back.'

I walked down the stairs with her. The rain had stopped. Showers had given way to patches of blue sky, as is April's way. But Water Lane was aptly named. In the time we'd been inside, a rivulet had appeared on the far side of the alley and was streaming down towards Fleet River. A shaft of sunlight pierced the darkness of the narrow alley, catching the soft down on Kate's neck. I put my hand on her arm and tried to draw her to me.

'Don't, Matthew. If I'm away too long, Frances will never let me come again.'

'You will come again?'

She gave a wry smile. 'I have to be sure that Alice is recovering. If you truly care for me, then care for her. But yes, I will return.'

I squeezed her hand. 'I'll do my best.' She pulled gently away. 'Before you go, tell me, what does Lady Frances think happened to Alice?'

'That she fell from a wherry into the Thames. Rochester told her in a letter. She receives letters from him most days.'

'Was Frances distressed?'

'She thought it a sad accident.'

'Is that all?'

'She said she liked Alice, but she couldn't mourn for someone she's not supposed to have met.'

'Does she really think Alice is dead?'

'Yes. Why do you ask?'

'Frances instructed me to ensure no harm came to Alice,' I said. 'But she didn't speak of it when I last met her.'

'If she thinks it was an accident, why would she? She is greatly troubled at the moment.'

'I know. She hates being married to Essex, and she wants the nativity that Forman cast for her deciphered.'

'There is much else besides, Matthew. Much that you don't know.'

'Tell me.'

'I can't. Frances told me in confidence. Now I really have to leave.'

She declined my offer to escort her back to Essex House, reminding me that it wouldn't be wise for us to be seen together. But she did allow to me to kiss her goodbye and assured me she'd come back when Frances next gave her the time.

As she walked off and turned up Water Lane towards Blackfriars Playhouse and Fleet Street, a crow that had been pecking at a pile of waste flew off.

I sat awhile with Alice, who slept on, often stirring, but not waking. It gave me time to think. If Frances had been in the slightest distressed on hearing of Alice's death, she would surely have been angry with me. I'd seen for myself in Hannah's hovel the heat of her rage when she thought she was being crossed. I'd believed Frances when she insisted that Alice wasn't to be harmed. She might even have believed it herself. But the truth was she cared no more for Alice than she did for me. I'd recognised her sharp mind and fierce intelligence when I first met her. Now I could see how hard-hearted she could be. Rochester was easily outwitted. But not Frances. When the time came and she wanted rid of me, it would happen quickly, with no warning.

24

What's good for a witch

For several days I sat beside Alice. In all that time, I rarely left the rooms, except to empty the chamber pot into the Fleet. Whenever I was out, I locked the door behind me. When I was in the room, she slept for much of the time, albeit fitfully, often twitching, sometimes kicking and screaming in her sleep.

'You've rescued her body,' said Kate. 'But her mind is still in The Bridewell.'

A full week passed before she began to emerge from her mental fevers. She still looked haggard, and there was fear in her eyes, but by then her scalp was soft with downy hair and colour was returning to her face. Whenever Kate came into the room, Alice grew more animated. She was beginning to look more like the Alice I'd taken to Chartley than the stick-thin creature I rescued from the female factory.

'She cannot stay here much longer,' I said to Kate. 'She's tried to leave several times. She's angry. Says I've merely taken her from the prison of The Bridewell to one in Water Lane.'

Kate took my hand and looked me in the eye. 'Then you must get her out of London. Take her somewhere truly safe. Take her to Canterbury.'

'Why Canterbury? I don't know anyone in Canterbury.'

'Alice does. Her brother's there. You told me so yourself. She looked after him in London. Now he can look after her in Canterbury.'

'She'll never leave her family behind.'

'Then take them to Canterbury too.'

I was minded to refuse. What business of mine was Alice's mother and her ragged brood of Dutch urchins? Then Kate squeezed my hand and smiled. Alice was asleep in the bed chamber. Kate and I were sitting on the floor before the fire in the front room. I leaned forward to kiss her. She put her hands to my cheeks and held me firmly. 'Not yet,' she whispered. 'We must wait until Alice is safe and my mind is wholly here with us.'

'It will take time to make the arrangements. If the whole family is to go to Canterbury, I'll have to find a carter willing to make the journey, a carter who can be trusted to be discreet.'

'You must go with them, Matthew. Be sure they arrive safely.'

'Canterbury and back. That's the best part of a week.'

She drew close. 'Do it for me, Matthew.'

'I can't be away from London for that long.'

She took hold of my hand. 'Matthew.'

'Frances has given me instructions. If she thinks I'm ignoring her, she'll prevent you from seeing me.'

'Alice cannot stay in London. Leave messages with Richard Weston to deliver to Frances while you're away. Assure Frances that you're doing your bidding.'

'She's impatient.'

'I know that all too well. But if she's asked you to do something, it's because there's no-one else she trusts.'

All this time she was looking into my eyes, and I knew that in time I'd agree. 'Very well. But I have to make preparations. As soon as I've done what I have to, I'll seek out a carter.'

She leant forward and brushed my lips with hers. It was hardly a kiss, but despite everything that's happened since, I'll remember it for the rest of my life.

'While I'm away, what do we do with Alice? I have business to attend to. And when I'm out I cannot leave these rooms unlocked.'

'I'll talk to her.'

And that's what she did. Kate told her that she'd soon be reunited with her brother and her family. Alice believed her and agreed not to leave the rooms. And I promised to spend as much time with her as I could, however pressing my business.

Long before I reached the clearing, I could smell burning hanging in the early morning air. There'd been frequent thunderstorms over the past few weeks, but that night had been cloudless, and when I reached the mossy bank where I'd first looked down at Hannah's hovel, the sun was edging up into a clear sky. Fingers of mist rising from the grass below, mixing with smoke from what remained of Hannah's little sanctuary.

The thought of what they must have done to her churned my gut. So easy to throw in flaming tar torches, block the little doorway and leave her and the cat to burn inside.

I dreaded what I'd find, but felt compelled to look. I walked slowly down the bank and across the clearing. The smell of burning flesh warned of the worst. And there, inside the circle of smoke-blackened stonework that had been the base of the hovel, lay a disfigured corpse. But it was the body of a man, not Hannah, that lay crushed beneath a fallen wooden beam, his head half covered with smouldering turf from the roof. All that remained of his clothes were charred rags and half burnt leather. But recognisably a man.

No trace of Hannah nor the cat.

I shuddered – unable to rid myself of a picture of Jacob with his head crushed beneath the fallen stone at old Spital Priory.

If Hannah had been smoked out, what was the dead man doing there? Perhaps she had a premonition, abandoning the hovel before they got there? Or perhaps they destroyed it to prevent her returning? And the dead man inside? From the way he was lying, I guessed he'd been kneeling when the roof collapsed, and the beam had fallen and broken his back. They hound out the witch, set fire to the hovel, and this man goes back in to look for something.

The scrying mirror?

Knowing that I must never even glimpse it, I blindfolded myself before prodding and raking the ashes with a stick. Nothing. No broken obsidian fragment, no trace that Hannah had ever been there, nothing that told of what might have happened. But my lungs were filling with the smell of darkness that hung about the place.

I made my way to Highgate Pond, where I stripped and bathed to wash the soot and ashes from myself and my clothes. The shock of cold water gave me blissful respite from thoughts of what had happened at the hovel. I should have known there'd be worse to come, although months would pass before I'd discover how much worse.

I lay down on the grass and dried myself off. The sun already hot, wisps of steam forming on the dark surface of the waters, the woods alive with a chorus of blackbirds and warblers.

I thought I heard Hannah's voice in my head. Something she said when I first found her. *The hovel isn't mine. Merely a roof above my head for the time I'm here.* Then the roof falls in and Hannah disappears.

I could understand a mob of men coming out from Highgate, driving out a woman they thought was a witch. I could understand them killing her, burning down her hovel. I had no time for such lunacy, but I could understand it. But this made no sense at all. Then it struck me that if a mob had come for her, there'd have been some sign of a gathering in the clearing. But there were no broken branches, no trampled undergrowth.

I made my way to The Cock and Hen in Highgate Village. I thought to tickle Madam Gossip, hear what she had to say. Hounding out a witch wasn't something people would keep to themselves. I was expecting to hear that all was well now that she'd been driven out. Their dogs would never again go off howling in the night for a mate and come back as rats to infest their miserable houses. Milk would never curdle in the summer heat, butter wouldn't turn rancid. And Master Limpcock would soon be fathering a dozen strong boys.

I spoke to a score or more people at the inn. One old fellow told me he'd got up in the night to use the chamber pot and smelt wood smoke. He thought it must have been the baker starting early. I went to the bakehouse, bought a loaf of bread. I passed the time of day with everyone I saw. What a chattersome fellow was Matthew that day. But not one word did I hear about witchcraft. And nobody spoke about anybody missing. Wide-eyed and innocent, I asked whether there were foxes big as wolves lurking in those nearby woods. They laughed at my gullibility. But it was the good-natured laughter of people who are used to mocking fearful Londoners venturing out into the country, not the tense, nervous laughter that would have told me I'd hit on a guilty truth. If Hannah had been driven out of her hovel, nobody in Highgate knew about it.

But whatever had happened, she was gone. And she was of no use to me until I could find her. On another day I might have tried to track down the identity of the man who'd lost his life in Hannah's hovel. But Alice was still in my lodgings. And if I couldn't find Hannah quickly, I'd lose Kate too, because Frances would surely put a stop to things.

I headed back to London. Those damask cushions – burnt in the fire – and something Hannah herself told me – had given me an idea where I might find her. *They say I should be cast out. Cast out to a place where madness can be cured.* Where other than Bethlehem Hospital? Bedlam. Less than a hundred yards north of the City walls, close by Bishopsgate and Saint Botolph's church.

The jangling of keys, a bolt drawn back, the gate screeching open on rusty hinges. A wizened man with raven's beak for a nose, jaundiced skin and wild grey hair stood blocking the doorway.

'Visitors' gate,' he croaked.

'I'm here to see the master of the hospital,' I said.

'Today's Tuesday. Visitors on Saturdays.'

'I've not come to visit. I want to speak with the master.' I reached for my purse, put sixpence in my palm. He turned his head slightly to one side, as if about to peck at the gleaming silver coin. 'Speak to the master?'

'Yes.'

'You got a patient for us?'

'I have to speak to the master.'

'Two sorts of patients we have. Fools and madmen. All of them under the whip. What you got for us?'

'I need to see the master about it,' I said quietly. You'd be surprised how good-natured I can be when needs must.

'Fools and madmen. We has both – twenty-three here this week. Fools play the ape, make you laugh, make you smile. Madmen we has too. Devil's in them. Roaring mad and fierce as bears. Cunning as crows. You name it, they'll try it. You been warned. You go in with a weapon, they steals it off o' you. Silky smooth and slippy as a silent fart.' Then he held out his hand, and snarled, 'So... Dagger. Hand over your dagger.'

'I carry no weapon,' I said, looking the man straight in the eye and lifting my arms above my head, inviting a search. He looked at me as if I were the madman to be wandering around without a weapon. He didn't bother with a search. Then he took his sixpence and stepped back, inviting me to step through the gateway into the grounds of Bedlam, slamming the door, bolting and locking it after me.

My sixpence didn't include the services of a guide. I walked through the gatehouse passage into an open cobbled courtyard with four sets of stocks and a pillory in the centre. To the right stood small stone buildings that might once have been barns, to the left an old church. The hospital itself, two storeys high, lay straight ahead. The reek of a cesspit overwhelmed the smell of rotten fruit that lay around the stocks, but the three lost souls who were wandering round the yard took no more notice of the stench than they did of me.

A ghastly clamour from within the hospital echoed round the cobbled yard.

I tried the only door I could see. Locked. No response to my knocking. I was walking back to the gatehouse to ask the keeper how to gain entry, when one of the Bedlamites came shambling towards me. He was wrapped in a blanket. I called out to ask directions.

'Do not tempt me. Do not tempt me,' he said, brandishing a carrot in my face as if it were a crucifix. 'I know why you have taken this shape. You do not deceive me. Do not tempt me or I shall strike.' I looked away. He shuffled by.

Another Bedlamite was sitting cross-legged by the stocks, picking through the rotting fruit strewn across the cobbles. His tongue lolled out as he inspected a mushy apple, earnest as a pawnbroker considering a bracelet.

'Good day to you, sirrah,' I said. He gave a start and looked up.

He grinned. He had a round flattish face, high wide forehead and strangely elongated eyes. He mumbled something that might have been 'Good day', then lunged forward, wrapping his arms around my legs and clinging to me as a small child to its mother. When I tried to break away, his grip tightened. My instinct was to kick him off, as I would a dog or a beggar scrounging food. But he looked up with a grin that defied a history of beatings, witnessed by the bruises on his arms and lower legs.

'Kind sir.' I think that's what he said, but his lips were swollen, and he had difficulty forming words.

'I prithee, take me to the master of the hospital.'

He scrambled to his feet, beaming such a smile that his eyes almost disappeared in folds of flesh.

'Friend. Friend. Friend to master.' He clasped my hand and kissed it.

Despite my disgust, I reckoned I'd get more sense from this poor fellow than from the gatekeeper.

'What's your name?'

'Name,' he drawled.

'My name is Matthew. What's yours?'

'Jemmerry.'

'Jeremy?'

His grin engulfed his whole face. 'Jemry.' He grabbed me by the hand and led me round the side of the building to an unlocked door which opened onto an unlit corridor. He pointed me to the master's room, but hung back, flinching as I knocked on the door. No response. The door wasn't locked. I let myself in.

The Master had drunk himself senseless. Arse on a chair, upper body sprawled over the table, hand clutching an empty goblet. I lifted his hand to take his pulse. He stirred, groaning in his slumbers, before collapsing back onto the table.

With the Master too drunk to beat him for his pains, Jeremy insisted on acting as my guide. The inmates were chained up in rooms with no doors and nothing more than straw for furnishing. A man hurled curses at us as we passed. An iron collar round his neck and fetters on his ankles had chafed wounds blood raw from constant straining to break free. In the next room, a cowering wreck of a fellow, squatting on his heels in a cage no more than four feet high, rocking back and forth, holding his head in his hands and quivering in panic at every sound from his neighbours. In another, a man lay naked on his straw bed, cock in hand, fetching his mettle. Jeremy pointed, squealing with mirth.

How could anyone who'd lost their wits recover them here? The noise was so hideous, so frightful, so relentless that I feared I might soon lose mine. My head came close to bursting with all the clattering of chains, the screeching and the wailing, the ever louder screams of agony and frenzy.

We reached the end of the corridor. 'Hannah?' I said.

Jeremy grinned. 'Name.'

'That's right. Hannah. Is she here?'

He grinned.

'Hannah.' I said it slowly. 'Do you know where she is?'

'Upstair women, downstair men,' said Jeremy, pointing to a narrow stone staircase. But he refused to go up himself.

In the world outside, women might be the fairer, gentler sex, but not in Bedlam. The noise on the upper floor was deafening. Passing from room to room was more harrowing, for I needed to get close and examine faces.

In the last of the rooms on that first floor, a patient was curled up alone and silent on a pallet of straw, hugging her grief to herself, one ankle shackled to the wall. She didn't look up when I walked in.

'Good day to you, mistress.'

She didn't move. I approached slowly. One eye was bruised a puffy blue black. There was a large bald patch on her scalp. She stared at me with a look of incomprehension, then covered her face in horror, as if she'd just conjured a fiend from Hell.

'The devil is in me. Stay away.' Despite her mumbling through swollen lips, I recognised the voice. 'What's good for a witch is Bedlam,' she said. 'Bedlam will drive out the demons.'

25

Mermaid talk

'They say I'm a witch. They say that I'm mad.'

'You're a seer, not a witch. And whatever they say, you're not mad.'

'I didn't.' She shook her head. Put her hands over her eyes and sobbed.

'Didn't do what, Hannah? What didn't you do?'

She mumbled something behind her hands which I couldn't make out. Then wailed loudly, setting off a ghastly howling which echoed down the corridor. Gently, I tried to ease her hands away from her face, but she clenched her whole body, curled herself tight, and cried. The howling turned to shrieking. The whole place shaking with chains hammering on wooden floors.

I could have dragged her out of Bedlam. The master was blind drunk and the gatekeeper would have taken bribes – that's what coins are for, Hannah. But where could I have taken her? Not for safekeeping to The Bridewell. Not to my lodgings in Water Lane with Alice still there. And not to Essex House. I don't think Lady Frances would have taken in a lodger.

How did I know she'd be in Bedlam? I didn't. But I guessed. Her own words when I first went to the hovel. *They said I should be cast out to a place where madness can be cured.* Only one place in London where they claim to cure madness. I knew she feared Bedlam when I first spoke to her.

Hannah was incapable of answering my questions, but I was beginning to piece together a story of what might have happened. The damask cushions were a clue. They surely came from some fine house. It seemed unlikely she'd been paid for her services in cushions, and she wasn't a thief, so perhaps she'd taken them with her when she'd been banished from her home. I reckoned that someone in her family had found out where she was, and forcibly taken her to Bedlam, where they thought madness could be cured.

It didn't explain the dead man or the fire. But she was in Bedlam, so most of it was right.

When I next saw Frances, I invented a different story. I'd gone back to collect Hannah, only to find she'd left the hovel and was living with her sick mother in Barnet. A place plucked from the air. I said I'd tracked her down and spoken to her. I was sure she'd come and meet Frances again, but for the moment she was refusing to leave her mother.

I couldn't tell her the truth. Frances would never have put her trust in a woman she thought was mad. I didn't know why she was so obsessed with that second nativity, but so long as I was useful to her, she'd let Katherine keep visiting.

In the meantime, quite by chance, I'd heard something deeply worrying. Madam Gossip may be unreliable, but she has a keen nose for trouble.

I usually met with Richard Weston at The Mermaid. Sometimes he was there before me. On the days I had to wait for him I made it my business to cultivate the tapster, Albert Trimble. I asked him how the place got its name. You might expect a Mermaid close by Billingsgate or Blackwall docks, but in Paternoster Row? How come? It's further from the river than Paul's church. There are more Mermaids in London than there are King's Heads, but all the others are within a seagull's wing beat of the river. To tell the truth, I couldn't give a fig about the name. It was the tapster I was interested in. Get him talking. Show an interest in his world. Little by little he starts to open up. Tells me stuff I really want to know. Tells me more about Richard Weston than he'd ever tell me himself.

'Well…' says he, talking about the tavern now. 'What I heard when I first come 'ere was there's this first mate to Pirate Drake. The crew catches a mermaid somewhere in the Fortunate Isles. They all think it's an ill omen. But not the first mate. He keeps her safe and well. First port they come to he sells her to some rich Frenchie. Makes hisself a small fortune. Then when his sailing days is over, he uses the money to buy this little tavern in Paternoster Row. What else could he call it? Had to be The Mermaid, didn't it.'

'And how do you keep a mermaid safe and well?' I say. 'What do you feed it? Fish or fowl?'

'How would I know? It's a story I was told.'

'And what's the story you tell, Albert?'

'Most people what drinks here, they're so legless by the time they leave they might as well be mermaids.' He thinks this funny. So I laugh. And the laughter brings a few others round. And soon the talk moves on, like it does, from Mermaids to Frances.

'You hear what they're saying about the Countess of Essex?'

'Her what bedded Prince Henry?' This from a wiry fellow with long ginger hair and thin red beard.

'*And* the Vice Cunt fucking Rochester.' One of Redbeard's mangy acolytes.

'Same night I wouldn't be surprised.'

'Go on. What they saying?'

'Husband's gone and fled the country. Taken ship to Amsterdam.'

No news in that for me. Kate had told me about Essex's departure. It was what came next that was so alarming.

'Lord Essex, you mean? Him locked her away in his place in the north?'

'That's the one,' says the tapster. ''Cept she never went, did she. Sent a whore from Southwark stews in her place, so the fucking Countess never actually left London.'

'Good yarn,' says Redbeard, smug and superior, not wanting anyone else to take centre stage. 'But you're wrong. Because she lives in Essex House. Bloody great pile on The Strand.'

The tapster gives him a scornful look and says quietly, 'I'm not talking about what she's doing now. I'm talking about last summer. When she was supposed to be up North. That's when the whore took her place.'

'Make a good play would that,' says John Marston. Calls himself a playwright does Marston. Often in the Mermaid picking up stories.

'What you going to call it? *Bedward Ho!*?'

'*The Insatiate Countess.*'

'Going to write it are you, John?'

'Maybe.'

Madam Gossip's outpourings often owed more to Cousin Malice than to any passing acquaintance with Truth. But that was neither here nor there. What mattered to me was what would happen when talk of a bed trick reached the ears of Rochester. And what mattered even more was where he thought the story came from.

I was also growing suspicious that Kate was being followed when she came to visit. She said she always did as I'd asked – walking past the house where I was lodging and waiting in another alley twenty yards or so closer to The Thames, before turning back. She confessed to taking pleasure in the trickery of it, and was certain that nobody knew where she was going, and nobody ever followed her. But Kate knew little of the world I came from, and I suspect she thought it more of a game than a matter of life and death.

26

Soft and precious

Bill Carter was short and stout, with arms as thick as table legs, nose as red as raw beef and face as round as a baby's arse. Strong as an ox, with a voice to match. His stables and yard were on the Deptford road out of Southwark, near the edge of town. There was just one empty cart in his yard, two-wheeled with high sides. Not a lot of room for Alice, her mother and three children, but when you see a possibility, you make it happen.

The stable doors were open. Carter was inside, waxing a harness. I like to see a man taking care of his tackle.

'Good day to you, Master Carter.'

He grunted, and continued what he was doing.

'You got any other carts than these?'

'The one in the yard and two others. I've got a man out working. The other cart's being repaired.'

'And this one's good, is it?'

'New wheels and axle just a month ago. My carts is my living.'

'This will do well enough. I've something special I want taken to Dover.'

'Dover's a week's work. Three days there, three days back.'

'I know. I'll pay you well.'

He hung up the harness and led me over to the far corner of the yard. A rat scurried off the flat bed of the cart and down a rope hanging loose from the back.

'Been carrying grain?'

'Grain. Coal. Hay. Turnips. Flour. You name it, we carry it.' But not as often as you'd like, I thought, or that cart wouldn't be standing idle in the yard.

'I'll pay you for the full week if we can leave tomorrow.'

'What you want taken to Dover?'

'Nothing of interest to the excise men.'

'Can't give you a price til you say what we'll be carrying. I need to know how heavy. One horse or two.'

'Two. And you'll be driving.'

'I've a man can drive. He's good. I don't leave the yard these days. I need to be here for business.'

I looked him in the eye. There are times when a slowly fermenting silence is the best persuader. No surprise that he had to break it. 'Never been to Dover,' he said, as if getting there was as dangerous as crossing the ocean.

'But you have been to Kent.'

'Oh, I been to Kent. Yeah. Apples and hops in autumn.'

'Dover's in Kent.'

'Is it?'

'Oh yes. Dover's in Kent.'

I reached into my doublet. Found my purse. Untied the drawstring and fumbled around inside. 'Thing is, Master

Carter. I can see you're an honest man. I trust my judgement. And I trust you. But I haven't met your driver. And I don't trust people I've not talked to. But you don't want the work, and that's a shame. But I can see your time's precious, so I'll waste no more of it. Who'd you recommend in these parts who would want the work?'

But he did want the work. One cart being repaired, one cart waiting up, not in use. He needed the work. And I wanted him and not his man. But if he was going to be away for the best part of a week he'd need a story to tell his wife. So I told him he'd be taking bales of woven silk for a merchant who wanted them shipped to Paris. And so we struck a deal. You might wonder that I didn't hire someone in the north of the city, nearer Spital Fields. But that would have meant crossing The Bridge, which would have run the risk of the cart being stopped and the load inspected.

I walked out to Spital Fields and told Alice's mother what she needed to do. She looked frightened. The boy, whose English was better than hers, did his best to translate.

'Do you want that we walk?'

'Only as far as Southwark. Not to Canterbury.' But she didn't understand. I was glad I'd befriended the boy on my earlier visit. He'd not forgotten me. Maybe Kate was right after all, and a little kindness does have its own rewards. I don't know what he said to the mother because he spoke in Dutch, but I recognised the words *Aeltje* and *Pieter*. He was excited about seeing them again.

I told them how to find Bill Carter's place, and asked him and the mother to repeat my directions back. She agreed to be there soon after daybreak the next morning.

I'd have collected them myself, but I had to escort Alice. Kate and I had given much thought to how we might disguise her. I suggested she could be a nun or a corpulent midwife, as Frances had been on her journey to Sherborne. It was Kate who suggested man's clothing. She'd turned Frances into a man when she visited Hannah. She could do the same for Alice. I waited outside while the two of them went about it. I took no part in it, though I heard Alice's squeals as Kate bound her breasts. Alice did what was needed with her face. By the time she was done, she looked as ruddy as Bill Carter, though not so stocky.

Just over a month had passed since Alice first came to lodge in Water Lane. I spent more time with Kate in that month than I'd spent with any woman since my own mother died. We were growing easy with each other. Kate promised she'd come again as soon as Frances allowed after I got word to her that I was safely back from Canterbury. My delight in Kate's company was already clouding my judgement. I should have given more thought to why Frances was so willing to let her venture out. I told you this would be a whole truth. Even as I write these words, I realise that it's fast becoming a catalogue of my own carelessness.

Alice and I set out from Water Lane early the following morning. She didn't talk much. The sky was clear and the air already warm. A stinking pile of garbage had built up on the corner of Bow Lane and Thames Street. As we approached a kite flew off with a bone in its beak. No sooner had it gone than the rats scurried back, and crows dived down to pick through the filth.

We crossed The Bridge without incident, although it was already thronging with people. 'Stay close,' I urged. 'Look ahead.' She'd never crossed before and was looking in wonder at the houses and shops. 'The walkway's narrow. People get knocked by carts.'

We made our way to Bill Carter's yard. He nodded to Alice, who was wearing my best cloak and wide-brimmed black velvet hat.

'Good day to you, sirrah,' said Carter.

Alice tipped the hat and looked away. I'd instructed her not to speak.

'He's going to sit in the back and look after the load,' I said.

Carter looked quizzical.

'Hardly any English,' I explained. 'He's going on with the silk to Paris.'

'Where is it then? This silk of yours.'

'It's on its way.'

'You said you wanted to leave early.'

'We're not leaving without the load. You'll get paid, I promise you.'

Alice was nervous. And although I didn't let Carter see it, I too was getting worried about the load that hadn't yet showed up. Alice would never go to Canterbury if her family weren't with her.

The two horses had already been harnessed. They swished their tails, they each took a shit, and occasionally they stamped their hooves, but they were more patient than me.

'I can't leave the horses out here any longer,' said Carter. 'Not in this heat.' He unbuckled the girth on one of the harnesses. 'Take them into the stable. Out of the sun. You and your Frenchie friend can help.' I made a poor excuse about my companion not being good with horses. But I showed willing.

We had one of the horses back in the stable when the family appeared. The mother came first, holding hands with the girls. The boy behind. The mother looked like she suspected a trick. Frans was the first to recognise Alice. She crouched down to hold the little lad in her arms. I held my finger to my lips. I shut the gate and bolted it. Carter ran over. Grabbed my arm.

'What the fuck you doing?' he said.

'The gate stays shut until we leave.'

'My yard. My business. My gates. Now move.'

My hand stayed on the bolt. Carter was a big man, a deal heavier than me, and stronger too. He could have picked me up and thrown me to the ground.

'Hear me out,' I said. 'If, after that, you don't want the work, so be it. You can open the gates, keep the money I gave you as surety, and we'll trouble you no more.'

He didn't move. But he didn't hit me.

'This is the silk,' I said, pointing to the family.

'What the Hell you mean by that?'

'Silk's precious, isn't it. Soft and precious. That's what we got here.'

'You said nothing illegal.'

'That's right. Nothing illegal at all. And I'll tell you now what I didn't tell before.'

He looked across to where Alice was on her haunches, talking quietly with the children.

'All I ask is discretion. Tell no-one what I'm about to tell you. Not one word to a soul.'

He stared at me.

'See the old woman?' I whispered, pointing to Alice's mother. 'She's a widow. Husband's dead...' Pause for a moment,

show him how distressed I am by what happened. 'It was...'
Pause again. 'My doing.'

'You killed him?'

'Shhh! Not me. No. But I blame myself. The husband
brought his family here from Holland to find work.'

'You said they was French.'

'They're going to Paris, yes. But they're Dutch, not French.
He brings his family here to London, but there's no work for a
Dutchman. Spends all his time looking. But soon as they hear
him speak, they turn him away. Nobody hires a Dutchman. I'm
in The Mermaid one night. He comes over to me. Introduces
himself. His English isn't as bad as his accent. His name's
Johan. Did I know anyone might have work for him? Me and
Johan, we fall into conversation. He has good English, but no
money. No money for rent. No money for food. Barely enough
to buy me a drink.'

'Why they want to go to France?'

'Johan's cousin's in Paris. And he's got this letter telling him
there's plenty of work in Paris for a hard-working family. But
how's he going get to France with no money?'

'And how they going to pay me?'

'Don't you worry about it. Me that's going to pay you,
Master Carter. Me and Johan, we was both in our cups that
night. And he's desperate. So I taught him a thing. I taught
him to cheat at gleek and primero. Then I take him along to
The Dagger at Holborn. But my face is known at The Dagger,
so I can't go in with him. But nobody's seen our Dutch friend
before. He was quick, was Johan. I give him ten shillings. My
own money. And I tell him so long as he never goes back in
The Dagger, he can walk away with ten pounds from a night's

gaming. I wait for him in The Mitre nearby. And sure enough, two hours pass. And there he is, wearing this smile like you never seen. Every muscle in his face is smiling. Even his beard is smiling. He's made enough to buy passage for himself and his family on a ship bound for Calais. I should have slapped him, shocked him out of it. But I don't, 'cos I'm excited too.'

'What's wrong with that?'

'Nothing wrong with winning. But that's not the end of it. We had a deal. He pays me back my ten shillings and one fifth of his winnings. And that's why I blame myself. Because he counts it out. There. At a table in a corner of The Mitre, he pays me my share. And I let him do it. I'm so damn pleased for him that I don't even see he's been followed. Not a day gone by since I haven't cursed myself for that. Three of them. Two on him, one on me. That was their mistake. 'Cos I can look after myself. I deal with my attacker, but my Dutch friend's already down, bleeding like a stuck pig. I pretend I'm badly wounded, moaning and groaning, breathing my last – which distracts them, gives them time to relieve Johan of his purse. They're counting the coins out between them when the man they'd left for dead – that's me – slits their throats.

'Now it's me kneeling beside Johan. And he's not faking it. As he lies there dying, he begs me to get his poor family to Paris. And here's the rub, Bill Carter, I make him a solemn promise that I'll do it.' Tears in my eyes as I'm telling Carter this. 'I swear to you, Johan, I say, I will get them all to Paris, come what may. Then Johan squeezes my hand. His last word on this earth, a whispered thanks.'

Carter was wearing a puzzled expression. Maybe a touch of admiration, maybe a whiff of fear.

'Well,' he said, looking across at the family. 'Seems you're a good man, Master Farnworth.' You might have guessed I'd be Martin.

'Tell me one thing, though. The fellow with the hat? Who's that?'

'Johan's son. A troubled fellow. Trusts no-one – specially not the English. Blames all of us for what happened to his father. Best stay clear of him.'

There are big stories and there are little stories. For Carter, this job was the big story. For me, it was a little one. We had our problems and our adventures. But I'll not tell of the journey, except to say that the road from Southwark to Deptford was rough and rutted. And after Deptford it got worse.

I might tell you that we were set upon by highwaymen in the forest around Shooters Hill, and that Carter and I despatched them all. But that would be as big a lie as Johan's card tricks. The journey was memorable only for its tediousness. Carter was a talkative sort, but a man can tire of endless tales of rutted roads and strange loads. I've no doubt other carters were enthralled by the story of the sow that gave birth to a litter of piglets in his cart or the samphire that turned out to be cabbage, but I was soon missing Bradshaw's steadfast, ill-tempered silence.

We stopped for the night at a coaching inn with stabling for travellers, just outside the city walls of Canterbury. Carter stayed in a room above the stables. I took two rooms at the inn – one for Alice and the family, and another for myself. I fell asleep to thoughts of Kate and yearnings for the time when she and I would share a bed and much else besides.

In the morning we carried on to Dover. It was essential that Carter believed the story I'd told him, and that he took that story back with him to Southwark. He dropped us at the gates to the port. I thanked him and paid him what I'd said I would. He turned round and headed for home. We gave him time to get ahead of us, then we all set out on foot back to Canterbury.

I helped them find Pieter Vancy. It wasn't difficult. Anybody who'd ever seen him remembered the giant of a man with half his face stained like a plum. He'd got himself work with some Frenchies who'd set up as weavers.

The little girls curtsied and said their thank-yous in Dutch, as did the mother. I asked little Frans to look after them all. He was tearful. As for Alice, she'd not forgotten her six months in The Bridewell, but despite that she had the grace to thank me for getting them to Canterbury.

I was footsore and weary when I got back to London, but I made my way straight to The Mermaid. Richard Weston was sitting in his usual corner. After the usual London tittle tattle, he agreed to get a message to Frances's maid.

Then I waited. Father Time must have been sleeping off a heavy hangover. He hardly stirred as one day became two, and two became three, each day passing slower than the last. And no word came back from Kate.

27
Matters of the bedchamber

The Mermaid lived up to its name. Neither one thing nor the other. A respectable inn with panelled walls, but the bare earth floors of a low tavern. It served best Canary sack, fine claret wine and ale as good as any in London. Just don't try the food. The bread's stale, the cheese is mouldy, and what passes for a pie comes with a filling as rank as anything the night men take away.

And what of that other-worldly siren? Her sign on Paternoster Row was freshly painted. She sat with bright red nipples and green scaly tail on an island of yellow sand in a dark blue sea. But the wooden figurehead within was a dismal sorry sight. Fixed to the wall above the fireplace in the room where Weston and I usually met, she might once have graced a navy galleon, as Tapster Trimble claimed, but she'd lost her arms, and all traces of paint on her face and her tail had long since flaked off.

Four days had passed since I returned from Kent. Twice I'd been back to Bedlam to try to get sense from Hannah.

Twice I'd come away disappointed. And still no word from Katherine.

I asked Weston if he thought I'd offended Lady Frances. Had my absence angered her?

'Had you not heard they've moved?' He beamed with pleasure that for once he was ahead of me. 'The Countess and her retinue now live in Salisbury House. She'll have been too busy to have time for a foul temper – or give the maid time to see you.'

Kate had said nothing of moving, so I guessed it had taken her by surprise as much as it did me.

'You know the lady's husband's gone to Amsterdam?' said Weston.

'Madam Gossip talks of nothing else.'

'I promise you, I gave the maid your message. I handed it to her in person. She said she'd see you as soon as her mistress allowed.'

I thanked him for delivering the message safely, and bought him another cup of sack. If the plan I had for Kate and myself was to hatch and thrive, I'd need time. I was already in deep. I had to go in deeper yet. And although Richard Weston didn't know it, he could show me the way.

'Do you remember when we were drinking together here a few weeks ago?' I said. 'An excellent evening, though I suffered much for it the next day.' Which gave him permission to boast of his own sore head. I laughed, as if I enjoyed nothing better than getting drunk in the company of this closest of friends. He grew more relaxed, perhaps relieved that he wasn't going to be blamed for Kate's silence. He liked his Canary. I bought us a jug. Every time I filled his glass, I filled mine too.

I poured most of mine away, though Weston thought I was drinking heartily. It was well that The Mermaid had a bare earth floor and not flagstones. He was the easiest of men to convince I enjoyed drinking with him. And when he was just drunk enough to accept without question whatever I told him, but not so drunk that he'd forget it on the morrow, I asked him about Anne Turner.

'What about Anne Turner?'

'Your mistress.'

'Ahh,' his eyes widened.

I leant forward. 'How was she, Richard? When her husband died?'

'She changed her fashionable yellow clothes for mourning dress.'

'Did she come to you for consolation?'

'Well…'

'Does she prefer the liberty of widowhood to the prison of marriage?'

'Master Edgworth, I …' He paused, feigning embarrassment, but loving the flattery.

'I'm sure you stepped into the breach. When the husband died? How was she, Richard? Is it true what they say?'

'What they say about what?'

'The old saying. About the lusty widow and the tailor.'

He shrugged, playing modesty with little conviction, before breaking into a grin. 'For a few months, I gave her some comfort through her lonely nights.'

'And now Mistress Turner has taken a young lover?' My voice now heavy in consolation. I should have been an actor. Maybe I will be yet.

'You heard about that?'

'You told me so yourself, my friend. But…' I drew closer. 'You know why, don't you?'

'Why what?'

'Why she took the young man to her bed.'

He mumbled something neither of us heard.

'I'll tell you why,' I said, 'And it's not what you fear.'

'What then?'

'Mistress Turner is a woman who greatly values her reputation, is she not?'

'Yes.'

'A young lover does that no harm at all. But when it comes to matters of the bedchamber, you and I know very well that youth is sadly over-rated. A young man's enthusiasm has him boiling over all too soon. Mistress Turner's lover is nothing but a rank beginner. She may boast about his ardour to her friends, but I warrant she yearns for you to warm her bed.'

'You really think…'

'Oh, Master Weston, I've seen the way she looks at you.' He didn't ask me when I'd seen them together. It suited him not to. I'd never spoken to Mistress Turner, and thought it unlikely that I ever would. And I'd no idea what went on in Weston's britches. But I did know this – I wanted access to the letters he carried between Frances and Lord Rochester. There might have been other ways to get hold of them. I could have hired a gang of common cutpurses to fall upon Weston and rob him. But Frances and Rochester would have known their letters had been stolen. And I also wanted Weston's complicity.

When we'd gone into The Mermaid that afternoon, the place had been full of people and thick with tobacco smoke. Most folk had now gone about their business, leaving Weston and me snug in a dark corner close to the armless wooden mermaid. Just a few weeks from midsummer and the first really hot day of the year. Tapster Trimble had left the front door wide open. A shaft of late afternoon sunlight coming through the doorway made the room seem even darker. I bought us another jug of Canary, walking back from the buttery bar with great care.

'Slow and steady,' I said, stumbling a little as I slurred my words. 'One foot in front of. One foot. And then. The other.' He laughed. He was easy to amuse.

'My dear friend Richard.' I held my glass to his. 'I need advice. And I do believe there is nobody better to give it than you.' He looked pleased. 'Tis the thing with flattery. Make a man feel good enough about himself, and you become the person he needs to believe.

'Richard, my friend, promise me you'll not to breathe a word of what I say. Not one word to anyone.'

He was delighted to be asked, and eager to promise.

'You remember when you and I first met?'

'In the stable block at Cope Castle.'

'You brought a message for me.'

'To meet with Lady Frances in the Chapel Royal.'

'You know why she wanted to meet me?'

He didn't. But I had his interest.

'She had an errand for me. A small task that's neither here nor there. I'd worked for her a couple of times before. I was flattered that she trusted me. I thought nothing of her wanting to meet me again. Until … Until.' I stopped for a moment. Let Weston wheedle it out of me. 'Oh, I don't know… Why am I telling you this?'

'You want advice.'

'I do. Indeed, I do.'

'She met you in the chapel.'

'She had an errand for me. A small matter. A trifle.'

'And?'

'I was happy to agree. But she…'

'She what?'

'She… Me and her. Me and Lady Frances. Alone in the chapel. She explains the errand. I stand up to leave. She takes hold of my arm. Pulls me down to sit beside her. Close to her, Richard. Closer than you and me sitting here. Talks to me about things… Things she…'

'Things?'

'No, no, no. I shouldn't say.'

Weston insisted he was sworn to secrecy. He was gazing into my eyes, rapt by my every word. 'Go on. Go on. What she say?'

'Don't remember the words. But the husband. He can't. Can't. Husband's Lord Limpcock. Very unhappy lady. But you and me. We knew already that. Stuff of every street corner gossip. What she tells me. And here's the rub, Richard. My master. Lord Rochester. What Lady Frances tells me is he hasn't … he can't…'

'What?'

'Raise an interest. Not like that. Cut from the same cloth as the husband, you might say. And all this time she's holding my arm with both hands. Very close. I can feel her breath on my skin.' Now's the time to take a player's long pause.

Weston looked wide eyed. 'And what's? What's the advice you want from me?'

'Why? That's what I want to know. Why'd she tell me all that?'

He looked at me intently with a faint hint of a smile.

'Richard?' I wondered for a moment if I'd fed him too much drink. 'Richard?'

'Dropping hints. That's what it is. She's dropping hints. What she wants from you's what Anne Turner wanted from me.'

'Still does, Richard. Still wants from you, my friend.'

'The Lady,' he whispered. 'She wants you to pleasure her. That's my advice.'

I acted shock. 'I hardly dare to … No… Do you really think so?'

'I'm sure of it. Why else does a lady tell a healthy man she's not satisfied with her husband *and* her so-called lover?'

'You flatter me, Richard. I'm no match for Lady Frances.'

'She's not looking for a match. She's looking for experience. You wouldn't be the first servant to pleasure his mistress.'

'Too dangerous,' I said.

'Maybe that's what excites her.'

I smiled broadly and raised my glass: 'May love and Fortune take good care of us both.'

We drank to that. I'd enjoy spinning yarns in the coming weeks about how my wooing was progressing. But there was more to my little game than mischief. I pretended to think about what he'd just said, and then, as if the thought had just occurred: 'If I'm to play bold Lancelot, there's a small favour I need to ask.'

He was keen to help.

'Is it true you act as post between the Countess and my master?'

He gave a small nod, as if by not speaking he wouldn't be breaking the secrecy he'd been sworn to.

'Then let me see those letters before you deliver them. If Rochester's to be my rival, I need to know his thinking, and what the Lady says about me in her letters.'

'Always sealed.'

'Have you never forged a seal?'

He looked embarrassed that he hadn't.

'Easier than coining a sixpence. I'll read the letters, reseal them. And I swear to you that none will be the wiser.'

'They trust me, Matthew.'

'I trust you, too, Richard.'

He hesitated.

'How often does Mistress Turner's young gallant come visiting?'

'Maybe two, sometimes three times a week.'

'So she has four, five days a week when you can remind her what real pleasure feels like.'

He shut his eyes and moaned quietly to himself. They say you can never know what someone else is thinking. They're wrong about that.

Time to seal the deal. 'Did you ever accompany Mistress Turner when she used to visit Doctor Forman?'

'I never went to his house, but she always spoke highly of him on her return.'

'I saw him once. He made up a little potion for me. I paid him well.'

'A potion?'

'A love potion. I still have several vials.'

'For your own use or –'

'Oh, for the ladies, Richard. For the ladies.'

He was grinning.

'A couple of drops in their drink and their passion knows no bounds. But a word of warning, Richard. When you unstopper the vial, don't so much as take a sniff yourself, or you'll find yourself even quicker to the point of evacuation than the young gallant.'

And thus it was done. He'd lend me the letters for an hour or so. I'd give him a vial of Forman's magical love potion.

Two days later I followed him discreetly to Whitehall Palace. He went in by Scotland Yard Gate as the clock struck twelve. The gatekeeper knew him well enough to let him in without question. I waited in the shadows. He came back out in short time. From Whitehall he headed east down King Street, past Charing Cross, along The Strand and on to The Dolphin in Temple Bar. And there we made the exchange: one of Doctor Forman's small vials containing an exotic golden liquid. In return he gave me a letter bearing Rochester's seal.

Whitehall Palace
June 1612

My sweetest dearest Frances,

Your letters bring with them such joy and comfort. It is a source of shame to me that I cannot write to you more often. The King has been greatly exercised of late with matters of the Treasury and the Court of Wards, and this has taken much of my time. But I do swear that you are always in my thoughts, my dearly beloved Frances, even when I am with the King.

With Lord Essex departed for his business in Holland, I had thought you and I might be able to meet again, but I understand the wisdom in your great uncle counselling so strongly against it. Even if we could meet freely, I fear you would find me poor company at this time. And thus I come to the dreadful matter of Thomas Overbury, a matter which has been causing me great distress. I cannot rid myself of my fury against him. I had thought that he and I were reconciled. I had persuaded myself that he must have thought better of those monstrous calumnies against you, and was regretting having ever voiced them. It is therefore with a very heavy heart that I tell you that Overbury's libels and slanders against you have started again, and it is causing me great distraction. I would not wish to trouble you with such disagreeable news, my dearest, sweet Frances, but I would rather you heard it first from me than from some loose-tongued lady-in-waiting. I can, however, assure you that I have the matter in hand. James has confided in me that he considers Overbury to be disruptive and meddlesome, an unconscionable slanderer, vile and full of malice. James is wholly sympathetic to my desire to silence Overbury.

I would that you and I can be together soon, but I am willing to heed your great uncle's advice if it means our happiness will eventually be vouchsafed.

Until then, I am and always shall be your devoted and loving,

Robert

I read and reread the letter, committing it to memory even as I was warming the wax to remake the seal. Frances had mentioned Thomas Overbury when she was with cunning Hannah. She despised the man. I knew little about him, except that he and Rochester had been the closest of friends, and Colquhoun loathed him. I had, however, seen *A Wife by Thomas Overbury*, a pamphlet being sold by the peddlers in Paul's churchyard. I'd not thought to read it before then but determined to buy a copy as soon as I'd returned the letter to Weston.

I read those last sentences again before returning the letter to its envelope and resealing it: *I am willing to heed your great uncle's advice if it means our happiness will eventually be vouchsafed.*

Did he imagine there'd come a time when he and Frances would be openly together? *Happiness vouchsafed.* Did that mean marriage? Had he resurrected the idea of murdering Essex? Was that what was so troubling for Frances?

28

The maid and her rogue

The stench was visible. Hot air shimmering above garbage piles on street corners, hanging over the rivers like layers of old glass. Nearly a month had passed since last I saw Kate. It hadn't rained in London for several weeks. The Fleet had dropped at least a foot and was slithering slow and dark, making hardly a ripple where it joined the Thames. The slower it runs, the worse it reeks. Being inside or outside the walls of the city made no difference. London stank worse than an overflowing cesspit. Many of those who could afford to had escaped to the country, as they usually did at this time of year. I'd thought Frances might spend the rest of the summer at Audley End, taking Katherine with her. I guessed she stayed in London to be closer to Rochester, even if she couldn't see him. Certainly, the letters went back and forth between them every day.

Whenever I saw Weston, he asked me what progress I was making with 'herself'.

'Slowly, slowly. She's a Countess, remember. She'll not be rushed and harried.' Then I taunted him with tales that owed more to what I saw in the theatres that summer than anything I could dream up in my lonely bed. In truth, I'd seen no more of Frances than I had of Kate. And I'd still not coaxed Hannah out of Bedlam.

I asked Weston about his own attempts with Anne Turner. He enjoyed my gentle prodding and teasing. But I was growing tired of other people's love affairs, and ever more hungry for Kate. The letters between Lady Frances and Rochester dripped with lust, thinly disguised in the noble language of the court. They were laying themselves open to blackmail. But blackmail's a foolish way of making a living. However much power you might think it gives, you turn into the kind of problem that's best solved with cheese wire. The letters were most valuable for what they told me about Sir Thomas Overbury. I knew he detested Frances and poured vitriol on her reputation at every opportunity. Rochester's letters gave me a better sense of why, despite Overbury's slanders, he still sought the man's company. Overbury did his thinking for him. What came as a revelation was that Overbury was probably in love with him, and deeply jealous of his affair with Frances. Rochester clearly found that flattering. He needed to be adored.

I decided to make myself known to this Sir Thomas. What I had in mind was more subtle than blackmail. The plan had been thin and flimsy at first, but was growing more solid as the days passed. I could see a door to my own future, and Overbury had the key. If he could advise Rochester, I could persuade him to advise me. I could imagine my own country estate, a retreat for the summer months. I could even imagine respectability – after a few grievances had been forgotten. I'd had enough of creeping from one dark alleyway to another, living forever in the shadows of those I helped to thrive, whose intentions were darker than any deeds of mine.

I asked Weston to take another message. He assured me he'd delivered it to Kate in person. She told him she'd write back as soon as she could. But no letter came, no arrangements to see me again. A dark nagging fear was growing that Frances had changed her mind about letting Kate liaise with a scoundrel such as me. Or worse – that Kate had lost interest, and I'd been as fanciful in my affections as Weston was in his.

Most wealthy families abandon their grand houses in London and Westminster for the summer months. For me, an empty house is an open house, whatever the locksmiths might claim. I go in to borrow books – a book's hardly a book if it's not being read. If trinkets and jewels have been left behind, that can only mean they're not wanted. But there are people who do want such things, and they pay well for them.

On the third of August – I'll not forget the date – I returned to my lodgings just before sunrise. I'd been abed for just a few hours when the bells of Saint Andrew's church rang out eight in the morning, calling the faithful to mattins, and Matthew to rise from his bed and take breakfast.

Although my lodgings were close to the Thames and the Fleet, my rooms were at the top of the house, where the air was not so rank as on the street. I opened the window and door to let the breeze blow through. I was sitting at the little table, still in my nightshirt, when I caught a hint of Kate's scent. I'd been dreaming about her just minutes before. Was Forman's scrying mirror still turning tricks in my mind? I looked up. She was standing in the open doorway, as real as ever I could wish.

'Matthew.'

I gasped in astonishment, which made Kate laugh. A silver trill of a laugh that I'll never forget. She wore stockinged feet and was carrying her shoes.

'I didn't mean to startle you,' she said, plainly delighted that she had. 'I've been very careful. I've not been followed. I went down Water Lane as far as the quay before turning round and walking slowly back. I made sure nobody saw me when I turned into the alley. Then I took off my shoes because I didn't want anyone in the downstairs rooms to hear.'

Had I known she was coming I'd have washed my mouth with vinegar and cleaned both rooms.

'That's good. Best be safe.' I reached out. Took her hand. Squeezed it. I was still in my nightshirt. She was still in the doorway. She came inside. I shut the door behind her and kissed her chastely on the cheek. I'd lain awake for night after night, imagining this day: both of us so consumed by passion, there'd barely be time to lock the door, and not a word spoken until after bed.

There were times that morning when I looked at myself in some amazement. Matthew Edgworth transformed as if by some cunning woman's enchantment from lecherous rogue to elderly gentleman-usher welcoming some distant relative into his master's house. I led Kate to the table, where she took my seat. I stood before her fumbling for words, trying not to let her see the fellow beneath my nightshirt straining at the cloth.

'Sit with me, Matthew.'

'I have only one chair. Shall I sit on your knee?'

She grinned. 'There's a joint stool beside your bed. I used to sit there when I was caring for Alice.'

I fetched it through, carrying it before me to conceal the swelling thing that led my way. Who would have thought I'd be so embarrassed by my own desire?

In the tussle between cock and brain, brain was winning out – for the moment. I sat demurely, the very model of patience and attentiveness.

'Master Weston gave me your message,' she said. 'Thank you for taking Alice and her family to Canterbury. I'm glad they're all safe. I'm sorry I didn't reply straightway. I wanted to be able to say when I could meet you. And every day Frances promised, "Tomorrow, Katherine, I can give you some time." But when the morrow came, she said she needed me after all.' She paused for a moment, but barely long enough to take a breath. 'And there was never any time to write. Each day busier than the last. Every day she went to court to see friends, and every day she said, "Tomorrow, Katherine, you may have some time." But every day – '

'Kate, Kate. Slow down.'

She smiled and took another breath.

'Frances and I no longer live in Essex House.'

'Weston told me.'

'While you were away in Canterbury, we moved to Salisbury House. I wanted to get word to you, Matthew. But time swirls by like autumn leaves chasing in eddies. And Frankie kept saying that very soon – '

'Kate. You're here. I have never been so happy to see anyone.'

I leant over the table. We kissed. Now perhaps, now would be the time. Now that she had made her apology, the rest of the talk could wait. I stood up, went round to her side of the table, making no attempt this time to conceal the strength of my desire.

'Come, Kate. I have yearned for you so much.'

Gently, she eased me away, though her eyes were smiling.

'And all this past month, Matthew, I have wanted nothing more than to be here with you. And yes, to kiss. But first I need to talk.'

'I didn't mean to hush you, Kate.' I sat back down, wanting so much to fondle and caress. But I restrained my desires. 'I have ached for this, and now that you're here... Now that you're here...'

'What?'

I shrugged. Maybe Matthew, the patter merchant, should keep quiet for a while. Let the storm of words blow through!

She smiled. 'Matthew Edgworth lost for words?'

We smiled at each other, like young cousins meeting for the first time.

'Why Salisbury House?'

'It was her great uncle's idea. Henry Howard.'

'The Earl of Northampton?'

'She trusts him more than she trusts any man.' More than she trusts Rochester, I noted. 'She calls him Uncle Henry. He came down to stay at Audley End for her mother's birthday celebrations. There was dancing and music and banquets. All the things she loves that had been denied her by her husband. Except that it was all ruined because she thought that might be a good time to ask her father for help in seeking annulment of the marriage. He was cross and dismissed the very idea.'

'Who was cross with her?'

'Her father. He was furious. That's what she told me. I'm sorry. I'm talking too fast again.'

'I like to hear you talk.'

'Uncle Henry was there at Audley End. And he thinks it is possible, provided she's discreet. Which is why he advised her not to see Robert.'

'Robert?' If this was going where I thought it might, best play ignorant.

'Rochester.'

'Even while her husband's away?'

'Especially while he's away.'

'Salisbury House is much more comfortable than Essex House. She called that place Purgatory on Thames. The rooms were barely furnished, the fires didn't draw properly. Through the cold nights of March and April even our rooms were smoky. If Lord Essex didn't drink like a sot, I'd say that he was a Puritan. He hates music and dancing. Salisbury House is so different. There are books everywhere, and wall hangings and paintings and statues in the gardens. And proper chimneys.' She paused for a moment, but only long enough to take a breath. 'And glass in the windows so smooth and thin you can see through them clearly. Curtains as well as shutters and rugs and Turkey carpets on the floors.'

'Is that why she moved? To be more comfortable?'

'Uncle Henry suggested it would silence the gossips while her husband's away. Her sister, Elizabeth, lives at Salisbury House and Elizabeth's married to Lord Knollys, her husband's uncle.'

'So by living at Salisbury House, she makes herself appear to be the ward of Lord Knollys? A shrewd move.'

'Lord Knollys takes great pleasure in her company. So long as she sees him every day, and is charming and polite, she can do as she pleases – anything except for seeing her beloved Robert.' I thought I detected a note of disdain.

'Would that make her happy? To see him?'

'I don't think anything will make her happy until her marriage is ended.'

'Is that possible? Ending the marriage?'

She shrugged and turned her palms up, as if testing for rain. 'One day she's full of hope, the next she sinks into despair. She goes to court regardless of what mood she's in, to see her friends and talk, to dance and be seen to be spirited and cheerful.' To perform a version of Frances that none will forget, I thought. 'On the days when she's despondent, we take longer to prepare her face for the world. But nobody would ever know how she feels, except for me – and Robert.'

'But if she doesn't see him, how – ?'

'They write to each other. She insists on being alone while she reads his letters. And then she burns them. I'm sorry. I shouldn't be telling you that.'

'What we say here goes no further, I promise you.'

'I sometimes wish she wouldn't read his letters for they leave her most distressed.'

'Does he not care for her?'

'It's not him. It's his friend, Thomas Overbury.'

'Oh?' I said, as if this were a surprise. I didn't want to drag her into the dark corners of my world.

'Overbury hates Frances. He's trying to poison Rochester against her. He says such hateful things. The servants talk about it all the time in the kitchens.'

By then, everybody who'd stayed in London for the summer knew at least one person who'd seen Overbury's wretched pamphlet – or claimed that they had, for there weren't that many in London could read.

I squeezed her hand. 'You surely didn't come here to talk about the cruelty of the gossips.' She attempted a smile. We had never before been so close. Her lips were full, as was the swelling of her breasts beneath her linen dress, but it was the mist of downy hair on her neck, just below her ear, caught in sunlight, which truly aroused me.

'You wear no face paint. Is that your choice? Or does your mistress not like to think of you as competition?'

She laughed, but didn't answer.

'You are beautiful. Your skin so smooth and soft.'

'You flatter me, Matthew.'

'No. I speak truth. And who wants a mouthful of oils and powders?'

She laughed again. 'I've talked too much. Men don't like women who talk.'

'I like to hear you talk.'

'But enough's enough?'

My turn to laugh. I stood up again, still holding her hands. She got to her feet. I led her through to the bedchamber. She came willingly. Neither of us spoke. We sat on the bed. Matthew still in his nightshirt. I untied the white ribbon that fastened her ruff and laid it on the bed beside us. Her bodice was laced at the back. I untied the bow at the top and slowly loosened it. I kissed her neck. With one hand on her breast, the other behind her head, I pulled her to me, and we kissed. A long, slow, lingering kiss.

I put my hand on her knee and slid it gently, oh so gently, up her bare thigh. Such soft skin. Cool to the touch. Slowly, slowly. Cool getting warm. Soft becoming moist. She took hold of my arm. 'Matthew.'

I paused. We looked at each other eye to eye.

'I want you, Matthew. But not today. I'm still a maid. I don't want to rush.'

'No rush, sweet Kate.'

'Frances is visiting her friend Mary Herbert at Greenwich this afternoon. She wants me to accompany her. If I'm late, she'll not let me come again.' She was still holding my forearm. My hand slid a little further up her thigh before she grasped it firmly.

I felt a sudden surge of irritation. Why come at all if she was planning to leave so soon? Why kiss, then deny me anything more? My balls were aching, my cock still standing proud. I've had dozens of women and never worried myself about their scruples and hesitations. But no woman before had ever been Katherine.

'Maybe next time, Matthew. When Frances allows me more time.'

'And when will that be, Kate? When will Lady Frances let you come again?'

'Maybe tomorrow. Maybe next week. Maybe not til next month. I don't know. In company she's as spirited as ever I've known her. When she's alone with me, her moods waver. One moment she rages at me, as if I'm to blame for all her woes, the next she….' She stopped herself. I looked in her eyes. My cold impatience melted. I took hold of her hands, kissed them. Then on her lips. A gentle kiss.

'I've ached for you these weeks. Ever since we first talked at Chartley. I've been dreaming of you. I don't want to be subject to the whims of Lady Frances.'

'She will let me come again. I'm sure she will.'

I waited a while. 'You were about to say something.'

She looked away. 'I've never known her like this.'

'Like what?'

'Even in the darkest moments at Chartley, when she sank into the depths, she was kind to me. I did what I could to lift her spirits. And she always thanked me. Now I vex her, even when she seems cheerful in herself. She's told me several times that I'm a slovenly maid and a tedious companion. And then this morning,' she stopped to sniff back tears and wipe her eyes. 'And then this morning, after I'd helped her dress and brought her breakfast, she told me to spend the rest of the morning with you. She didn't ask if I wanted to see you. She just told me to go. As if she wanted rid of me. But I thanked her just the same. And then she snapped, "Why do you go out of your way to make me feel so ashamed, Katherine?"'

I kissed her gently on the cheek, savouring the salt of her tears. I took a kerchief and wiped her eyes. Then I put my arms around her and held her close, as if comforting a child.

'She frightens me. I've done nothing, said nothing to make her feel ashamed.'

She pulled away and looked at me directly. 'What are you thinking, Matthew?'

I walked over to shut the window.

'This morning she specifically told you to come here?' I said quietly.

'I wanted to come. I've been wanting to see you ever since – '

'She instructed you to come to me? Is that right?' I didn't want to frighten her, but she must have heard my concern, seen it in my face.

She looked worried. 'Yes.'

'Are you sure you weren't followed?'

'I did as you taught me. I stopped several times. Even on the hump of Fleet Bridge. I was trying to imagine what The Bridewell would have looked like when it was a royal palace. But I also looked to see if anyone was watching me, if anyone else had stopped. Nobody followed me, Matthew. And nobody saw me come into the alley. I promise. Frankie knew I've been wanting to see you. That's why she – '

'Kate. You and I know things we shouldn't. That puts us in great danger. We know more than Alice ever did.'

'I've done nothing wrong.'

'Nor did Alice. Listen to me, Kate. Frances knows what's planned for both of us. That's why she's ashamed.'

'No, no, no, Matthew. That's not right. You're making me cross now. I've been with her since before her tenth birthday. And the only time we've ever been apart was while she was at Sherborne after the exchange. She used to say she loved me as a sister. She would never do anything to hurt me.'

I knelt before her. Kate sitting on my bed, her bodice half undone, her ruff discarded on the floor, her hair hanging loose. If anyone ever tells you that men never change, take a look and see Matthew, kneeling before the woman he desired, still desires, more than anything in this world and talking quietly, earnestly, tenderly, not forcing her to his will. That picture and the words we spoke as vivid to me now as then.

'If there is one thing I want more than sharing a bed with

you,' I said, 'It's to wake beside you each morning.'

She laughed. 'I want that too, Matthew. But Frances would never allow that.'

'Then maybe you and I should disappear.'

'Did Forman teach you his conjuring tricks?!'

'Hear me out, Kate. Think what happened to Alice.'

She pulled back a little, as if to see my face more clearly.

'You told me she's safe in Canterbury.'

'Is that what Lady Frances thinks?'

She shook her head.

'Frankie's irritable, that's all. She's got a mind full of worries. She would never allow me to come to any harm.'

'Rochester has a list. Alice was on that list. I'm on that list. And hateful though it is to say it, you're on that list.'

She stared at me. Neither of us spoke. From outside came a shrieking of gulls – a common enough sound when fish are being landed at the quay, but it put us both on edge.

'What did you mean just now?' she said. 'When you said we should disappear.'

'Leave London.'

Her hands were clasped together, held to her mouth as in prayer. She sniffed. And then: 'If what you say is true, then Rochester would still have us hunted us down.'

'Alice is safe, Kate. Nobody's trying to track her down.'

'Because they think she's dead.'

'Exactly.'

She closed her eyes.

'Let me tell you something, Kate. A secret between me and Frances. When I was escorting her to Sherborne she confided in me.'

'I know. She asked you to collect the nativity that Doctor Forman cast for her. She told me.'

'She also made me swear that if ever Lord Essex took her back to Chartley I was to rescue her. I remember her words: "Take me and Katherine to a port where we can take ship for Virginia. If I cannot live as I choose in this country, we will make a new life for ourselves in the New World."'

Kate shook her head. 'No, Matthew. I will not leave this country. My family are all here. I want this world. I don't want to go to the New World.'

'I don't want to either, Kate. But if Frances and Rochester are convinced that's where we've gone…?'

She shook her head slowly, as if still trying to deny the magnitude of what I'd told her. But she knew the danger she was in, I'm sure of it. She and Alice must have talked of it. She was sniffing as she asked me to lace up her bodice. I sat beside her on the bed, and would have done as she asked, but I couldn't stop myself kissing her neck. I wanted one last taste of her before all was hidden to the world. I slipped my hand beneath her breast.

She moaned and whispered that she couldn't be late back to Frances. I squeezed her nipple. Then let go and started to tie the lacing. Cock and brain, for once in harmony, each reckoning that Kate would want me more if I could show a little self-restraint.

She started sobbing.

'I'm sorry, Kate. I didn't mean to distress you.'

She looked at me. 'It's not you, Matthew.' Tears running slowly down her cheeks.

I kissed those tears.

'I'm frightened, Matthew.'

I put my arms around her, held her close.

'I don't want to wait,' whispered Kate.

We neither of us spoke another word until we were in bed, both of us naked. At the time I thought of nothing else except being there with Kate, breathing in the softness of her skin, tasting the sweetness of her breath. Looking back, I realise now how unfamiliar those feelings were to me. You don't get to work as the Boy of the House in a place like The Hat or The Vixen, and not get to sample the wares. But never before had I felt so alive, so aroused by the very presence of a woman, never before experienced such delight in kissing, such pleasure in feather-light touching and stroking. It was as if it were me, not Kate, who was in a virgin state.

'I don't want to cause you any pain.'

She took my face in her hands and looked into my eyes. 'I know what to expect, Matthew. I have an older sister. And Alice told me many things. Any discomfort will soon pass.'

'Are you certain?'

'Hush, Matthew. My monthly courses are regular. I'm at a time in the month when I'll not fall pregnant.'

She gasped as I entered her.

'Am I hurting you?'

She said not, but later, as we were dressing, I noticed blood on the sheets.

'Your eyes were shut,' she said. 'Next time, will you look at me. I want to see you. I want you to see me.'

She kissed me. A quiet, gentle kiss, filled with so much promise, so much love.

We lay together, arms wrapped around each other. I wanted to doze and wake with her beside me. And that, too, was a first: wanting her as much afterwards as before.

But Frances had threatened to stop Kate from visiting if she was late back to Essex House. When she was dressed and tidy and ready to walk back to Salisbury House, we started making plans. At some point in the next few days, when Frances was in better spirits, Kate would say that Matthew had carelessly mentioned his desire to make a new life for himself in the New World as soon as he'd fulfilled his obligations to Frances. Kate would say how disappointed she was because she had no desire to leave England, and it meant that Matthew would soon be abandoning her. Meanwhile, I'd make enquiries at Blackwall docks about the cost of a berth on the next ship bound for Virginia. 'Let Madam Gossip do the rest,' I said. 'When we disappear she'll assume we're on that ship.'

She smiled at that, and my immediate thought was that she was amused, imagining it to be some kind of game, the kind of fantasy that her mistress might enjoy in a play performed in court, so I was surprised when she asked, 'Where will we meet, Matthew? When we disappear?'

So we made our arrangements, and I insisted on accompanying her as far as The Strand.

'Is Weston to be trusted?' she said as we were crossing Fleet Bridge.

'Why do you ask?'

'I want us to write, Matthew. Every day. I write very slowly, so my letters may have only a few words. But I will write. Will you write to me?'

'Every day. I swear it.'

And with that we took our leave.

'God be with you, my dearest Kate. I would dearly love to kiss you, but – '

'It would not be prudent. And we will be together soon.'

'When we'll wake in each other's arms.'

You see a possibility, you make it happen. I felt the future changing.

29

A consummate deceiver

I was still reading some of the letters that Weston took between Rochester and Frances. Weston was in so deep by then that he had no choice but to continue with the arrangement. I didn't read them all. Rochester's protestations of love were tedious, making me wonder what in the name of madness Frances saw in him.

Weston also brought me letters from Katherine. She was true to her word. She did indeed write every day. Her letters were as short as she'd said they would be, but I cherished those few words in her own painstaking hand, which contained no hint of regret. I was true to my word too, writing to her every day.

'Are you playing the maid as well as the mistress?' said Weston.

'How else am I to know what the mistress is thinking?' That seemed to amuse him. He seemed to get vicarious pleasure from thinking of Edgworth as the rogue who'd stop at nothing to slake his lust.

I saw Weston every day. Ten days. Ten letters from Kate. Until one evening he was late. The weather had broken by then, and I thought he'd been delayed by flooding, for it had barely stopped raining for several days. When he appeared in The Mermaid his cape was dripping. He brought his own shower with him. The bare earth floor was turning to mud. Despite his sorry state, he wore a foolish grin.

'I have something for you, Matthew.' He unbuttoned his sodden doublet, drew out a sealed letter, put it on the table. But kept his hand on it as if about to reveal a prime hand of cards. I couldn't afford to lose his goodwill, so I went along with his game. I bought him a jug of Canary. He passed me the letter. The seal was Frances's, but it wasn't addressed.

'For me? Are you sure?'

'Frances made me swear I'd give it you today.'

'Ahh!' I said, as if this was what I'd been waiting for. It suited very well for Weston to believe I was making headway with Frances.

'Will you not read it now?'

'There's not enough light in here.'

He borrowed a lantern from the tapster. I broke the seal.

'She wants to see me. In private.'

Richard Weston went on his way that night convinced that his friend Matthew Edgworth would soon be adding the Countess of Essex to his conquests. I knew otherwise.

The kitchen door of Salisbury House at the stroke of nine.

It was still raining when I made my way back to my lodgings that night. Water Lane was living up to its name, awash with slurry pouring down from Blackfriars. Another reason to be thankful that I'd taken rooms at the top of the house. The roof was leaking, so I put a bucket under the drips. My bed was dry, but I hardly slept that night. I was dreading the meeting with Frances, convinced that she'd lost patience and decided to prevent Katherine from seeing me again.

'Where is she, Edgworth?'

'Where is who, my lady?'

'How dare you be so insolent? You know very well who I mean.'

'The cunning woman is still with her family. But I promise you – '

'Stop your gabbling. Katherine Garnam. My maid. Where is she?'

'I don't know, my lady. She last came to my lodgings on the fourth of August. She said that was with your blessing. I've not seen her since.'

'You expect me to believe that? You are a consummate deceiver.'

'I swear to you, I tell the truth.'

I'd knocked the kitchen door as she demanded. An usher had taken me through to a small withdrawing room on the ground floor, where I now stood before her.

'I thought you must be angry with me, my lady, for not bringing the cunning woman to Anne Turner's. I thought that's why you didn't want Katherine to see me.'

She lifted a hand to stop me. I stood where I was. Neither of us moved as she scrutinised my every blink.

'The fourth of August, you say. That was the last you saw her.'

'Yes, my lady.'

'A Tuesday as I recall.'

'Yes, my lady.'

'Katherine accompanied me to Greenwich Palace that afternoon.'

'She told me she had to get back because you wanted her with you.'

'And you swear you've not seen her since?'

'I swear it.'

She was still staring at me, seeking out the tiniest flicker of deceit.

'Do you like this room?' Her tone lighter.

Whatever her game, I had no choice but to play. I glanced round. 'The plasterwork is magnificent.'

She waited.

'And the panelling is very fine.'

'You have an appreciative eye. You will therefore understand how much I prefer living in this house to Chartley, or to Essex House.'

'I can well imagine. Yes.'

'Every room boasts exquisitely crafted furniture. The chairs are wrought from best English oak, Turkish carpets on every floor, French silk cushions, Dutch wall hangings. There have been days when I've enjoyed living here.' Not what Katherine said, but who was I to argue? 'I do not wish for that pleasure to be taken from me. You understand?'

I nodded.

'Do you understand?'

'Yes, my lady.'

'Good.' She performed a courtly smile. It wasn't intended to set me at ease. 'There is also a fine garden with fruit trees and statues from Greece. Did Katherine tell you about the garden?'

'No, my lady. But she did speak highly of the furnishings and tapestries.'

'Did she?'

'She said she was delighted that you were in good spirits. She thought that was because you were able to see friends in court and were living in greater comfort.'

'Did she tell you about the statue of Medusa?'

'No, my lady.'

'Lord Knollys had it brought here from Delphi, at great expense. But it's an ugly thing. Katherine and I came upon it as we were strolling through the covered walkway. Rain was dripping off the snakes that writhed through its hair. It frightened her. She said it looked like they were dripping venom. Did she not tell you about that?'

'I haven't seen her, my lady.'

Her smile turned ice cold. 'Nor have I, Master Edgworth. Not since yesterday morning. I gave her leave to see you again. I was tired. I needed to rest until the evening. She left here just before ten in the morning.'

'I didn't see her yesterday.'

'She didn't return.'

'I swear I have not seen Katherine in ten days. I give you my word, my lady, I don't know where she is.'

'The word of a cheater, a scoundrel who knows the filth of London better than I know my own hand.'

'I have never deceived you, my lady. Nor your maid, Katherine.'

'Let me tell you what I think, Edgworth. I think you grew

impatient. I know you were out of London for a week in late July. I too have my spies.'

'I had to go to Kent.'

'You went to Dover.'

That gave me pause. How in Hell's name did she know that? Had one of her intelligencers spoken to Bill Carter?

'Yes, my lady.'

'And this past week you have been seen at Blackwall docks.'

'I don't deny it, my lady. I last saw Katherine on the morning of the fourth of August. She said she had to get back to Salisbury House because you wanted her to accompany you to Greenwich Palace that evening. I swear to you, my lady, I am as concerned as you are.'

'How dare you compare yourself to me? Your only concern is that I will have you hanged for kidnapping.'

I could feel sweat trickling down my forehead. I let it run. I wanted her to imagine I was shocked by Kate's disappearance. And I was, indeed, shocked. Of course I was. This wasn't how we'd planned it, but I had a good idea what she'd done.

'The only reason I don't hand you over now to the officers of the watch, Master Edgworth, is because you will find her. And you will bring her to me. She can tell me herself where she's been. I will decide what's to be done with her. If she is not here by noon tomorrow, you will be swinging from the gallows tree at Tyburn before the year is out.'

30

Disappeared

I assumed that Kate had chosen to disappear, but that something was stopping her getting word to me. I guessed she'd be in one of the hiding places we'd talked about, and was expecting me to seek her out. I was eager to find her, but wary of a possible trap. If Frances had become suspicious, she could have had Kate followed. So I took my time and a meandering route from The Strand to Saint Olave's, but I was already making plans to get her safely out of London. After that I'd have to clear my name with Lady Frances. Neither would be easy.

Saint Olave's was our special place. There was no Kate in the churchyard, and nothing left as a sign for me that she'd been there. I looked into the church itself. Nothing. Was it possible she'd taken refuge at Mountjoy's place? I wasn't expecting to see the Frenchie himself, but he was in the shop, tightening the curls on a wig sitting atop an eyeless mannequin.

'Master Mountjoy.'

'Is it you come for to collect, or for to commission or do you have some more hair for me?' I was impatient, and his Frenchie accent irritated even more than usual.

'I've nothing for you, Mountjoy. I seek information. Katherine Garnam, the Countess of Essex's maid. Have you seen her in the past two days?'

'I am working.' He was twisting a lock of hair around his little finger. Not what I call work.

'Have you seen the maid?'

'She is not been here for several weeks.'

Perhaps she'd let herself in to my lodgings while I was with Frances. She still had a key. No Kate. And that was the moment, as I stood there alone in my own rooms, that my keen anticipation began to turn to dread.

I walked from Water Lane to Blackwall docks in case she'd sought me there. Nobody had seen her. I even spoke to the warden at The Bridewell, thinking it possible that Frances had grown jealous of Kate and had her despatched as a wanton woman. The warden looked worried. I assured him I had no argument with him. And I believed him when he swore that he'd received no prisoner meeting Kate's description.

This wasn't the disappearance we'd devised. My stomach was knotting with fear. Again and again, I went over what Frances had told me.

Could it be that she and Rochester had a way of secretly communicating without using Weston? Were they colluding against me? Could Kate's 'disappearance' be a way of luring me out of my lodgings? My search for Kate would give someone to time to break in. I checked my wooden chest of treasures. Everything as I'd left it. Nobody had tried to pick the lock. I sat for a while, chasing thoughts in circles, like autumn leaves. A picture Kate had painted in sweetly spoken words.

I'd assumed that with Alice gone, I'd be the one in greatest danger. But suppose it was Kate? In less time than one swing of a pendulum, possibility became certainty. There was no point in my looking for her. I was alive because I was still useful. She was dead because she wasn't.

I tried to shut out the thought, to persuade myself that she understood the danger she was in, that she'd have taken great care. Again and again, I went over our last conversations. Her voice. Her touch. Her kisses. Her skin. Her lips. The scent of her breath. The future we were planning. I tried to hold back tears – until my jaw started twitching and my whole body shook. I never cried like that when I lost all my family. I wiped my eyes and blew my nose. But every time I thought I was gathering my senses, I started shaking with sorrow. Until finally, I felt hollow and cold, drained as the Thames at low tide.

My thoughts were still racing. But, try as I might, I couldn't persuade myself that Kate was in hiding. I knew it in my bones. She hadn't chosen to disappear.

I'd no idea who'd actually murdered her nor how they might have done it. But I was convinced it was Rochester who'd commanded her death. And Kate wouldn't be the last to pay for what she knew with everlasting silence.

Why Rochester? It could only have been him or Frances. And although Frances was more cunning than her lover, I couldn't believe she'd contemplate murder. Kate irritated her from time to time, but more because they were so close than for anything Kate had done to offend her. When the time came, they might collude against me, but not against Kate. Frances needed her too much. It was Rochester who commanded me to dispose of Alice, Rochester who wanted poison to murder Essex. I didn't doubt for a moment that Frances's threat to have me hanged at Tyburn was genuine. But she would never commission a murder.

So much I didn't know. The only certainty was that Katherine had roused feelings I'd never had for anyone else. I was grieving for her as I never grieved for my own family. Many might mock – what could a miserable rogue such as I know of such noble sentiments as love? But I certainly knew about fury. If there were a hundred names for rage, none would come close to what was pounding through my veins. Rochester might have had Kate extinguished, but he would never douse the flames that she'd kindled in me. My desire for vengeance, however, was ice cold. Killing Rochester would have been easy. But I wanted much more than that. I would bring him down. He'd be shamed and ruined, begging for the mercy of a quick death while I ensured he suffered the long and lingering one I had in store for him. It might take a while to finalise the details of my plan, but I can be patient when needs must.

I went back to Saint Olave's. The rain had stopped. The clouds had cleared. The early evening shadows fell long on the ground. I sat on the wooden bench in the churchyard where Kate and I had sat together. I closed my eyes and tried to work the same magic that conjured her from my dreams in my lodgings just ten days before. For a moment, I caught a hint of her on the air. But it was the evening scented honeysuckle climbing over the church porch. The magic didn't work this time. She didn't appear in the church doorway.

I went inside and knelt to pray that Kate wasn't dead, that she was in hiding. But I haven't prayed for years. And God wasn't easily fooled. The unbearable silence of God. I tried again, asking that Katherine's sweet soul might rest in peace, wherever her body might lie, for I don't think peace comes easy in a weighted sack on the bottom of the Thames – which was where I feared her corpse would be.

I stayed kneeling in the church a good long while, although I soon gave up on prayer. I was using the time and the quiet to take stock and gather my wits.

From St Olave's I set out to find witnesses. Rochester would have had to pay somebody well to commission a murder. And when that somebody got paid, they'd want to spend it. In the kind of circles that I move in people have a nose for the trails that money leaves behind. I called in at a dozen inns and taverns. I heard nothing suspicious.

According to Lady Frances, Kate left Salisbury House just before ten in the morning the day before. I walked to The Strand, following the route that Kate would have taken. Along The Strand and Fleet Street, over Fleet Bridge to Blackfriars and down Water Lane – about half a mile all told. I asked in every tavern and alehouse close by. I spoke to the constable of the ward and his officers of the watch. Had anyone been murdered in the past two days? Blood had been spilled in tavern brawls, two men had been stabbed, their assailants were already languishing in Newgate Jail. I congratulated the officers on their good work. Neither of the victims had been women.

I retraced that same route again. The cobbles of the roadway over Fleet Bridge were greasy with all the recent rain.

I stopped at the top of the hump to look at the river, for no other reason than that was the place where Kate and I had said our last goodbyes. I felt a spot of rain on my cheek. I was back in my lodgings, kissing the tears on Kate's cheek, savouring the salt of her tears. The Fleet was now in full flow, close to washing over its banks. It didn't smell so bad when it was running fast. I had only stopped because it was a way of honouring Kate's memory. I wanted to see what Kate had seen when she imagined The Bridewell as a royal Palace. I saw only grim dark walls and ferns growing in cracks between the stones. I was also put in mind of Bradshaw at the bridge in Ilford while we were bringing Alice back from Audley End. 'If you was walking, you wouldn't want to meet a carriage or a cart coming the other way.' Bradshaw's words.

Something large and dark floated by beneath. The bloated body of a drowned dog.

That's when it occurred to me. Nobody would have witnessed her murder because it would have been an accident.

I went back to the taverns, asked a few more questions, bought several rounds of drinks. The sun had long gone down when I found three men who'd seen what happened.

31

Truths and half-truths

We presented ourselves at the servants' entrance of Salisbury House as the bells of Saint Clement Danes rang out nine. Lord Knollys' steward was waiting with an officer of the watch. I explained about the three men with me. We were led through to the same small withdrawing room on the ground floor where Frances had seen me the day before. The steward and the officer stood guard at the door.

'Master Edgworth has brought witnesses, my lady. They saw what happened.'

'Show them in.' She looked drained. She seemed to know already, as if the mere presence of witnesses confirmed her worst fears.

They bowed as I introduced them. William Benson, an ostler who worked at The Dolphin, Daniel Whitby, a costermonger who'd been pushing a handcart of apples to one of the great houses on The Strand. And Edward Powell, a young scholar training to be a lawyer at the Middle Temple. They'd been more than willing to talk the night before, and on our way to Salisbury House that morning. In the presence of a Countess they all stood silent. 'Speak. One of you,' said the steward. 'We didn't bring you here to show you the house. The Countess of Essex wants to know what happened to her maid. Speak.'

Benson, the ostler, stepped forward and bowed again. 'I seen it my lady. Yesterday. About noon. I seen a cart being driven too fast. Much too fast. I'm about to cross the bridge myself. I'm walking behind the maid. Just ten yards or so. Not following her, you understand. Just that we was both walking in the same direction.'

'It's not you we're interested in. It's the Countess's maid, Mistress Katherine Garnam. What happened? What did you see?' The steward impatient, stern. Frances looking at Benson, then back at me. Saying nothing.

Benson cleared his throat. I thought he might dry up and forget everything. Then he started up again. 'The maid's walking up the slope of the hump on Thames side of Fleet Bridge. I'm on the North side. I hear this cart coming from behind. Clattering. Banging. I turn round. Just in time. I have to jump out the way. Near as dammit hits me. I curse him as he drives past. He swerves to the other side. The maid's on the brow of the bridge. Standing, staring out over the Thames. I'm thinking, what's she looking at? Then I can't see her 'cos the cart's in the way. Next thing I hear a thud and a scream and a splash.'

Frances flinched. Benson stopped.

'My Lady?' The steward.

Frances took a deep intake of breath, then gestured that Benson should continue.

He cleared his throat again. He was having trouble swallowing. 'Then I runs on to the bridge. See if I can help. But the maid's not there. I'm thinking did I imagine that? Then I looks over. And she's down there. In the river. Splashing, spluttering, trying to call out. Bonnet floating. Skirts white against the dark waters. And she's – '

'Enough,' said Frances, under her breath. Shaking her head and looking away, as if that would shut out the horror of it.

But now he'd started, Benson couldn't stop himself. 'Nothing I could do. I swear it. I called out for help. First thing I did when I – '

'Thank you. That's enough,' said Frances.

Benson stepped back. The steward asked Frances if she wanted to hear the testimony of the other two men. She asked them to keep it brief.

Daniel Whitby had been walking in the other direction, pushing his loaded barrow up the slope of the London side of the bridge. 'Everything what he said, I seen it too. Carter driving much too fast. Maid looking out, like she's seen something at Paris Gardens. Cart reaches the brow of the bridge. Like the horse is out of control. Then the maid cries out and she's gone. Drop the handles of my barrow. Apples everywhere. I run onto the bridge. She's down there in the water right enough.'

Edward Powell, the lawyer, finally found his voice, but in his nervousness he had been picking at the skin around his fingernails and was trying to hide the bleeding. He spoke as if he were addressing a court. 'My name is Edward Powell, and this is my true testimony of what I witnessed soon after the bells of the church of Saint Clement Danes chimed out ten on the fifteenth day of August.' Despite his carefully chosen words, his voice was thin and high pitched. He sounded younger than his years. 'I saw the maid walk onto Fleet Bridge. I noticed her because I remarked to myself that I thought she was unusually tall for a maid. When she reached the hump of the bridge, she stopped to converse with a gentleman who had been walking in the other direction and was pointing to something in the Thames. I thought perhaps he had seen a porpoise. Several have been seen this year, my lady.'

'Yes,' said Frances. 'I know. Continue.'

'Your testimony,' said the steward.

'The gentleman who had been speaking to her went on his way, but the maid stayed where she was. I also saw the cart that these men spoke of. It was indeed being driven too fast. When I realised that the maid had been knocked from the bridge into the river beneath, I immediately stopped another carter. I borrowed a rope from him and threw it for her in the hope that she might take it and we could save her. But with all the recent rain, the River Fleet has become a muddy torrent and the maid could not reach the rope. I had never met these men before that day, but we stood there together, the three of us and others too, helplessly watching on as the maid was swept away, out into the Thames before anyone could reach her.'

Frances looked pale as moonlight, appalled at what she was hearing. She asked but one question, and that to Edward Powell. 'The man you saw conversing with her. Was it anyone you recognised?'

'No, my lady.'

'Step forward, Edgworth.'

I did as the steward bad me.

'Was it this man?'

'No, sir.'

Frances shut her eyes and covered her face, seeming too numb to ask further questions. She sat for an age before bidding the steward to escort us from the house. As we were leaving, she called out and instructed the officer of the watch to question the men further, to have the carter tracked down and arrested, and to seek out the man who'd been talking to Katherine on the bridge in the moments before the accident. The officer took my arm to escort me from the room. Frances remained where she was, gazing far into space, before calling out, 'Do what needs to be done, officer.'

'God be with you, my lady,' I said.

She didn't reply.

We walked in single file, the steward leading the way, followed by the three witnesses with me and the officer of the watch taking up the rear of our little procession. I asked him what the punishment would be for the carter when they arrested him. He ignored me – a sign I took to mean I was still being blamed, and he'd be taking me straight from there to Newgate. Stay calm, I thought. Keep your wits about you. Stay alert. Appear relaxed. Set him at his ease.

'Beautiful house,' I said. 'Such fine oak panelling.' He showed no interest.

I was reminded of the corridors in The Bridewell. How long before the ornate plasterwork ceilings gathered mould and crumbled, and weeds took root in the crumbling mortar on the outer walls? London and Westminster were always quiet in the hot summer months. In all the time I lived in London, the plague was never far away. Just two years since the last bad outbreak. The summer stench wasn't the only reason that so many wealthy families left town. How long before the great sickness returned, the theatres all closed and these grand houses on The Strand fell prey to rot? Just as men and women meet their end, so too the finest churches and the grandest houses. The Priory at Spital Fields can attest that.

Just as we reached the kitchens, a young manservant caught up with us. Walking fast, not running, the rules of the house strictly applied. He pushed past me, and whispered to the steward, who brought our procession to a halt.

'The Countess of Essex will talk further with you, Master Edgworth.'

Frances was sitting in the same place, a light blue satin kerchief on her lap, stained dark with tears. She asked the usher, who'd led me back, to wait outside and shut the door.

'You may sit, Edgworth.' She blew her nose, wiped her eyes. 'Allow me a moment to compose myself. This has been most distressing.'

I thought she'd question me further about the incident on the bridge. But instead came this, spoken slowly, words chosen with care: 'I will speak candidly. You must do the same. I apologise for doubting you. Many people would think me foolish for trusting you. But I do. You have always behaved honourably with me, and with Katherine too, if what she told me about you was true.'

'Thank you, my lady. For better or worse, I have always been a man of my word.'

'Then answer me this.' She hesitated again. 'Katherine told me you had plans … to go to Virginia. Is that true?' She sniffed and wiped her nose again, but didn't take her eyes off me.

I took a gamble, even though I knew the risks of half-truths. 'I was sounding out possibilities, my lady. I didn't want to go. But I felt I had to.'

'Explain yourself.'

'I was besotted by Katherine, as I'm sure you know.' She nodded. 'But I have a reputation here in London. I wanted to escape my past. If Katherine and I were to be together, I wanted to start afresh, I wanted to be known as an honest man. For me and for her. And for the two of us together. So long as I'm in London, I cannot escape the web of my own dark deeds. I asked Katherine if she'd come with me to Virginia. She said she could never leave your service. She made that very clear. She told me that she loved you more than she could love any man.'

Frances sniffed. 'She told me the same.'

'I decided that if I could not start afresh with Katherine, I would make my way alone. So I did indeed make enquiries at Blackwall and at Dover. But I had no intention of going until I'd honoured all my promises and fulfilled my obligations to you, my lady.'

'I sent her to you that morning to give her the chance to bid you goodbye.'

I thanked her for that, although what she meant by it, I couldn't tell. Was that a veiled threat? I knew better than to seek clarification.

'You claim to be a man of your word, Matthew Edgworth. So tell me. The cunning woman, Hannah. Where is she? I have been very patient.'

I had no choice but to tell her what I knew – with a little added decoration: 'She has been with her family in Barnet, caring for her sick mother. But Hannah has the gift of prophecy. She is a true seer. There are many people who find that deeply troubling, including her own father and brother. They had her taken to Bedlam.'

'Has she turned mad?'

'No, my lady. Nor is she a fool. But they call her prophecies madness, and they want her cured.'

'You mean they want her gifts beaten out of her?'

'Her father is frightened. Knowing how much you want to see her again, I visited her in Bedlam. I offered to bring her out. She refused to leave. She says the devil is in her and Bedlam will drive out her demons.'

'Is she possessed?'

'I believe not, my lady. But it's what her father told her. "You stay in Bedlam until the demons are driven out." She cannot help but tell what she sees. He doesn't like that.'

'She speaks truths, and they call it the chatter of demons,' whispered Frances, as if she feared the day when some might say the same of her. And then to me: 'I want her to finish what she started.'

'I understand.'

'What will it take to get her out?'

'I can bribe the Master of Bedlam but getting her out isn't the only problem. The last time I saw her, she was too frightened of herself to speak truth to anyone.'

'What will it take?'

'Time. Patience. Gentle encouragement.'

She sighed. 'Everybody urges me to be patient. There is a limit to my patience.'

'I understand, my lady.'

'I don't think you do.'

Who was I to argue?

'My sister, Elizabeth, will appoint a new maid to replace Katherine. She will surely be diligent, she will be polite and efficient. But she won't be Katherine,' as if to remind me that I could still be held responsible and that if I failed her, Newgate Jail and then Tyburn Gallows weren't far away. 'I took Katherine into my confidence. She understood me better than any of my brothers and sisters. I already miss her dreadfully.' She got to her feet, walked to the window. She stood there for some time, looking out over the inner courtyard. Then she turned. It seemed she'd made up her mind. She walked over to the door and spoke to the usher, who'd been waiting outside in the corridor.

'You may leave now, Latimer. The business I have to discuss with Edgworth will take some time.'

It started with an explanation. When Frances got back to London, she and her friend Anne Turner had talked about the sad and mysterious death of Doctor Forman. Anne Turner had known Forman well, and it was she who first recommended Forman to Frances, persuading her that he was neither the charlatan nor the necromancer of popular ill-repute. She'd been as distressed as Frances to hear of Forman's death.

'Anne offered to find someone who could take Forman's place. That was before you found Cunning Hannah. It took her several weeks, but then she sent word that she'd found someone with true wisdom. We agreed I'd go to Anne's house in Paternoster Row. She took me to her private parlour on the third floor. The shutters were closed, and wall lanterns had been lit. Two chairs and a low table were set out before the fireplace.

A Doctor Savory was waiting for me. He disgusted me from the first. He leered at me constantly, as if appraising wares at a market. But he assured me he could cast my nativity. And I wanted to believe him. I held out my hand. His stubby, greasy finger felt like a slug on my palm. He called out some canting talk, leafed through an almanac and wrote a few notes. But he asked not one question about where I was born nor the time of my birth. When I saw Doctor Forman, the consultation took several hours and a week of calculations. Savory's took less than an hour all told. I timed it by the bells of Paul's. And he told me exactly what he thought I wanted to hear. I have enough wit to know that to be a sure sign of trickery.'

I chose not to remind her that I'd warned her about Savory back in February. 'There are a great many cheaters in London, my lady. You did well to see through him.'

'But it was foolish of me to lose my temper. He insisted I owe him his fees. I refused to pay. He presented me with a bill. I tore it up. Did he think I was some common housewife who carries a purse? He threatened me if I didn't pay. I told him he was a charlatan who tarnished the memory of good Doctor Forman.'

I agreed with her wholeheartedly – which was what she wanted to hear, although she didn't take that as a sign of trickery. But there was something Frances wasn't telling me. Savory's threats of blackmail would be empty if she'd only asked him to cast her nativity. I asked how I could help.

'Find him. Silence him. Whatever it takes, Edgworth. You understand?'

'Yes, my lady.'

She thanked me. I got to my feet.

'Stay. There is something else.'

She steepled her hands together and put her lips to her fingertips as if about to say grace before a meal. There was nothing to be done with the silence except breathe it in – and such exquisitely painful pleasure there was in that, for there was a hint in the room of the scent Katherine brought with her when she came to my lodgings. Two large bowls filled with rose petals and lavender had been placed on the hearth.

'Have you ever met my husband, Lord Essex?'

'You spoke of him when we were staying at The Crown in Wells. But I have never met him.'

'Did Katherine speak of him?'

I was wary, wondering whether she was laying a trap by getting me to talk about Katherine.

'She always spoke of you with the greatest affection, my lady. But the only time she spoke of Lord Essex was when she told me about the way he treated you at Chartley Manor.'

'Did you know he spent several months this year in France and Holland?'

'I'd heard, my lady.'

'Then maybe you've also heard that he's now returned. He brought a ring back with him. A gift. For me. A ring with a diamond. He said the jewel was an heirloom from his mother. He'd had it set by a jeweller in Amsterdam. My heart sank. There is nothing he can give me, nothing he can do to ever make amends for who he is and what he's done to me. But I accepted the gift with good grace. What else could I do?' She retreated briefly into silence again, perhaps deciding how much, or how little to tell.

'The ring has been stolen. If Lord Essex thinks I've lost it, he will blame me. He can be viciously vindictive. If he sees I'm not wearing it, he will be furious. I want you,' she paused for barely a moment, but that was long enough. She was gazing into my eyes, the hint of a smile flickering around her mouth. Such easy flirtatious charm, as if this business of the ring was a lover's game between us. 'I want you to get it back.'

'Do you know who stole it?'

'I have my strong suspicions.' She covered her mouth with a hand. Was she nervous? Or was this a calculated performance? And as the silence swelled, I had a ghastly thought. Not Katherine. Surely, she didn't think Katherine had stolen it.

'Have you ever heard of a woman named Mary Woods?'

The Mary Woods I'd met was a cheater from Norfolk who set up in Clerkenwell. I played ignorant. 'No. My Lady.'

'She used to work here in the laundry in Salisbury House. I've not seen her for more than a week. I fear it's Mary Woods who stole my ring. After Essex gave it to me, I wore it at all times. Except at night when I placed it on my dressing table before going to bed. It was too big for my finger. I didn't want it slipping off and getting lost in the bed linen.

'Then one day I was late for a dance at court, and in my haste, and with Katherine indisposed, I asked Mary Woods to accompany me to Whitehall. I feared the ring might fall off if I were wearing it while I was dancing, so I asked Mistress Woods to look after it for safekeeping. It was late when the dancing ended. I was tired. I forgot to ask for it back. When I went to put it on the next morning, I realised Mary Woods still had it. But she had gone. And none of the staff here know where she might be. I want you to find her. And bring the ring back to me.'

When a story tumbles out so fast, no matter who's telling it, I am always suspicious. Frances would never have danced at court without Katherine in attendance. And the Mary Woods I'd met in the back room of a tavern in Clerkenwell would never have been given work at Salisbury House. I suspected Frances had consulted Mary Woods and paid for her services with the ring. And now Essex had decided he wanted it back.

'I will find Mary Woods, my lady, but how will I know your ring? I wouldn't want her passing off some cheap imitation.'

'The diamond is set in a gold band decorated with simple twisting plaits.'

Assuming the interview was at an end, I again got to my feet.

'One moment. Wait.'

'My lady.'

'Do you think Katherine's death was an accident?' I was flummoxed by the question, but before I could mumble an answer, she continued: 'Your witnesses spoke of a cart driven too fast by a reckless driver. But knocking Katherine from the bridge without wrecking the cart. That must have taken great skill.'

I'd been thinking the same myself. Surely, she wasn't trying to lure me into speaking of my suspicions of Rochester?

'I don't understand, my lady.'

'My question was very simple. Do you think it was an accident?'

'I don't know. To my knowledge Katherine had no enemies.' No enemies, but certainly a certain someone who wanted her dead.

'Maybe not an enemy,' said Frances. 'But there is a man who once tried to rape her, who raged against her for what he called her insolence and what I call loyalty. And you, Matthew Edgworth, you have enemies. It's in the nature of what you do. And for very different reasons, so do I. Katherine was far more to me than a mere servant. She'd been my close companion for many years. Any harm befalling Katherine was always going to wound me deeply.'

She let that lie. She was looking at me eye to eye.

'Let me tell you what I think, Matthew. I think that Katherine's death was indeed a terrible accident. I think that whoever paid the carter didn't intend for Katherine to be killed, but to be terrified. My guess is that the plan was for Katherine to survive the accident and be brought back to me with cuts and bruises and a story of how close she came to death. Soon afterwards I'd have received a letter containing an anonymous warning. But Katherine is dead, so the someone who paid the carter dare not write that letter.'

I remained silent.

'I will do anything to get my marriage annulled. There are certain men who would do anything to prevent that happening. One writes loathsome libellous tracts against me, the other would have me locked away. That man already threatened violence against Katherine. Did she tell you that Matthew Edgworth?'

'Yes. She did, my lady.'

She stared at me, her head turned slightly to one side, as if curious about my response. Her expression, as so often with Frances, was hard to read. I almost caught a smile, but certainly a challenge.

32
Antichrist in a lewd hat

I ignored the usher's well-meaning pleasantries as he escorted me from the house. I was too knotted in a turmoil of sorrow and rage to trust myself with idle chit-chat. Maybe Frances was as distressed and as hurt as she'd said she was, but her talk about the theft of Essex's ring had seemed to stir more passion in her than losing Katherine.

So much rage. So many held back tears. So much confusion. And there was a part of me that still refused to believe she was dead. I went again to Saint Olave's churchyard. I didn't expect to find her there. But maybe I'd find some sign that she had been? There was nothing, nothing except my own memories of us sitting together in the churchyard. So that's what I did. I sat on that old wooden bench. I shut my eyes and tried to still my thoughts. Breathe deep, breathe slow. A trick I learnt when I first started picking locks.

I slowed my racing heart, but not my thoughts. Frances's talk of the 'accident' that led to Kate's death was certainly plausible, but seemed unlikely. I was still convinced that Rochester lay behind it. It was indeed possible that the carter had been instructed to injure, not to kill. But the fact of it was that Kate was dead. And that was exactly what Rochester wanted. Bradshaw, Colquhoun and Edgworth, we'd all be disposed of in due course. I was thankful that Frances still valued my services. For so long as I was useful to her, I'd surely be safe – at least for now, at least from her. But I was deeply puzzled by her talk of Kate's death as an accident. What was she doing by talking like that? The obvious was that she was inciting me to avenge Kate's death. But the obvious with Frances was rarely what lay beneath. She certainly wasn't idly musing to herself while Matthew just happened to be in the room. Had she been trying to convince herself that Katherine's death hadn't been intended? In much the same way that I still wanted to believe she wasn't dead. Maybe she spoke without thinking? I'd seen the rash, impetuous side of her nature in her fight with Hannah.

But as I sat there in Saint Olave's churchyard, another much darker thought started nagging at me – that it was a deliberate attempt to distract me from suspecting Rochester. And that implied that Frances had colluded with Rochester in organising Kate's murder. It was almost unthinkable that Frances was in some way involved, or even that she'd got wind of the plan, and not stepped in to prevent it. But the more I thought about it, the more things fitted into place. At Audley End Frances had insisted that she wanted Alice unharmed, yet Kate told me she'd not been unduly troubled on hearing that Alice had drowned. 'Ensure no harm comes to Alice' had been nothing but a half-hearted attempt to salve her conscience.

She'd been furious about Kate's disappearance, but even her distress about that seemed to pass too quickly. She called me a consummate deceiver. She could have been describing herself.

I would indeed avenge Kate's death, but it would take time, and in the meantime I had to ensure that neither Frances nor Rochester saw the faintest hint of my suspicions.

Frances had given me three tasks: persuade Hannah to cast a new nativity, silence Savory, get Essex's ring from Mary Woods. The easiest of these would be to silence Savory. It was the kind of work I enjoyed – not too demanding, yet sufficiently taxing to keep me focused on the matter in hand. Having paid him a visit earlier in the year, I knew where Savory lived. I set out late afternoon as the shadows were already lengthening. The sky was deep blue, the sun was warm, but after all the recent rain, the track was muddy, and ruts were still brimmed with puddles. I was wearing the same courtier's clothes that had got me entry to Audley End, and I wanted to keep them clean, so the walk out to Savory's in Hackney took more than an hour.

His small cottage stood alone on the northern edge of the village. My long boots, painted face, velvet cape and wide-brimmed feathered hat not at all out of place as I strolled past the large houses. Such a fashionable area.

I knocked Savory's door and waited. No sound nor movement within. I picked the lock, let myself in, removed my boots and looked round the house in stockinged feet. Savory kept a tidy house. He wouldn't want to come home to muddy floors. Two rooms downstairs, a kitchen and a back room. Between them a low door that opened onto a staircase. At the top of the stairs two bed chambers. In one, a desk and small chair. In the kitchen I found several bottles of wine and two glass carousing cups. Savory made a good living from his quackery. Lady Frances might have had the sense not to pay his fees, but others were clearly taken in, or too frightened to refuse his demands.

I took the glasses and one of the bottles through to the back room, where I eased myself into a comfortable chair.

Plenty to occupy my thoughts as I waited for Savory to come home. I'd managed to channel my rage against Rochester into cold determination. The key would be to ensure he could see his ruin coming but be unable to prevent it. And all the while for Frances to feel she could never be free of her husband without my services. I could yet make this business of dealing with Savory and Mary Woods work in my favour.

I heard a key jiggling in the lock. The click of the latch. The squeak of the door. Indistinct grumbling as he locked the door behind him.

I called through: 'Good evening, Doctor Savory.'

He went through a rigmarole of outrage. Who was I? How dare I break in? What was I doing? He was gripping a heavy looking dagger, his fingers knuckled white around it in a way that suggested he'd never put it to use.

That fashionably lewd hat on my lap concealed my own much finer stiletto. I made no attempt to answer his torrent of questions. The windows were small with thick old glass, but I'm sure he could still see my genial smile. That may not have been what finally calmed him, but like a fat old man climbing a hill, he finally ran out of puff.

'How did you get in?' It was the third time he'd asked.

And now that he'd calmed a little, I answered – in the voice of Sir Haughty Disdaine: 'I knocked on the door. There came no reply, so I opened it. I walked through. I sat down. I've been waiting an hour or more.'

'I locked the door. I always lock the door when I leave the house.'

'Maybe you forgot this time.'

'I never forget. I have the key with me.'

'Then maybe I slipped through the walls.'

He snorted.

'I was, after all, a close friend of the late Doctor Forman,' I said, in hushed tones. 'I am sure you must have heard of the great man's death. Such a terrible loss. But I do have his scrying mirror. He bequeathed it to me.' As if that might explain my appearance in the house.

That gave him pause. He looked at me as if his own fake sorcery had conjured the Antichrist Himself. Hackney's very own Faustus.

'What do you want?'

'The Countess of Essex sent me. I understand she owes you money.' I removed a bulging purse from beneath the hat on my lap. I still didn't let him see my dagger. He looked amazed.

'Come, Doctor Savory. Put your weapon away. I mean you no harm. Bring a chair and sit down. We must talk about how much she owes you.' I held up the bottle of claret. 'Shall I pour?'

'That's my wine,' he said.

'Then you must drink with me.'

I passed him a glass, which he accepted. I poured – for him and then for me. No harm in good manners I always say. It's how the moneyed charm their way to greater wealth.

'Now, tell me, Doctor Savory, how much does the Countess owe you?' I untied the drawstrings of the purse.

'I um… I… I can't be certain,' he bumbled. 'I work with Master Gresham. He keeps our accounts.'

'I came to you, Doctor Savory, to settle the business. I cannot go chasing over London to find Master Gresham.'

'I think … Um… I think two pounds…' I reached into the purse. 'And ten shillings,' he added hastily.

'You think?'

'I'm sure.'

'And that would settle the business?'

'Oh yes… Yes, indeed.'

'That will be the end of it? She'll hear no more from you?'

'Most certainly.'

'Very well.' I took a drink, then put my glass down on the floor. I started counting the money, from the purse to my right hand. 'A sovereign, two angels, making two pounds. A crown. And one, two, three, four, five shillings. Two pounds, ten shillings in all. Is that right?'

He looked as if he'd never seen so many coins before.

'Now, before we conclude the business, tell me, Doctor Savory, exactly what the Countess is paying for.'

'That's between me and her. It was a private business.'

I turned my head a little to one side. 'It was indeed a private business – which is why she sent me. But you surely don't expect me to pay you before we agree what's being settled.' One by one, I put the coins back in the purse.

'That … that …. two pounds and ten shillings,' he burbled. 'That will settle all … all her debts. I assure you.'

'I need to hear from you, Doctor Savory, exactly what I'm paying for.'

He was sweating and although I couldn't see his throat, the

twitching of that straggly beard told me he was having trouble swallowing.

He took another drink. 'The Countess wanted me to cast her nativity for her.'

'And was she pleased with what you told her?'

'I told her what she wanted to hear.'

'Yes. That's what she told me.'

I waited. Give him time, and his nerves would do my work for me. He emptied his glass. I filled it for him. 'How long, Doctor Savory? How long did it take? For you to cast her nativity?'

'I don't know. Fi… fi… five, five hours, maybe, maybe six. Most of the day.'

'Doctor Savory, I'm here to pay you what the Lady Frances owes. As you've seen, I have the money here. But if I'm to pay you, we have to be honest with each other. What passes between us goes no further I promise you. The Countess didn't think it took as long as five hours. Was Father Time playing tricks?'

'Maybe not quite five hours.'

'She also told me there was something else she wanted from you.'

'She asked about a potion.'

'Ahhh. A potion?'

'I said it might take several days to find the ingredients for the … erm… for the…'

'For the recipe to make up the … potion?'

'Yes.'

'And to make the potion you would have to charge a high price? Yes?'

'Yes.'

'And this debt that Lady Frances owes you, is that for the casting of the nativity or for the potion?'

'Both.'

I sat back in the chair and took a slow drink of wine. 'I'm intrigued, Doctor Savory. How much for the horoscope? And how much for the potion?'

'I... I erm... I don't know exactly. I ... I need... I'll need to talk to Master Gresham.'

'Roughly?'

'Maybe one pound for the horoscope. One pound ten shillings for the potion.'

I reached into the purse, took out a sovereign and gave it to him. He clutched it in his greasy little palm.

'You look surprised, Doctor Savory.'

'No, no, no. I'm delighted.'

'Good. Now, I need to know a little more about the potion, and then I'll pay for that.' I leaned forward, dropped my voice to a whisper. 'I'm here as Lady Frances's representative. I need to know that once this debt is paid, she will not hear from you again. You understand?'

'Yes.'

'So... Tell me. About the potion.'

That beard of his was twitching again and he was pursing his lips. 'Poison,' he mumbled.

'Poison?'

'For ... her husband.'

'Ahh. And you've delivered that, have you?'

'She changed her mind. She sent a letter. The letter said she didn't want the potion after all. She didn't use the word poison.

Not in a letter. But I knew what she meant.' Now he was gabbling. 'But I'd already bought the ingredients -- '

'To make the potion. I understand. And you want your payment?'

'Yes.'

'Very well. I've paid one pound. You said another pound and ten shillings.'

'Yes.'

'Have you noticed it's getting dark?' I said. 'Best have some light I need to see the coins if I'm to give you the right money.'

He got up, found a tinderbox and lit a couple of candles.

I got to my feet. 'Come, Doctor. Let's through to the kitchen. I'll count the money at the table.'

We went through. He set the candlesticks down on the table.

'A little more light, I think. You have a lantern?'

He did. He used a candle to light the wick.

I counted the money onto the table. 'One, two, three, four, five shillings. A crown. Two angels. Yes?'

He leaned forward and looked carefully – as if I might be trying to pass off counterfeit coins. When he reached to scoop them up, I put my hand on his. Sir Haughty Disdaine has a surprisingly strong grip.

'Before you take the money, I'd like you to give me the potion.'

'She said she didn't need it after all.'

'No. She doesn't. But she would like to have it in her possession. And I need to show her something for her money.'

'I don't have it here.'

'Then what do you think we should do? About payment?'

He blustered and struggled to get his arm from my grip.

I'd been playing patient and polite for long enough. I let slip the manners of the courtier. And grabbed hold of his beard, wrapping it round my wrist, like a sailor with a yank of rope.

He shrieked.

I was wrong about the beard. I thought he'd stolen it from The King's Men, when they kicked him out of the acting company. But if it was false, it was stuck on with good glue. I've never had a beard myself, but I'm told they hurt when pulled. You'd think so from the noises he was making.

'Hush, hush, hush. It only hurts if you struggle.' I let go his arm and seized his hair. He tried to fight me off, flailing with both fists. But I had his face turned away and he couldn't see what he was doing. He was fighting the air.

'Hush the noise. Be still.'

I gave him fair warning, but he persisted, so I slammed his face down on the table. His nose spouted blood. His shouts turned to snivels.

'Time for some truths, Doctor Savory. You have no potion because you never made one.'

He whimpered.

'You've been lying to me. There is no poison. And the Countess of Essex was so displeased with the horoscope you cast that she dismissed you as a charlatan.'

He blubbered a half-hearted protest.

'You threatened her. She doesn't like that. She commissioned me to silence you. You know what that means?'

He squealed. I took it as a yes.

'They owe you that mean to pay you, Doctor Savory. The Countess of Essex owes you nothing. I owe you nothing. But you, Doctor Savory, you owe me your silence.'

I pulled him towards the candle. He tried to hold back. 'Don't struggle, or I'll cut you.' I held the end of his beard in the flame. Burning beard. Not a smell I like. And nor did he. He liked it even less when I stubbed out the flames on his cheek.

'What do you want?' he wailed.

'Your silence.'

'It was a misunderstanding.'

'Yes indeed, Doctor Savory. The misunderstanding was thinking you could threaten a lady. The misunderstanding was thinking she owed you anything.'

'Yes.'

'So how can we ensure your silence? Should I cut out your tongue? Would that be enough?'

'I swear to God I'll be silent.'

'Have you even met the Countess of Essex?'

'Never.'

'Good. Now, look at me, Doctor Savory. What do you see?'

He shrugged and made strange noises.

'I'll tell you, shall I? I'll tell you what you see. What you see is a man who knows how easy it is to cut out a man's tongue.'

He sobbed.

'It's not pleasant. Cutting out tongues. Messy business. Lot of blood in tongues. I don't like it. But if needs be, I do what I have to. Trouble is though, Doctor Savory, you're a learnèd man. You can read and write. So even if I do cut out your tongue you could still write letters. You could still make threats.'

'I won't. I swear it. I won't.'

'How would you cast a nativity without your hands and without your tongue?'

'I swear that I will never, never, never – '

'Shush, shush, shush. Now, Doctor Savory, listen carefully. Put both your hands in front of you, palms up on the table.' He did as he was told, letting go the sovereign he'd been clutching all this while. It spun round a few times, then lay glinting in the candlelight.

'Now. I let go your beard. But you stay where you are. You don't move. Do you?'

He shook his head.

'You read palms, don't you, doctor.'

He whined and nodded.

'Then tell me what you see in yours. What does the future hold for you?'

'I don't … can't read my own palm.'

'Mmmm. Then let me read it for you.'

I took out my dagger. Laid the blade on his left palm, for I had noticed that he, too, was a sinister sort of fellow. Then I pressed down into the flesh and pulled the blade back. Give him something to remember me by.

'You have never met the Countess of Essex. You understand?'

He did. He understood.

I picked up the sovereign, put on my hat, and took my leave. Antichrist in a lewd hat. I left Savory sobbing at his table. And the only blood shed was from his broken nose, and that cut on his left hand – which was well because I hate getting my courtier's clothes messy.

But all was not well.

The next morning, I walked out to the tavern in Clerkenwell where I'd met Mary Woods in February. She'd been in the day before, trying to sell a ring, claiming she'd taken it from a childless woman in payment for a special remedy to make her husband fertile.

I visited every inn and tavern in Clerkenwell. I spoke to tapsters and landlords, saddlers and maids, whores and drunkards. The story came in various guises. Most had heard of Mary Woods. Several had seen her trying to sell a ring. When, at last, I found her lodgings, her room was empty. She'd taken all her belongings. Left without paying the rent. I cursed myself for being such a dull and stupid creature. My distress at Kate's death was churning me up more than I knew.

If I'd gone in search of Mary Woods in Clerkenwell instead of toying with Savory, I could have had the ring from her myself and given her a special remedy of my own, the special remedy I have for cheaters. But Mary Woods had left for Norfolk the previous afternoon, while I'd been playing games in Hackney. She probably still had the ring.

Colquhoun had left one of his coded letters. Rochester wanted to see me. You might think I'd have been unable to hold my rage in check, but I welcomed the summons. I still needed time to fashion my revenge. What I had in mind needed to be served up cold, not in the heat of fury. Being in the same room with him strengthened my desire to draw out his humiliation and suffering. Kate might have disapproved of my vindictiveness. But Kate was dead. And Rochester was alive – his usual self: impatient, short-tempered, demanding. All fuel for my revenge.

'Do you know Thomas Overbury?' he asked. Not 'Sir Thomas' I noted, although it was Rochester who'd persuaded the King to give Overbury a knighthood.

'I know of him, my Lord.'

'You know where he lives?'

Of course I knew. I make it my business to know such things.

'No, my Lord.'

'Ask Colquhoun. Have him show you. Tell me who goes to his house. How long they spend with him. Where he goes. Who he sees. What people say about him in the alehouses and the taverns. I want to know everything. Report to me here next week. And every week.'

Rochester and Frances both loading me with work. It seemed I was back in favour. I was pleased to be busy. That would at least keep me safe while I worked out what needed to be done.

33
The best laid plans

I sent a message to Frances through Weston that I had news which would please her. She had me meet her in Salisbury House again. I told her that Savory wouldn't trouble her again. She seemed impressed by the speed with which I'd gone about the business.

'I also found the place where Mary Woods was living. But by the time I got there she'd fled to Norwich. I would offer to track her down, but I don't have a horse and if she plans to sell the ring, then the matter is urgent. But I need to visit Cunning Hannah again. I fear that if I don't visit regularly, she will sink deeper into melancholy, and we will never get sense out of her. There's a man named Richard Grimstone who works for Lord Rochester. He's a better horseman than me.'

'You suggest sending him?'

'He knows Norwich well. It's where he was born.'

'I will make enquiries.' She gave a mournful, heavy sigh and put a hand over her eyes before looking up. 'They have

283

still not found the carter who killed my dear Katherine. Do you think he has also fled from London?'

I thought it highly likely. But fudged a response, without even hinting at the conclusions I'd reached about Kate's death.

'I am determined to see Hannah again, so you're right, it is best you stay in London and do what needs to be done. I will have another deal with Mary Woods. Richard Grimstone, you say?'

'Yes, my lady.'

'I will have him called in and speak with him myself. Thank you for the recommendation.'

She paid me well for dealing with Savory. Then she fixed me with her gaze. 'Do not fail me, Matthew Edgworth.'

I would have visited Hannah in Bedlam that same day, but Colquhoun sent word that Rochester wanted me. For once he didn't keep me waiting. His face was almost as red as Bill Carter's. Rage does that to a man.

He produced a small vial from an inside pocket. 'Remember this?' he said. Of course I remembered the vial. The liquid inside had once been golden yellow. It was now dark brown, the colour of Canary sack.

'Two drops,' he held it up to show me. 'That's what you said. Two drops enough to kill a man. No effect for several days. Then the victim loses appetite, sickens and dies within six weeks. Well, Master Edgworth. We now have a use for it.'

He'd changed his mind again. He'd lost patience, and wanted me to dispose of Lord Essex. I suspect his rage was a symptom of despair – just as sweats and shivers are a symptom of plague. But it was rage nonetheless. I thought it very unwise, but not wanting to offend my beloved master by challenging his judgement, I said nothing. But I still asked for a substantial purse – 'For bribes, my Lord. I'll need access to the kitchens at Essex House.'

When Savory claimed that Frances had asked him to make poison, I thought it a lie. I assumed she'd merely let slip that she was unhappy in her marriage, and Savory had seen that as a sign that she'd be easy prey to blackmail. Now I was wondering whether Frances might be behind Rochester's change of mind about murdering Essex, and that they'd schemed together to concoct the theory that Essex hired the carter who killed Kate, as a way of setting me up. Frances was highly intelligent, but she underestimated me. It was all too clear that she wanted to incite me to take my own revenge against Essex, but she didn't understand the way my mind worked. Rochester's raging outburst had convinced me that Essex had nothing to do with Kate's death. Nevertheless, I couldn't help but go back to that conversation with Frances. Kate's

There were a number of reasons for believing that Frances's death had indeed been an accident, and that the carter had been hired to frighten her, not to kill her. For a start, the timing was wrong. If Frances was indeed involved, she wouldn't have wanted Kate disposed of until after the annulment of her marriage. Living in Salisbury House might have been much better than in Essex House, but Frances was closer to Katherine than to any of her own siblings.

She'd spoken of her enemies – men who'd do anything to prevent the annulment of her marriage.

But there was another: a man who was far more devious than Essex; a man who could play the King himself through his puppet, Rochester; a man who wrote 'loathsome, libellous tracts against me' in Frances's own words. When offended, Essex would lash out in rage, he would attempt to take out his frustration on Kate, but he wasn't the kind of man who could think things through. Holding Frances in Chartley was evidence of that. But that other man, who was determined to drive a wedge between Frances and Rochester, he would certainly have the wit and the wherewithal to threaten Frances by harming Kate. Frances had certainly planted a seed, but it wasn't the one she hoped would take root.

I sought Colquhoun, hoping he could tell me what specifically had left Rochester in such foul spirits. It was always the steward who suffered most when the master was raging.

Colquhoun's breath already smelt of beer, and his speech was slightly slurred. It wasn't hard to wheedle it out of him. I'd known that our dearly respected master had spent the previous evening in the company of Thomas Overbury. He was, after all, paying me to be his eyes and ears! What I didn't know was that Rochester and Overbury had nearly come to blows.

I played the innocent. 'Is Overbury not his closest friend?'

'Nae when the fellow rails agin Lady Frances. He's obsessed wi' 'em both.'

'Master Colquhoun, you and I should find a tavern and share some brandywine, my friend.'

I took him to another Mermaid – tongues get loose around Mermaids – but not the one in Paternoster Row. I didn't want Richard Weston to see me with Colquhoun.

The deeper Colquhoun sank into his sack and brandywine, the more slurred his speech and the more incensed he became about 'The Vice Cunt's obsession with that damn O'Brae. Thing is, Edgworth, why's he ever visit the fucking man? Why? Why do that when...? When all he ever hears is. Is the Lady. Lady Frances. Slandered. Why? Why visit at all?'

'I don't know.'

He beckoned me closer. 'Ye see, the King, God bless him, the King has appointed the Vice Cunt, his beloved Rochester to be Lord High Treasurer of Scotland.'

I'd already heard, but feigned surprise.

'Aye. And made him a Knight. Knight of the fucking Garter.'

'Does that mean a pay rise for you and me?'

'Ye're missing the point. Has duties. Has responsibilities.' He took another drink. 'Has to have. Has to make. Has to. Decisions. Ye understand? Has to give. Opinions.'

'Who does?'

'Rochester. Has to advise the King. But O'brae does the thinking for him. Advises Rochester to advise the King. O'brae does. And then the. Then Rochester. Advises the King. D'ye see? So O'brae. Without O'brae he's ...' He trailed off. 'Without O'brae he's. He's...'

'He's fucked,' I offered. He found this funny.

'Aye. Aye. Aye. 'xactly. And me...'

'What? And you, what?'

'Alexander. My name.'

'Alex?'

'Aye. To friends.' I felt flattered. The friends of Alexander Colquhoun – a small and very select group.

'To friends.' I raised my glass. But I needed more from my friend Alex before he sank into a stupor. Did he remember

Rochester having any unusual meetings in the last weeks of August? He didn't.

'Are you sure?'

'Nothing I recall. Unless … the day he went to Cope Castle. Last week. But that was to meet you.'

'Last week? When?'

'Aye.'

'When?'

'Tuesday. Wednesday. Don't remember.'

'Not me, Alex. He wasn't meeting me. Until this afternoon, I've had no dealings with him for three weeks or so.'

'Then it wisnae you he was meeting.' He shut his eyes and groaned. He was turning surly, withdrawn. Things he didn't want to think about.

'How did Rochester react when he heard about the accident that befell Lady Frances's maid?'

'I dinnae ken.'

'Were you with him?'

'I wisnae wi' him when he heard the news.'

'Was he distressed?'

He shrugged. 'I've told ye he's a dark fucking pool. I've nae idea. Only time I know what he's thinking is when he curses me.'

'One of us is next, Alex. Have you thought about that?'

'Next for what?'

'You and me and Bradshaw. We're the only ones left who know about the exchange. The whore from the Vixen's dead. The maid's dead. Which of us is next?'

He put his cup down and stared at me. His eyes were bloodshot, but in every other way he seemed suddenly sober. 'I've nae mem'ry o' no exchange. The woman I saw at Sherborne was his cousin Isobel. Saw nothing, heard nothing. Ma eyes are milked o'er, ma ears are blocked with wax.'

'But Rochester's aren't. He's not forgotten. And he'll not forget til there's none of us left alive can bear witness to what happened.'

He shrugged and took another drink.

I escorted him back to Whitehall, where Rochester was in residence, although 'escorted' isn't quite the right word. I led. He stumbled, all the while insisting he was sober. Same way Rochester was supposed to believe him deaf and blind and cursed – or, rather, blessed – with a fading memory.

Colquhoun thought himself a canny Scot, but in his cups he always gave away more than he thought he was telling. I still hadn't found out who'd been driving the cart that killed Kate, but I'd spent hours quietly talking to each of the witnesses. It had taken too many rounds of ale to get there, but I now had a sense of how it had happened. At least two men were involved. The carter and a fellow on foot who followed Kate until she got to the bridge. Then he ran up and passed her and held her there in conversation until the cart arrived.

I was determined that Rochester would pay the price. Revenge needs careful crafting, but I already had the framework. And that conversation with Alexander Colquhoun was more helpful to me than he could ever know. Within weeks of starting to work for him I'd known how dependent Rochester was on Overbury. Indeed, I was increasingly convinced that Overbury was implicated. Colquhoun's ranting about our beloved master's reliance on Overbury confirmed the plan would work. All this talk of poison. I'd merely be following the example of my betters. I arrange for Overbury's poisoning. He dies. A little time passes. Then strange rumours are heard about the manner of Overbury's death, whispers growing louder, the first drops of rain before a storm. And then, in due course, Rochester's charged with murder most foul. He's imprisoned in The Tower. And only then, when my beloved Lord and Master is waiting for his appointment with the executioner on Tower Hill, I pay him a visit. I would hate for him to die without knowing the true author of his disgrace and ruin. There was plenty yet to work out, and maybe there'd be pitfalls on the way. But I had the plan in essence. The beauty of it was that Rochester would see his death coming, but there'd be nothing he could do to prevent it. He'd lose everything he'd ever won. Titles, riches, the King's favour, property, influence, his closest friend. And, yes, oh yes, sweet Frances too.

Why not simply kill him? Would that not be true vengeance? Meet with him in the stables at Cope Castle, cut him and be there to watch him bleed to death? Too quick. He'd suffer, but not enough. So why not find a poison that would cause a long, painful, lingering death? Because that would gain him public sympathy. The King would sit mournfully at his bedside. The last thing I'd want for the man who killed Katherine. My true revenge would be his long, drawn-out public humiliation. Scorned by all who'd fawned on him. Brought low. Disgraced. Then execution at the command of his beloved James.

But Overbury had to be first. And although he didn't know it, Colquhoun had given me a start. In the midst of all his ranting he told me how irritated our dear master had been when Overbury served up small tarts at the end of a meal. Overbury loved nothing better. Rochester couldn't abide the taste of pastry, and thought Overbury served them to annoy him. Colquhoun thought this a sign of Rochester's childish self-absorption. I thought it prime intelligence. And given my new role as Rochester's spy, I could reward his faith in me with slow drip-dripping malice against his former friend. Rochester would soon have good reason to want to be rid of Overbury, and I'd make sure that everyone would know it. So when Overbury died unexpectedly, the rumours would start even before I tickled Madam Gossip.

I started my enquiries the very next day. I did as my master had bidden. I watched the Overbury house. I wanted to know which grocers and costermongers the cooks used, where the kitchen boys bought fish and meat. Did they go out for flour and milk, or have it delivered? I made enquiries. More ale, more wine, more talk. Nothing direct. Just passing tittle tattle. And ever so discreet. It wouldn't have done for a stranger to be showing an interest in Overbury's kitchens.

It wasn't easy. Overbury's household kept mostly to themselves, seldom venturing out. But there was a kitchen boy who often called into The Stag off Fleet Street on his way to Newgate Market. It was shabby little place. One room, a bare earth floor, a few tables and benches. I kept my eyes on the boy, a short, skinny little fellow, with pinched face and darting eyes. He thought himself sharper than he was. He claimed he was fifteen. Going on twelve, I reckoned. Time for Martin Farnworth to make another appearance. Poor Martin. So easily gulled, even by a twelve-year-old boy.

Jack, the kitchen lad, notices poor nervy Martin, challenges him to a game of dice. Martin loses, curses his ill luck and takes his leave. And there's young Jack thinking he's the trickster.

You'll have already guessed the plot, I'm sure. I cast my line, Jack takes the bait. I give him a few days before reeling him in. Jack wins pennies the first day, sixpence the next, a shilling the day after that. Martin's feeling sorry for himself before he comes into luck and wins it all back. And a little more on top. Then poor young Jack can't pay his debts. What's to be done? Well, what's to be done is don't frighten him off. Such a kind man is Martin. He tells him there's no urgency to pay what he owes. Play a little more. Jack wins a game or two. But however many games they play Jack just can't win it back. And all the while that Martin's playing dice and cards, Matthew's learning who is who and where is where in the Overbury household. That's when I should have struck – demanding he pay his debts by letting me into the house in the early hours one morning. But I waited and gave the little fellow another day of stewing in his debts. My second bad mistake in less than a fortnight. First Mary Woods, now Jack the Lad.

Next time I saw him, Jack couldn't stop himself from grinning. 'Where you been, Martin Farnworth?'

'I had to visit a cousin in Kent.'

'Thought you was going to let me off what I owe you.'

'No, no, no. I've not forgotten.'

'What do I owe?' said Jack, though he knew very well.

'A shilling and fourpence, as I recall.'

To my horror, he produced a purse and paid what he owed.

'Where you get that money?'

Jack tapped his nose. Not Martin's business. Which surely meant he'd stolen it.

'You be careful, young Jack.'

He chuckled. 'I know what I'm doing.'

I had my money back, and he'd already told me as much as I needed to know about the layout of the Overbury house, its comings and goings, and the habits of Sir Thomas. I could have walked away and let him get caught, which he surely would be. But the ghost of Kate was whispering in my ear that I was in some way responsible for young Jack. And there was part of me that was beginning to like the little fellow.

'You know the punishment for thieving?'

'Who said I done thieving? I've not filched nothing.'

'I had a brother. His name was Tom. He worked in a great house. He borrowed some of cook's money. Just a few pence. Never got the chance to pay it back. 'Cos they caught him, then they hanged him at Tyburn one Mayday Gallows Day.'

'What's that to me?' He frowned, sounding aggrieved. But his show of innocence looked more like a sulk.

We played a few rounds of cards. I won. We played again. I won again.

'Your luck running out?' I said.

'You cheating me?'

'You shuffled the cards, Jack. My hands have never left the table.'

'You never won five rounds in a row before today.'

I leant forward. Martin's thin, apologetic little voice slipped away. Matthew talking now: 'I'll show you how it's done, young Jack. On one condition. Never take money from where you work. I don't want you going the way of our Tom. Don't want that on my conscience. Because when they catch you, you will sure as hell be hanged for it.'

'I know what I'm doing. They'll never catch me.'

'You've a sharp mind and a quick wit. I like you, Jack. But the steward of the house has already set traps. You can be sure of it.'

He sulked for a while. Then I offered him a deal. If he agreed not to borrow or steal, in return I'd teach him tricks. And I did. Simple sleights, like loading dice, palming a card, dealing from a hidden pack. He was proud of himself, called himself my prentice boy. But if teaching him tricks kept him out of trouble, it also made him cocky. That didn't bode well. Not for him, not for me.

34

The Sunne gone out
of our Firmament

While I was teaching Jack to be a cunning gamester, Rochester changed his mind again about Lord Essex. That didn't surprise me, for without Overbury's guidance he had no compass.

By then, Richard Weston was becoming uneasy about letting me read the letters between Frances and my master. 'Only a matter of time before we're caught. And we'd both end up on the gallows.' He could have been parroting what I'd said to Jack. There was good sense in what he said, but I needed to keep track of the correspondence. I persuaded him to let me see just one letter each week. It was one from Frances that explained my master's change of mind.

She'd been talking to her Great Uncle Henry, the Earl of Northampton.

... I now have good reason to believe that Lord Essex can be persuaded to seek the annulment himself. Dear Uncle Henry says my father has become sympathetic to such a course of action. At Audley End last year, father was dismissive. But he intends to come to London before the end of the month and has agreed to meet Uncle Henry and discuss how best to proceed. Together they will then meet with Lord Knollys... and convince him that my husband should seek the annulment himself. If anyone can persuade Essex of this, it is Knollys. I firmly believe, dear Robert, that my unbearable marriage will soon be ended.

There followed the usual babble of affectionate folderol. And then this:

I know how impatient you are with the situation, but I beg you, please do nothing that might jeopardise the possibility of annulment.

Towards the end of the letter Frances complained about her new maid.

She is polite and efficient. She goes about her duties quietly and with diligence. She knows the household well, for her parents have both been servants to Lord Knollys for many years. But she is not the companion I had hoped for, and she will never be the confidante I need.

No mention of Savory or Mary Woods. No mention of Matthew Edgworth. Not even any mention of Katherine by name. That alone seemed to confirm what I'd been thinking. But nor was there anything about having her nativity cast a second time. I wondered if the prospect of the annulment had made the business with Hannah less urgent.

You might think that I'd have welcomed the unexpected idleness. Far from it. I wanted to further the plan I had for Rochester. For that I needed access to the Overbury house. Little Jack's thievery had put paid to that for a while. And with nothing much to occupy me, I found the loss of Kate increasingly painful. I'd thought that with time, my grief might lessen. I was unprepared for the sudden waves of anguish that came washing over me.

Nearly a year had passed since she and I talked in the Wilderness at Audley End. Two months since she was murdered. But she was more present in my dreams than ever. At first, I welcomed her. She made my memories more real. I woke to feelings of tenderness. But the dreams had turned darker, and I was starting to dread what lurked in my sleep. Again and again, I see her knocked from Fleet Bridge, silently screaming as she falls into the river. Her gaping mouth slipping down into the deeps. Kate in the churchyard at Saint Olave's – disappearing into smoke-dark London fog before she can voice the words she wants me to hear. Me on the Gallows Tree at Tyburn. Kate looking on and calling. Wherever she appears, she's always calling out. For help? Or to tell me something? I call to her to speak more loudly. But it's me who's dumb, me who's had my tongue cut out. She comes to my lodgings. Slipping through walls.

I wake. She's sitting beside me, where she once sat to nurse Alice. Then I realise that the waking is itself a dream. So real I have to go to the door to check that Kate's not standing on the tiny landing outside.

I wasn't the only one in turmoil. London and Westminster were awash with surging rumours. Prince Henry, heir to the throne, had been taken sick, and was lying abed with a high fever, headaches, and a bleeding arse.

Rumour and Gossip never sleep. Never easy to distinguish between what's grown from a germ of truth, and what's sown by Envy and Malice. What seemed certain, however, was that the Prince was confined to his bed, his life in danger, and King James refusing to visit him. Whether this was because he feared for his own fragile health or because he resented his son's popularity depended on who was talking and the tavern where you heard it. But there were some who said that there was so little love between father and son (the King and his heir) that James was secretly pleased that the Prince was ill. Some were already whispering, 'Poison'. That took me back to the conversation I had with Appleby the cook at Sherborne Lodge. He'd been convinced that when Prince Henry came of age, he'd insist on Sir Walter Ralegh's release from The Tower, and the Sherborne Estate would revert to its rightful owner. But if the Prince were to die, Ralegh's hopes of freedom would dwindle to nothing. And that would suit Rochester very well.

My head was full of what-ifs. Rochester might have had nothing to do with Prince Henry's sickness, but he did see poison as a solution to his problems. Was that what Kate was trying to tell me in my dreams? Did Rochester's recent silence mean he no longer had need of my services? How long before I too fell sick? I stopped eating in taverns and inns, and bought all my food in the Cheapside shops and markets. Wherever I ordered a drink, I watched the tapster pour the ale. I even accompanied Weston to the buttery bar when he bought drinks in The Mermaid.

I was fearful in my waking hours. By night, I slept fitfully. The margin between dreams and waking was growing murky.

I woke one morning to the first London fog of autumn. I could smell it in the air even before I rose from my bed, like some monstrous creature had slithered up from the riverbed and was lurking just outside the door. Its foul breath an unearthly choking mixture of Thames mud, coal smoke and the vapours of slurry from flooded cess pits.

But I was hungry, and fog doesn't fill your belly.

I was walking slowly along Knightrider Street, barely able to see the ground beneath me. Sounds so muffled I could hardly hear my own footsteps. Blurred shadows passing. And then, of a sudden, from out of the murk, Kate's face no more than half a yard from mine. She floated silently by before I'd recognised her. The fog had swallowed her again before I called out. I tried to follow. I caught up with someone. Not Kate.

The fog clung on for three more days. I ventured out every day. Retracing my steps as best I could. Leaving the house at the same time in the morning, just after Saint Andrew's muffled bells rang out their nine o'clock peal. No Kate.

I saw her again about a week later.

A gale had blown up and dispersed the fog. I was sheltering under an awning as I queued for bread at a bakery on the north side of Cheapside, just beyond Gutter Lane. I don't recall the date nor which day of the week. But I do remember that the skies were grey. A piercing, cold wind funnelling through the streets. Hubbub and chaos in Cheapside. A flock of sheep being driven to Stocks Market, the most hideous din accompanying them as they approached Cheapside Cross. Sheepdogs snapping at the hooves of ragged stragglers; feral curs circling, baying like stalking wolves. When shepherds and drovers bring livestock in to markets there is always commotion; but the flock couldn't move. An overloaded hay cart had struck the Cross and keeled over, its front wheel splintered and wrenched from the hub. Tempers fraying. A dozen or more carts queued behind. No going forward, no going back. Horses steaming in the cold autumn air, shit piling in the street. One of the carts was loaded with pigs. The carter backed up. I guessed he planned to head down Friday Street and avoid the chaos. The shepherd meanwhile was frantic, whistling his own dogs, lashing out at the neighbourhood curs, shouting and cursing. Then the pig cart backed up and knocked him over. The shepherd struggled back to his feet, dragged the carter from his seat, hurled him to the cobbles, mashed his face into a pile of dung that a horse had dropped just minutes before. He should have known better. Carters look after their own. The fight soon turned into a raging brawl. Dogs barking furiously, pigs shrieking and bellowing, cattle loosing their bowels and bladders in panic. Cheapside as raucous and rank as the holding pens outside a slaughterhouse. The crowd down both sides of the street looking on and cheering as if we were at the bulls or the bears. That's when I caught sight of Kate.

She was at a costermonger's stall on the other side of the street. The uproar had caught her attention. Then she turned back to the costermonger, handed over some coins, put half a dozen apples in her bag. I recognised the movement of her arm, the turn of her head, the curls of dark brown hair poking through from beneath a plain headscarf.

'Kate,' I shouted. 'Kate. Katherine.' But with so much din, she wouldn't have heard me had she been just a yard away. She walked away, clutching her bag. I climbed onto a crate and saw her turn down Bowe Street. By the time I crossed Cheapside, she'd long since disappeared. I asked the costermonger if he knew the woman. He didn't know his customers by name, but he didn't remember having seen her before.

A couple of days later, the clouds lifted, the air was clear, the sun unusually warm for the time of year. Steam rising from slippery cobbles and muddy lanes. I made my way to London Bridge, where I had some business with a silversmith on the south end. The business went well – which was pleasing, for in my troubled state of mind nothing else was. Knowing there'd be thieves keeping an eye on the shop, I stood in the doorway, eyeing the traffic. Not much heading south at that time of day. Hordes going into town: pedlars and traders, mules and donkeys, housewives and gallants; carts and mules. Wheels and hooves clattering on shit greasy cobbles. The chaos of the Bridge makes life easy for even the clumsiest cutpurse. And my purse was full. So I decided to walk the few yards to the south bank, then take a wherry to Blackfriars from Paris Gardens. I walked through the gatehouse and out into sunlight. And there was Kate, about to enter the Bridge.

'Kate.' She didn't respond. I stood before her. Her face more ruddy than when I'd seen her last – no longer the pallor of the court. She was wearing a heavy, undyed linen skirt and dark brown shift.

'Katherine?' She looked quizzical, wary. I held my hands to either side to show I meant no harm. People stared as they sidled round.

'I don't know you,' she said.

'I'm Matthew.' A foolish thing to say, for I already knew she wasn't Kate. I apologised. She smiled and went on her way. I stood, watching her disappearing into darkness as she walked through the gatehouse arch. I'd wanted her to be Kate. She wasn't. But I knew it, so at least I wasn't going mad.

The wherryman didn't stop talking as we crossed to Blackfriars Quay. I heard nothing of what he said. My head was filled with an impossible conundrum. If the woman at the Bridge *had* been Kate, what would she have been doing on the south side of the river?

I knew what had happened on Fleet Bridge. The witnesses told the truth. I'd not bribed them to tell Frances a story of my own. But I began to ask myself questions I should have asked before. I talked again to Edward Powell. What exactly had he seen when Kate had been so cruelly knocked into the river? Once he realised that I intended no harm, he was helpful. The River Fleet had been in full spate. The tide in the Thames was high, and about to turn. The wind was blowing strong from the north. I called on John Butcher in Cheapside. Bought a pig's bladder. From there to a blacksmith, whose name I forget, who had a small forge on Saint Peter's Hill. He used his bellows to inflate the bladder for me. And then, with my pig's bladder blown up like a football, I painted it red, using face paints from the Blackfriars Playhouse.

I waited until conditions were as close as possible to the way they'd been when Kate had been forced from the bridge.

With a north wind blowing and the Fleet still running high, I watched the tides in the Thames as closely as any sea-captain about to set sail. When the time was right, I dropped my red football into the churning waters below. And I watched it bobbing out into the Thames, the current from the Fleet taking it swiftly into the middle of the river. A curious wherryman rowed over to take a look. I cursed and would have shouted if there'd been any chance of being heard. Thankfully, his passengers were impatient to get where they were going. My red football carried on its way, blown by the north wind to the opposite bank, where maybe some lucky lad would salvage it and struggle to explain to his mother why anyone would paint a football red. How else to keep sight of it as it drifts across the river?

Pigs' bladders can be put to stranger uses – as this tale will shortly tell. But what was the tale my red football told? It was possible. That's all. It was possible that Kate had survived. Tree branches fell into rivers during gales. If there'd been one close enough when Kate fell in, she could have grabbed it. The wind and the current could have carried her across to the south bank. It was possible.

I lay awake for hours that night, tormented by visions of Kate pulling herself out of the Thames and staggering up the muddy shore near Paris Gardens. Then what? If she was, indeed, still alive, why hadn't she found her way to my lodgings? Or at least sent a message of some kind?

I eventually fell asleep, but was woken about an hour before daybreak by the slow and regular tolling of a deep single bell in Westminster. I knew immediately what it was. The sickness that took Prince Henry to his sickbed had despatched him to his death. Tuesday November 6th. It's a date that Londoners will never forget. Frances would be distraught. Rochester would do his best to appear sympathetic, but no doubt he'd be secretly relieved.

The death knell tolled on.

Later that day a pamphlet was circulating on the streets, outside the churches, in every drinking house.

The Sunne gone out of our Firmament

I saw people asking strangers to read it to them. I saw women wearing mourning habit, as if they'd been personally bereaved. I saw grown men weeping in public.

I was distressed too. Impossible not to get caught up in it. But that didn't stop me thinking about Kate. The sun might have gone from their firmament, but I was daring to wonder whether it might yet rise again in mine.

35

Hellfire in Bethlehem

The beautiful Prince's funeral.

So many Londoners lining the streets to watch the funeral procession. I'd never seen so many ladies on the streets, so much frustrated lust disguised as tears of grief. I paid my respects, but didn't follow the procession to Westminster Abbey. A man has to make his living, and Rochester had paid me nothing for several weeks. Such was the general state of mourning that many grand houses were left unlocked. There were books to be borrowed, silverware to take to my friend on London Bridge. I could have probably walked through Greenwich Palace unchallenged.

The funeral was the talk of every tavern for weeks. King James not present. Little fuckwit Charles giving the oration. And this:

'Just as the prince's body's lowered into the ground – '

'A madman runs naked, stark bare-arsed naked, all through the mourners, yelling at the top of his voice, "I am the

305

ghost of Good Prince Henry." Jumps into the grave. Lies bare bollock naked on top of the coffin.'

'Should have left him there.'

'Best place for a ghost.'

But a man can't spend his days listening to tattle. Rochester could change his mind again if Lord Essex refused to countenance the annulment. And, besides, I had my own reasons for seeking out a poison that would do what I'd claimed for my little vial of piss. Just a few drops. No effects for a month or more, by which time too late to find an antidote. I paid another call on James Franklin.

I knocked his door. No sound from within. Nearly a year since last I was there. He could have died of the pox in that time. I knocked again. Louder. Nothing stirred within. I found my way round to an alley at the back of the house, picked the lock to the back door and let myself in. The place smelt worse than Mountjoy's workshop. It was all I could do to stop myself from gagging. But it was sulphur from hot coals and bubbling acid that filled the air, not the smell of death.

The house was maybe a hundred years old or more, stone and timber built, two rooms at ground level and one floor above, reached by a wooden staircase, curtained off with hessian sacking. If he was at home, he must have heard my knocking – unless he'd drunk himself to oblivion.

His workshop at the back of the house was a poor man's version of Forman's. Rough shelves on every wall, sagging under the weight of jars, boxes, vials and measuring scales. But no books. I guessed he probably couldn't read. Herbs hanging to dry from two thin ropes strung from wall to wall, a crucible bubbling atop a hot stove. I pulled back the curtain and called up the stairs, 'Master Franklin.'

Still no sound.

'It's Matthew Edgworth. I've not come to call in a debt. Me that owes you.'

That roused him. Footsteps clumping down the wooden stairs. His own stench preceded him. His beard, which had once been red, was turning white. He hadn't trimmed it in months.

Behind the pock marks and peeling skin, he looked embarrassed.

I gave him a coin.

'What's this?'

'A shilling.'

He looked bemused.

'You gave me excellent advice. You remember telling me of a cunning woman who lived in the woods out near Hamsted?'

'You paid me sixpence then.'

'And you're an honest man to say so, Master Franklin. I like that.'

So many scabs on his face that his smile looked painful.

'I'm not paying twice,' I said. 'I'm paying because she was everything you said she'd be. And more. Twice as good. So here's another sixpence.'

Despite his suspicions, he pocketed the coin.

'I need some powders. A friend of mine has difficulty sleeping.'

'A friend?'

'A friend who lies awake all night, ever watchful, ever restless. Can you make me some powders will help my friend sleep soundly?'

'Do you want this … friend of yours to wake in good health?'

'Most certainly.'

'And how long d'you want this him or her to sleep?'

'What my friend needs is a good night's sleep, and to wake in the morning refreshed. Six hours for a man. Isn't that what they say?'

He looked at me.

'Can you do that for me?'

'When do you want them?'

'How long will it take?'

'I'll need herbs that can't be bought at market this time of year. And other ingredients too. Come back in two weeks.'

'Then the contract is this Master Franklin. I pay you one third now for the commission. One third when I take delivery of the powders. And one third after my friend has enjoyed a good sleep.'

He offered to shake on the agreement. I declined his hand, which even in that freezing weather was sweating. But I did put a silver angel on the table.

I waited until the end of January before going back. The powders were ready. A man of his word, as I am too. I paid him the second instalment. The way he looked at me with a lecherous grin suggested he thought I had a woman in mind. And in a way he was right, but perhaps not the way he thought. The powders were for the Master at Bedlam, but the commission was also a test. I wanted to know whether Franklin could do as he claimed. If he was going to make poisons, I'd need to be sure he could deliver what he promised.

Hannah was the woman I had in mind. I planned to get her out of Bedlam so she could cast the nativity for Frances – and for my own purposes too. I hoped she could help me in my search for Kate. After my experiment with the pig's bladder football, I'd spent a lot of time on the south side of the river. I spoke to wherrymen. I asked in taverns and inns whether anyone had seen a poor maid climb from the river. Most people don't remember yesterday, never mind the middle of August. But a maid in soaking clothes, a maid covered in Thames mud, surely they'd remember that. They recalled a lot of rain in August, a lot of wet clothes, but no-one climbing from the river.

I asked in the south bank churches. A few strangers had taken shelter from the rain. Nobody'd seen a poor maid half-drowned, in fear for her life.

I even went to the Forman House because Kate told me that she'd once visited the house with Frances. It was possible she'd sought sanctuary with Widow Forman. The house was empty. The furniture and furnishings removed. Forman's physic garden long since abandoned and overgrown.

I'd started my enquiries full of hope. My moods lurched wildly between a despondency so deep I sometimes considered throwing myself from Fleet Bridge to join her, and an ever-growing rage against Rochester. It was that rage gave me the will to live; that, and a bewildered determination to follow things through. I grasped hold of any possibility that Kate had somehow survived. That was the other reason I was keen to see Hannah. She understood possibilities. If anybody could tell me if Kate was still alive, and where she might be, it would surely be Hannah.

The rigmarole with the gatekeeper was much as before. But he let me in without much argument. Perhaps he didn't recognise the pale-skinned courtier wearing the fine cloak and wide-brimmed hat that Alice had worn for the journey to Dover. The courtier had urgent business with the Master of Bedlam.

It had been raining heavily for much of the morning. The cobbles in the yard were as slippery as a frozen pond. Fruit thrown at the pillory had turned to pulp, creating a film of grease. Even the madmen hadn't ventured out. No Jeremy to greet and guide this time.

The Master was at his table. His door was ajar. He was eating a pie.

'By your leave, sirrah. May I speak with you?'

'Visitors on Saturdays,' he said, without glancing up.

'I'm here on business.'

'And this is my business,' he said, poking at the pie.

I walked in. Closed the door behind me. It muffled the screaming of inmates from deep in the bowels of Bedlam. He looked up.

'Good day to you,' I said. 'I'm here to seek your advice.'

'Visitors on Saturdays.'

'I cannot wait until Saturday.'

A gob of pastry splattered onto the table. He wiped it off with his finger and stuck it in his mouth.

'Do you have any women patients here?' I said.

'If you're here for sport, see one of my nurses. You got money, one of them can fix you up.'

'I'm not here for sport. I need advice. I have a sister. Isabella. She was betrothed to be married. Abandoned at the church by a rogue who ran off with her dowry. My dear mother's a widow and she's distraught with the shame of it or she'd have come here herself.'

'You want to bring your mother in? Who's paying her board?'

'Not my mother. My sister. Isabella. Her poor heart is broken. She's turned quite mad with grief. And I will be paying whatever it costs.'

He looked interested now there was money in it. 'Advice? Want me to tell you what to do with the rogue that walked out on her?'

'I seek advice about dealing with my sister. Do you think you can cure her?' I asked in all innocence, although I knew the answer, for I've never heard of anyone leaving Bedlam cured.

'Fools and madmen, we has both in here, sir. Men and women. Fools we keep under the whip. For the mad we have a doctor comes in. It's his trade to cure the mad, sir.' He stuffed the last of the pie in his mouth, wiped the crumbs from the table, then got me a chair. He seemed to be warming to the task.

I sat down, leant forward, covered my head with my hands and sniffed loudly.

'I must apologise.' I sniffed again. 'I am more distressed than I knew.' I wiped my eyes with a kerchief.

'I understand,' he said.

I took a flask of brandywine from my bag. 'Would you mind if I …?'

'Not in the least.'

I took a swig, though nothing passed my lips. I passed the flask to him. He protested a little, but I knew from my earlier visit that he enjoyed his drink.

'When might you be able to take my sister in?'

'Bring her tomorrow morning.'

While we were talking about the arrangements, he started coughing. He put his hand over his mouth and his cheeks blew out like a toad seeking a mate. He coughed again and spluttered. I eased my chair back.

He groaned. 'Mustn't eat so fast,' he mumbled. 'And last night. Too much.' He yawned. 'Too much to… I'll be alright. Now. Your sister. Sorry for the… Forgive me.' He yawned again then tried to return my smile, but his eyelids were growing heavy.

'I've taken too much of your time,' I said. 'Until tomorrow.'

He folded his arms on the table and laid his head to rest. James Franklin's powders were as good as he'd promised.

'Sleep well,' I said, before relieving him of his large iron ring of keys.

Hannah's hair had been shaven, her face was badly bruised. One eye was surrounded by puffy blue-black bruising. That's what they meant by a cure. She stared at me with a look of incomprehension, then covered her face in horror, as if she'd conjured a fiend from Hell.

'Hannah?'

'The devil is in me,' she mumbled through swollen lips.

'It's Matthew. I came to you in the wood near Hamsted.'

'Stay away. Never go to that place.'

'Hannah. You shouldn't be in here.'

'What's good for a witch is Bedlam. They drive out demons.'

The wailing, the howling, the clatter of chains against stone, the devils in the other cells, that's what was driving her mad.

'Hannah. This place is for madmen and fools. You're neither.'

'Here or the gallows.'

'I can get you out of here.'

'I have to be here.'

If she couldn't be talked into leaving, perhaps she could be walked to her senses. I worked my way through the keys until I found one that unlocked the shackles on her ankle. I took her by the arm and lifted her to her feet, thankful that she had a cell to herself and none of the other patients could see what I was doing.

'No. Mustn't go.' She sank back down to the rush strewn floor.

I knelt beside her. 'Who brought you here, Hannah?'

She shook her head.

'I can take you out of here. I can escort you to a safe place, wherever you want to go.'

She stared at me wide-eyed through the gloom. No candles were allowed outside of the Master's own room, but her small cell had a window high up, although sunlight barely penetrated the lacework of dusty cobwebs.

'Who brought you here, Hannah?'

'Adam.'

'Who is Adam? Why did he bring you here?'

'I killed him.'

We were still crouched together on the floor of her cell. Somewhere down the corridor a woman was screaming that Bedlam was burning, that the fires of hell were taking hold. I wanted to be quiet, to be gentle, to make Hannah feel safe, but I had to raise my voice to be heard above the chaos.

'Did Adam bring you here?'

'I killed Adam. Cursed him. I still see fire.'

She'd been staring into the distance, face racked with pain. She turned away, as if she could feel the flames.

'Who brought you here?'

'Adam was my brother. Now he's dead because I showed him.'

'Showed him what, Hannah? What did you show him?'

'Wanted to take me home. Couldn't go. Can't go. I'm a danger.'

'Was it Adam who wanted to take you home? I can help you, Hannah.'

'They said they could help.'

'Who? Adam and who else?'

'Adam and David.'

'Adam was your brother?'

'And David is my brother.'

'Was it David brought you here?' I was piecing together the fragments. Was it David who paid the Master to admit her?

'Your two brothers came looking for you. They found you. Did they try to persuade you to go home with them?'

'I killed Adam.'

'You showed him something. What did you show him, Hannah?'

She shook her head.

'Was it the scrying mirror?'

Her silence convinced me that it was. And Adam had been entranced by whatever he saw in that dread darkness. Had she really cursed him? Or had she not been able to prevent him getting drawn into the darkness, just as I had been in Forman's workshop?

'Come with me, Hannah. You can walk free.'

She shook her head. Bedlam was the punishment she had to serve.

'Hannah. Please. Listen to me, please.'

Her eyes were looking in my direction. But not focused on me.

'Do you still have the scrying mirror?'

She didn't answer. Didn't so much as nod. But she did clutch her stomach as if protecting herself. And from that small movement I reckoned that she had it concealed about her person.

'Can you use it for me?'

Her eyes flickered.

'Katherine Garnam. She was the maidservant to Lady Frances. Is she still alive?'

'I killed Adam.'

'You didn't, Hannah. His death wasn't your doing.'

Her gaze briefly met mine.

'Katherine is the woman I love. Please Hannah. Tell me. People say she drowned. I don't believe them. Is she still alive?'

She shut her eyes and whimpered.

'People saw her knocked off Fleet Bridge. Into the river. They thought she drowned. Did she? Did she drown?'

She gave what seemed to be the smallest of movements. Was that a shake of her head?

'Is she truly dead?'

Nothing. No movement. No words. But she'd shut her eyes, and I wanted to believe she was trying to conjure a vision of Katherine.

'Is Katherine dead?'

'Don't know.'

'Would it help to use the scrying mirror?'

'Not in here. Can't use it here. Can't think. Can't see. Can't let the mirror be seen.'

I tried again to persuade her to leave, to come with me to a place of peace where she'd be safe and could recover her wits. She insisted she had to suffer the punishments of Bedlam. But she had spoken with me, and some of what she said made sense. Small steps.

I went back to the Master, who was still asleep. I nudged him. He stirred, but didn't wake. I put his keys back. Franklin's powders were everything he'd claimed. I'd not hesitate to commission other potions from him when the time came.

36

Life and debt

Later that same day, I returned to The Stag. It was the tapster told me. Sam, the red-nosed landlord whose breath stank of a rotting liver.

'That little fellow you play dice with.'

'Jack?'

'Owe you money, does he?'

'A little.'

'Won't get it back.'

'Run off, has he?'

'How much he owe you?'

'Half an angel, give or take,' I said.

'You won't be seeing that, my friend. Nor will he. Ain't no angels where he's going. Got hisself arrested. Thieving from his master. In Newgate Jail, he is. Going to hang at Tyburn next gallows day.'

I had another dream about Kate that night. She's in my bed holding a new-born child. Our child. I'm sitting beside her, stroking her brow. The child's a boy with Jack's face. He pulls a deck of cards from his swaddling clothes. Next, I'm protesting my innocence. It was Jack persuaded me to play dice. He was looking for someone to teach him gleek and primero. It was me, Matthew, warned him not to thieve. But the patter soon dries up, and Kate has an answer to whatever I say. The Kate of my dreams is the angel of my better nature, a nature which hadn't been seen much before I met her.

Maybe it was fanciful to think she might be still alive. But even if she was dead, the best way of grieving was surely to do right by her.

Early morning's best for a visit to Newgate, when the jailer's recovering from the night before. He was a squat, heavy, thick-limbed man, bald and square faced, with eyes as dark as cavities in a skull. His pate glistened, dank as the walls.

'You have a young prisoner, named Jack?' I said.

'We got a dozen young prisoners. You think I remember names?'

'Caught thieving, he was, at the Overbury House.'

'And what if we do have him here?'

'I'd like to speak with him.'

'And he'd like to walk through walls.'

'I work for a rich lord –'

'I've heard it before. Don't waste my time.'

I turned my head a little to one side – the scar's always more effective when the light's low, a reminder that I'm a man who knows about violence. Then I placed my fist on the heavy table between us, slowly lifting my hand to reveal two gold sovereigns. More than he'd earn in a year without bribes. Sticks and carrots. Scars and money. He grunted and looked up. Something inside that blockhead skull met my gaze.

'Take him to a cell on his own,' I said. 'When I've spoken with him, the coins are yours.'

'Tell your rich master. Ten times that, and he could buy the little fucker's escape.'

'I don't need his escape. I need information.'

'Dead man is your Jack. He'll hang inside three weeks.'

'He can hang tomorrow for all I care, so long as I get the information I need. I get half an hour with the prisoner. You get two pounds. No escapes. No risk to you.'

'Half an hour?'

'Alone. Just him and me. I need information. That's all.'

'I'll have him moved' he growled. 'Wait here.'

More waiting. Locked in the jailer's little room above the gatehouse, I waited.

'Follow me,' he said on his return. None of Franklin's powders for him – I needed a guide. I'd never before been into the depths of Newgate. He took a lantern for himself and gave one to me. I followed as he clumped past prisoners in the holding pen, down steep and narrow stone steps into the hellish depths. Three cells on each side. They call them the bowels of the prison for good reason. Air heavy with the stench of shit and piss and rage and terror. I'd sooner die in a knife fight than end up in Newgate.

We walked slowly to the end of the corridor, the stone floor slimy with sweated confessions. The jailer slipped a key in the lock.

'Your boy in there,' he mumbled.

'I speak with him alone. That was our bargain. Leave me with him.'

'There'll be a guard on the stair,' he said. 'He'll bring you back when you're done.'

I kicked open the door and stood there with my lantern. Jack was cowering in a corner. I watched his eyes for the glance behind the open door that would warn me of a trap. But he was staring at me, terrified, bewildered.

'Over here, boy.' I held out a small loaf of bread. He was starving. He got to his feet and walked slowly over.

'I never stole nothing.'

'I don't care what you stole or didn't steal. I'm not here as your accuser.'

'Don't want to be hanged.'

'You won't hang, Jack,' I whispered, and put my finger to my lips.

'The Justice said I'm gonna hang. Justice said I'm an evil urchin. The Justice – '

'Hush you. Listen. Do what I say, and you won't hang. You have three weeks in here before they take you to Tyburn.'

'Don't want to hang.'

'Listen. Just listen. You're in the hangman's cart. There's a commotion in the street. The cart comes to a stop. The guards won't be bothered about you. They'll be looking out for the big fellows. When you jump out of the cart, I'll be there to whisk you away.'

'But I'll be shackled.'

'Yes, you will, Jack. You will indeed. Which is why I'm going to teach you how to use these.' I broke the bread and pulled out some picklock wires. He was wide-eyed as I showed him how to pick the lock on the cell door. 'Watch me.'

He was clumsy at first, but a quick learner.

'I couldn't have asked for a better prentice boy,' I told him, and gave him the bread. I'd not seen him smile like that since he first won a penny off Martin Farnworth. 'Now listen, Jack. The bigger the keyhole, the easier it is. But shackles have small locks. So you need to practice whenever you can without being seen. Not by guards. Not by prisoners. They'd beat you to pulp to get their hands on these. Don't try to escape from here. Too many guards. And if you think they're going to search you, put the wires in your mouth. Bend them round your top teeth.'

Time was ticking by. And what I'd told the jailer hadn't been entirely fanciful. I did want information from little Jack. And after the bread and picklock wires he was glad to give it – the easiest way into the kitchens at Overbury's House, which days of the week the master of the house took pastries, when they were made and where they were stored.

The guard's heavy boots clunking on the stairs.

'Quick, Jack. Wires away.'

I was pleased with myself. That alone should have been a warning. The guard leads me back to the jailer's room. He unlocks the door. Follows me in. Another guard comes in. Slams the door shut. Two of the burliest guards. Shorter than me. But bigger, and heavier. The jailer's sitting behind his table. I walk over. Stand facing him, the table between us. The guards move over, lean against me, one on each side, stinking of the lower depths.

'You'll get what I promised,' I say.

'But what you promised's not enough,' says the jailer. 'You don't leave Newgate til you pay the going rate. And the going rate for half an hour with a ripe young boy is five pounds.'

'I don't carry five pounds.'

'But you carry a purse 'cos I seen you take two gold sovereigns out of it. Put your hands on the table.'

I nod and smile, like he's got the measure of me and I'm full of admiration for his guile. Except I take my time. And that's not thinking time, it's calming time. I'm not going to fight. How could I? Three of them and one of me. They can relax.

Slowly, my hands go palms down onto the table.

One of the guards grabs my hair, pulls my head back. The other rips open my doublet. I don't struggle. I let him do it. He finds my dagger and the purse. He keeps the dagger, empties the purse out on the table. The sound of coins clattering and spinning.

'Well, well, well,' says the jailer. 'Look what we got here.'

'Can't look,' I cough out.

'Show 'im,' says the jailer. The guard on my left forces me to look down.

'Count it,' says the jailer.

'Four pounds,' I say.

'And?'

'Five shillings and threepence ha'penny.' What a miserable, defeated wretch I must sound.

'Should have paid us four pounds when you had the chance,' says the jailer. 'That way you could ha' walked away with what's left.'

I whimper out a plea for him to leave me the pennies. He thinks this is funny.

Both guards still leaning on me, eager for the jailer to give the word to take me for a beating. But they'll be waiting a while because what they're all forgetting is that weapons come in all shapes and sizes. The heavy oak table for a start. I've slipped my hands to the edge. I hurl it back at the jailer, the edge hard into his chest, pinning him against the wall. He's gasping, choking. Broken ribs I'd say from the blood he's coughing up. As I let go the table, both guards reach down to grab my arms. More fool them because as they bend, my elbows smash into their faces. Elbow to nose. Elbow wins. Roars of pain. The guard on my left's sprawled out on the floor, blood spurting from the pulped mushroom he used to breathe through. The one on the right's still standing, and not snorting blood. I must have missed his nose. But he's dazed and can't see properly. He's still got my dagger though. He takes a lunge. I swerve. The dagger misses, but he lurches against me. I'm off balance. I fall to the floor.

The one who fell is down there with me, blood pouring from his nose, scrabbling around, trying to get back to his feet.

But the other one, the fellow with the dagger, is still standing. One kick to my head and I'm dead. So I get my retaliation in first. I kick hard, aiming the heel of my boot at his knee. Knees bend one way. It's not sideways.

He doubles up with a great roar of pain. Drops my dagger as he collapses. It falls with its blade facing me. I scramble. Reach out to grab it, but can only grasp the blade, not the hilt. By then mushroom nose is back on his feet. He stamps down, forcing the razor-sharp edge deep into the flesh of my palm, trapping my hand beneath his boot.

I'm at his feet, pleading. His blood dripping onto my face. He keeps his boot where it is. Puts more weight onto it. He's used to meting out torture. I'm nearly passing out with the pain. He's making the most of this. Teasing out the agony as long as possible. That's his mistake – the gloating. He loves it when his victims beg for mercy. What he's never met before is the speed of my reactions. One moment I'm screaming in pain, the next his knee's gone too. I'm back on my feet. And neither of the guards can walk.

I didn't kill them. I collected my money, took the jailer's keys, locked them in, and left them there in their bloody mess. On my way out, I threw a few pennies into a cell that held a dozen prisoners. The shouting, the brawls and the chaos drowned out the cries for help coming from the jailer's room.

And Jack? If I hadn't gone back to release him, the jailer and the guards would have taken their humiliation out on the little fellow. And Jack would never have got as far as the gallows' cart. Newgate Jail's not a good place to die.

Once we were out on the street, I gave him the loose change from my purse and advised him to get away from London. But he'd have to make his own way from now on. So somewhere there's a cunning little picklock owes me one.

I've no regrets about getting Jack out of Newgate, but I should have paid attention to the advice I gave him just weeks before. When things are easier than they should be, it's either a trap or a trick.

37

The cat's taste for pastry

If Hannah hadn't been so determined to serve her time in Bedlam, I'd have asked her to heal my hand, for if anyone knows about healing it's a cunning woman. If Forman's heart hadn't given out on him, I'd have asked him. But as things were, the only person I knew who might be able to offer healing was Doctor Franklin. So I braved the stench and paid another visit. I told him how impressed I was by the powders to help my friend sleep.

'Did they work as I said they would?'

'Yes indeed, doctor. My friend was far more restful the last time I saw him.'

I showed him my hand and asked what he could do for me. He made a dressing, covered the wound with lint and made up a paste for me to take away. I had to repeat this dressing each morning and night. The pain slowly eased, and with it the bruising and the swelling. But I'd lost the use of the thumb and two fingers. And there was nothing he could do about that.

But I still went back to him, for by then I thought I could trust him. 'There is something else I need from you, doctor.' I put it to him straight and plain. I feared he might react as Forman had done and claim he was a man of faith who would never do anything to harm God's creatures. He had no such qualms. His reply was as plain as my question.

'What kind of poison?'

'Something slow acting, Doctor. Something that can't be traced back to me. Something that could go into a quince tart and not spoil the flavour.'

'Much mischief hidden in a pudding!' He gave a fruity little chuckle.

It took Franklin two weeks to acquire the ingredients. In that time, I acquired a cat. I'd assumed it would be easy to catch one. Leave a bowl of milk in a place the local dogs couldn't reach. Get a net and take my pick. Not so easy. Every night, I put out milk. Every morning the milk was gone. I made a snare. I caught a rat one night, a fox the next. Neither of those much use to me. So I went to the Mermaid and asked the tapster if he'd let me have one of his, for every tavern in London has at least half a dozen cats in their yard.

'I've a terrible plague of mice in my lodgings,' I told him.

He told me to see his cellar man. Next time I called he gave me a sack. Inside was a mangy, flea-ridden mog. I fed it milk and fish scraps from the wharf at the bottom of Water Lane. A feast for lucky Mog. She began to grow quite tame.

A fortnight later I returned to Franklin.

'Will you be making the tarts yourself?' he said.

'Do I look like a baker?'

He gave this more thought than it deserved before agreeing that I didn't. 'Then you'll have to buy the tarts. Slice them open, then smear the quinces with this paste. Be sure to wear gloves.'

I did as he suggested. I'd grown quite fond of Mog in the time I'd been feeding her, but she recognised the sack when she saw it. She'd as soon have scratched my eyes out as submit to it again, but with a deal of yowling that's where she went. And with the sack slung over my shoulder we made our way out through Ludgate.

I'd chosen a dry night, but there was a frost in the air. I followed Jack the Lad's advice about getting into the kitchen garden of the Overbury House. After that, the lock on the kitchen door should have been easy. The keyhole was big, the lock was old. Just a fortnight before I'd have been able to do it with eyes closed. But my left hand was useless, the air was freezing, and I was shivering. Never before had I felt so cack-handed. I blew on my fingers, then tried again. I thought I heard levers click in the lock. I tried the door. It didn't move. I put my hand down my britches and tried warming my hand on my bollocks. I'd had no other use for them since that morning with Katherine. And I silently repeated to myself all those words of wisdom I'd trotted out for Jack. Patience. Take your time. Steady your breathing. Listen for the tiniest movement in the lock.

I tried one last time. If that had failed, I'd have tracked down Jack to be my prentice boy. The lock moved this time. I opened the door. I picked up the sack with Mog inside and found the larder. There on a shelf was a small tart freshly prepared and ready to be set before Thomas Overbury on the morrow – just as Jack had said it would be. I wrapped the tart, put it in my bag. I let Mog out of her sack. She screeched and ran off. The first servant down to the kitchen in the morning would find a stray cat had crept into the larder, a stray cat with a taste for pastry.

I crept quietly back to the outside door. Something brushed my leg. Mog. She purred. I picked her up. She was supposed to be here in in the morning, not coming back to Water Lane with me. I've never much liked cats. But she liked me. I'm ashamed to say I took pity on her. I found her some milk and cheese. I told her I'd be back for her the next day. I don't suppose she understood. But she seemed happy enough lapping up spilt milk while I crept out the door, taking care to lock up behind me.

I found a baker, showed him Overbury's tart, and asked him to bake another, exactly the same. The following morning, I collected it, took it back to Water Lane, cut it open. After putting on gloves, I smeared Franklin's secret ingredients on the quince filling, then put it back together. In due course I'd maybe need half a dozen, but Sir Thomas would want his pastries fresh.

I planned to return to the Overbury house that night. In the meantime, I sought out Richard Weston. I'd been lying low since losing the use of my fingers, and wanted to know whether Lady Frances had been trying to contact me. Weston was in his usual corner.

'Have you heard?'

I hadn't.

'Sir Thomas Overbury?'

'Isn't he a friend of Viscount Rochester?' I said.

'He was.'

'What do you mean, *he was*? Have they had a falling out?'

'Overbury...' he paused – not that he needed to because he already had my attention. 'Overbury has been accused of treason. He was taken to The Tower this very morning. So, what do you make of that?'

'Well, well, well,' I said. 'Now there's a thing.'

Getting quince tarts to Overbury was going to be more difficult than I'd anticipated.

38

I see blood

Richard Weston hadn't yet found his way back into Anne Turner's bed, but she was taking him into her confidence, and Frances had confidence in Anne. Piecing together what Weston told me and what I gleaned from Colquhoun, I gathered that Frances had taken my advice and suggested Rochester send Grimstone to Norwich in pursuit of Mary Woods. Grimstone had always been an easy going, cheerful fellow with hopes of rising in the household. He'd been pleased to be trusted with finding the Woods woman, and thought he'd done an excellent job, for he tracked her down and, even though she'd already sold the ring, he had her arrested. Mary Woods was now languishing in a Norwich jail. When he reported his success, Rochester was delighted. Two days later he was furious.

I could hear Frances behind that fury. If Essex saw she wasn't wearing his ring, he'd feel slighted. That could put paid to her hopes of getting the marriage annulled. And if Mary Woods' case came to trial, she'd have tales to tell about how she truly came by Frances's ring. I feared that Frances would blame me for Grimstone's failure. There was only one sure way of getting back in favour.

I paid straightforward bribes this time. I said I wanted the Hannah woman for myself. It was the kind of deal Bedlam's gatekeeper and its Master both understood.

The Master looked embarrassed when I went to his door. The last time I'd seen him he'd fallen asleep in the middle of our conversation. He remembered me, but little else from that day. He'd forgotten about my imaginary sister and had no idea I'd borrowed his keys. He perked up when I asked him if I could take one of his female patients for the day. Ten shillings for him – a pretty little gleaming silver angel.

'And another for surety,' he grunted. 'Returned when you bring her back.'

I argued, but in the end I paid him what he asked. If Frances thought I'd failed her I could pay with my life.

The Master collected Hannah for me, then escorted us to the gatehouse. Hannah mumbled to herself, but didn't resist. In the time she'd been in Bedlam she'd learnt that defying the master got her a whipping.

There was a queue to pass through Bishopsgate. Staring eyes and chattering tongues followed our every step down Cheapside. I'd given Hannah a cloak and pulled the hood over her head, but I hadn't brought shoes. Nobody could see the rags of Bedlam, nor her shaven head. But they could see she was walking barefoot, arm in arm with a well-dressed courtier.

She clung to my arm, unquestioning, unspeaking. We made our way to Paternoster Row. Anne Turner was expecting us. Weston had made the arrangements. He led us up a narrow creaking staircase to a small third floor room at the back of the house.

'You can leave us now, Master Weston.'

He slunk off, disappointed. He did well as a go-between and a dogsbody, but he was far too curious to make a gentleman usher.

Two chairs on opposite sides of a small, low table. Thick grey window glass letting so little light into the room that wall lanterns had been lit in the middle of the day.

'Why have you brought me here?' said Hannah.

'To meet with Lady Frances.'

The name meant nothing to her. Had they whipped her memories out with the demons?

'Lady Frances. The Countess of Essex. I brought her to see you before.'

Hannah shuddered. Was she still haunted by her brother's death?

'You interpreted the horoscope that Doctor Forman cast for her.'

She looked down at the floor.

'She asked you if you could cast a new nativity for her.'

She mumbled, without looking up.

'The Lady Frances is coming here for you to cast her nativity.'

'I cannot.'

'You must.'

'I need peace of mind. I need to be close to the earth, to the trees, to the wind.'

'We haven't the time, Hannah.'

She lifted her head and shut her eyes. 'There is no time,' she said. 'No time.'

I fought back my instinct to shake sense into her. There had to be some way I could strike a bargain.

'She trusts you, Hannah. You alone. You above anyone.' She was drifting away again. 'Just tell her what she wants to hear.'

'Who am I to know what she wants?'

'Tell her that her marriage will be annulled and that she'll be allowed to remarry whoever she wants. Tell her she'll have the most wonderful wedding. Tell her that her second marriage will have the blessing of the King.'

'I cannot cast a nativity.'

'Then use the scrying mirror. Listen. Lady Frances will be here very soon. If you don't tell her what she wants to hear, things will get worse.'

'Nothing can be worse. I live to be punished.'

'Just tell her what she wants to hear, damn you.'

She was gazing straight ahead. Then it came to me. I leant forward. 'Your brothers. Adam and David. Were they twins?'

Her head moved slowly from side to side.

'Adam,' I said. 'Adam who died in the fire. Was he the older or the younger?' I had her interest now. She didn't answer. 'David, who put you in Bedlam. Where is he now?'

She shook her head.

'I can find him, Hannah. And I will. The Master at Bedlam knows where he is.'

'No.'

'Yes, he does, Hannah. Because David pays to keep you there.'

'No.'

'Does David die like Adam? In a fire like Adam?'

333

She was staring at me.

'Do as I ask, Hannah. And no harm comes to David.'

She was about to speak when there came footsteps on the stairs. Richard Weston opened the door without knocking and ushered Frances into the room. I stood and gave a small bow. Hannah didn't move. Frances sat down.

'Leave us, Master Edgworth,' said Frances.

'I don't wish to gainsay you, my lady, but I think it best if I stay.' I'd have to prompt Hannah if needs be. I took the liberty of whispering in Frances's ear that Hannah was in a dangerous state of mind.

Frances waved me off to stand by the door. I stared at Hannah and, unseen by Frances, gestured for her to start.

'I know why you have come,' said Hannah. 'But I cannot do it.' The moment I'd been dreading. 'To cast a nativity I need to be in a place of calm, a place where my mind is free.'

'Then you have wasted my time. I trusted you, Edgworth. I do not take kindly to those who betray me.'

'Forgive me, my lady. But Hannah can yet be of service. She knows another way to see possible futures.'

I glared at Hannah. She whimpered, as if in her mind's eye she'd caught a glimpse of her brother David in a fire. Then she produced the scrying mirror and laid it on the table. I looked away, knowing what would befall me if I allowed myself to be drawn down the well of the mirror's darkness.

Hannah spoke quietly, as if murmuring some mysterious incantation. But what she said was almost word for word what I'd told her to say, though where she pulled the details from, I've no idea.

'I see a gathering of men in a large room,' said Hannah. 'A great hall. I see men behind a table. A woman standing alone. The woman questioned. I see ...' She faltered for a moment, as if trying to make out what was there in the darkness. 'I see parchments and papers. Documents. Large books. Shafts of sunlight on the table. I see... men arguing between themselves. It may be they are shouting. I see the King.'

Silence. And then: 'I see a proclamation. And...'

Silence.

'And what?' Frances speaking.

'I see blood. There is blood.'

'What does that mean?' Frances again. 'Blood? Whose blood?'

'Don't know.'

'When?' said Frances. 'When is there blood?'

'No time. There is no time.'

'You saw a proclamation. Tell me about that.'

That seemed to break Hannah's trance, for the tone of her voice changed. 'The proclamation. Your marriage will be annulled. You will be allowed to remarry. You will be allowed to marry whoever you desire. There will be a fine wedding.'

I was glad to be looking away, for if Frances had caught sight of my face, she'd have seen me wincing at my own words parroted.

'And this new marriage will have the blessing of the King.'

Silence filling the room. Silence, sticky and cloying, like the smell of overripe cheese.

'Look again,' said Frances. 'After the wedding ceremony. What do you see?'

From outside on the streets around Paul's, hawkers were shouting out to sell their wares. 'What do you lack? What do you lack?'

And then, barely audible, 'I see horses. Four horses.'

'Where? Where do you see that?'

'In a white mist. Four gleaming black horses in a white mist.'

'In the mirror? Is that what you see in the mirror?'

Silence.

'Forman looked in the mirror and he saw the same. Four black horses in white mist.'

From outside, that regular chiming chant, 'What do you lack? What do you lack?'

Hannah speaking softly, soft but clear: 'And blood. I see blood.'

'When? When is that? After the wedding?'

'No time. There is no time.'

The screech of a chair pushed back over wooden floorboards. Frances on her feet.

'Thank you, Matthew. You have done well to arrange this. Do not leave London. There is another matter I need you to attend to. I will have Weston call for you.'

Then she was gone.

39

Bethlehem to Epping Forest

'Cover the scrying mirror, Hannah.' No sound except the hawkers' cries from Paul's, and Hannah's breathing, as heavy as if she'd just run up Hamsted Hill. 'Cover it now. And tell me when you've done it.'

I heard no hint of movement. So I covered my own eyes and walked over to the table, picked up a cushion from the chair where Frances had been sitting and placed that, by touch, on top of the scrying mirror. Only then did I open my eyes. Hannah was sitting at the table staring a hundred yards ahead, a hundred years into the future for all I knew.

'Hannah. We must go.' If she'd not played the seer quite so splendidly, I'd have taken her to Paul's and left her to fend for herself. But she'd somehow done as I'd instructed, blending what Frances wanted to hear with what must have been true visions.

'Hannah.'

Still nothing.

I put my hands on her cheeks and forced her to look at me. 'Hannah, listen to me.'

She moaned, as if waking from a long sleep. 'Where do we go?' Her voice barely louder than a whisper.

'I'm not taking you back to Bedlam.'

'I have to be punished.'

'You have been punished, Hannah. You've suffered enough. It was the scrying mirror killed your brother. Not you.'

She seemed to be focusing on me at last, so I tried again. 'Listen to me, Hannah. I will never take you back to Bedlam. I will take you to a place that's safe. Wherever you want to be.'

'Close to the earth, to the trees, to the wind.'

'A forest then?'

If I thought the doctor at Bedlam had a genuine cure for madness, I should have presented myself to him, for I must have been the one who was truly mad, abandoning the money I'd left for Hannah's safe return, and ignoring Frances's insistence that I remain in London. But I was sick of waiting for her beck and call, sick of playing the timid lap spaniel.

In my madness I bought Hannah some clothes and I walked with her to Epping Forest. There was mud everywhere, but the sky cleared as we walked. At first she was withdrawn and tense, glancing behind her every few steps, shoulders hunched, barely speaking. But the further we got from London, the easier she became. And little by little, she began to relax, although I think it was the trees, the birds and hedgerows she was responding to rather than Matthew's loving kindness. As we walked, I managed to tease out a little more of her story. I'd got some of it right. She did come from a wealthy family. But they hadn't thrown her out. It had been voices in her own head that told her she must live in the wilderness if she wanted to see real truth. But even a cunning woman cannot survive on truth alone, and her brothers had occasionally brought her food and drink. I asked her about the fire that destroyed the hovel. She wouldn't answer me directly, but she did tell me enough for me to work out what happened. Adam, her brother, was visiting. He built up the fire, then caught sight of the scrying mirror and wanted to know what it was. He was gazing into it when her store of tinder and dry sticks caught light. Her cat fled, and Hannah ran outside in pursuit. It was only when the hut was ablaze that she realised that Adam hadn't followed her out. It was hardly her fault, but she still blamed herself for his death because she'd allowed him to become entranced by the scrying mirror.

We walked a mile or so into the forest before finding another abandoned charcoal burner's hut in a clearing flanked by ancient yew trees. I went back to a nearby village to buy food. When I returned, she was sitting where I'd left her, wearing an expression of strange contentment. There was still light in the cloudless sky, and warmth in the air. I did what I could to make the hovel watertight, and together we collected wood and tinder for a fire. Then we sat and shared the food I'd bought.

'New life,' said Hannah, delighted by the sounds of the forest ringing with birdsong.

But my thoughts were elsewhere, and she knew it. She asked what was troubling me.

'There is no time, you said. What does that mean?'

'It means I don't see time. I see what I see. I don't know when it is.'

'I came to Bedlam a few weeks ago. You remember that?'

She looked at me. That puzzling, seemingly vacant look that was so easy to misread.

'I spoke about to you about Katherine. I thought you might be able to tell me whether she is dead.'

'I am not a magician nor a witch.'

'But you have the scrying mirror.'

She nodded slowly. 'Yes. I have the scrying mirror. But I never met this Katherine you speak of. If she is indeed dead, her ghost will not come haunting me. I do not commune with the dead. I am not a necromancer. If she's alive, I have no way of telling where she is.'

'Is there nothing you can do?'

She closed her eyes. 'You have been kind to me, Matthew Edgworth.'

'I wouldn't want anyone to suffer the way you did in Bedlam.' That wasn't strictly true, for I would have loved to see Rochester in Bedlam, head shaven, hands shackled, thrashed every day and gawked at on Saturdays when the noble gallants and their ladies came to visit, wondering at the terrible fate to have befallen the man who'd once shared the King's bed. Bedlam would be even better than The Tower, where I was planning he'd end up. Or perhaps better yet – Bedlam, then The Tower.

'You have been kind, Matthew Edgworth. And maybe you know more about Katherine's whereabouts than you think. Come. Sit close to me.'

When I first met Hannah, I'd been wary of her. But, even though she had no herbs to sprinkle on the fire, and I don't much like being out of the city, I felt more at ease with her there in the depths of Epping Forest than I did alone in my lodgings back in Water Lane. I sat beside her on the moss-covered bough of a fallen tree. She placed her hands on my forehead.

'Tell me what you know.'

'I don't understand.'

But I did. And I told her again all that I knew about what had happened to Katherine on Fleet Bridge, and how I thought there was still a possibility that she might have survived.

A woodpecker flew yaffling through the trees. The screech of an owl. Light fading, the sky reddening. Night would soon fall.

Hannah spoke softly. Her words lilting like a mother's lullaby. 'Allow yourself to think about Katherine. Be with her again that last time you saw her. The last time you saw Katherine... Did you speak to her about anyone who lives south of the river?' Hannah's voice, somewhere between a dark velvet murmur and a single white cloud, high in the sky on a summer's day. I was drifting.

'My master spends much time at Greenwich Palace. I've never seen it – except from afar, from the top of the hill near Highgate Village.'

'But you sometimes have business south of the river ... Did you speak to her about that?'

'Doctor Forman. And his widow, Anne. I've been to the Forman House. Kate went there too, with her mistress. I tried that, Hannah. There is nobody there. Widow Forman's abandoned the place.'

'Shut your eyes, Matthew. What else do you see?'

I saw the Cardinal's Hat. I saw myself there as the Boy of the House. I saw the gallants and the guinea-birds, I saw my sweated education. But I'd never mentioned any of that to Kate.

'See it, Matthew.'

I saw the smoke from our fire. Moths flickering in firelight, drawn to the flames. Bats squeaking unseen around the edge of the clearing. The half moon rising behind the shadows of trees.

I'd had very little business south of the river these past few years – except for visiting the theatres and the bear pits. But Kate wouldn't have asked for sanctuary in a theatre. Actors had their own little world, and Kate wasn't part of it.

And then… it was so obvious. Why had I not thought about Bill Carter before? Kate questioned me intently about him taking Alice to Canterbury. Why hadn't I been to see him before? Because my head had been full of whoever knocked Kate from Fleet Bridge. Because the people I'd spoken to about that all had their business north of the river. Because southside carters viewed those on the north with great suspicion, and Bill would have known nothing of their doings. Because when I thought about Bill Carter I thought about Alice, not Kate.

Hannah still had her hands laid on my head.

'Did she go to Bill Carter? Is she alive, Hannah? Is that what you see?'

'How can I know?'

'You saw the future for Frances.'

'I cannot work magic. It's you who saw this man.'

'Kate would have left a message for me if she'd had Bill Carter take her to Canterbury. I know she would have.'

'Maybe she did.'

342

'Is that what I'm thinking or what you know?'

'No magic, Matthew. It's what I'd have done if I'd been her.'

I stayed with her in the forest that night, setting out for London soon after daybreak. The bells of St Botolph's were chiming their midday twelve as I walked through Aldgate. From there to The Bridge and on to Bill Carter.

His yard was empty. Either his business had picked up and his carts were all in use, or he'd fallen on hard times and there was no business. I called his name. A stable boy came to greet me and took me through to a room up new wooden stairs. My wonderings were answered.

'You paid me well, Martin Farnworth. I thank you for that. But I can't take another load to Canterbury. Not for at least another three weeks. Far too much work round here.'

'I don't have work for you. I have a question.'

I described Katherine, and asked whether he'd seen her at the end of last summer, and whether she'd hired him to take her to Kent. He looked at me as if I were laying a trap.

'Did she leave a message with you?'

He shook his head. 'I owe loyalty to all my customers.'

'I'm very glad to hear it. Did she leave a message for Matthew Edgworth?'

'What's it to you?'

'I'm Matthew's cousin.' He didn't look convinced. 'Do you remember the message she gave you?'

He took a deep breath. 'I've told you. I – '

'Or was it in writing? A letter in a sealed envelope?'

'I've nothing more to say.' He'd not have been a good card player. His gaze flickered away, and his Adam's apple bobbled.

I'd hit on something. 'Now, Master Farnworth,' he said. 'If you're not here to hire my services, I have business to attend to.'

'Just tell me one thing before I go. Did you deliver the letter to a Master Weston at The Mermaid?' That had always been how Kate and her mistress got word to me.

'Begone with you, Master Farnworth. I have nothing more to say to you.' But the twitching of his top lip and the shortness of his breath told me what I needed to know.

40
Too many Mermaids

'Have you ever met a Bill Carter?' I asked Weston after a couple of glasses of Canary.

He gave my question some thought, then shook his head. 'No. Don't know any Bill Carter.'

'Works his trade from a yard in Southwark.'

'No.'

'Last summer. Late August, early September. Somebody gave Bill Carter a letter, paid him to deliver it for you to give to me.'

Weston looked quizzical. 'Complicated arrangement.'

'Indeed. But I never received the letter. And I've only just heard about it.'

'I don't know any Bill Carter. Anybody gives me a letter for you, Matthew, I give it you soon as I see you. Lady Frances and that maid who was sweet on you. They're the only ones use me to carry messages for you. Them and Rochester's steward.'

'You've never had dealings with any carters from Southwark?'

'Only dealings I have south of the river are the plays and the bear baiting.'

'And you've heard nothing of Katherine Garnam? Lady Frances's maid.'

He looked at me suspiciously, like I was playing games and trying to catch him out.

'I thought ... Didn't she have that accident on Fleet Bridge?'

I said nothing for a while. He carried on talking – about this and that and nothing very much, but it wasn't the chatter of nerves. If he was lying about Bill Carter and the letter, he was a more skilled deceiver than I'd credited.

'Could it be your man delivered his message to the wrong Richard Weston? A lot of Mermaids in London. The others are all closer to the river than this one. And Weston's a common enough name – for my sins.'

'Most likely,' I said. If I sounded calm, I didn't feel it. Kate could still be alive. She could have gone to Bill Carter, left a message for me to be delivered to Richard Weston at The Mermaid, but didn't know which one. That made sense. Kate had spent her childhood near Audley End and all her adult life as Frances's close companion – except for those few weeks in Chartley. She'd probably never been to any London tavern. She only knew about The Mermaid because I told her that's where I met with Richard Weston. And she wouldn't have wanted to seek me out in person because that would have been too big a risk for both of us. If she had sent me a message it must have gone to the wrong Richard Weston at the wrong Mermaid Inn.

'I like you, Bill Carter. I have the greatest of respect for a man who keeps confidences. But I will not be fobbed off this time. Let me tell you what I think happened. A young woman, Katherine Garnam, comes to you. She asks if Matthew Edgworth still uses your services. You've never heard of Matthew Edgworth. And you tell her so.'

'I've told you, I don't know any Matthew Edgworth. And I don't know Katherine Garnam either.'

'She's quick-witted, and she says she'll pay you to take a letter for Matthew Edgworth, to be delivered to Richard Weston at The Mermaid.'

He looked impassive.

'Is that what happened?'

'I don't know Matthew Edgworth and I don't know Katherine Garnam.'

'But somebody came here, and somebody gave you a message which you took to Richard Weston at The Mermaid.'

Silence.

'You can admit to that. That's not breaking a confidence.'

Still nothing. I described Katherine. 'Did she use a different name?'

He shook his head.

'You are a good man, Bill Carter. An honest man. And I will not hurt you, nor your business. But I beg you, tell me what you can. That message was important. My cousin, Master Edgworth, is sick. That's why he can't come here himself. And he hasn't received the letter that Katherine Garnam promised him she'd write.'

I don't know why he changed his mind. Maybe because the Martin Farnworth who'd paid him to take a family to

Dover had been true to his word. Maybe because Matthew's patter dried up. Or maybe because he saw in my face a sense of true despair, and maybe an honest man responds to honest feelings.

I stood up to leave and was at the door when Carter called out, 'Wait. I'll tell you this. Very few women come in here. A carter's trade isn't women's business. And I'm no messenger boy. It's a while ago, but yes, I do remember. A woman come in here September last year. Not the one you described. She had a letter. Sealed. Said it was for Matthew Edgworth. And I was to take it to Richard Weston, like you said, at The Mermaid.'

'Which Mermaid?'

'I only know the one. Corner of Bread Street and Thames Street. Near Queenhythe Wharf.'

'And that's where you took the letter?'

'Master Weston wasn't there. But the landlord took it for him. Said he'd pass it on.'

'Do you know what was in the letter?' I asked.

'It was sealed. I'd never read a sealed letter addressed to someone else.'

Rafe, the landlord at The Mermaid in Bread Street had squirrelled the letter away in a drawer somewhere and forgotten he'd even received it. He'd long since stopped wondering who Richard Weston might be. But it was addressed to Matthew Edgworth and that's who I said I was, and if he had any doubts about confidentiality, they were eased by the angel I gave him 'For taking such good care of it.'

Rafe was a jovial fellow, and his Mermaid was a great deal more convivial than the one in Paternoster Row. I stayed for a fine fish supper. But I remember little else about my surroundings, for I read the letter while I was eating.

My dear Matthew,

I am dictating this to Anne Forman because I write very slow, and I do not have good spelling. This is in Anne's hand, but the words are my own with Anne's help.

I was knocked from Fleet Bridge by a cart. I thought I would drown. The current was very strong and it took me to the south shore of the river. I was pulled from the mud by a woman close to Paris Gardens. She took me inside. I do not remember much about the place except that it was very noisy. The woman asked me if I knew anyone who could look after me. The only person I knew who lives on that side of the river is Anne Forman. She had been friendly to me when I went with my mistress to see Doctor Forman.

Anne cared for me while I was sick with a fever. Anne says she thought I might die, but she has many good remedies that she learnt from her husband, and she harvests herbs and plants from Doctor Forman's physic garden. She says I was sick for more than three weeks. I do not remember.

I thank the Lord and my dear friend Anne that I have now recovered my strength. I told Anne everything that you told me about the danger we are in, and about Alice too. I had to explain to her because when I regained my health she wanted to take me back to my mistress. I hope you will not be angry with me for telling.

I am safe. And now I am well. Anne said that it would be very dangerous for me to leave her house. I know you are a friend of Richard Weston and I know that you meet him in The Mermaid. And I remember that you told me that Bill Carter is an honest man so Anne will give this letter to Master Carter to deliver.

Anne has a son. He is five years old. His name is Clement. We are all going to leave Lambeth soon. I will go with her. When Anne's father was alive he worked as proctor at the cathedral in Canterbury. She thinks that someone who remembers him will offer us lodgings. She thinks that we will be safer in Canterbury than in Lambeth. The neighbours have accused her of being a witch.

God bless Anne for nursing me back to health and God bless you, Matthew.

Your loving,

Katherine

Those last three words in her own hand.

God bless me indeed, I thought, for my good fortune. And God bless Rafe for holding the letter all those months.

41

Piglets and mischief

I could have made my escape there and then. It would have been easy enough to lay a false trail with Colquhoun, Weston and maybe a few others who worked for Rochester or Frances, then make my own disappearance and follow Kate and Alice down to Canterbury. Instead, I decided to stay in London and finish the business that I'd started.

If I were a playwright I could write the scenes that played out in my head that night. I have all the voices. Most were telling me to go. But the loudest insisted I stay until I'd taken my revenge on Rochester. I'd also need money in my purse when I left London. I wanted to make an honest promise to Kate that I'd put my rogue's life behind me. It was the same mistake I'd coaxed dozens of gulls into making at cards and dice. Just stay a little longer at the table. One more round and you'll not need to come back. So that night I persuaded myself that I was in control – despite my broken hand, despite knowing full well how cunning and ruthless Frances was.

A message came through Weston the next day. Lady Frances wanted to see me again. It was urgent. Anne Turner's place. The same third floor room where Hannah had peered into the scrying mirror and seen her visions. I was there before Frances. Keep us waiting. That's what they do. And I still thought I was in control!

The wall to the right of the door was panelled, but the wood was cracked in several places. Black mould stained the plaster round the window and there was a lingering smell of damp and coal smoke, although no fire had been lit that day. It was an old house, maybe a hundred years old, not much better than many of the places I've lodged. It puzzled me that Frances should spend so much time with a woman like Mistress Turner. I have sometimes wondered what dark secrets lay behind their friendship.

I opened the window and looked out over the nearby roofs. The great bulk of Christ Church loomed not far off to the north. I looked for Saint Olave's. But for a London church it was a trifle, a small thing with no spire. Not unlike Frances's husband if Madam Gossip was to be believed.

I couldn't see Paul's, but I heard the great clock strike twelve. I was taken by surprise when the door opened. Frances had climbed the stairs silently. She was wearing stockinged feet. Was Mistress Turner not to know she was in the house? I bowed. She thanked me for arranging the meeting with Hannah. 'Shut the window, please.' That 'please' a sure a sign of trouble. 'I do not wish us to be overheard.'

She sat down. 'Do you remember Alice?' she was kneading her hands together and whispering, as if speaking her name was dangerous.

I swallowed. Had her spies followed Alice to Canterbury? 'I do, my lady.'

'You thought I didn't know where you found her. But Alice told me so herself. My two days with Alice at Chartley were an education. There is something she talked about.' She stopped, as if wondering whether I was after all to be trusted with what followed. Despite the sounds of hawkers round Paul's, our silence filled the room. Then she lifted her head, half smiled and looked me directly in the eye, those deep blue eyes sharp with steel resolve. 'If… If Alice, were still alive I would ask her to get something for me, but she is no longer with us – so I'm asking you. I will pay you ten pounds now, and double that later. But do not breathe one word to anyone of what I'm about to ask you.'

'I swear you have my silence and discretion, my lady.'

She handed me a purse.

'A Nullity Commission has been convened at Lambeth Palace.'

'I had heard.'

'My husband has admitted that he has been unable to consummate the marriage.'

'I didn't know that.'

'It may be tactful to be ignorant, but this is a time for plain speaking between us. I shall be direct with you. I expect you to be the same with me.' She didn't wait for my response. 'Things get quickly distorted – as much by lawyers as by gossips. The proceedings of the court will all be published, and there is nothing I can do to prevent that, so what I tell you now is for you better to understand exactly what I'm asking and why.'

'Which court, my lady?'

'They call it a commission, but it is effectively a court. And it's me, not my husband who's on trial. But if that's what it takes to get my marriage annulled, so be it. My lawyer's statement to the court was very plain. *The Countess of Essex desirous to be made a mother, yielded herself to her husband many times, and offered herself and her body to be known …. But the Earl could not have copulation in any sort which the married bed alloweth… The Countess of Essex therefore remains virgo intacta…* There. I agreed the wording with my great uncle at the beginning of May, a week before the Commission was convened. I learnt it and I have it pat. You will no doubt be able to read it all in street corner pamphlets in due course. But you have it from me first.

'When they called me to the court – the Nullity Commission – at Lambeth Palace I wasn't even permitted to read my own statement aloud. The Archbishop, three bishops, six lawyers. Ten commissioners sitting in judgement. No seat for me. I had to stand while my statement was read aloud by a clerk. They glared at me as if I were in the dock, and my own statement became an arraignment against me. A clerk, a jaundiced, pock-ridden, lank-haired clerk declared to the court that *The Countess of Essex asserts that she knew nothing of the Earl's impediment before the marriage. She is, however, fit and able to have copulation with a man…* My uncle insisted on including that clause.'

Frances glared at me, as if daring me to damn her as so many others had. Only a true aristocrat could have been so forthright.

'I heard a little of the proceedings, my lady.' Something of an understatement. The street corner gossips were full of it – the Countess of Essex had declared herself fit to fuck.

'So now we come to the crux of the matter. My husband has cast doubt on my virgin state. I therefore decided to take matters into my own hands. I proposed to the Commission that I submit to an inspection by matrons and midwives of the commission's choosing.'

She would never have spoken like that to her servants, nor to her friends. This made me at once the privileged confidant and something quite other. It was safe because I was barely human. I was lower than a dog.

'In the language of the court, Matthew Edgworth, I have to prove that I am *virgo intacta*. But I cannot leave the findings of the midwives and matrons to chance. Alice told me things that no other woman has ever spoken about to me.'

She stared at me, daring me to look shocked.

'Alice told me about the market in young virgins at The Vixen and the stews of Southwark. I am not so innocent that I found that shocking. What I didn't know is that some young girls, who are indeed *virgo intacta*, do not bleed when first penetrated.' She looked away, as if trying to shield herself from the connection she was making between herself and those girls in The Vixen.

'The bawd at The Vixen taught Alice the trickery of such places. She didn't want to speak of it. I insisted she did. Knowledge is power, Matthew Edgworth.' And dangerous too, I thought.

'Do you know what I'm talking about?'

'Alice never shared her tricks with me, but yes, my lady.'

I'd learnt the secret she was talking about from the bawd when I was the Boy at the Cardinal's Hat. Soak a piglet's bladder in strong water for a minute or two, then wash it clean. The acid makes the bladder delicate, the skin then tears when lightly prodded. And out pours the blood. Leave it in acid too long and it ruptures too soon. Not long enough, the blood stays safe within – which defeats the purpose. At the Cardinal's Hat I learnt to get it just right. With a little careful schooling, a girl could work in the stews for several weeks, and still be sold dear as a virgin.

I assured Frances I knew what was required. I got to my feet, bowed and was about to leave, when she raised a hand to stop me. She seemed to be considering how to broach whatever was on her mind. Was there something more troubling than the virginity test?

'You did well finding Hannah, and bringing her here. I didn't thank you at the time. I do now. I am most grateful. You have been very resourceful.'

'Thank you, my lady.'

'You and I had a conversation at The Crown at Wells. You promised me then that you would do whatever I asked of you. You remember that?'

'I do. Yes.'

'I want advice, Matthew Edgworth. There is a man imprisoned in The Tower for treason. A former friend of Viscount Rochester.'

'Sir Thomas Overbury?'

'He is supposed to be a close prisoner. No letters in, no letters out. He is there on a charge of treason. The King offered him a post as his ambassador to the Grand Duchy of Muscovy. He turned it down. He offended the King. He has also offended me. Even in the Tower he maligns and libels me. Can you read, Edgworth?'

She knew very well I could read. She often summoned me by letter. 'Not Latin or Greek, but English. Yes.'

'Have you read any of that mean-minded, scurrilous poem of Overbury's, *The Wife*?'

'No, my lady.' An outright lie. You only had to walk twenty yards from Mistress Turner's house to find one of the Paul's pamphleteers flogging a copy for threepence. I disliked Overbury's puritanism, but the poem made me laugh. Made most people laugh. And everyone knew it was about her and Rochester.

'Overbury is insufferable,' she said.

I nodded agreement.

'And so the advice I seek is this. How can we …' That 'we' was carefully chosen. 'How can we prevent these outpourings of his libellous bile?'

I did my best to give the impression I was giving fresh thought to the 'Overbury problem.' Tentatively, I suggested, 'My understanding is that your uncle, the Earl of Northampton has the ear of the King – '

'My great uncle. He's already had the Lieutenant of the Tower dismissed and his own man appointed in his place. He's supposed to be allowed no correspondence except with Viscount Rochester. Yet Overbury's bile still leaks out.'

'If you and the Earl of Northampton are on good terms, might I suggest, if I might be so bold – '

'To the point, Edgworth.'

'That you ask him to have Overbury's jailer dismissed as well. And someone of your choosing appointed in his place.'

She laughed. 'You are nothing if not bold, Matthew. Should I suggest you take the jailer's place?'

'I work for Viscount Rochester. A jailer has to take residence in The Tower. That would prevent me from serving my master. That wouldn't please him.'

She gave a wry smile. 'So who would you recommend?'

I pretended to give this some thought. 'Perhaps... Richard Weston? Anne Turner's man.'

After due consideration, 'Yes. Yes, indeed.'

Frances was more cunning than any of her sex I've even known. She never once said she wanted Overbury dead. And she knew better than to remind me that she'd hinted at Overbury's involvement in the 'accident' that befell Katherine. Instead, she asked my advice to put a stop his libels. But she and I both knew what she was asking.

I knew about Frances changing places with Alice. I knew about her consultations with Forman and Cunning Hannah. I knew what she planned to do at her virginity test with the midwives and matrons. And now she wanted Overbury silenced. As soon as she had what she wanted from me I'd be more vulnerable than ever. But I blocked my ears to the alarm bells that were ringing. The letter from Kate had buoyed me up, given me a strange confidence that I could make my own disappearance at a time of my own choosing.

Easy enough to obtain and treat the bladders. The problem was making sure the blood was fresh and warm. She wouldn't want it to clot before she put it to use. I went to John Butcher of Cheapside.

For the first delivery we met again in the room at Anne Turner's. I assumed that first was for practice. A couple of days later Richard Weston brought me a sealed letter.

30th May. Noon. Whitehall Palace. King Street gate.
Bring a fresh nosegay.

The Countess of Essex, as she then still was, arrived at the Palace in a grand carriage, accompanied by her new maid. As she stepped down from the carriage, Sir Haughty Disdaine, that elegantly dressed young gallant, stepped forward, made a deep bow, then offered a small bouquet of flowers.

'A token of my deep respect and admiration,' he said.

The maid tried to take the flowers, accusing the gallant of insolence. She would have thrown the flowers into the gutter and sent the fellow away if the Countess had herself hadn't intervened.

'A stranger offers me kindness,' she snapped to the maid. 'He understands what it seems you don't, that being sent to trial to prove my own suffering is deeply distressing. Leave me. I have no need for you here.'

The maid seemed close to tears. The mistress accepted the bouquet, and held it to her nose, looking carefully to see what delicate flowers it contained. She sniffed it, and smiled.

Puddings and tarts are not the only delicacies that can conceal a little mischief.

42

Quince tarts and stage tricks

All very well having debts to call in, but once debtors get wind of a weakness, every debt becomes a grievance. In the world I live in, grievances get settled sooner than debts. I was wearing gloves all the time in company. But word was getting out about my damaged hand. I'd once been a master of disguise, but what used to take me an hour of preparation was taking half a day. How could I call myself a picklock when I was defeated by anything a master locksmith had fitted in the last five years? I could hold a dagger in my right hand, but had no strength in my left. As for gaming and cards, there's nothing like an infirmity to make an honest man of you.

Finding my way into the kitchens of Overbury's house on The Strand was one thing. Quite something else getting access to The Tower. And I couldn't ask Weston to deliver quince tarts for his prisoner. I didn't want to be connected with Overbury, directly or indirectly.

I needed a courier. It had to be someone well-known to Rochester and Overbury, someone that Overbury himself would trust, someone who would be linked to Rochester but not to me when the investigations started. Now Jack the Lad was not that someone, but he might well know who was.

He'd got himself work as the Boy of the House at The Three Pigeons, a better class of bawdy house in Brainford. Following my advice, and following in my footsteps. Doing well for himself, was Jack.

'I don't owe you nothing,' he squeaked when he realised who he was talking to.

'You don't owe money, but you do owe a favour. And listen to what I say, young Jack, because the jailer at Newgate has every constable in London on the lookout for you.'

I wanted the name of a household servant who was well liked by Overbury and Rochester.

'Lawrence Davies. Always full of it when Rochester comes. Grinning after he's gone. He gives him little tips, you know what I mean.' I did. I knew exactly what he meant. And the name Davies was familiar from the intelligence I'd undertaken for Rochester. I suspect Rochester had been using him as a spy within the Overbury house. Perfect for my purposes. I thanked Jack and gave him a few coins.

I dressed myself in courtier's clothes, powdered my face and wore gloves. Then I called at the Overbury household and asked to speak to Master Davies. I told him I was in the service of Viscount Rochester and that my master wanted a letter delivered to Sir Thomas in The Tower. Davies looked suspicious.

'Rochester told me that Sir Thomas thinks highly of you.' He was still wary. 'The thing is this. My master and yours had a falling out. Viscount Rochester wants to make amends, but he imagines that your Sir Thomas won't open the letter if it's delivered by one of Rochester's servants. Which is why he thought it best to ask you.'

'Your master wants me to deliver a letter to Sir Thomas in the Tower?'

'He will pay you well for your trouble.'

We agreed to meet at the King's Head in Fenchurch Street, just ten minutes' walk from the West Gate of The Tower. I had a small purse for him, and a carefully wrapped package.

'I thought you said a letter.'

'I thought so too. But my master changed his mind. A small gift on this occasion. Be sure to tell him who it's from. If the jailer asks questions, tell him it's a gift from Viscount Rochester. Be sure to tell him that. And anyone else who asks.'

Later that day we met again. Davies reported that Sir Thomas was delighted. 'He unwrapped it while I was there. He said he hoped to savour it with his dinner.'

I hoped so too. But there was no poison with the quince on this occasion. I needed to be certain the tart got as far as Overbury. I had no quarrel with Richard Weston, and didn't want him snaffling it for himself.

I left it a week before having another batch of tarts baked. If a man in Overbury's predicament has a fondness for a delicacy, then I say let him have it. It's surely an act of human kindness to grant some relief from the bleakness of a prison cell. I wrapped another tart in waxed cloth – this, too, in its virgin state, untainted with poison – and gave it to Davies. The report came back from Weston that his prisoner had much enjoyed some gifts he'd received from Rochester.

No indication that Weston knew I had any connection with Davies or the tarts. If Davies were ever questioned about the tarts, he'd talk about a smooth-faced courtier in the employ of Viscount Rochester.

Knowing the tarts would be delivered safely, I prepared the rest with poison, confident that they'd get to Overbury.

I met regularly with Richard Weston in the King's Head whenever he could take time off from his duties in The Tower. Weston was more interested in talking about the Nullity trial than his prisoner. I'd thought it would all be over once the matrons and midwives declared Frances a virgin – but you couldn't cross the Thames without every wherryman bending your ear with theories about her virginity, though I never once heard mention of piglets. As the trial rumbled on, the tattle surrounding it grew ever more scandalous. I didn't envy the maid who'd taken Kate's place and would be suffering Frances's temper.

I was ready to send in the first of the poisoned tarts, when Weston asked me, 'Did you ever go to Overbury's house for Rochester?'

'The steward, Colquhoun, went often enough. But I had no cause to. Why do you ask?'

'You never had dealings with a Lawrence Davies?'

'No,' I said.

'He's a Welshman.'

'I don't know him. Why do you ask?'

'Davies first came in a month or so ago. Brought a couple of tarts for Overbury. Gifts from Rochester. Now he's in at least twice a week. Tarts, pies, sweetmeats, allsorts. And letters. Letters between Overbury and Rochester.'

'I thought he was a close prisoner,' I said. 'No correspondence allowed.'

'Except with Viscount Rochester. Special instructions from The Lieutenant of the Tower.'

'Have you been corrupted, Master Weston?' We both laughed.

'I do as I'm told,' he said. But the twitch of an eyebrow told me he was doing well with bribes.

'And how's Sir Thomas coping with imprisonment?'

'Ailing, I fear. Not well at all. But in good spirits for a man so sick. Says Rochester's been a very good friend, and even though they've had their differences they've settled all that. He reckons Rochester's been using his influence with the King, and he'll soon be released.'

'Really?'

'Could well be true. The king's own surgeon's been to visit. De Mayerne. A Frenchie. Strange fellow. Strange remedies. But I'm sure he knows best.' Same way he knew best with Prince Henry, I thought.

'Ah well, good luck to him,' I said.

And good luck to me, I thought. Because by then it had dawned on me that when Overbury died, which he surely would, it wouldn't be my doing. But I was going to be blamed for it. I wasn't the only one who wanted the end of Overbury. And far from me setting up Rochester for a fall, I was going to be the one who'd hang for it.

Frances had been playing me from the first, using most of the tricks I used. From the moment she came to my room at The Crown in Wells, she'd wanted to convince me that I was special, that I was the only one she trusted with her most dangerous assignments. She thought me reliable, ingenious, resourceful, cunning. She even told me that I intrigued her. And I congratulated myself on assuming that because I had the wit to realise she was playing me I could somehow remain untouched by her charms. She'd cast Katherine as the bait, and slowly reeled me in. And I'd swum willingly into her net. But there was fight in Matthew Edgworth yet.

I reckoned I'd be safe so long as Overbury still lived. But I didn't have long. I'd surely be arrested within hours of his death. And then, no doubt at all, an accident would befall me in Newgate before my case came to trial.

Time to contact Gervase Chapman.

I made my way to The Phoenix in Lombard Street and asked the ale-wife if I could speak to Richard Bowden, the landlord.

'Died six months since. This place is mine.'

'I'm sorry to hear – '

'Don't lie to me,' she snapped.

'May I speak with you alone?'

'My daughter will entertain you sir, if that's what you require.'

'It's you I need to speak to.'

'Don't run a tavern to stand here and chatter.'

A small crowd was gathering, enjoying this stranger's discomfort. I asked for a pint of double beer.

'Penny ha'penny.' She held out her hand for payment. I tendered a groat, waved away the change, and met her look. 'I need to talk to the landlord. If that's you, Widow Bowden, then so be it.'

'Talk then, stranger.'

'In private.'

She considered the groat, then called for a maid to take her place. She led me down an unlit, narrow corridor to a small room at the back. I told her that it was Gervase Chapman I needed to see.

'Hundreds of men drink here. You think I know all their names?'

'Did your husband know him?'

'My husband got his throat slit for asking questions. So I don't ask names.'

'I was told I'd find Gervase Chapman here.'

'And I don't hear 'em either. That way I don't have to forget 'em.'

I wasn't done yet. I went back to the tavern and joined a game of dice. The glove on my left hand raised suspicions. I said I'd been bitten by a dog. By the end of the week I was no longer an object of such curiosity. But Gervase Chapman was never mentioned. So I took up Widow Bowden's offer of entertainment with the daughter.

The little penthouse room had but one small, shuttered window. The only light came from the small lantern that Nelly Bowden hung from a hook on a beam. I chattered mindlessly in the way that some men do when they secretly fear the pleasures of the flesh. I asked her about Michael and Wilfred and Barnaby. Names of men I'd played dice with downstairs. Did they amuse her? Did they keep her busy for their allotted time? She humoured me, doing her best to raise my interest with babbling talk and fluttering tongue.

'And Gervase Chapman? How was he?'

'Don't know nobody of that name.' But her look suggested otherwise.

'When next you see Gervase Chapman, tell him that he and I have a friend in common. Amos Appleby from Sherborne in Dorsetshire. And I have something from Master Appleby that will be of great interest to Master Chapman.'

'Never spoke to no Gervase Chapman.'

'But you will, Nelly Bowden. Won't you. You will get word to him. Tell him that Matthew Edgworth would like to meet him.'

I returned to The Phoenix every day, with one of Rochester's letters hidden in a secret pocket, one of the letters I'd taken from the Forman house. A week later, a lean man with jaundiced complexion and more hair on his chin than his pate called me over and asked if I wanted to join him and two others in a game. They called him Nate. We'd played three hands when Bald Nate proposed moving to a room at the back reserved for gaming. It reeked of cozenage. It was a risk I had to take.

The room was bare, except for a table and four chairs. We took our seats. A maid brought in a jug of Canary wine, four cups and a large trencher with bread and cheese to share between us. We drank each other's health, and agreed the stakes.

After several rounds, Nate left the room to 'visit the privy'. He returned with a man I'd not seen before. He looked Spanish, with black hair, dark brown eyes and tidy beard, but he spoke the English of a nobleman, and his clothes implied he was a man of wealth.

One of the players gave up his seat. Nate locked and bolted the door. Four of them. One of me.

'You have something of interest to Gervase Chapman?' said the Spanish looking fellow.

'I do indeed,' I said. 'And I would speak with him alone.'

Nate pulled a knife from beneath his doublet. The other two followed his example. Three men with knives. The new arrival stayed sitting, looking at me directly. I lifted my hands from the table in surrender.

'And what is it you wish to speak of?' said Chapman, for it had to be him.

'Stand up,' said Nate before I could answer.

I did as he said.

'You have a knife?' said Chapman.

'I do.'

'Hands high,' said Nate.

'One on my belt and one in my boot,' I said. 'Take your pick.'

'Take them,' said Chapman.

I let Nate take both knives. He gave one to Chapman and tucked the other in his own belt. Chapman held the stiletto before him as if he were a Roman priest with a crucifix. He pursed his lips and nodded, recognising quality when he saw it. Nate and his cronies were on edge. They suspected a trick. I let them search me. If they'd smelt fear or hostility, I'd have met my end.

Chapman waited til they'd finished. Then spoke quietly, 'What is so important that you risk your life to find me?'

'If you and I are to talk, it has to be alone.'

He dismissed Nate and the others, although I knew they'd be just outside the door.

'You're late, Master Edgworth – if that's your real name. I

was expecting you months ago. Appleby sent word that you wanted to make contact.'

'I'm surprised he remembered who I was. Last time I saw him he could barely remember his own name, let alone mine. He is not so simple as he seems.'

Chapman wanted to know why I was offering my services to Ralegh's faction. I could have said that I wanted to right the injustice of good Sir Walter Ralegh imprisoned in the Tower. But Chapman wouldn't have believed me.

So I told him straight. 'I had to bide my time. Being the servant of two masters is the stuff of plays. I used to work for Rochester. Now I don't. He has wronged me, and I'm done with him. I want to bring him down. What I have for you will destroy him. If that speeds the release of Ralegh, so be it.'

'What is it you have for me?'

I gave him a letter from Rochester to Forman. Chapman read it carefully. 'This will indeed create a scandal,' he said. 'Rochester and his mistress visiting Doctor Forman. The court thrives on scandal. But so does Rochester. It will hardly ruin him.'

'I offer it as my letter of introduction. Proof I can deliver what I say. Meet me here again two days from now, and I will bring you evidence that will take Rochester to the executioner's block on Tower Hill.'

In the meantime, I sent a letter to Frances assuring her that the task she had set me would very soon be completed. I wanted her to believe that I thought myself wholly responsible for Overbury's failing health. I would have sought a meeting with her in person, but I didn't trust myself to conceal the rage I felt about Katherine's 'accident', for I was now certain that Frances was complicit in that.

I was at Mountjoy's place early the next morning. The Frenchie was in his workshop. As he recognised my face the colour drained from his. He led me straightway to the private room where he met with special clients.

'I have an urgent commission for you, Mountjoy.'

'I have already too much work. The ladies of court, they have returned to London, and they are all impatient – '

'You're a busy man.'

'*C'est impossible.* I cannot agree new work.'

'You're a fine craftsman, Mountjoy. That's why your services are in such demand. I understand you sometimes make devices for the King's Men.'

'*Mon enterprise* is to make tiaras and periwigs. And *parfois je fais… Pardon. Pardon.* Sometimes I make some costumes for the masques of the court.'

'Believe me, Mountjoy, I am far less patient than any court lady. So stop your whimpering and listen. I know you sometimes make devices for the King's Men.'

'Devices? *Je ne comprends pas.* I know not what you mean.'

'Devices, stage properties, actors' toys, call them what you will. But I know you make them. I have friends who are actors. They think very highly of you.'

'*Qu'est-ce que vous voulez?*'

'A stage knife.'

'You have a stiletto. You show me before.'

'Then I don't need to show you again. But I will if I have to. I want a stage knife. It's different.'

'*C'est impossible.*'

A knock at the door. I stood in Mountjoy's way and opened it myself – just a few inches. A prentice boy had a letter to hand.

I waved him off. 'Master Mountjoy is busy. He must not be disturbed.' I shut the door, but not before the acrid stench of glue and vapours of strong water came seeping through. I gagged. My eyes watered. I bolted the door.

'A stage knife,' I said. 'You know exactly what I mean. How long will it take to make one for me?'

'*C'est impossible. J'ai une commande*, a commission from the Princess Elizabeth.'

'Answer me. How long? To make a stage knife.'

He sniffed. Maybe the vapours were affecting him too. 'A week. *Peut-être* ten days. But it is impossible for me.'

'Impossible is not a word I ever want to hear again. French, English, no matter. Never again. You understand? I need a stage knife, Mountjoy.'

'*Ce n'est pas –* '

'It is. It is possible. Because I stay here. Day and night. Until it's ready. Do you understand?'

'*Oui. Je comprends. Mais –* '

'You do understand. That's good.'

He sat down at his desk, pulled out a drawer, removed a small parcel. He unfolded the leather wrapping to reveal an English dagger in the old style. 'Monsieur Burbage himself, he bring this to me for to repair.'

'Ahh. Richard Burbage of the King's Men?'

He nodded.

The blade glinted in the shaft of morning sunlight that fell on Mountjoy's desk. 'Let me see.'

He handed me the knife. I remembered what Henry Condell, an actor friend, had once told me. For the illusion to work, the hilt and handle have to be as solid as any fighting knife, the blade must be real. During the play, the actor shows the audience how sharp it is by creating some stage business and slashing through parchment or cloth. And then, when the time comes for the bloodbath at the end of the play, the actor moves a hidden lever, and the blade retracts into the grip.

'I'll take that. Make a new one for Burbage. I will pay you well.' I reached for my purse.

'*Non*. You cannot take this. It is not safe.'

I slid the blade slowly in and out. 'Looks safe to me.'

'*Non, non, non.*' When a man spends most of his life wearing a curmudgeonly scowl, his face rarely gives much away. But he was nervous. 'I have need to make it good.'

'How much will you charge to make it good?'

'To me please.' He held out his hand. 'I show you.'

He took the knife in his fist, stuck it hard into the desktop and left it there, quivering. Condell's words of warning: 'Actors are wary of those knives. If the blade jams and doesn't retract, they're as murderous as any stiletto.'

'See. It is not safe.'

'How long will it take you to make it safe?'

'I have to make the costume – '

'For Princess Elizabeth. I know. But I'm here, Mountjoy. And she's not. And I'm not leaving until you make it safe.'

'Do you want blood?'

I laughed. 'Do I want blood?! Not yours, Mountjoy. Not unless you deny me what I ask.'

'Blood for when you use the knife.'

'Ahh, yes. Yes, I do indeed. I need to feign a death.'

'Then I will make the adjustment. The blade will … pull back into the … *le manche du poignard…*'

'The handle of the dagger?'

'*Exactement*. Except for one half of one inch.'

'I understand. And that half inch is enough to puncture the pig's bladder filled with fresh blood, but not the skin beneath.'

'*Très bon*. You do understand.'

He worked at it until we were both satisfied that the blade would slide smoothly back into the grip, however hard it was thrust. It took him the rest of morning. He's a very skilled craftsman and works fast when he has to. I paid him well. I don't think I could ever grow to like Mountjoy, but I was beginning to respect him.

I sought out Colquhoun. He met me at The White Hart in Drury Lane.

'I have to speak to Viscount Rochester. It's a matter of great urgency.'

'D'ye imagine he's at yer beck and call?'

'Tell him I have news about Overbury's death. He'll want to talk to me then.'

Colquhoun chuckled. 'D'ye plan to blackmail him?'

'No, my friend. I plan to kill him.'

Colquhoun seemed more amused than shocked by this. He cocked his head to one side, waiting for more.

'To kill him before he has me killed. And you'll be next. You or Bradshaw.'

'He'll have nae need to kill Bradshaw. Poor fellow. He tripped while running down the stone stairs in the stable block. He cracked his head and broke his neck.'

'Bradshaw was never in a hurry.'

'He was in a hurry to get to the bottom of those stairs.'

I'd been half expecting it, but I still felt a sudden shock of nausea. Bradshaw was as innocent as Kate. He'd only ever done as he was bidden.

'There's a list, my friend. Five names on it. The first three have already been crossed out. Alice, Katherine Garnam, Bradshaw. You and me are next.'

'I can look after myself.'

'I don't doubt it, but if our dear lord and master owes his life to you, that might give you a little longer.'

He laughed.

'You think I jest?'

'Ye're a dark horse Edgworth. I'll ha' nowt to do wi' killing.'

But he was intrigued. We talked some more. Eventually he agreed to the plan and accepted the little bauble Mountjoy had made for me. I showed him how to use it. It made him smile.

'A canny toy,' he said.

'You not seen one before?'

'When I use a knife, I mean it to hurt.'

'You never been to The Globe or The Blackfriars?'

He shook his head, and grunted disapproval. Colquhoun was a puritan in all but name. He'd have had the theatres all shut down.

'A shame,' I said. 'There is much to be learnt in theatres.'

That same evening, I went back to The Phoenix. Bald Nate was expecting me. He took a break from his game at the table by the fire, and set off down Lombard Street. An hour or so later he reappeared, and waved me through to the private gaming room. Gervase Chapman arrived soon after. Nate left us alone.

'I believe you have something for me,' said Chapman.

I laid the small clay effigy on the table. Chapman held it to the light.

'The Earl of Essex if I'm not mistaken.'

'I took it from the Forman house. It was Rochester commanded the sympathetic magic.' I pointed to the pin stuck through the little fellow's bollocks.

'Painful.'

'I thought you might be able to use it in evidence against Rochester.'

'The figurine's amusing and damning of Doctor Forman, but without proof of connection to Rochester, it's merely an amusing ornament.' Gervase Chapman was a man of plain speaking. I like that in a man.

I gave him two letters taken from the Forman house. 'From Rochester to Forman. In this he commissions it. And this refers to payment.'

He read them slowly, a smile gradually lifting the corners of his mouth. 'Excellent. Our good King James abhors anything that reeks of sorcery. When this comes to his attention, Rochester will surely fall from favour.'

From the floor below came a sudden roaring. Another game of cards ending in a brawl.

'I have one more letter that might be of interest. From the Countess of Essex to Doctor Forman.'

He hesitated before taking it, as if he didn't want his opinion of Frances soiled. His face fell as he read.

'Before reading this I had thought her much maligned,' he said. I guessed he too had once been charmed by her.

'And your price for these?' said Chapman, quickly

returning to the business in hand. 'You don't strike me as a man who sells things cheap.'

'Indeed I'm not. They're priceless. I want no money. But swear to me you'll use what I've given you to destroy Rochester. That's all I ask. Think of it as a parting gift from a man who may not have much longer.'

'Are you sick?' He looked worried, as if by shaking hands I'd just given him the plague.

'Not sick, no. But I am in great danger. And if I survive the next few days, I shall have to leave London. Whether I live or die, you'll not see me again. And there is something else, Master Chapman. Even better for Ralegh's faction than what I've just given you. Had you heard that Sir Thomas Overbury is very sick?'

'I had indeed. Poor man.'

'He's being poisoned. I can give you another name, Lawrence Davies. A servant in the Overbury household. He's been taking poison to Overbury on Rochester's instructions. Have him arrested and follow the trail, and you'll have Rochester take Ralegh's place in the Tower.'

We spoke no more about Frances, but that third letter was from her to Forman thanking him for potions he'd made to deny her husband his potency. When Rochester fell, he'd take Frances down with him. I was already picturing the day.

Chapman took my hand and shook it warmly. 'I thank you, Master Edgworth. Thank you indeed. I must warn you, though, that we will have to bide our time. Rochester's star is still rising. It seems likely that the Countess will be granted her annulment, and if that happens, she and Rochester will want to marry – which they will surely do, and with the King's blessing.

There are eminent men in court who despise Rochester. None more so than Sir Ralph Winwood. But Winwood is a politician and a pragmatist. He and others will try to buy favours with lavish wedding gifts. The happy couple will be grateful. But Rochester will soon forget their generosity. That will be the time to start whispering in ears, when generosity turns to grievance. The more lavish the gifts, the greater the grievance.'

So now the plan was complete. I go to the Cope Castle stables. I attack Rochester. Colquhoun saves our master by stabbing me with the stage-dagger. Rochester watches me bleed to death, then orders Colquhoun to dispose of the body. While Rochester thanks the Lord for his fortunate escape, Colquhoun assists me with mine. And in the months after the wedding, Gervase Chapman casts his net. Rochester and Frances are both arrested. Accused of Overbury's murder and commissioning Doctor Forman in the most hideous sorcery. All titles stripped from him. All property confiscated. He loses Frances. He loses Sherborne. The King throws off his favourite. Rochester is shamed, destroyed, humiliated. Then publicly hanged at Tyburn. He's even denied a private execution on Tower Green – that's for nobility, not for common murderers.

The pity of it is …

43

His master's saviour

… It seems I'm dead. It's not the way I'd choose to be. But there comes a time when you have no choice in the matter.

I'm there in the stable block long before Rochester. I light the fire in the grate. He's told Colquhoun he'll meet me at noon. Colquhoun's early. I give him the stage dagger, and remind him what we'd planned. I show him again how it works.

Rochester's late. Heavy boots on wooden stairs. The door flies open. Rochester out of breath and angry. And surprised to see Colquhoun, who gives a small bow. Always the good steward.

'I dinnae trust Master Edgworth,' says Colquhoun. 'If ye ha' nae objection, my Lord, I will stay to ensure your safety.'

I'm standing with my back to the fire. Colquhoun a yard or so away. I don't wait for Rochester to respond. No point in starting with pleasantries. When the business to be done is my own death, 'twere best it be done quickly, so Rochester will remember all happening in the passion of the moment. And Colquhoun won't have time to get stage fright.

'Did you ever meet Lady Frances's maid, Katherine?' I ask.

'How dare you address me like that! You think I've come here to answer to you?'

I pull my stiletto and have the point on his windpipe. My real stiletto, with honed point and honest blade.

'It might be wise to answer.'

I enjoy that look of terror on his face. I ask again.

'Katherine Garnam. What happened? Who drove the cart that knocked her from Fleet Bridge?'

His expression's changed. This is more than abject terror. He knows about the cart. It was indeed him who commissioned Kate's murder.

Time slowing, as it did in Forman's workshop with the scrying mirror. Does that mean I'm close to a real death? Such a clever plan. Except I'd not reckoned on the heat of my own rage. I want to kill him there and then. I want to watch him bleed to death. Even if it means I'm hanged for murder.

'Colquhoun,' squeals Rochester.

'Don't move, Colquhoun. Stay back.' My dagger still on Rochester's throat. First blood trickling from a graze. Not good that. It means my hand's shaking. 'Who did you pay to kill her?'

Colquhoun's worried. He sees my rage is real. He rushes forward. Knocks the stiletto from my hand. Throws himself at me, plunging the stage-dagger into my chest.

I feel a sudden searing pain. Time very slow now. I remember Mountjoy's words of warning. I remember what Henry Condell told me. Actors are wary of stage-daggers. They're dangerous toys. They don't always work as they should.

Blood spurting through the gash in my doublet. I fall gasping to the floor. Colquhoun crouched over me. Blood bubbling from my mouth.

Rochester stumbles back against the wall. Falls to his haunches as if he's the one who's injured.

'Katherine,' I whisper, in a voice as faint as feathers, but loud enough for Rochester to hear.

'Finish him off,' says Rochester.

Colquhoun bends over me, takes hold of my wrist, feels for a pulse. 'He is already dead, my lord. I fear I had no choice.'

'You did well,' says Rochester. 'The body must be disposed of. You never met an Edgworth. I never had dealings with a man of that name You understand?'

So that's that. I no longer exist. Now Colquhoun has the task of ensuring I never did.

'Get rid of the body, Colquhoun. And clean this floor.'

A body. My body, lying in a pool of blood. Head flopped to one side.

If he had his wits about him Rochester would see what I can see. The blood's the wrong colour. Too dark. Thickening already. Flowing too slow. But his voice is trembling. He's not looking at the floor. That could have been his blood. He can't bear to look at the corpse of his would-be killer. He wants to escape. Get away from this place while he can, for if Matthew Edgworth, such a loyal and trusted servant, can turn against him, where will the next attempt on his life come from?

Colquhoun covers my body with a cape. That's what we agreed. Boots clumping on wood. Rochester leaving the room. The door slams shut.

'Is he coming back?' I say. It hurts to speak.

'He cannae bear the sight of blood.'

'He's lucky it's not his own.'

I try to throw off the cloak Colquhoun's used to cover me. Nothing fake about the searing pain in my chest. I can't stop myself from crying out. Like I've been kicked by a mule.

Colquhoun standing by the single window, looking out onto the yard below, where Rochester is barking orders. He scurried down those stairs quicker than a rat. Hooves clattering on cobbles. Back to his nest in Greenwich Palace, lined with royal favours. Much safer there, in the company of his beloved King James. A narrow escape like the one he's just had makes a man see danger even where there is none. But for Rochester there's plenty. Danger wherever he tries to hide. And he can't spend the rest of his life locked away from trouble. Royal grace and favour turns sour quicker than milk in midsummer.

'Rochester will nae be back today,' says Colquhoun, turning round. 'Ye can get up now.'

'I can't. I'm hurt. I told you we should have rehearsed.'

He stares at me, glowering. What does he have to be so angry about? He's his master's saviour, and he just earnt himself a special place in his master's affections.

'Ye think I ha' time for your damned play acting? Ye're nae better than him. Always complaining. I did as ye instructed. You're nae dead. And he thinks ye are. What more d'ye want? You're a bloody mess Matthew Edgworth. And you'll nay get out of here wi'out ma help. I'll get ye a mop and a pail o' water. And when I come back, you'll scrub the damned floor.' And with that he leaves, locking the door behind him.

My stiletto lies where it fell. Just reaching for it makes me gasp. I undo the buttons of my doublet, remove the pig's bladder which I'd filled with fresh blood earlier, and feel round the undershirt. It's bloody, but not torn. The knife hasn't penetrated. But when I press my chest it's agony. I spit out the small bladder of blood I had in my mouth.

I'd spent hours oiling and checking the mechanism, ensuring the blade would retract all but that small half inch needed to puncture the bladder. The knife did what it should. But Colquhoun's lunge has cracked a rib.

He's been gone too long. If he comes back with a groom and stable hands, I stand no chance. I can barely get to my feet unaided. If he decides to turn my counterfeit death into a real one, he'll have witnesses when he disposes of my corpse.

A heavy wooden door banging shut somewhere in the stables down below. Boots on wooden stairs. I stay where I am, sitting on the floor, surrounded by drying blood. In my present state, cold reasoning and warm persuasion will serve me better than a blade.

A key in the lock. The door flies open. Colquhoun's alone. He stands still for a moment. Sees I've hardly moved. He turns back and brings in the pail of water, mop and brush.

'Ye're still here,' says Colquhoun.

'You were right. I can't leave here without your help.'

He glares at me, saying nothing.

'And I will clean up. I owe it to you.' He looks suspicious. The Matthew Edgworth he knows isn't the kind of man to play the scullery maid.

'Here, Alex. Help me to my feet. Getting killed's more painful than I expected.'

He looks at me like this must be another trick.

'I'm grateful to you,' I say. 'You did well.'

'I only did what ye said. I did nae mean ye no harm.'

'I know. My first time too. When it came to dying, I was a virgin.' He chuckles at that and offers me his hand. I grimace and hold back a cry. It's breathing deep that hurts so much, and bending to either side. And as he and I both struggle to get me to my feet, I see that for him this counterfeit killing has been a mark of rare friendship. But he allowed me to persuade him to deceive his master. And the deception troubles him. That's why he was angry. He's said many things when drunk that reeked of deep resentment against Rochester, but that doesn't count as disloyalty in his mind because he never remembers in the morning. Steadfast loyalty, the one quality he's truly proud of. A man who needs to live by certainties. In the end, he'll always do as bidden. And obedience will surely be his downfall.

I drop back to my knees and start scrubbing the floor. He stands there watching for a while, and then, to my amazement, he gets down with me and helps.

'Where will ye go?' he says, sounding almost rueful.

'I shall walk to Winchester. Money to be made in Winchester. But I shan't stay long. From there to Exeter. As far from London as I can.'

We waited til midnight, then Colquhoun helped me make my way to a gardener's gate in the estate wall. I needed to be well away from Cope Castle by sunrise.

Breathing was painful, but I could walk. I was on my way from London with half a moon for company.

I had no intention of going anywhere near Winchester, nor Exeter come to that. But when Colquhoun next fell into his cups, and he let slip what happened that afternoon in the stables at Cope Castle, his careless indiscretion would lead Rochester's thugs away from Canterbury, where sweet Kate would surely be waiting for me.

44

Epilogue

On the 15th of September 1613, in the room where he was being held as a close prisoner in the Tower of London, Sir Thomas Overbury died in great pain. He had been coughing and vomiting for days.

On Tuesday the 24th of September 1613, in the great hall at Lambeth Palace, George Abbot, the Archbishop of Canterbury, read from a prepared document. After a brief legal preamble came this:

> *Some secret, incurable and binding impediment has prevented Lord Essex from having carnal knowledge of his wife. .*

And then, finally;

> *The marriage between Lord Essex and Frances Howard is therefore declared to be utterly void and none effect.*

Utterly void and none effect. Words Frances had been yearning to hear for years. Words that blazed through her body.

Frances waited a week before allowing Robert to visit. He waited a further week before asking her to marry him. They agreed to wait another week before announcing to King James and then to the court that they were to be married.

The King was delighted that George Abbot had been overruled and the Nullity Commission had finally done his bidding. But he was worried about losing his own beloved Robert. And so, in the hope of binding Robert to him, he not only gave the wedding between Robert and Frances his blessing, but insisted that it should be as lavish an occasion as the wedding of his own daughter, Elizabeth, had been at the beginning of the year. It took place on the twenty sixth of December 1613 in Westminster Abbey. The King and Queen were both present.

The public celebrations lasted well into the new year. On New Year's Day there was a great banquet in Merchant Taylor's Hall. And on the fourth of January a magnificent torchlight procession through the streets of London to the court. The men all rode on horseback, the ladies in coaches, and Frances in the finest of all, a new coach, beautifully appointed with fine leather seats and gilded fittings.

So many candles, so much smoke. On a clear, moonless night. It was like riding through mist.

'The horses that drew my coach, Robert, are they yours?' Frances asked in a quiet moment later that evening. I don't recall seeing them before.'

'They are a gift, my beloved Frances. A gift to us both. From Sir Ralph Winwood.'

She had seen them before. In Doctor Forman's scrying mirror. Hannah had seen them too. Four gleaming black horses in white mist. The most lavish of all the wedding gifts.

HISTORICAL NOTES

The Invisible Exchange is a work of fiction, woven around historical records.

Of the named characters, Matthew, Alice, Pieter, Katherine, Colquhoun, Bradshaw, Gervase Chapman and Cunning Hannah are fictional. Most other characters in the novel are based on real people. The following notes are offered as a guide.

PEOPLE
FRANCES HOWARD was the daughter of Lord Thomas Howard (Earl of Suffolk). In 1604, she was married at the age of fourteen to Robert Devereux, 3rd Earl of Essex. The arranged marriage was intended as a political reconciliation between two immensely powerful families.

In 1610, Frances Howard met Robert Carr. They began a passionate love affair. Although Frances's marriage to Essex was never consummated, he was intensely jealous of her, and throughout the summer of 1611 he insisted she live at Chartley Manor, his moated mansion house in Staffordshire. There is no firm evidence in the historical records that she was spirited out of Chartley, but throughout the period when Essex kept her under virtual house arrest, rumours persisted that she was seen in and around London.

King James was persuaded by Lord Knollys and Henry Howard (Frances's great uncle) to set up a Nullity Commission. Proceedings started in May 1613. Frances underwent a virginity test before the Commission finally agreed in September 1613 that Frances's marriage to the Earl of Essex should be annulled.

On 26th December 1613 Frances Howard and Robert Carr were married. Their wedding was a lavish occasion paid for by King James, who bestowed on them the titles Earl and Countess of Somerset. What happened after they were married is explored in the second volume of this trilogy, *Creatures of the Deed*.

ROBERT CARR (Rochester) was a page to the Earl of Dunbar when he met Thomas Overbury in Edinburgh in 1601. The two became close friends and travelled to London together. In 1607 Carr broke his leg at a tilting match attended by King James. James was deeply concerned and visited him several times while Carr's leg was healing. He soon became James's personal favourite and was appointed as Gentleman of the Royal Bedchamber. Whilst there is some dispute about whether their relationship was sexual, it was certainly passionate, as is clear in many of James's letters. In March 1611, James ennobled Carr, making him Viscount Rochester.

ROBERT DEVEREUX was the third Earl of Essex. His father was executed for treason in 1601 after a failed coup against Queen Elizabeth. He was married to Frances Howard when he was just thirteen years old, and she was fourteen.

Rochester's close friend **THOMAS OVERBURY** was an intelligent and skilful political operator. Rochester relied on Overbury for advice which he passed on to the king as his own. Overbury was initially amused by Carr's fascination with Frances Howard. He even helped compose letters for him to write to her. When the relationship became more serious, however, he strongly disapproved. He wrote a pruriently polemic poem entitled *The Wife* (one of a series of *Characters*) with Frances in mind. In April 1613, he was imprisoned in the Tower of London on a trumped-up charge of treason. He died in the Tower on 15th September of that year. The strange circumstances of his death and the subsequent murder trials became known as 'The Overbury Affair' and was one of the great scandals of the Jacobean age.

SIMON FORMAN was an excellent, if maverick, doctor. His enemies accused him of being a sorcerer and necromancer. He was heavily implicated in the Overbury Affair – even though he had himself died two years before Overbury's death in September 1611. It seems likely he had a heart attack, but the circumstances of his death are very curious. They weren't investigated at the time, and remain unexplained to this day.

Many of Forman's casebooks survive (most are stored in the Bodleian Library in Oxford). They give us a wonderful first-hand account of late sixteenth / early seventeenth century medical practice. They also contain vivid first-hand accounts of theatre-going (including visits to The Globe to see *Pericles* and *Macbeth*) and detailed references to his own adulterous relationships.

Although he remained active as an astrologer and a doctor until the week of his death, the whereabouts of the casebooks from 1610 and 1611 is not known. It was during this period that he was consulted by Frances Howard.

ANNE TURNER was a close friend and confidante of Frances Howard. It's thought she introduced Frances to Forman. By 1611, she was a widow, but she'd been conducting an affair with a younger man for many years before that.

RICHARD WESTON had been a tailor before taking employment with Anne Turner. Despite having no previous relevant experience, he was appointed jailer to Sir Thomas Overbury in the Tower of London in May 1613.

Soon after James took to the throne in 1603, he had **SIR WALTER RALEGH** accused of treason and imprisoned in the Tower of London. James confiscated Ralegh's family estate at Sherborne, and later leased it on a peppercorn rent to his favourite, Robert Carr (Rochester). Ralegh was a hugely popular figure who had a great many supporters, amongst them the playwright Ben Jonson and Henry, Prince of Wales.

HENRY STUART, PRINCE OF WALES was rumoured to have had a close relationship with Frances Howard before she took up with Robert Carr. Henry held Ralegh in the highest esteem, regularly visiting him in The Tower. He publicly argued with his father, King James – not least about his treatment of Ralegh. Henry died suddenly in 1612, at the age of eighteen. Medical historians now think that he probably died of typhoid fever, but at the time there was much speculation that he'd been poisoned. After Prince Henry's death, his younger brother Charles became Prince of Wales, and subsequently King Charles I.

CHRISTOPHER MOUNTJOY owned a house on the corner of Silver Street and Muggle Street (now Monkwell Street), where William Shakespeare lodged. He also had a shop and a workshop there, running a business making wigs and elaborate headgear, much of it in the fashion of the French court. He supplied costumes and properties to several of the London theatre companies. He was a notoriously mean man.

JOHN MARSTON is best known for his plays, *The Dutch Courtesan* and *The Malcontent* He was briefly imprisoned in Newgate for a lost play that was deemed to be offensive to King James. This seems to have deterred him from finishing his draft of *The Insatiate Countess*, which was completed by William Barksted and Lewis Machin, and published in 1613.

Mary Woods, **Doctor Savory**, **James Franklin**, **Richard Grimstone** and **Lawrence Davies** were all real people whose stories approximate closely to the glimpses we see of them in *Edgworth*.

PLACES
In and around London
I have used the spelling most common in the early seventeenth century, for example: Hamsted, rather than Hampstead; and Brainford, now Brentford.

BEDLAM, as Bethlehem Hospital was commonly known, was founded in 1247 as part of the priory of St Mary of Bethlehem and stood near what is now Liverpool Street station. It was an institution for housing the insane. Visitors were allowed – partly as a way of raising funds. Bedlam is referred to as a tourist site in several of Ben Jonson's plays; and, thinly disguised, features as the sub-plot in Middleton and Rowley's *The Changeling*. Edgar in *King Lear* disguises himself as Tom o' Bedlam. Bethlehem Royal Psychiatric hospital is now in Beckenham, about eleven miles south of the original site.

BLACKFRIARS PLAYHOUSE was the winter home of the King's Men (who played at The Globe in the summer months). It was one of the first commercial theatres (i.e., outside of the royal courts) to use artificial lighting. The Sam Wanamaker Theatre (at the present-day Globe Theatre) uses candlelight for performances. Many productions there are performed in conditions which approximate to those at the seventeenth century Blackfriars Theatre.

BRIDEWELL PALACE was built for Henry VIII, with fine river frontage and its own quay. The king often stayed there with Queen Katherine (Katherine of Aragon). When Henry had the palace built, it was sited with one side facing the Thames and the other overlooking the pretty banks of the Fleet River. By 1612, it had long been known as The Bridewell, and had been a workhouse for more than half a century, a House of Correction, a place of fearsome reputation.

COPE CASTLE, built in 1605, was a magnificent mansion, commissioned by and named after Sir Walter Cope. It stood near the village of Kensington. After Cope's death, the house passed by marriage to Henry Rich, Earl of Holland, and was renamed Holland House. It was destroyed during a bombing raid in the second world war. The grounds of what used to be Cope Castle are now known as Holland Park.

FLEET RIVER flowed through Kentish Town, King's Cross and Clerkenwell before joining the Thames at Blackfriars. It is one of the many 'lost' rivers of London which have been buried underground. **Fleet Bridge** was a narrow, stone built, humped back bridge to the west of Ludgate.

LONDON BRIDGE was the only bridge over the Thames in London. In the early seventeenth century, there were some two hundred buildings on the bridge, standing up to seven storeys high and overhanging the road, forming a dark tunnel through which all traffic had to pass. The only alternative for Londoners wanting to cross the Thames was to use a wherry, a kind of water taxi, or (for those who could afford it) the horse ferry, which plied between Whitehall and Lambeth.

SAINT PAUL'S was the second church to be built on this site. It had been completed in 1240 in the Gothic style. In the early seventeenth century, the church was a popular meeting place. Notices and job offers were posted near the door at the west end – which became known as the *si quis* door. The churchyard to the east of the church was used by pamphleteers and booksellers to sell their wares. The church was destroyed in the Great Fire of London (1666). The present-day Saint Paul's cathedral (the third church on the site) was built to a design by Sir Christopher Wren.

SPITAL FIELDS. By the fourth century AD, the largest of the cemeteries serving Roman *Londinium* was in the area that later became known as Spitalfields. Saint Mary's Priory was founded around 1197 in that area. It soon established itself as a hospital for the sick and incurably diseased. The area to the east of the priory became known as Spital Fields. In 1539, during the dissolution of the monasteries, the priory was surrendered to the Crown. Some buildings were demolished, some simply abandoned and left to go to ruin. The large-scale settlement of Huguenot refugees in Spitalfields did not take place until the 1680s. But the persecution of Protestants in France and Holland had started long before that. This novel speculates that some families, such as Alice's, had already tried to settle in the area in the early seventeenth century.

By the early seventeenth century, **WHITEHALL PALACE** had become a rambling maze of apartments, great halls, chapels, tennis courts and courtyards (one named Scotland Yard). One side fronted the River Thames. It was said to contain at least

2,000 rooms and was probably the largest palace ever seen in England. King James disliked it, however, much preferring Greenwich Palace. Having survived the Great Fire of London (1666), which did not reach so far to the West, Whitehall Palace was destroyed in a massive fire in 1698. The Banqueting House (built in 1620 to a design by Inigo Jones) is the only part of it to survive into the twenty first century.

TAVERNS AND INNS

All the inns and taverns referred to in *Edgworth* were real places (many of them featuring in city comedies of the period). The only one to survive to the present day is The White Hart Inn on Drury Lane.

BROTHELS

There were numerous ways to refer to brothels in early seventeenth century England. Whorehouses and stews were perhaps the most commonly used, but plays of the period also include references to trugging houses, vaulting houses, common houses, bawdy houses and nunneries – all slang terms for brothels. Many of the areas known for their brothels were outside the jurisdiction of London. One of these was Hog Lane, which later took on the nickname of Petticoat Lane. Prostitutes working in Southwark (south of the river) were known as Winchester Geese. Southwark was also outside of the jurisdiction of London and from the Middle Ages had been controlled by the Bishop of Winchester, who had the power to licence brothels – hence the name 'Winchester Geese'. *The Vixen* and the *Cardinal's Hat* are fictional names. Given the way that individual brothels were named, they could well have been real places.

OUTSIDE LONDON
AUDLEY END

Thomas Howard (Frances's father), the Earl of Suffolk had the vast house built on the site of an earlier Tudor manor. When completed in the early seventeenth century it was the largest private house in the country. A descendant of Thomas Howard sold the house to Charles II, who used it as a country retreat when attending the races at nearby Newmarket. Audley End today is approximately one-third the size of Howard's original house and is mostly Victorian.

CHARTLEY MANOR was a moated manor house in Staffordshire. It was the family home of the Earls of Essex. Mary Queen of Scots had been imprisoned for almost a year at Chartley Manor from 1585 to 1586. The house was destroyed by fire in 1781. The present day Chartley Manor had been Chartley Manor Farm until the 1980s.

SHERBORNE LODGE

Queen Elizabeth I leased the medieval twelfth century Sherborne Castle to Sir Walter Ralegh. He and his wife found the old castle unsuitable to live in, however, so Ralegh had a smaller, beautifully proportioned house built to his own design. He called it Sherborne Lodge. The architecture was much admired. After King James had Ralegh imprisoned on a charge of treason, James leased the house and estate to Robert Carr. Although Ralegh's lodge has been considerably extended over the years, many of the original features survive. It is now known as Sherborne New Castle. The house and gardens are privately owned. They are, however, open to the public from April to November.

BIBLIOGRAPHY

A small selection of books referred to while researching the background to the novel.

FRANCES HOWARD AND THE 'OVERBURY AFFAIR'

The Trials of Frances Howard by David Lindley. Routledge, 1993.

Unnatural Murder by Anne Somerset. Weidenfeld and Nicholson, 1997

SIMON FORMAN

Dr Simon Forman by Judith Cook. Chatto and Windus, 2001.

Simon Forman: Sex and Society in Shakespeare's Age by A.L. Rowse. Weidenfeld and Nicholson, 1974.

SOCIAL AND GENERAL BACKGROUND

The English Housewife by Gervase Markham, Ed. Michael R Best. Republished by McGill-Queen's University Press, 1986.

The Elizabethan Underworld by Gāmini Salgādo. Sutton Publishing Ltd, 2005.

The Complete Coney Catching by Robert Greene. Ex-classics Project 2017 Public Domain.

https://www.exclassics.com/cony/conyintro.htm

The Black Book Thomas Middleton (first published as a pamphlet in 1604).

Ex-classics Project Public Domain (from Complete works of Thomas Middleton, Vol. 8. Houghton Mifflin, New York, 1886).

https://www.exclassics.com/bbook/bbookintro.htm

LONDON

Ben Jonson's London by Fran C. Chalfant. University of Georgia Press, 2008.

A Survey of London written in the year 1298 by John Stow. Republished by The History Press, 2009.

Shakespeare's London 1613 by David M. Bergeron. Manchester University Press. 2017.

PLAYS

Most of the following are available in several editions:

Ben Jonson: *Epicoene – the Silent Woman*

The Alchemist

The Devil is an Ass

Bartholomew Fair

John Marston *The Dutch Courtesan*

The Malcontent

The Insatiate Countess (published version completed by William Barksted and Lewis Machin)

Thomas Middleton *A Chaste Maid in Cheapside*

The Honest Whore (co-written with Thomas Dekker)

MAPS

London: A Life in Maps. Edited by Peter Whitfield. The British Library, 2006.

Map of Early Modern London "The Agas Map." Map. Ed. Janelle Jenstad. MoEML, 2012. Web. Open. https://mapoflondon.uvic.ca/map.htm

Ogilby's Road Maps of England and Wales. Facsimile edition republished Osprey Publications, 1971.

ACKNOWLEDGEMENTS

The map of Matthew's London is loosely based on the Aga's map. It was drawn by Cathy Guerin.

Many thanks also to John, Jane and Robbie Airs; Tracy Baines; Chris Ball; Matthew Ball; Ann Bauer; Rib Davis; Tim Grana; Lesley McDowell; Mike O'Byrne; Judith Ramm; Stevie Simkin; Debbie Weinstein; and all at Village Writers.

The typeface for the title and map graphics is IM Fell DW Pica Pro. The Fell Types are digitally reproduced by Igino Marini. www.iginomarini.com.

ADDITIONAL MATERIAL

Additional information about the background to the novel can be found at:

http://www.brianwoolland.co.uk/the-invisible-exchange.html

Readers who sign up for *The Invisible Exchange* mailing list will receive advance information about the second and third novels in the trilogy. They will also be offered a free subscription to an occasional blog about early seventeenth century London and the world of the novel.

Edgworth mailing list info: edgworth1612@gmail.com